BELOVED SON, AISLING TRILOGY BOOK 3

Newfound love might not be enough. Trust holds the possibility of both salvation and damnation.

Circumstances having forced them to seek asylum in Lind, Wil and Dallin find themselves at the center of an approaching convergence they're not sure they're strong enough to face. The power of the land and the Mother wait for Wil in the bowels of Lind, but it comes with strings attached. With Dallin's help, he must find a way to defeat the soul-eater and save the Father, Her Beloved, and manage to keep his soul in the process.

Friends are not necessarily friends. Trusted mentors are not necessarily to be trusted. And good intentions are sometimes the most dangerous sort.

Through deduction and magic and mutual strength, Dallin and Wil must accept their roles as the Guardian and the Aisling, and stand together against a ruthless god in a climactic battle of dreams and wills, the fates of both of their souls and those of all mortals hanging in the balance. Except, what good is the strength of love, if the one who needs it doesn't know how to trust?

Beloved Son

Aisling Trilogy, Book 3

Carole Cummings

ROCKY RIDGE BOOKS

Beloved Son, Aisling Trilogy Book 3
Copyright © Carole Cummings 2020
Cover art © TL Bland
Interior layout and design by P.D. Singer

Maps created using a template courtesy of freefantasymaps.org

Print ISBN: 978-1-62622-092-8

First Edition published 2011 by Prizm Books

Second Edition published 2017 DSP Publications

Third Edition published 2020

Rocky Ridge Books
Box 6922
Broomfield, CO 80021

For Julia

GLOSSARY

Æledfýres

(āel-et-fēr-es) God of fire. Brother of the Father. One of what are known as the old gods. Also referred to as dearg-dur or daeva.

Ælíf

(āel-if) Given name of the Mother; literally translated as "eternal."

Aire

(ə-rā) Literally translated as "danger."

Aisling

(ă-ēsh-ling) Literally translated as "dream." In Ríocht's culture the Aisling is also referred to as the Chosen, a holy figure who is called on once a year to ask the Father for His favor and blessings, and then convey those blessings onto the people.

Brethren

A band of priests cast out of the Guild and reformed as a more fanatical sect dedicated to the Father.

Brionglóid

(briŋg-löid) Given name of the Father; literally translated as "dream."

Célnes

(sāl-nəs) Goddess of the wind. Sister of the Mother. One of what are known as the old gods, or the gods of the Four Corners.

Chester

A midsized city south of Lind.

Chosen

See Aisling.

Cildtrog

A holy place in Lind; literally translated as "cradle."

Cliabhán

(klē-ə-bän) Cradle.

Coimirceoir

(kim-ól-ēk-āórr) Literally translated as "guardian."

Commonwealth

See Cynewísan.

Cynewísan

(kin-ə-wiss-än) Also referred to as the Commonwealth. A conglomeration of united provinces with a democratic government overseen by their elected Elders. Bordered to the north and east by Ríocht.

Daeva

Vampire.

Dearg-dur

Incubus; soul-eater.

Deartháireacha

(dē-ath-air-rēch-ə) Brothers.

Díepe

(dē-əp-ā) Goddess of water. Sister of the Mother. One of what are known as the old gods, or the gods of the Four Corners.

Dudley

A small village south of Putnam.

Ealdordéman

(al-dór-de-món) Chief judge.

Eorðbúgigend

(ē-ərthpā-gēg-änd) God of the earth. Brother of the Father. One of what are known as the old gods, or the gods of the Four Corners.

Father

The patron deity of Ríocht. God of music, harmony of the seasons, beauty, the stars, and dreams.

Fæðme

(fa-äm-ə) Womb.

First Tongue
The language of the old gods and the first clans.

Flównysse
(flō-win-üss-e) A major river that runs a southeasterly course from the mountains on Lind's northern border.

Foreládtéowes
(fär-eläd-tā-äw-es) Chief; leader.

Gníomhaire
(gə-nēv-əm-h'er) Literally translated as "agent."

Guild
The governing body of Ríocht.

Lind
A province of Cynewísan known for its Old Ones, a governing assembly of magic users and healers. Its denizens are devoted to the Mother and are highly secretive, keeping themselves as isolated from the rest of the Commonwealth as is possible. It sits in the northeast corner of Cynewísan. Ríocht sits at its northern and eastern borders.

Mother
The patron deity of Cynewísan. Goddess of cultivating, reaping, comfort, nurturing, protection, and war.

North Tongue
Native language of Ríocht.

Old Bridge
A tiny hamlet in northern Cynewísan, northwest of Putnam.

Putnam
A major city in the mideastern region of Cynewísan (also referred to the Commonwealth).

Ríocht
(rē-äkht) Also referred to as the Dominion. A highly religious

and patriarchal country governed by priests sworn to the Father, their patron deity. Bordered to the west and south by Cynewísan.

Wæpenbora

(wap-en-bär-ó) Weapon-bearer; warrior-knight.

Wæterþéotan

(wat-er-thā-ät-an) Conduit; floodgate.

Weardas

(we-órd-ós) Watchmen; guards; ones who stand post.

THE STORY SO FAR

The Story So Far....

BOOK ONE: *Guardian*

Putnam's First Constable, Dallin Brayden, is called upon to question a man brought in as a witness to murder. From the moment Dallin encounters the man who claims to be Wilfred Calder, things begin to skew off-kilter—from the not-quite-recognition Dallin feels when he first lays eyes on Wil to the fact that one man beat another to death, apparently as a result of an argument over Wil himself. Before Dallin can get answers, Wil skips town and Dallin is sent after him. It seems Wil is actually the Aisling, the Chosen of his country—Ríocht—sporadically at war with Dallin's country, Cynewísan (also known as the Commonwealth), for as long as anyone can remember. And the return of Wil to Ríocht is the only thing that will keep the war horns from blowing this time. Dallin is commanded by the chief of Putnam's constabulary to track Wil down and bring him back.

Dallin sets off on Wil's trail, and notices there are others on it as well, others who have burned an entire village and murdered its denizens in their pursuit. Dallin finally catches up with Wil in Dudley just as Wil's pursuers do. A violent confrontation ensues, and once Dallin takes care of those who are after Wil, Wil once again tries to run from Dallin. Dallin jails him with the cooperation of Dudley's sheriff.

Under Dallin's interrogation, Wil tells a tale of decades-long captivity and addiction, and a man, Síofra, who kidnapped an infant Wil and had been keeping him prisoner in order to control his magic until the Brethren—Wil's other pursuers, and self-appointed agents of the Father, Ríocht's patron deity—stormed Ríocht's citadel and took Wil away. It wasn't a rescue, Wil says, just another kidnapping, and his captivity no less horrifying than it had been with Síofra. Wil is the Aisling, he tells Dallin, one who can enter the dreams of others, and manipulate them into doing his bidding. Wil also says Dallin is the Guardian, a being of magic meant to guard against the Aisling and his power.

Dallin doesn't believe in magic, but he's seen plenty of evidence that Wil is in danger, and that returning him to Ríocht and Síofra would be no less perilous—both to Wil and Cynewísan. Despite his orders to capture and return Ríocht's Chosen, Dallin decides he needs to protect Wil, if he can get Wil to trust him. Before he can even try, the Brethren attack the jail. Dallin and Dudley's militia manage to fight them off, after which Dallin and Wil flee into the wilderness.

They decide to head to Lind, the northern country where Dallin was born, the place out of which Dallin's mother smuggled him when he was twelve and Lind was attacked, apparently by forces sent by Síofra and looking for Dallin. Dallin barely remembers it, but he thinks it's the place there might be answers, and they have nowhere else to turn.

On their way, they stop at an inn for the night, during which Dallin dreams things that seem to confirm what Wil has told him. The Mother comes to him in the dream and tells Dallin he is indeed the Guardian, and he's meant to protect the Aisling, not protect against him. She calls on Dallin to guard her precious Gift.

Dallin wakes, still disbelieving, but then he makes a joke that Wil should prove it all to him by making it rain. Wil does.

BOOK TWO: *Dream*

Having accepted the fact that he is the Guardian, meant to protect the Aisling, Dallin must rethink everything, including who to trust and where they need to go to find answers. He and Wil agree to travel to Lind—the place of Dallin's birth—in the northern mountains to consult with the Old Ones, Lind's holy men. Wil doesn't want to go there, since he's believed all his life that going to Lind will mean his death. But he knows they need to learn what they can, so he agrees.

On the road, they get to know each other better and begin a tentative trust. Wil admires Dallin's dagger, after which Dallin gifts it to him. He also gives Wil a rifle and teaches him to shoot. It turns out Wil's an excellent shot.

They stop in Chester, just outside of Lind, to find a place for Wil to stay while Dallin goes to Lind to find out what he can. There's a confrontation at the city's gate, during which Dallin makes an enemy of the gate guard. Once they're in Chester, Dallin spots a man who appears to be watching them. His build and his dress seem to indicate he's from Lind, but he appears and disappears, so Dallin's not sure he's actually seeing what he thinks he's seeing. Meanwhile, Dallin is feeling off his game, reflexes dulled, which contributes to his delayed responses when he and Wil are ambushed by the gate guard and his cronies. During the fracas,

Dallin is stabbed in the back and injured quite badly. Wil manages to take down a few of the assailants and scare off the others. He's trying to get Dallin to his feet so they can look for help when the man who's been watching them appears again.

Barret Calder turns out to be a former Old One and the father of the real Wilfred Calder, having cut the Marks from his cheek when he left Lind to find out what happened to his son. Wilfred had been a seeker, sent out into the world to try to find the lost Aisling, but when he did, Wil ran and the Brethren murdered Wilfred. Wil took Wilfred's papers and named himself Wil. Barret Calder knows what Wil and Dallin are, but he doesn't know the part about how Wil got his name. He helps Wil get Dallin to the local Temple, where Calder and the Temple's priest, Thorne, heal him as much as they can. It's not enough.

That night, Wil meets Dallin in a dream and convinces him to accept all of what the Guardian is—including a healer. Dallin heals himself, after which Wil kisses him.

They spend a few days at the Temple, during which they learn how Wil's magic works, and they discuss with Calder everything that's happened. They still don't trust Calder, but they all agree Lind is their only choice and they'll head there once Dallin is fully recovered. Before they're ready, Síofra arrives with some constables from Putnam and a contingent of Cynewísan's soldiers. It's obvious they're after Wil and Dallin, so Wil and Dallin attempt to flee. They're caught, but Dallin gets Wil to take off without him. Wil gets away, but Dallin is arrested by his old friend and fellow constable Corliss. Dallin convinces Corliss to listen in while Síofra questions him. She does, after which Corliss and another constable break Dallin out. Just as they're making their escape, Wil comes barreling back to rescue Dallin.

They're surrounded by Cynewísan soldiers. Síofra tries to manipulate Wil into coming with him. Wil refuses, and there's a magical battle between them. Wil wins but as he's digging into Síofra's mind to finally learn his real name, he confronts a malevolent presence—Æledfýres. In his haste to escape, Wil pulls his magic back too quick and too hard, and gets caught in his own dreams until Dallin finally finds him there and brings him back.

When Wil wakes up, he's in Lind.

Beloved Son

CHAPTER 1

Touched by Her own hand. Wil could feel it. Could feel Her. Almost overwhelming strength wrapped inside soft benevolence. Terrifying might and boundless love. Impassioned wisdom and fierce defense. All of it in his palm, striating all through him. He wanted desperately to hurl the thing away from him, and just as desperately to curl it so tight in his fist it melded with skin and tooth and blood and bone.

"Wil?"

Dallin was leaning close, eyeing Wil with concern, sandy brows drawn down over a thoughtful gaze.

Wil blinked. "Mm?"

Dallin's eyebrow went up. By the small twitch of a wry smile at the corner of his mouth, Wil guessed Dallin had been trying to get his attention for a while now.

"I asked if you had any questions before we get into everything else."

"I have lots of questions, but...." Wil frowned. "I'm not quite sure...."

He'd been asleep for four days, and then he'd spent the

morning getting pummeled by pure and unfettered power—raw and crude, almost primitive, but ancient and sophisticated at the same time. For a while it had seemed as though he knew everything, every thought from every living thing. Knowledge, its threads too raw and too pure, and he'd nearly strangled himself in the weave. Everything else had lost its importance, until now. There'd been no real chance to talk, to find out how precarious their position might be, how much these people knew, and how much they *should* know.

Fortunately Wil didn't need to explain it to Dallin. "They know all about you." Dallin's tone was steady, maybe even defiant. "What blanks Calder left, I filled in." Dallin shot a pinched grimace over to the three Old Ones. "And then some."

Marden shook his head at Dallin, light reprimand. "You must be more forgiving of our brother." It was sad, but with a soft bit of pleading beneath it. "You have not yet received your Marks—you cannot know what it means to lose them."

"He didn't lose them. He cut them away so he could—"

"So he could step into the shoes of the lost Guardian." Siddell's hazel gaze was straight and unbending but not quite harsh. "So he could honor his son, lost to us now in some anonymous grave, buried without the graces or so much as a lock of hair from one of his kin so his ghost can remember who he was or that his death was an honorable one."

"In the service of an Aisling he didn't even know existed."

Siddell frowned now. "You have much anger in you, Dallin Brayden." He held up his hand when Dallin's lip curled. "I do not reproach. I only observe. But I would ask that you try to think more kindly of Brother Calder. Within the space of a year, the man lost his wife and his only son, both of whom he loved more than life. His calling was all he had left, and his faith is strong, yet he consigned it all so that he might wipe away the Mother's tears and restore Her lost one to Her." His thin lips pinched, and he shook his head sadly. "You have seen and spoken to Her," he went on quietly, shifting his sharp glance to Wil. "Can you now imagine the silence if you were to call to Her and She could no longer hear you?"

Wil swallowed. He'd guessed as much, but now the empathetic pain of the truth pierced him. "He didn't just cut away his Marks," he told Dallin softly. "He cut away his connection to Her —*for* Her." He shook his head and frowned at Siddell. "It seems... very unfair."

Siddell waved a bony hand. "Ours is not to question." He flicked a sly glance at Dallin. "Others have taken up that task."

Wil almost smirked as Dallin rolled his eyes with a low grumble. Instead he pointed a curious gaze at the old men. "He is very suspicious of me."

Thorne shook his head, but it was Marden who spoke. "He fears for you, lad," he offered in his gruff baritone, "but he shares the fears of all of us as well."

"Fear of me." Wil peered at every one of them closely. No one negated the statement. "I wouldn't... I *won't—*"

Except he would. He had. Almost destroyed a city, almost took Dallin's head off, almost set half the *Weardas* on fire.... Why should they believe a word Wil said, or trust any good intention, when it was all too plain he hadn't the strength or power to control himself, let alone... everything else?

"You do not know your own power," Siddell put in as though reading Wil's own thoughts. "You cannot control it. Bringing you here is like teasing a match over a mountain of gunpowder. Yet there was no other way. There *is* no other way. Yes, we fear for many things—ourselves, you, the very world." Siddell shook his head. "You are not only dangerous to your enemies, lad. You must understand, we cannot—"

"Look." Dallin's teeth were clenched. "You cannot judge and accuse when you don't even—"

"You would tell us truthfully, Dallin Brayden, that our fears are unjustified?" Siddell's voice was challenging, colder than before.

"I would tell you that they are premature and pessimistic." Dallin's voice, on the other hand, was rising and heated. "He controls it better every day, and he's stronger than you think he is. This place was crushing him, and yet here he sits, calm and sane and willing to talk reason, when—"

"Because you have set your shoulders beneath it," Marden cut in.

"That isn't true. Wil's taking most of it. I just—" Dallin waved a hand, irritated and edgy. "I've channeled it." His gaze hardened. "Isn't that my job? Isn't *all* of this my job?"

"And do you truly feel qualified to take up that 'job'?" Thorne wanted to know. "You are as untested as the Aisling, and yet you—"

"Just *stop* it!" Until that very second, Wil had been unaware he intended to speak at all, but the bickering was making him more anxious than he would have thought possible. Pressure was building at the back of his throat, making his heart pound and his palms sweat. Panic was flittering at the bottom of his stomach, weighting his previously pleasant breakfast like a lump of cold lead in his gut. "Just... *stop* for a moment. Please."

Amazingly they did, as Wil tried and failed to gather his scattered thoughts. They were all looking at him, Dallin too, waiting patiently while Wil's mind stumbled and his hand fisted reflexively around the warm stone in his palm.

"I never meant to hurt anyone." It sounded so inadequate, but it was all Wil could think to say. "I only wanted to be let to live." His eyes were burning; he shut them tight for a moment until the

4

heat receded. "What's inside me... I don't want it. I'll give it back, if you want. I'll let you have it if you'll just show me how." He turned to Dallin. "You can take it away, right? You know how—like what you did before."

"I'm sorry, it doesn't work like that." There was sincere regret in the roughness of Dallin's voice.

It didn't make Wil feel any better. He turned back to the Old Ones. "Calder told Dallin he should kill me." Bald and flat. Despite the panic welling in him, he lifted his chin, defiant. "Is that what this is about? Is this a tribunal?" He set his gaze on each of them, trying not to let the fear show. "Am I on trial?"

He hadn't realized how close to the edge of hysteria he'd been until the warm weight of Dallin's hand came to rest on his shoulder. A message. A reminder.

You're not alone. Whatever happens, I won't let you face it by yourself, and I'll do everything in my power to keep them from hurting you.

Wil sagged beneath it, warmed and calmed by the simple touch.

Thorne had been silent, watching and listening. Now he laid a hand on Wil's knee. "It is true that we have long feared what might have been happening to you, what you might have become." He patted once, then drew back. "Now that you are here, we can see that your heart is astonishingly untouched by the darkness through which you have waded."

Wil looked down. His heart didn't feel untouched.

"You are a good man," Thorne went on. "But even the best of men can have the worst effect if he possesses power he cannot control."

Wil's gaze went unwillingly to the healing burn on Dallin's cheek, then quickly skimmed away, focusing instead on his own hand still fisted around the charm.

"My Guardian has been teaching me. I'm learning."

"Certainly," Marden agreed. "But your Guardian, while more powerful than we'd expected, is unschooled himself, and now we understand there is another consideration." He paused when Wil shot a narrow glance up through his fringe. Marden shrugged. "There is a deeper connection between you than that which was meant." His broad face pinched with mild worry. "Your Guardian owns the priorities of a lover, when he should—"

"Now wait just a damned minute," Dallin cut in, his hand tightening on Wil's shoulder so hard that Wil almost winced. "That's no business of yours, and you've no right to—"

"I beg to differ." Thorne's tone was more stern than Wil had heard it yet. "It is not our business to sit in judgment upon either the Guardian or the Aisling, but you must think about it as the Shaman now. Here we are, presented with an Aisling who possesses more powers than any before him—some that even we do not understand, all of them raw and untamed—and a Guardian who loves him above all."

Wil couldn't help but blink at that one, then quickly snap his glance over to Dallin.

Dallin flushed, but he didn't look at Wil.

"Our task, our calling, requires us to—" Thorne shook his head. "No, it *demands* that we do not unleash upon the world one who will loose that power unfettered. Chester is but one example, and a small one, of your destructive potential."

"But—!" Wil couldn't help the little flail. "But I wasn't even conscious! I didn't mean to... I wouldn't—"

"And that is our concern." Marden's expression softened. "You are a good man, as Brother Thorne testified. We know it. You wear your heart like a crown upon your head, visible to all and shining bright through the darkness. But even a good man's neck may bend beneath the weight of what you carry." His mien went stern. "You

6

nearly destroyed a city in your pain and anger. We are told the storms alone were violent enough to wash away small animals, the hailstones large enough to knock grown men unconscious in the streets. You moved the very earth, lad—uprooted structures from the bedrock as though you were plucking weeds. And all of that in your *sleep*."

Wil was mute. He hadn't known the destruction had gone so far.

"Countless were injured," Siddell put in. "We have no word yet if any were killed. Besides Síofra, of course."

Wil flinched—he couldn't help it.

"*That*," Dallin said slowly, quietly enraged, "is extraordinarily unfair. Síofra—"

"Síofra," Thorne interjected grimly, "was an evil little man who has done unfathomable damage—not only to our countries and our world, but to Wil himself." He looked at Wil steadily, his gaze just this side of hard. "Do you even know what you did to him, lad?"

Wil held the gaze for as long as he could, then tore his own away, pointing it unseeing to his curled fist. He nodded.

"What does it matter what he did to that... *man?*" Dallin seethed. "If you're going to sit here and tell me that he didn't deserve every damned—"

"I crushed his mind." Wil opened his hand and stared at the charm. It was almost pulsing in the wavering light of the fire, as though it had twined with the beat of his own heart. He let his fingers curl over it loosely. "I held everything he was in my hand, and then I closed my fingers." He paused, looking first to the three old men and then to Dallin. "I found his thread, and I tore it out. Father...." Shame he hadn't even considered before took hold of him. He felt his cheeks flush with it. He looked right at Dallin, ignoring the others. "We're not meant to meddle and change.

Before you knew me, the very thought horrified you. Now you condone it."

A flash of hurt skittered over Dallin's features, a harsh flicker of betrayal. "That's hardly what—"

"No, I'm not criticizing you—in fact, I'm grateful." Wil set his hand on Dallin's knee. "But they're right. You're here for me, not the Aisling. You said it yourself. They *should* be afraid of me. *I'm* afraid of me." He jerked his head toward the Old Ones. "They've a right to be concerned. But they don't know you." He sucked in a shaky breath. "You'll do what's right, even if it means I don't live through it. I know that." Dallin looked away. Wil leaned in, relentless. "Swallow your pride and tell it to them."

Dallin was staring out the mouth of the cave, his jaw set—just as angry with Wil as he was with the three old men. Slowly Dallin turned his head and set a wrathful gaze on Wil.

"Should it come to it," he said through his teeth, dark eyes nearly black but steady and burning into Wil's, "I claim the right—no one else."

Wil was a little ashamed that he was yet again forcing something from Dallin that Dallin was so profoundly and morally against. Still he pushed it, reluctantly ruthless.

"Tell them what you claim. Say the words."

Impossibly, Dallin's jaw set even harder, so tight Wil could hear his teeth grinding. Dallin stood abruptly, knocking Wil's hand from off his knee, stalked over to the cave's opening, and looked out.

"I claim the right of *murder*." He ground it out coldly. "Execution. Slaughter. How many more ways d'you want me to say it?" He turned his burning glance to the Old Ones. "I'll *kill* him. Is that what you want to hear? If he proves too dangerous, I'll snuff him out. Snap his neck, he said to me once, handed me a bloody knife and demanded the promise. You're a little late with your concerns, y'see—he's already beat you to it. So, if we're *done* with this, I suggest we move on. Because this is *not*, even remotely, what I was told you wanted to discuss."

The Old Ones—three men heavy with years, skilled in magic, and rich in wisdom—sat shamefaced before their Shaman, heads bowed beneath his wrath.

Wil's cheeks tingled with his own bit of contrition, but beneath it there was the confidence of necessity mixed with a selfish warmth blooming from the core of Dallin's fury. It confirmed Wil's faith, not only in Dallin and the emotion from which the anger sprang, but in the promise itself.

Wil waited until Dallin's dark, furious gaze clashed with his. "I'm sorry, I—"

Dallin gave a sharp shake of his head, teeth still clenched tight. Slowly he paced back over, then just as slowly lowered himself beside Wil again.

"*Fuck* your apologies." It was a growl, low and dangerous. Dallin glared at the Old Ones. "You've three seconds to start talking, or we're done."

It was very telling, this slip of self-possession. Wil didn't often think about how events affected Dallin—he so often didn't allow them to affect him at all. The pressure must be getting harder and harder to contain, right along with his temper.

Thorne gathered himself first, lifting his head and turning his gaze to Wil. "You sit now in the Mother's Cradle, the place from which all life sprang. You have felt the power here."

It had been more like being pounded relentlessly by an invisible sledgehammer, but Wil nodded acknowledgment.

"I venture to say you feel it more keenly than any other," Thorne went on. "It knows you and calls to its own."

"Tell him what that means." Dallin was keeping his hard gaze on Thorne and deliberately away from Wil.

All three of the old men were shaking their heads.

"We are not sure what it means to you, lad," Marden answered. "We have meditated, asking, and always the answer to any one of us has been *The heart of the world is born in Fæðme*, nothing more." He peered at Wil, hopeful. "Do you know what that means?"

Wil blinked and turned to Dallin. No help there—Dallin was still brooding and avoiding Wil's gaze. Wil turned back to Marden with a frown.

"No. Should I?"

Marden sighed, disappointed, and sat back with a shake of his head. "We do not know."

"It means that you are more than you were meant to be." Dallin turned his gaze slowly to Wil, the concern beneath it crowding out the anger. "Ordinarily the Aisling is brought here when his Guardian receives the call. He is taught and tutored, and when he is deemed ready, he is taken to Fæðme—to the Mother." His gaze softened further when he saw Wil's unintentional flinch. "You're different. The power here is vast—it almost staggers the mind. No one could take it all and keep their sanity. No one but you." Dallin held up a hand when Wil opened his mouth. "It gathers at you—it isn't just asking you to take it, it's begging, demanding. I could feel it when you pushed the pain at me. Eventually, if you stay here for much longer, you're either going to have to let it in or it's going to crush you." He tapped at Wil's chest, setting the little crystal bobbing and knocking against Wil's breastbone. "*You* are the heart of the world. Or you will be, once you take what's being offered."

Wil was... staggered. "I—" He turned to the Old Ones, but

they were staring at Dallin with a mix of enlightenment and chagrin on each wrinkled face and no help at all. "Offered?"

"Ahhh." Sudden illumination was blossoming over Thorne's weathered face. He offered Dallin a small sad smile. "Power to power. Blood to blood."

Wil snapped his glance at Thorne. "What does that mean?"

"Blood kin to the Father." Siddell's expression was also moving toward sorrow, sympathy. "And so, therefore, blood kin to His own."

Wil's stomach dropped all the way down to the floor. "Æledfýres."

Thorne nodded slowly. "Your Guardian tells us he stood right at the very edge of you and felt Æledfýres emerge from a mere memory."

Wil's dazed glance went slowly to Dallin's, hung there.

Dallin merely looked back, steady as ever, supportive and encouraging despite his genuine rage of a few moments ago.

"If a mere memory was that powerful..."

"...then imagine what the reality must be," Wil supplied hoarsely.

Pulling and tugging and twisting, laughing and whispering....

Blood to blood.

Wil shut his eyes tight and only opened them when he felt Dallin's hand settle back on his shoulder. "A minor god."

Dallin nodded, mouth twisting. "This place—it's handing itself to you. *She's* handing it to you."

"She wants me to fight for Him." A cold shudder worked through Wil.

"And She's giving you the tools."

"How d'you know all this?" Wil slid Dallin a sideways glance, hoping for... something. Confusion. Reservation. Doubt. He found none of those things. "Did She...? Have you...?"

Dallin shook his head, rueful but not doubtful. "No. I've not seen either one of Them since that time by the river."

"And yet...?"

"Yes. Yeah. I'm sorry, but I'm sure."

Sure. Just like all the other times when Dallin had been sure for no reason and turned out to be entirely right. And yet if anyone dared suggest it was anything other than reasoning and logic, Dallin would likely give them the same disgusted roll of his eyes he'd been directing at Calder since they'd met him.

Dallin didn't need to talk to the Mother. He really did know. Because he really was the Mother's creature. And he didn't even know how much She'd given him.

What more did Dallin know that he didn't even know he knew? And what would it mean for them when he finally let himself see the end?

Did he really think the Mother was doing any of this for *Wil*?

Dallin was looking at Wil sharply. "What are you thinking?"

"A lot of things." Wil looked away. "But not what you probably think I'm thinking."

It didn't matter. Any of it. Wil had known when he'd touched Síofra's memories, slammed face-first into that cold, bitter presence, that this was his—that it was his place to stand for the Father, put back the balance somehow. And if She was going to hand him what he needed to do it, childish resentments and grudges had no place in it.

Except it didn't even feel like resentment anymore. Embarrassment. A strange humiliation that Wil had allowed himself to be so tricked, and by someone like Síofra, someone so small and weak. Síofra had kept Her from Wil just by convincing him he wasn't loved, that *Wil* was weak and didn't deserve to be loved. A fear of standing before Her and feeling rebuke, of being measured and found lacking. A bone-deep wish for that unconditional love only a mother could bestow, and the terror of not finding it when he finally got the courage to go looking for it.

Childish. Oh, indeed.

Time to grow up, Aisling. If not for Her, then for Him.

"It doesn't matter what Her intentions are toward me." Wil lifted his chin. "Well, it matters, but not... not with this." He eyed the Old Ones, one by one, then looked again to Dallin. "What do I have to do?"

Thorne was shaking his head, dismal. "It is not that simple, young Wil. This is... even we do not understand what all of this means."

"He wants my name. And once he has it, he can push me away, send me out into the dark." Wil looked squarely at the three shamans. "I'd rather not let him have it."

"The risk is far too great," Marden put in. "Brother Calder was right, in this at least. We cannot allow it, not without the Mother's blessing, and we cannot know yet if She will give it."

"It is not your place to 'allow' it at all," Dallin put in with quiet authority. "But I will concede that it would be unwise to proceed without Her endorsement." He tipped his head at Wil. "Tell him what that means."

The Old Ones went silent for a moment, brooding quietly to themselves, a subvocal conversation flitting between them by way of long looks and twitches of eyebrows. Wil kept from writhing through it only by virtue of the numbness that had seeped in with his realization that, whatever it turned out to be, it couldn't be worse than facing that cold, hungry presence again—real this time, no weakness of mere memory—and on purpose.

"Fæðme," Thorne finally said softly. "You must empty yourself to the Mother and accept what She gives back to you."

Wil couldn't help the bit of a shudder.

He will empty you at the feet of his whore-goddess....

It was almost as though Dallin heard the echo of it too.

"We go to Fæðme to settle things with Her once and for all," he told Wil steadily. "Or we don't go at all—we take our chances with the Brethren and everyone else on our own. I've been assured of safe passage out of Lind, if that's what you want. We show this place our backs and never look back. It's your choice."

Wil drew up his knees, noticing his hand was clenched around the stone again, so tight it was making his fingers tingle numb. He pressed his knuckles against the crystal at his breastbone. Several long, deep breaths weren't nearly enough to calm him, but they helped. He locked his gaze with Dallin's.

"What do you think I should do?"

Dallin's mouth went tight. "Don't ask me that unless you want me to tell you."

With that, Wil knew exactly what Dallin thought he should do. He wanted to hear it anyway. "What do you think I should do?"

Dallin scrubbed at his hair. "I felt him in there with you." He kept his eyes steady on Wil, open and honest. "All he needs is your name, and the Brethren have it. It's only a matter of time." He shook his head sadly, as though he wished he could say something other than what they both knew was coming. "I know what the damned prophecies said, and I know what all this must sound like to you, but—" He sucked in a long breath, girding himself. "—I think you should do it. If you've ever trusted me in anything, trust me in this. She loves you. It isn't all some trick, it isn't a cage, and even if that's what it turns out to be, I'll keep my promise." There was still anger and resentment beneath that last, but it made the sincerity all the more real and... touching. "And you won't be doing it alone. If it means anything, if it helps, I'll be there right behind you."

Even through the sick fear, the grieved dismay, Wil managed a small smile before he dipped his head down to his knees and closed his eyes. Could Dallin really not know what it meant? Had Wil been that stingy with confirmation and validation? He'd have to work on that.

"It means everything. And it helps."

Wil opened his eyes. Slowly he uncurled his fist and stared down at the little charm. It must have been a trick of the eye—it still seemed to glow in light that wasn't there, thrumming against his skin in rhythm to his own heart. He shut his eyes again, accepting the cadence of it, letting the sensation of *Mother* seep into his skin, wind inside him, touch his heart.

"All right." Wil sighed and lifted his head to look at Thorne. "What next?"

What next seemed to be a whole lot of more or less polite arguing about whether Lind as a whole should be told about the truth of the Aisling and the Guardian, and if so, exactly how it should be done. Dallin, being Dallin, wanted a gathering and an announcement, and then criers to all points to make sure the farthest reaches were informed. The Old Ones, as a whole, preferred to maintain their traditional silence as a policy. And if they couldn't have that, they advocated a whisper campaign with no confirmation from themselves or Dallin.

"Let the people believe what they want to believe," Marden had argued. "Gossip can sometimes be most useful."

To which Dallin replied, somewhat heatedly, "Right, and they'll either have Wil burned at the stake or crammed on a makeshift throne."

Expecting me to shoot fire from my eyes, Wil had put in

silently, but since that wasn't too far off the mark, he kept his mouth shut.

He tuned them out. It didn't truly matter to him one way or the other. He was going to be stared at and whispered about no matter what they were told. And since Dallin was likely to get his way anyway, the entire thing seemed rather pointless.

Wil occupied himself with his new gifts, opening himself to their lethargic magic and the lambent nuances of their sleepy songs. He could spend decades listening to one single slice of awareness, absorbed through miniscule pores and drawn out across time. Every single thing that had touched the pieces had left a mark of some sort, and the stone had kept it, added it to its... well, character, Wil supposed was as good a word as any. There didn't seem to *be* a word to describe it.

"...then we shall have to prepare," Thorne was saying. "A celebration."

"It'll take days we don't have," Dallin argued.

Thorne laughed. "You have been too long away from home, my boy." His tone was sincerely amused. "Allow us to send word ahead."

Dallin thought about it for a moment, frowning. "Fine. We strike camp in the morning. Send a runner to the Bounds as well. I want to know what's going on out there. We still don't have...."

Wil tuned them out again. Apparently the Shaman had prevailed and was as uncomfortable about it as he'd been since... well, at least since Wil had woken and been able to observe the grimacing and twitching every time someone gave in to Dallin's demands. For someone who was so used to giing orders and having them followed, Dallin was damned ill at ease. More of that blind faith he so derided, Wil supposed. Ha. If what Wil had seen so far was any indication, Dallin would have to get over that pretty quickly or spend the rest of his life scowling.

Gently unheeded and mutually heedless, Wil quietly rose, stuffed the charm in his trouser pocket and the crystal inside his shirt, found his coat, and ambled slowly over to the cave's opening. Breakfast having been over for some time now, most of the small fires had been left to smolder, their owners having wandered off past the paddocks and now occupying themselves with either throwing knives at a target or betting on others who were throwing knives at a target. Wil spotted Hunter standing a dozen or so lengths away from the caves, not joining in either the betting or the throwing but merely watching from a distance. Wil peered over his shoulder and caught Dallin's eye. Dallin tilted his head, asking, and Wil answered with a nod toward the green and a small smile. Dallin returned the smile and turned his attention back to the conversation.

Freed from the pretense of caring about whatever details they were discussing, Wil stepped from the cave and once again out into the sunshine. He paused for a moment to close his eyes, reaching tentatively. If he was going to get pounded again, he'd rather it happened right here so he could crawl back inside and not have another collapse out in the middle of the *Weardas*. The dull throb of the headache still remained, but it neither subsided nor grew—it was the same as when Dallin had gone flying backward, perhaps a little less intense after the doctored tea. Comparatively speaking, it was nothing.

Satisfied, Wil made his way over toward Hunter. He approached from behind, noting the stiff set of Hunter's shoulders, the straightness of his spine. Now that Wil was paying attention, he noticed the way Hunter's head swiveled, how his gaze swept the camp with slow regularity. Wil's eyebrows went up, curious.

Apparently Hunter heard him coming. He turned, squinting against the brightness, the sun having shifted behind Wil with the turning of the day. Hunter offered a shy, uncertain smile. He bobbed his fair head.

"Greetings, Aisling." His voice dipped down on the last, conscious of... well, nobody, really—everyone else was occupied with their games, the horses, or walking their watch.

A knee-jerk *Don't call me that* rose to Wil's tongue, but it stayed at the back of his throat. Yesterday, even this morning, he would have snapped and snarled at the name, but now... well, it was what he was, wasn't it? He couldn't give it back. He couldn't walk away from it. All his life he'd been used and hurt, imprisoned and punished because of that name, and he didn't suppose the ache of reminder would ever really dim. Still, it was more his than *Wil* was, and he supposed it was past time he stopped hissing and spitting about it.

His hand rose without his permission, fingers sliding into his hair, over the small scars—*I have a real name.* He turned the gesture into a casual brushing away of an unruly hank that he tucked behind his ear.

He returned Hunter's smile. "Perhaps 'Wil' would be better for now." He shifted a nod back toward the cave. "They're debating exactly how they're going to go about...." He shrugged. "Whatever they're going to go about."

Hunter's smile was slightly bemused. "It does not concern you?"

"Not really. Dallin will do what's right."

"As a Guardian should." Hunter's expression went solicitous. "Is there something I can get you?" He indicated the fire pit, still blazing and attended by a crew of one, but there was a notable lack of anything cooking over it. "It is not quite time to prepare for the midday meal, but if you're hungry...."

Surprisingly, Wil wasn't especially. Hunter and Shaw had brought him a huge chunk of what Dallin had told Wil was goat only a few hours ago, and Wil had gnawed it right down to the bone.

"No, thank you." Wil peered up at Hunter with a tilt of his head and a carefully friendly smile. "Have you been assigned to me or something?"

Hunter blinked. "Assigned?"

"Well, you...." How to put this politely, and so as not to hurt Hunter's feelings? "You're being very nice to me. Which is very good," Wil hastened to add. "I appreciate it, I just—"

He wasn't used to it. There was usually a reason why people were nice to him, and Wil didn't see that reason behind Hunter's eyes. The only one who'd ever been nice to Wil for no reason was Dallin, and... well, Dallin was different.

"It just... confuses me."

Hunter frowned. "Confuses you?"

Wil shook his head, embarrassed. "Never mind."

Idiot. Apparently social skills were something else Wil was just not good at.

"Are people generally not nice to you?" Hunter wanted to know.

Now that the question had been voiced so plainly, it made Wil's entire line of thought, and his questioning of Hunter, seem extraordinarily sulky and childish. *Nobody likes me, everyone's mean to me, boo-hoo-hoo.*

Wil rolled his eyes at himself. "I'm not generally a nice person, I suppose." He lightened it with a grin. "Are you on duty?"

"Duty? Oh." Hunter's cheeks went pink. "No, I—well, I thought it might be...." He stammered into discomfited silence, peering at Wil out the corner of his eye before quickly shifting his glance away. "It seemed as though you should not be disturbed. You were unwell, and then... well, the Old Ones, and everyone was trying to peer in, and...."

Wil blinked, the sudden remembrance of Hunter shooing everyone off earlier rising to the fore. He tilted a smile.

"Have you assigned yourself guard duty?"

To Wil's chagrin, Hunter reddened some more and swept a low bow. "I apologize, Ais—Wil. I meant no offense. I merely—"

"No, no." Wil took hold of Hunter's arm and pushed him straight. "I wasn't reprimanding you, I wouldn't have the right. I only...." He tried very hard to throttle the amused snort—the last thing he wanted was to offend Hunter or embarrass him further—but he couldn't help it. "I'm sorry." It was as sincere as it could be, considering it sort of huffed out amidst the snickers. "It's only that... well, the thought of the Guardian needing a guard. I mean, if you knew Dallin...."

Hunter's return smile was awkward, a bit stricken. "I didn't suppose the Guardian needed any such thing."

Wil's laughter dried up. "Oh." He cleared his throat. "Are you guarding me, or are you guarding against me?"

The shocked jerk of Hunter's head was answer enough. "Why would I need to guard against you?" The uncomplicated honesty in his eyes was just too palpable to mistake for anything else.

Wil only shot another glance back at the cave before giving Hunter a shrug. "Wait'll you get to know me."

Hunter's smile was confused but genuine.

Beyond the caves, the river was an ambient almost-sentience, a white rushing roar that clarified rather than crowded the air. It was such a presence it became merely a background hum when one didn't listen for it. Wil thought about asking Hunter to guide him to it—he was almost writhing to see it—but, as soppy as it was, he wanted that chore to go to Dallin. Instead Wil turned back to Hunter with a smile.

"You offered to guide me around camp before." The prospect of wandering around in the middle of all these people, standing out the way he did, was unnerving. Perhaps being accompanied by his own personal self-assigned bodyguard might take the anxiety out of it all. "I want to visit the horses, and then perhaps... well, I don't know. Have you got any suggestions?"

Hunter smiled, shoulders squaring. He tipped his head toward the men and women throwing and betting.

"Have you got a knife?"

He'd thought he was pretty good at knife throwing—he'd spent many a night in various solitary camps entertaining himself with his rusty little dirk, after all—but it only took Wil a few throws to realize he was quite overmatched here. The knife Dallin had given him was perfectly balanced, not at all what Wil was used to. The people of the *Weardas*, extraordinarily generous with their welcome even after Wil had nearly crisped a few of them this morning, were equally generous with their advice.

The lack of suspicion was surprising. After all, Wil was obviously not of Cynewísan, and he was well aware of this place's history with Ríocht. And this morning he'd been able to feel every chary thought that had gone through their heads. Now Wil felt none of it—only consideration and welcome.

Perhaps it was the fact that he'd arrived with their Shaman. There was also the fact that Wil actually *wasn't* shooting fire from his eyes... this time, anyway. He supposed it might even be Hunter's doing, with his obvious open acceptance.

Wil decided not to care. They were friendly and quite funny with their constant banter, and he'd never felt so comfortable in a crowd in his life. He was having *fun*.

One woman—exquisitely beautiful beneath her sunburn and tattoos—even went so far as to plant herself behind Wil, bully him into her preferred stance, and guide first his fingers into the proper grip and then his arm into the proper position. To Wil's sincere overfaced amusement, low whistles flittered through the rest of the crowd along with quite a lot of chuckles.

"Watch yourself, young Wil," one of the men called. "Thistle likes the ones that are smaller and can't get away."

Young Wil. He couldn't help the snort. If they only knew.

Strange. He was so used to people calling him "lad" that he actually felt like one most of the time. With the life he'd had, he supposed age was rather an esoteric thing. Sometimes he felt ancient and rickety and frail as the Old Ones, but most of the time, he felt like the twenty-something young man Dallin told him he looked like. Right now, Wil felt very young and very much alive.

"True," another remarked. "But her heart's doomed to loneliness, poor lass—she doesn't know her own strength and keeps crushing them."

Wil peered up and over his shoulder at the woman, mouth twisting wryly. "Thistle" hardly described her. Taller than even her peers, and twice as wide as Wil. No delicate flower, this one. And he doubted she ever had a problem filling her bed, when and with whom she pleased. Who would dare refuse, after all? Who would want to? Still, they must make an amusing picture, now that the size difference had been called to Wil's attention. Strange how quickly he'd stopped noticing it, fearing it.

Thistle grinned down at Wil, then smirked at the man who'd heckled her. "Aw, Free, don't be absurd. Wil's a guest. I'd never put a guest in an awkward position. It would be rude." She tipped a wink at Wil. "Guests get the top."

Wil almost didn't realize when Thistle guided his throw almost dead-on, he was laughing so hard.

Amazing. Bawdy and bold, jibes and innuendo flying in every direction, and yet Wil could feel nothing beneath it but humor and goodwill. No one was trying to manipulate him, no one stared at him just a little too long—or worse, glanced at him then looked away too quickly. No one was making sly little comments and waiting to see if he'd take their bait.

Candid. Open. Frank and accepting.

No buzzing *want* coming at him from unexpected directions. No *giveitgiveitgiveit* yammering beneath a face trying to be kind but sliding helplessly into greed.

He could live here. He could stay here for the rest of his life and never have to wonder what anyone wanted from him.

He could be *himself*—whoever that was.

What was it, Wil wondered? Was it the place itself? Did it somehow influence kindness and acceptance? Or did it merely overpower what he was, what others saw when they looked at him in the outside world? Were people like this everywhere, and he'd just never seen it because what he was crowded it out of them?

Determinedly pushing it away, Wil retrieved his knife. He had to really work to wrangle it from the tree's trunk—Thistle's strength had sunk it deep—suffering some more good-natured teasing in the process. Jokes about his strength, of all things, and yet Wil didn't feel weak—they didn't try to *make* him feel weak. Every single denial of weakness he'd snarled only hours ago seemed like so much ridiculous noise.

He didn't need to defend himself to these people. He *was* weak, comparatively speaking, but no one here cared, no one here tried to use it. They made him laugh at himself, and they laughed along with him, and it felt really damned *good*. He hadn't quite got up the nerve to throw his own barbs back—he was well aware that his sense of humor was a bit strange, and he didn't want to ruin anything—but he grinned and laughed and shook his head accordingly.

He hadn't noticed Dallin arrive, surprised to see him standing beside Hunter quite a ways away from the crowd. Dallin didn't look any the worse for his morning spent arguing. In fact he was smiling as he watched Wil, gaze serene and expression pleased as he leaned over and spoke quietly with Hunter. He gave Wil a wave and a nod. Wil waved back and started over toward him.

"Ha, there's your competition, Thistle," a young woman snorted as Wil passed, obviously referring to Dallin, and was immediately shushed.

Wil was about to turn, perhaps smile and wink, when another voice, reproachful and harsh, made him rethink it.

"That's the *Shaman*," a man hissed at her.

"Well, I know that, don't I? I wasn't—"

"It isn't appropriate," another voice put in.

Wil ignored it and kept walking. He didn't know what else he should do, or if he should do anything at all. Oddly, his cheeks were heating, and he had no idea why.

Why wasn't it appropriate?

He put it away, flipping the knife in his hand as he walked, watching the sun flare and scatter over the blade with each revolution and listening to nothing but the *slap* of the metal against his skin, the muted chatter of the river at the back of his consciousness. His smile was back in place by the time he reached Dallin, and he peered up with a squint.

"You're lucky I didn't still have your purse with me. You'd be a very poor man just now."

"Outclassed by the competition?"

"In every way."

"He's being modest," Hunter put in. "He did quite well."

"He's lying," Wil told Dallin with a wink toward Hunter, "but he's forgiven, because he means well." He held up the knife, waggled it, then leaned over and dropped it into his boot. "It's too perfect, y'know. Apparently I'm only any good with a crap knife."

"My apologies." Dallin dipped a little mock bow. "I promise to only give you crap from here on." He jerked his chin over his shoulder. "We've had a runner from the Bounds. My presence has been *requested*."

"Requested. By whom?"

"Well." Dallin ran a hand through his hair. "The captain there has apparently been suffering harassment from Corliss—at least that's the gist I'm getting. His message arrived with one from her, in which she said, and I quote: 'Get your great arse down here—talking sense into these people is your job.' You should have seen the messenger's face when he had to recite that one at me." He rolled his eyes with a bit of a grin.

"I hadn't realized she was there."

"Neither had I. But it sounds like she's perhaps making some headway. I'm not surprised. If I recall, the captain is younger than she is, and she's got this... *mother* thing about her. People listen—they can't help themselves." Dallin shook his head. "Anyway, I'm told General Wheeler himself is on the way with a full regiment, and the captain has asked to see me before they get here. There's not a whole lot of choice."

Wil sighed. "I suppose we should be grateful for the warning."

"A warning is exactly what it sounds like, which is what makes me think this captain might be coming around. With Corliss there, it just might be possible. Then again, it could just be a last chance to avoid bloodshed. I won't know until I get there and talk to the man." Dallin shrugged. "I wondered if you wanted to join me."

Wil blinked. Strangely, he hadn't been assuming anything from the conversation, neither that he would go nor that he wouldn't. And now that he'd been given a choice of preference, he didn't think he had one.

No, that wasn't true—what he *wanted* to do was to stay here and have another day like today had turned out, laughing and being laughed at and feeling like he belonged. What he *should* do was stand by Dallin's side, be at his back, and be ready for whatever was brought down on them. He was, after all, the whole reason there even *were* soldiers at the Bounds.

"I was hoping we might have a chance to go to the river." A light flush rose to Wil's cheeks at the faint note of pleading in his voice. It was *so close*, after all. "D'you think we'll have time?"

Dallin smiled, gentle understanding. "We'll be following it, in fact. And we'll camp by it tonight." He paused, thoughtful. "Why don't we go there now? We can't stay for long—we'll want to get down to the Bounds before sunset—but we've got a little bit."

Wil was ridiculously pleased. Perhaps there'd even be time to doff his boots and stockings and dip his toes into it. The water was likely freezing, but that was wholly beside the point.

"I'd like Hunter to come along." Wil tipped his head when Hunter's blue eyes went wide and hopeful. "To the Bounds, I mean. If you get caught up in negotiations, he can help me with Lind's customs and... whatever." Wil grinned. "He fancies himself my bodyguard."

Dallin's eyebrow went up. "Does he, then?"

"Don't be jealous. I'm sure he'll protect you too."

Hunter had gone red to his roots. "I.... No, I didn't... I wouldn't presume—"

"Presume all you like." Dallin shot a sardonic glance at Wil. "This one needs all the guarding he can get." He turned to Hunter. "You know which horses are ours?"

Hunter bobbled a nod.

"Good. Shaw is coming with us. Get someone to help you saddle them up. Our things are already gathered and packed—bring them along. And see if you can't scare up something to eat on the way. Bring them 'round the path to the Stairs, and give us a whistle when you're done." He cut his glance to Wil. "Shall we?"

Dallin watched Hunter scurry off, then took Wil's elbow and steered him toward the caves. Now that Wil was looking, the tops of the formations did rather resemble a great staircase. They weren't walking directly toward the caves themselves but toward a well-worn path around the eastern side of them. It was only a few paces before Dallin's arm slipped over Wil's shoulders. Halfway conscious of the others—of what they'd said and the fact that they were probably now looking on and marking them—and halfway not caring, Wil leaned in slightly, matching Dallin's long-legged pace.

"All right?" Dallin gave Wil's shoulder a squeeze.

Wil thought about it for a second before he nodded. "The headache's still there, but it hasn't got worse. How about you?"

"No, I mean—" Dallin's voice dipped, somewhat quiet and hesitant. "Are we still angry?"

"We?" Wil peered up at him with a small frown. "I was never angry."

Dallin looked back for a moment, then dipped his head. "Good. Thank you."

Wil didn't quite know what Dallin was thanking him for but let it pass. Wil knew quite well, after all, exactly why Dallin had been angry, and... he had a right to it.

"So Hunter is your bodyguard, eh?" Dallin's mouth twisted. "D'you think it's wise to have another Calder so close?"

Wil rolled his eyes. "If you're suspicious of the boy because you've got a feeling about him, that's one thing, but if it's because of who his uncle is...." He paused, but Dallin didn't elect to fill the silence. "He should see his Shaman at work. He's been training for war his whole life, and despite his kind heart, he wants it. I think he should see someone he respects and admires trying to avoid it."

"Hm." Dallin puffed a dubious snort. "You really think that's how he'll see it?"

"I'm sure I don't know. But you're supposed to be the teacher. So teach."

Dallin pursed his lips. "I'm *not*—"

"Right, right, you're not a teacher. And you're not a cleric, and you're not the Guardian, and you're not anything else someone else says you should be, even if you clearly *are*." Wil elbowed Dallin in the ribs. "What difference does it make what you call yourself? Do what you do, and let Hunter watch what you do. If not for him, then for me, all right?"

Dallin groaned, sounding rather put upon, and shoved Wil ahead. "Fine. For you."

Wil smirked but kept silent. Dallin was kind of cute when he was annoyed.

To Wil's sincere chagrin and frustration, Dallin halted them as they rounded the bend in the path and demanded that Wil close his eyes and allow Dallin to lead him the rest of the way blind. The river was louder now, grown to an actual roar once they'd passed the muting barrier of what Dallin had called the Stairs. If Wil squinted, he could vaguely see blue-tinged whitecaps through the autumn-thinned trees, ages-old deadfall, and bramble sprouting from the swath of strand that stretched between them and the water.

"I'm not closing my eyes. There's bloody rock and moss everywhere. I'll break my neck."

"Not if you hold on to me and let me guide you." Dallin was resolute. "It'll be worth it, I promise, and I won't let you fall or anything—I'll be very careful."

Well, sure, but—"The deepest water I've ever been in was a bathtub. What if I fall in?"

Dallin didn't even dignify that one with an assurance. "Do you want this to be merely your first sight of a real river, or do you want it to be the most beautiful thing you've ever seen in your life?"

Wil failed to see how closing his eyes and stumbling about to get there could make that big of a difference. Still.

"Fine." Wil latched on to Dallin's arm with both hands. "But if I go down, so do you, because I'm not letting go."

Dallin grinned. He looked so young and boyish when he smiled like that—like the rest of the world and all the worries in it weren't weighing on his wide shoulders.

"The sun's perfect, just wait, you won't be sorry. No peeking, now. I'll have your word."

Wil rolled his eyes before he closed them. "Just get on."

It was unnerving, but Wil had more or less expected it to be. With every step, the rush of the water got louder, nearly deafening. He kept his head down as he clutched at Dallin's arm and followed along. He was surprised he wasn't tempted to open his eyes, but in case he did accidentally, all he'd see would be the ground.

Dallin led the way carefully as he'd promised, perhaps even too slowly, his steady instructions—*a big step down coming up, have a care, put your right foot... there you go, ah-ah, no peeking*—a corporeal counterpoint to the almost otherworldly ambience Wil's other senses were feeding him.

The air was getting close and damp, but it didn't press *down*, didn't constrict. On the contrary, Wil's lungs expanded. He dragged in the clean scents of chill autumn through his nose, tasting it sharp on his tongue—pine and loam and something else he could only describe as pristine and white. His ears were filled with the vast song of the water—he'd never guessed a real river would be so *loud*; no wonder he could hear it from the caves—the stone surrounding them snatching at it, echoing it back. The ground was by turns soft and spongy and then flat, slick rock beneath his boots, his feet settling into each step under Dallin's solid guidance with a surety that really shouldn't be there but just the same was.

Wil was—surprisingly and despite his impatience—enjoying the whole experience, overwhelming as it threatened to be. Still, there was relief and a mental *finally* when Dallin halted with a firm tug to Wil's elbow and a smooth turn.

"All right, this is it." Dallin had to raise his voice more than before to be heard above the shout of the water. "Open your eyes."

Wil blinked them open slowly, unexpectedly savoring the anticipation. He saw Dallin first—grinning with keen impatience, dark eyes shining and gold hair catching the sun behind him, russet and bronze sharding through and glancing over the unruly curls shifting on his brow in the cool breeze. He had this way of... *looking*, and it never failed to warm Wil all the way to his toes.

...or do you want it to be the most beautiful thing you've ever seen in your life?

Yes. Absolutely.

"All right now, are you ready?"

Wil blinked again. "More than."

Dallin only grinned wider, took hold of Wil's shoulders, and turned him in a gentle about-face.

Wil looked up, and... goggled.

"*Ohhhhhh....*"

There were no words. And even if there were, they wouldn't be enough.

Torrents of cobalt-curled froth plummeted from what looked like the very top edge of the world, great sheets of it blundering through a mossy breach in earth and stone, bellowing to the pool of gossamer-laced indigo at the bottom of its throat. Mist boiled up from its bosom, shatter-prismed and sparking with borrowed light and color, feathering out and up like the breath of a sleeping dragon.

Great, smooth slabs of granite step-marched up the hills. Chiseled gently through the ages, carved relentlessly by the might of the river. They stood now inside its face, an outcropping jutting out like nature's promenade. Like standing inside the river's heart, and watching as it made itself.

"*Ohhhhhh,*" Wil said again. He swallowed, reaching out, the river's breath tingling at his fingertips. "You were right." He was dazzled, dazed. "The sun is perfect." Flashing and fracturing through the water as it plunged over the rock, down and down, turning foamy white jets into gracile gold. Wil breathed in deep. "It's *all* perfect."

"It comes down from the mountains above Lind—actually passes through it. Fæðme sits... well, you'll see."

Wil almost pressed for more, but... he'd find out soon enough. And right now he didn't think he really wanted to know all that much about Fæðme or think about what was to happen there.

"I used to come here when I was a boy." Dallin was squinting against the light, tiny crinkles at the corners of his eyes, his expression far away. "My dad used to train *Weardas* before he went off to war—the caves, that's where they'd billet during training—and he would let me tag along, pretend I was his squire." He chuckled, rueful and small. "I don't think I was much use to him—I must've only been about six—but he pretended I was. In truth I spent most of the time here."

Strange. Wil had never heard Dallin talk about anything having to do with his life here. It hadn't even occurred to Wil that Dallin had been to this place before, that he'd spent time here, spent days shirking duties and perhaps daydreaming here. That he'd been a little boy here. That he'd been a little boy at all. So much responsibility, so much experience—it all sat on Dallin's brow in a quiet, understated frontispiece of honor and duty, dependability and constancy. It was sometimes hard to take that sporadic boyish grin and extrapolate it to the lad who grew into the man.

He'd never spoken of Lind as though he knew it, and Wil didn't think it was his own lack of observation. Lost Shaman or no, Dallin didn't seem *of* this place, of Lind. In fact he seemed very much apart. Apart from his home, and in turn apart from what he'd claimed as his home. And now apart from everything. Wil had spent the morning pretending at belonging, thinking he *could* belong if he pretended hard enough, long enough. Dallin didn't pretend at anything.

Wil leaned back until his shoulder blades settled against Dallin's chest. He rested his head back on Dallin's shoulder and just looked at the stunning scenery. Only a little while ago— bloody damn, could it really have been only a matter of weeks?— Wil had thought this whole *touching* thing incredibly uncomfortable. Too controlling, too intimate, too... risky. Dallin was a man who reached out constantly, and it had bothered Wil immensely. Now he sought it out himself, without even thinking about it. Reached back.

"Tell me what you did here." Wil said it quietly as he watched the water blossom over the top of the falls and boil down, listened as it shouted its songs.

Dallin's arm came around to drape across Wil's collarbones. He pointed.

"See that bit of a ledge up there? About three-quarters up, just to the left of the branch overhang?"

Wil squinted. "I see what looks like perhaps a bit of a jut big enough for a bird's nest, but I don't see a ledge."

"It's a ledge."

"I'll grant you 'protrusion,' but *that* is not a ledge."

"Right, well, whatever it is, I almost killed myself jumping off it."

Wil's eyes went wide as he stared at the little projection doubtfully. "Was someone chasing you?"

"Um... well, no."

"Well, you didn't jump on purpose, surely."

"Afraid so, yes."

Wil craned his neck to frown up at Dallin. "You were never that stupid."

"Ha. You say that like stupidity's a thing of the past." Dallin jerked his chin. "We climbed the Stair right up to the top. See how there's a dip in the formation, right above the ledge? Well, if you stretch and hang on to the willow whips, you can extend yourself just enough to drop onto that ledge. I suppose it would be less of a stretch now, but... anyway, we sort of dared each other. Can't back down on a dare, y'know." He chuckled. "It bloody *hurt* when I hit the water. Like slamming into a brick wall."

"I've no doubt." Wil eyed the expanse of thin air between what Dallin kept insisting was a ledge and the frothy surface of the river below the falls. "Who's 'we'?"

Dallin was silent for a moment, clearly startled. "Hm?"

"You said you dared each other." Wil peered up at Dallin again, bemused by the sudden scrim of tension in the line of the wide body at his back. "You must've come here with a playmate, yes?"

Another silence, this one stretching, uncomfortable. Wil just kept looking, watching Dallin looking at the fall of the water over the slick line of stone and not seeing it, maybe watching bits of his own history behind his eyes for the first time in... possibly ever.

"Yes," Dallin finally answered. "A playmate. One of the *Weardas'* lads, I expect."

Wil's frown deepened. "You don't remember?"

33

"No." It was brusque. "It doesn't matter. He'd be dead now."

They'd all be dead now.

Wil had lived with the knowledge of it for years, the guilt. Dallin had lived it.

Swallowing heavily, Wil laid a hand over Dallin's and leaned back into him a bit harder. He understood now. No wonder Dallin kept himself apart. This wasn't coming home for him—this was visiting graves.

"Have you got anyone left? Any family at all?"

Dallin rested his chin atop the crown of Wil's head. "No. I'm the last."

Something about it made Wil horribly, unutterably sad.

Wil didn't expect to live through what was coming. He'd felt the strength, the greed, the power. He hadn't been expecting to live through the next day for the past three years, but... but what if Dallin didn't? What if something happened to him? What if Dallin threw himself in front of another bullet? If Dallin were suddenly no longer here, who would be left to remember what a remarkable man he'd been? These people in Lind who barely knew him? Who looked at him as though he were some invincible, immortal being—no blood, no soul—merely another verse in the songs of their country? Dallin had mentioned friends back in Putnam; surely someone like him—someone who seemed to spend every waking moment worrying about others, who used up everything he was *for* others—should have more than a handful of people who had loved him, would mourn him. The whole world should know, the whole world should understand, and the whole world should keep tight hold of him, let him touch every life and make it better just by being what he was.

"You should've had a happy boyhood." Wil couldn't seem to make his voice rise above a whisper. "You should've had so much more than what you had. You should have so much more now."

"So shouldn't we all." Dallin dropped a kiss to the top of Wil's head. "You should laugh all the time, like you did today." He took hold of Wil's arms and pushed him gently away. Wil could almost *see* Dallin once again put away the small bit of his past he'd allowed himself to remember, bury it, and then move on. Dallin turned and gestured for Wil to follow. "C'mon, I want to show you—"

"Dallin."

"—how clear the water is. It's all rock here, so you can see right down to—"

"*Dallin.*"

Dallin paused but didn't turn. Wil took the few paces over to him slowly, and laid a hand to Dallin's arm.

"Do you put everything away like that? Do you bury every-thing that hurts?" Wil hesitated, but it had to be said. "You keep saying you see me, and I believe you do, because you bother to look. Well, what if I want to see you too?"

For a moment Wil thought he wasn't going to get an answer. Dallin bent his neck, mouth twisted tight as if he were angry, but it didn't feel like anger.

"We all do what we must, Wil." His voice was heavy, tired. "We take what the Mother gives us and do our best with it. This is my best."

Wil tilted his head, genuinely curious. "Pretending nothing hurts you is best?"

"Not pretending." Dallin was staring at the ground, lines of unease knotting his shoulders and vibrating beneath Wil's hand. "Accepting it and then moving on."

"Burying it."

"Wil, can't we just—?"

"And if I die?" Wil paused when he saw Dallin's jaw clench,

twitch. "Will you bury me twice? Once in a box and once in your heart?"

Dallin locked his gaze to Wil's, steady and hard. "We'll never know, will we? Because I don't intend to let it happen."

He stared, daring Wil to negate the statement Dallin no doubt saw as mere simple fact. Wil bowed his head, wishing he had the courage to say it wasn't really Dallin's choice.

"You're borrowing trouble," Dallin told him. "You always do. You're so much stronger than you think you are, and you keep forgetting that I'm not going anywhere. I won't let—"

"I don't think I can beat him." It came out more wobbly than Wil would've preferred. "I'd like to think I won't be another of your ghosts you pretend you don't see."

Wasn't that strange? He'd spent so much of the past few years willing people to not even notice him, to forget him as soon as they'd served whatever use he'd had for them the moment before. Now all he wanted was to know he'd be remembered—remembered by someone who'd looked at him, someone who'd seen and not looked away.

Not invisible. Not merely the sum of his sins. A real person, no one's dream, whole and the man he was reflected back in his Guardian's eyes, enhanced and cleaned of tarnish and imperfections of the soul.

...a Guardian who loves him above all.

How very terrifying.

How very... consoling.

Dallin was silent for some time, quietly seething and trying very hard not to. He took Wil once again by the arms, turning him so he faced the falls. Roughly Dallin wrapped his arms around Wil's shoulders, dipped his face to the crook of Wil's neck, and held on tight.

"Then don't die."

Wil shut his eyes. "I can't—"

"I don't want to do this now." There was a heavy note of pleading in Dallin's voice, and he squeezed Wil, just enough to constrict breath the tiniest bit. "Look up at that water, at the rock it carved its way through—scoring its way through everything to find its true path." He tightened his grip and gave Wil a small shake. "That's you. You *are* the river, Wil. Stronger than earth and rock— stronger than fire. And now you've got the strength of Lind behind you, or you will."

His voice... it blended with the song of the water, just as strong, just as sure and clear. He made Wil almost believe every word.

"And you," Wil said. "You're behind me."

"And me. Perhaps you can't beat him, but *we* can. I know how this has to go, and if you want prophecies, if that'll make you feel better, I'll give you one, all right? I'll get Thorne to put it in the songs—a prophecy from the Guardian to the Aisling. Are you ready?" Dallin didn't wait for Wil to answer. "It'll be dark, it'll be terrifying, it'll probably hurt, and you might even want to die. It'll be the worst thing either one of us has ever seen or lived through, but you *will* come out the other side, understand?"

Wil gripped Dallin's arms in both hands. "How—?"

"*Understand?*"

Understanding didn't really seem to be the point. Not even a little bit. Trust. That blind faith Dallin so despised. And here he was, asking for it, demanding it, and he didn't even seem to know it. And here Wil was, wanting to hand it over.

I will do whatever it takes. I want you to survive, Wil.

Do I look like I don't know what I'm doing?

Just trust me. I won't let anything happen.

Wil sank deeper into the embrace.

Trust and faith and give and take, and closing his eyes,

following blind and believing without thought that his Guardian wouldn't let him fall. That it was all right to be weak sometimes, because there was another there to be strong, to balance you, propping you up in your moment of frailty, not waiting to tear out your throat the minute you bared it. There was a strange sort of strength in that, one Wil could give back, because it didn't have to define him, and "weak" didn't have to mean "not strong."

Wil twisted his neck, and laid a soft kiss to Dallin's throat. "I understand."

He let Dallin support him as he leaned back and watched the falls. Watched the brown, sunlit ghost of a gangly, towheaded little boy plunge from the top of the Stair, laughing and shouting, and splash down, long arms and legs flailing, into indigo froth.

Wil closed his eyes, breathed in the day, and wished with all his heart it never had to end.

CHAPTER 2

W il, Dallin decided grimly, had already made up his mind. Accepted the end as if he knew what was coming and was perfectly all right with it. Sad, perhaps, a bit frightened, but not so much that he'd look for or accept another answer.

It was like holding on to someone who was already dead.

Dallin suppressed a shudder, took Wil by the shoulders, and pushed him upright. The chill hit right away, where Wil's warmth had swathed him a second ago, but Dallin didn't pull Wil back, though he almost wanted to. Instead he patted at Wil's shoulders, and pulled away.

Wil wasn't done looking yet, lost in the sight and sound of the falls, so Dallin merely withdrew, paced slowly back to the cliffside wall, and leaned his back to it. He stared at his boots.

It was very strange being back here, seeing things he'd forgotten existed, placing his feet on soil he'd walked before. The land itself vibrated through him, wanting to feel familiar, but somehow he couldn't let it. Like running into an old lover with whom things had ended badly and pretending you didn't recognize him, and after enough denials you might even start to believe it yourself. Walking away and feeling their eyes between your shoulder blades, accusing—*You remember, we both know it, what are you so afraid of?*

Ridiculous. Dallin had never done such a thing in his life, hadn't had enough real relationships that would afford the circumstance.

Have you ever loved?

His jaw tightened, and he scuffed his boot over shiny-damp granite.

What difference did it make? As if it were some sort of failure, as if he had any control over it whatsoever.

If he had even a semblance of control…. He'd what? Refuse it? Make it go away? Pretend it wasn't true until he believed it? Six weeks ago Dallin might've thought that possible, but now?

"You look tired."

Wil's voice was loud, to be heard over the rush of the water, but not loud enough that it should have startled Dallin as it did. Dallin cut his glance up, saw Wil's look of concern, and pulled his eyes quickly away again.

"Do I?"

"I should've noticed before." Wil seemed strangely hesitant all of a sudden, considering he'd been trying to plow Dallin under with unwanted memories only moments ago.

Dallin cast his gaze up to the top of the falls. "You only just woke yourself a few hours ago."

"Which is why I should have considered that you've not been taking the time to look after yourself." Dallin wouldn't look at him, but he could almost feel Wil's gaze go doubtful. "Have you been sleeping?"

The derisive snort whiffled from Dallin before he could stop it. He choked it back. *Sleeping* was a relative term these days.

"Yes, I've been sleeping." The lie came too easily. Dallin

pulled up a smile to cover it and tried to make it sly. "Although I'll admit I've been wishing I had something better to do at night to occupy myself, but since you were unavailable...." He waggled his eyebrows.

Wil twisted something that might have been a smirk. "Perhaps we can remedy that tonight." He took a step, right up close so his arm brushed Dallin's. Even through the thickness of both coats, the touch thrilled through like it had that first night. "I think I'd like to have you by the river." Wil murmured it low and right next to Dallin's ear, so the heat of Wil's breath seeped down Dallin's collar. "We'll make a few memories of our own it won't hurt you to remember, shall we?"

It was as though Wil had just taken him and tripped him into the water. Somehow Dallin managed to keep the smile, though he couldn't come up with a single bloody thing to say. And anyway, his mouth didn't seem to be working, so what was the point? What the hell was wrong with him? And why did whatever it was feel so much like fear?

"Dreams?"

Dallin snapped his glance up, narrowed it. "Sorry?"

Wil shrugged. "I recognize the look." He slipped a cold fingertip along the hollow of Dallin's left eye. "A few more days, and it'll look like someone blacked both your eyes. And you have a constant look about you, like you might draw on the next person who blinks too quickly." He tilted his head. "Want to tell me?"

"It's fine." Dallin tried to make his voice casual, but he only sounded tired, even to himself. He shook his head. "Same old thing, nothing new, and nothing to worry yourself about."

Everything about Wil went still. "Nothing to worry my pretty head over?"

"That isn't what I meant. I was only—"

"It doesn't matter what you *were* doing, it matters what you *weren't* doing—and what you *weren't* doing was being honest." Wil's mouth twisted, his gaze steely. "You're keeping something from me. And by the way you're trying to back yourself through that slab of stone, it appears to be something important."

"Wil, they're only dreams. They don't—"

"There is no such thing as *only dreams*. Haven't you been paying attention at all?"

Fucking hell. When had Dallin lost control over his own life, his proprietorship over his own thoughts and feelings, so damned completely? Two choices were possible right now, the way he saw it—fight over it, or give just enough to make it seem as though he was giving in. And he really wasn't up to a fight. With effort, he kept back a heavy sigh.

"It's only the one from... I think it was that first night in Chester. Or maybe the second. I can't remember. Like I said, nothing new."

"The one with the Watcher?"

"No, the one with Calder."

Wil's frown went hard, with a touch of fire beneath it.

Dallin realized his mistake right away. *Shit.* Why hadn't he said it was the one with the Watcher? Wil had just handed him an out, and Dallin had been too caught up in the half-formed lie to snatch it.

"You never told me about that one."

"No?" Dallin turned his gaze past Wil and back up to the water. "I expect there were other things more pressing at the time."

"Mm." Wil followed Dallin's gaze. "And now?"

Dallin rolled his eyes. "If you really want to know, I'll tell you —I've not been keeping any great secrets from you. It just hasn't come up, that's all."

Another lie. Bloody damn, he was getting good at them.

Then again, no, he apparently wasn't, because Wil turned

back to peer at Dallin closely, measuring. He was silent for quite a while before he nodded.

"I really want to know."

Of course he did. Wil really wanted to know *everything*, except for the things he *didn't* want to know, and Dallin was supposed to know how to tell the difference, and he was also supposed to not mind when Wil wanted to know things Dallin didn't want to tell him.

Which wasn't entirely fair, nor entirely honest, but Dallin really was fairly exhausted, and it was all he could do to keep everything that was going on in his head in some sort of order. Holding back this place from burrowing its way into Wil before he was ready for it, trying to listen to what Lind wanted to tell him— accept the things he wanted to know and block the ones he didn't —wrapping his mind around the fact that he could actually *hear* the land speak to him, and he had a feeling he could speak back if he wanted to, and it would hear him too.

Too unnerving, all of it, and almost too much to keep track of. And now Wil wanted a dissection of a dream Dallin didn't want to tell him about, after Dallin had spent all morning arguing with three old men over things as dire as Wil's very life and as unimportant as how many barrels of mead and beer would be needed for the damned celebration Dallin didn't want but they were planning anyway for when they finally made it up into Lind proper. And now Dallin had to make a trip down to the Bounds and use up *more* time they didn't have to deal with Commonwealth troops, when what he really wanted to do was hide here, watch the falls all day, watch Wil's face as he watched them, and not bloody *talk*.

What a fucking day.

Dallin gave Wil a level look. "It's nothing. A lot of nonsensical rubbish, really, but it's been coming almost every night, and yes, it bothers me. Everything about Calder bothers me, so I don't imagine I should be surprised he's a pain in the arse in my dreams as well." He sighed, a bit overdramatic, probably, but no less heartfelt. He waved his hand. "It's in that alley, and there's fire everywhere. I know you're there because I can hear you yelling at me to get up, but I can't see you." His teeth clenched. "That bloody stumpy little gate guard is there, but as usual he turns into one of the—" He cleared his throat. "He turns into one of the children."

Wil's expression went immediately from suspicion to sympathy. "Burnt?"

Dallin nodded. "And then Calder shows up, holding this stupid little gold figure shaped like a frog in his hand, only it's not really gold. It's alive, and it keeps staring at me, blinking its freaky bulging eyes at me, and Calder says—"

He stopped himself just in time, and turned his gaze back to the water. "Calder says things I can't remember, and then I'm in a boat in the middle of a gunfight."

He risked a glance sideways, saw the narrowed gaze, the slight pinch of the mouth. Wil wasn't buying the lie for a second.

"What does Calder say?"

He says you've been betrayed all your life, and implies I should be ashamed for planning to betray you further. Except I have nothing even resembling a real plan, and even if I did, it isn't real betrayal, because if I do what I think I have to do, I'm following orders from the Father Himself. How am I supposed to do otherwise? Just because you've made me promise—

He cut that one off and shrugged, annoyed. "What does Calder ever say but rot and nonsense? I told you, I don't remember."

Wil was quiet for a moment, staring at him. Dallin stared back, keeping his face blank and his gaze steady.

Eventually Wil looked away. "The frog is magic. Magic

untapped and unknown." He shot a sardonic glance at Dallin, then looked away again. "But I expect you knew that."

Dallin frowned. "No, I didn't." Though he thought perhaps Wil was saying he *should* have known it, but that didn't seem entirely fair either. "*You're* the one who knows these things. Why d'you think I should?"

"Mm."

And that was it, all Wil had to offer, as though they both knew what it was supposed to mean and Wil had no intention of dignifying the question with a response—*and* had every right to be angry that Dallin wouldn't admit it. Except Dallin really *didn't* know what it was supposed to mean, and damn it, how the hell had it gone from what it had been fifteen minutes ago to *this*?

"Look, Wil, I'm not trying to be difficult." Yes, he was—he just didn't want Wil to know he was being difficult. "It's all rather chaotic, and I really don't remember—"

"The gunfight is fairly self-explanatory," Wil cut in, terse. "Attack and counterattack." He slipped a wry glance up and over. "Typical when a person who likes to control everything around him suddenly can't anymore." It was all Dallin could do not to growl. Fortunately, Wil didn't allow an opportunity for response. "The boat isn't terribly significant—it's the state of the water. I assume it's somewhat... unsettled?" When Dallin frowned a bit and nodded, Wil merely shrugged. "So are you. P'raps if you'd admit you have emotions, it would calm down the next time."

The curt delivery and vague suggestion of a verbal slap surprised Dallin. "Hold on. That's hardly fair. How did this get to be about—?"

"Now, if you'll tell me what Calder says to you in the dream," Wil overrode him, "decent sleep might be a possibility tonight." He turned a bit of a glare on Dallin, sagging somewhat when he caught whatever pathetic expression of bewilderment he found.

He shook his head and laid his hand on Dallin's arm. "I'm only trying to help. I've been fairly useless at just about everything else, and I'll admit it's a bit unsettling that you won't let me in when you expect nothing but complete and total submission to your will from me."

That made Dallin's head jerk back. "*Submission?* Are you joking?" Perhaps the fairness of this conversation had been tipped in Dallin's favor since it started, but that one was not only unimaginably wrong but completely below the belt. "When have I *ever* asked you to submit to *anything?* When have I ever done anything besides—?"

"Besides make proclamations about what I do and do not need to know and expect me to trust and believe you?" Wil held up a hand when Dallin's mouth dropped open. "I *do* trust and believe you, don't misunderstand. But you're expecting of me what you seem to despise in others. And I'm willing to go along with it—up to a point. But I reserve the right to determine exactly where that point is."

"And keeping the things in my head to myself is somehow going beyond that point?" Real anger was sparking in Dallin's gut and searing down his spine. No one had a *right* to what Wil was implying, *no one.* "It's a bloody *dream,* Wil, and what Calder says in it means no more than anything he blathers at me while I'm awake."

"So you *do* remember."

"Oh, fucking *hell.*"

An interrogation tactic Dallin had used himself more times than he could remember, and he'd just fallen right into it. Where the hell was Hunter with those horses, and why was he otherwise underfoot constantly but notably *not* bumbling into conversations he didn't need to know about when Dallin really needed a diversion?

"Listen, I can't do this right now." Dallin tried to make his voice apologetic, contrite. "You're right, I'm very tired, and I haven't been sleeping well, and... and I'm sorry, but sometimes I really do know what's best." Bloody damn, his head was pounding, and the sound of the falls was abruptly filled with too damned much noise. Dallin sucked in a long breath, pushed it out on a weary sigh, and made himself meet Wil's angry gaze squarely. "Please. It's best, Wil. Just trust me and don't ask me anymore."

Wil's expression had gone incredibly hard. "How very noble of you," he said slowly, "to decide what's best for everyone else."

Dallin held back a growl. "It isn't like that. I—"

"You know what?" Wil shook his head and puffed out a dour snort. "Fuck off."

Dallin watched him turn, striding off too quickly and carelessly on the slick rock, which was too bloody typical and only made a bitter laugh rise to the back of Dallin's throat. He was tempted to follow after—and who knew, maybe Wil wanted him to —but Dallin truly didn't have the energy to catch up to the pace, nor the will to further the argument. He couldn't win it, not when Wil was so bent on being unreasonable about it. Dallin would give Wil some time to cool down, think about it, perhaps try to look at it from Dallin's point of view... which, all right, would probably be a lot more possible if Dallin actually *filled Wil in* on his point of view.

He shook his head, keeping a watchful eye until Wil had safely navigated the terrain. When he disappeared around the bend in the Stair, Dallin let his head fall back to rest against damp stone and closed his eyes.

It couldn't have been thirty seconds later that Hunter's whistle pierced through the hum of the falls. Dallin could have cheerfully choked him.

Not that Dallin had really expected the peaceful mood of the morning to last. Wil was too damned changeable, which was one of the more interesting facets of his jagged edges. Still, it had been nice while it lasted, and Dallin missed it already. Right at the moment, he suspected he was getting the silent treatment, though he pretended not to notice. It was probably only driving Wil's temper up further. Having dropped back to chat with Calder— most likely more to annoy Dallin than from any real affinity—Wil was making himself easy to pretend to ignore.

Anyway, Dallin had bigger things on his mind right now. Wil would come around. He had to. He just didn't know it yet. Which was, of course, Dallin's fault.

"...as it has always been," Calder was saying. Pontificating, in point of fact, but he wasn't doing it at Dallin, so Dallin only allowed an eye-roll instead of the growl that was threatening. "Lind could not have survived as it has, else. Her power depends on her people lending her the strength of their belief. Outlanders could only contaminate that strength, winnow it away, and dilute it."

"Well, yes," Wil agreed, "but belief does not depend on ignorance." His voice rose. "If a question is asked, it should be answered truthfully, and the inquisitor allowed to make of the answer what he will, not what another thinks he should know."

This time Dallin let the growl out, kicked his heels into his horse's barrel, and jogged her farther ahead—just enough that he could no longer hear the conversation or Wil's barbed responses to it that had very little to do with the subject matter and everything to do with scoring points on Dallin. Bloody hell, it had been a *dream*, for pity's sake. *Dallin's* dream, to be precise, and he had every right to keep the details to himself if he so chose. And with this one, he so chose.

He knows your purpose. And yet he gives you his trust. He was weaned on betrayal—would you cage him now?

Even if he wanted to, how was Dallin supposed to tell Wil something like that? It would only lead to more questions Dallin couldn't answer, which would no doubt lead to more arguments he couldn't win, so it was best to ignore it and hope Wil's anger dulled with whatever distance they could manage between them. Hopefully temporary distance.

I think I'd like to have you by the river.

Right. That *really* didn't help.

Though, considering the chill in Wil's voice and eyes....

Dallin sighed.

Perhaps it was too much to hope that a "temporary distance" would be enough to make the promise feel a bit more realistic. He'd be lucky to get Wil to look him in the eye again, let alone—

This time, the sigh was somewhat gloomy and pathetic.

Perhaps it was because it had to do with dreams. They were important to Wil—what they meant, how often they came, what the seeming-chaos of them might imply. Wil had lived in them for most of his life, after all. It probably shouldn't come as any sort of revelation that he took them seriously. Later, when Dallin was feeling more generous about it, he'd likely find some guilt with which to whack himself.

Perhaps Wil was regretting his pledge of trust, changing his mind. It wouldn't really surprise Dallin. Wil changed his mind like a fickle mink changed mates. Which, all right, generally worked out in Dallin's favor, since Wil usually ended up agreeing to do things Dallin's way—after making Dallin walk through bloody fire first, and then roll around in it for a while if Wil was being particularly difficult to convince—but this time was apparently different, and it wasn't even Dallin's bloody *fault*. And while trust was nice, Dallin could work around distrust if he had to.

Who was he fooling? Trust was more than nice—it was essential, and Dallin didn't want to work around anything. He just wished like hell he could depend on it when the time came. Because the time was fast approaching.

Shaking it off, Dallin peered over his shoulder, slowed his mare to allow the others to almost catch up, and tried to think about something else.

The curved stave of the crossbow, wedged between the saddle and the bedroll one of the *Weardas* had dredged up from somewhere unspecified, dug into Dallin's hip a bit, and he allowed a small smile. Just the image of Wil charging through the stables, lunging for the thing and snatching it from out that lad's hands.... It caused a reaction that wasn't conducive to a comfortable seat in the saddle, so Dallin tried to push that thought away too.

Except now that his mind was on weapons, it willfully wandered back to Wil's pleased expression when Dallin had handed him back the rifle. In the midst of giving Dallin the cold shoulder or no, Wil hadn't quite been able to conceal the brightness in his eyes when Dallin had handed the gun over, though Wil had tried very hard not to let Dallin see it. Dallin still wasn't completely certain there wouldn't be cause to regret it later, handing over explosives to a man who sometimes couldn't help setting things on fire, but he had to admit it felt damned good to have carbon and powder within reach now, instead of just the sword and knife he'd been carrying since they'd reached the caves. Of course, he'd have to continue to restrain himself from aiming one of the guns at a Calder—the uncle more than the nephew, but still—but at least they'd been relatively pleasant on the ride thus far.

He knew why he'd asked Shaw along. He wasn't so sure why

he'd allowed Calder to insert himself. Hedging all his bets, Dallin supposed. If he was going to drag Wil to the Bounds with him—and Dallin couldn't seem to let Wil out of his sight just now—and without the protection of the Old Ones, having Calder there was likely the safest alternative, if not the best. At least Calder used to *be* an Old One. Dallin had pushed another draft on Wil before they'd mounted up and left camp—had taken another himself, in fact, which Dallin suspected was the only thing that had kept Wil from throwing it at him—but the balance wouldn't hold forever. Balancing and channeling and keeping things at bay would only last for so long, and the drafts were going to be rather useless all too soon. Another few days, if they were lucky. Sooner, if Dallin was overestimating his own contributions.

Hunter was another story altogether, but Dallin hadn't decided which sort yet. Honest and forthright, surely, and he'd taken to Wil quickly, and Wil had taken to him. Still, Hunter was so very much *of Lind* that Dallin had decided to keep his reservations. And Hunter was a Calder, after all. In his defense, it didn't seem to take away from his determination to do right by the Aisling, so Dallin decided to keep an open mind. For now.

Anyway, with what Dallin knew to be skulking.... Well. It was best to have a few more guns about. And Shaw ought to prove somewhat useful once Wheeler showed up. Since Dallin had twigged to Shaw's little secret just outside of Chester, he'd been hoping Shaw would see fit to spill it himself eventually, though "eventually" didn't seem to be coming quickly enough.

Dallin eyed his little group, noting Shaw's posture in the saddle—the straightness of his spine, the jut of his chin—and how he was as attentive to his surroundings as Hunter was, eyes narrow and watchful. Certainly not the carriage of a man who'd spent his life praying in temples and hunched over sacred writ.

There was a touch of regret in Dallin's sigh. At least Shaw wouldn't be able to say Dallin hadn't tried for tact.

"...all along the border," Calder was telling Wil, sweeping his arm expansively along the river's southeasterly course. "It defines our Bounds. Lind sits between the Flównysse and Ríocht, but once you cross the Bounds to the east, the river is all that stands between Cynewísan and the Dominion. Besides the mountains to the west, of course. Some places, it's only a matter of stretching one's legs and hopping across. Others, you'd need a boat or a raft and a damned skilled river driver."

Wil had been swiveling his gaze continuously, taking in the riverscape and everything surrounding it while listening to Calder with avid interest, that curiosity Dallin had noted on the first day of their journey resurfacing and shining out from Wil like a torch in the darkness. Now Wil frowned, a touch of worry.

"But I see no guards. Shouldn't—?"

"And you will not," Calder answered. "But that doesn't mean they're not there. Since—" He shot a glance at Dallin, then back again to Wil. "The *Weardas* were increased just after your Guardian was lost. Men and women too old then and now too young, but they are ever-vigilant. You need not worry about its like again."

At least not for another day or two, Dallin thought, but he kept his mouth clamped.

Calder had said the entirety of it without ever once mentioning the words "raid" or "attack," implying but not saying that the sentries should be those of Dallin's generation but weren't because there were none. Nonetheless, by the way Wil dipped his head and went silent, Dallin assumed he'd heard it. Shaw saw it too, cutting his glance between the three of them, likely bracing for an argument Dallin didn't feel like pursuing. Dallin didn't suppose he could blame Calder for the sudden subdued quiet—it wasn't as though Dallin could expect anyone here to never mention the raid, since it was an historical fact, and one that had a damned significant impact on this place—but he'd like to.

"It's quite lovely in the spring," Dallin put in to the silence. He pulled up a small smile when Wil dragged his eyes from the reins twisting fretfully through his fingers. A peace offering. *I don't want to fight with you, not now.* "It's very subdued now"—Dallin gestured at the lazy flow of the water, burbling quietly now they'd left the falls and rapids behind them—"even with the recent rains, but when the thaw comes down from the mountains, it... it comes alive."

That wasn't quite right, but Wil seemed to understand what Dallin meant, because he smiled. A small concession.

"All of this," Dallin went on, heartened, indicating with a wave of his hand the soft, sloping swath of strand they were following along the river's edge, "it's all under water in the spring and most of the summer." He motioned past the trees that separated them from the rich farmland to the north. "Now and then it floods the valley, which is why you'll see lots of farm and grazing land but not very many permanent dwellings. Most who farm this land build only huts and the like, and only live here during season, so if the river breaks her bonds, they've not lost much more than some farming equipment and the few days it takes to build a dwelling. Not to mention the harvest, of course, but that's a different problem. Anyway, they move back to their homes on higher ground in the colder months."

Dallin looked away before frowning, abruptly uncomfortable. There he went again, remembering things he hadn't known he'd forgotten. Still, it did the job—Calder picked up the thread and turned the conversation toward agriculture and trade, and away from the violence of twenty-some years ago. Wil went agreeably along, asking questions and peering around himself with real interest.

Dallin figured it was safe to allow himself to disregard the buzz of conversation once more. A semiwelcome distraction from where his thoughts mainly dwelt these days, but a distraction none-theless, and he couldn't really afford too many of them anymore. Wil saw too much, knew too much, things he really shouldn't know, and there were some things Dallin didn't want Wil to see. What was coming, where it had to go. Unfair, certainly—perhaps even treacherous, if looked at from a certain perspective, and perhaps that was what the damned dreams were about—but Wil couldn't be allowed to see it, not yet, not until they were knee-deep inside it and there was no other choice.

The problem, Dallin thought, the *real* problem, the problem that superseded all problems in the scope of what was to come, was that Wil had stopped choosing himself. Somehow—sometime around when Dallin had got a knife in the back, he thought—Wil's razor edge had dulled, lost its bite. The badger was still there, teeth sharp and eyes wary, but not quite as vicious as it had been.

...that the Father had taught him too well in the ways of dreams, but not enough in the ways of men's hearts.

It had been bothering Dallin for some time now. Distrust was something Wil had learned, not something that was a part of him, and so trust came perhaps too easily when his back wasn't to the wall. What had it taken for Wil to trust Dallin, after all? Nothing but for the treatment Dallin would have given to any prisoner, with the exception of the fact that he hadn't shackled Wil. Dallin had merely fed him, sheltered him, spoken to him like he was an actual person—something he rather thought Wil hadn't got a lot of in the years previous—and protected him because, at least then, when it had all started, it had been Dallin's job as a constable.

I think you're the only person in the world I do trust.

And what had Dallin really done to earn that trust? And was the claim of exclusivity even true anymore? Wil trusted Shaw, albeit marginally. He was suspicious of Calder but accepted his presence a lot more readily than Dallin did or could. He'd spent the morning with Hunter, in the middle of a crowd armed and wielding knives, and he'd turned his back without thought on every one of them. And while watching Wil laugh and smile and have some actual fun had just about burst Dallin's chest with warmth, a cold tendril of unease had slithered beneath it.

Any one of them could just walk up behind him and cut his throat, Dallin had thought as he'd watched, *and he'd never see it coming. He's not even watching for it.*

The badger had been asleep on the job, and it worried Dallin. He wondered with no small amount of apprehension what might have happened if the Old Ones had sat there this morning and informed Wil that yes, he was on trial and had been found lacking. Would the teeth have come out then? Would he have fought for himself? Or would he have agreed with them, turned to Dallin and asked him what he thought, and then accepted his judgment?

What if they told Wil it was either him or Dallin? Wil had failed to run when Calder showed up in that alley. He'd failed again to run when Síofra's voice had echoed outside Chester's stables, and he'd failed to stay gone, to keep himself out of danger, when Dallin had finally forced him away. Three times now, Wil had chosen Dallin—perhaps not in a conscious way, perhaps not deliberately putting another before himself, but three times Wil had risked everything because he somehow trusted Dallin, cared about him, cared what happened to him— and while it almost made Dallin's knees weak, it also scared the shit out of him.

He chooses you, the Father had told him. *I would have you see to it that he continues to choose himself as well.*

A sentiment Dallin shared. Except how was he supposed to do it?

You have more than one calling. Guardian.

Unfortunately, Dallin was rather terrified that he knew what the other was.

You'll do what's right, Wil had told him, *even if it means I don't live through it. I know that.*

Would I?

Dallin honestly didn't know. And that, more than anything else, was a terrifying bit of reality he didn't want to see.

Where are You? Either of You? And why have You left me to figure this by myself? I couldn't get away from You before if I'd tried, and now—

Not true. Easier to believe, perhaps, but not true. She was here, at least, whispering to Dallin through the land itself—he could hear it, he could feel it—telling him things he didn't want to know, showing him things he didn't want to see, and he wondered how much of it Wil had let himself hear or know. Not much, judging by the easy way Wil had spoken to Dallin, touched him, looked at him. Real caring. Real affection. Real worry.

Fuck me, what have I done?

And the dreams... surely that was His handiwork. If Dallin ever saw Him again, he'd have to fill Him in on the fact that lack of sleep was not conducive to a sharp mind or an ability to cull strategy from chaos.

Fuck, he was tired.

He'd almost hoped Wil would hear it all in the songs of the falls. Almost hoped Wil would reach out, test his strength against the rush of the water, but he'd been content to merely look and enjoy and listen as Dallin had spun a tale about two little boys he hadn't even remembered before it had come out his mouth and hardly remembered now.

Do you put everything away like that? Do you bury everything that hurts?

Dallin rubbed at his eyes.

No. I live it until I can't anymore, let it gnaw at me until it hasn't got any teeth left, and by then it doesn't matter because I've bled everything I had anyway. But this....

This, Dallin *would* bury. This... he had no choice. Wheeler and his regiment weren't all that was coming. The Brethren skulked all around them, Dallin could feel every last one of them, out there and biding their time, waiting for it too. Something bigger was on its way, something that held the keys to Wil's cage and would close him inside it, so that all either of them would be able to do was wait for it to come, helplessly watch it send Wil outside himself, take everything he was, and make it... not his anymore.

Caught and caged.

Wil seemed to think there could be nothing worse. Dallin now knew otherwise.

Not on Dallin's watch. Not even if Wil ended up hating him for it and cursed his name forever after because of what Dallin was pretty sure he was going to have to do to prevent it.

Have you ever loved? She'd asked, knowing the answer before Dallin did. Knowing even then what She was going to ask of him, demand of him. Had Dallin even faced the truth of it before Marden had opened his big mouth and spilled Dallin's heart all over the cave's floor to be picked over and examined by three old men who probably didn't even remember what the word meant?

It was a sorry thing that the mere remembrance of it could color Dallin's cheeks. Fucking sentiment. It really was going to be the end of him one day. *Damn* them all.

It was the defeat—that was it.

None of it matters now.

...I'm beginning to think all of this has been a waste of time.

Anger crowded in Dallin's chest at Wil's remembered words, and he clenched his teeth.

I don't even think I care anymore, but you... I'll ask you not to make it... hurt.

They'd been heartfelt and sincere, and worse—recurring. The idea of facing down a monster frightened Wil, surely, but he'd accepted it without any real question, as though he'd been expecting it and expecting not to live through it. Surrendering himself to it all, when Dallin had never seen Wil surrender to *anything*—not shackles, not a cell, not even reality. The man fought everything, so why wasn't he fighting *this*?

You have heard the call. Now you must heed it.

I would have you see to it that he continues to choose himself as well.

So would Dallin. Even if it meant—

"...said we'd camp by it tonight, right?"

Dallin blinked, startled, and turned to Wil, who'd pulled Miri even and had been riding beside Dallin for... who the hell knew how long.

"Um?"

"Did you hear a word I said?" Wil's tone was impatient, but his eyes were touched by uncertainty, suspicion buried but not very deeply. "You haven't been listening at all, have you?" He tilted his head. "Is there something I should know?"

And if *that* wasn't a loaded question.

What are you keeping from me?

Doubt. A precursor to more anger, perhaps. Not that Dallin could consider the argument of this morning closed, he supposed. There'd been a silent truce a few moments ago but not a declaration of the end of hostilities by any means.

Did Wil know? Could he see into Dallin as easily as he could apparently see into those clever little gifts the Old Ones had given him? Wil had hit the core, and extraordinarily hard, when they'd stood at the falls—*Do you put everything away like that? Do you bury everything that hurts?*—and Dallin didn't even think Wil had really been trying. Was there even any point in trying to keep things from him?

Except then Wil had let it go, let Dallin push it all away with assurances neither one of them really believed, so... it was still possible Wil didn't really *want* to know.

Right. Possible. Possible in some other world, where purple dragons vomited rainbows and trolls pissed perfume. This *was* Wil, after all. And the acceptance hadn't lasted very long at all, had it, not when it came to withholding something Wil thought important.

Still... there had been that night in Chester, exposing deductions and theorizing their implications, and Wil hadn't wanted to hear it, not even a little. Dallin had forced the knowledge on him, and this time... this time Dallin couldn't convince himself it was the right thing to do. For pity's sake, the man didn't even want to know his own *name*.

Dallin looked away and rubbed at his brow. The headache was growing steadily again, and he didn't know if it was the stress of constantly keeping this place from pounding Wil, or if Dallin's brain was trying to bash itself against the inside of his skull to make him stop bloody thinking.

Is there something I should know?

Ha!

Well, let's see—I know how the power here works, I can see it all as clearly as you see your threads, and I know what they all want you for. I know the Brethren are here, waiting, and I know, whoever their Cleric is, he's coming, because I can feel him too. I know it's all coming together, converging down to one moment in time when it'll all narrow down to what you'll choose, and if I have to betray you to make you choose right, I'm pretty sure I will. I don't know who or how or when, but I know how this has to go, and you would too, but you're so busy pushing everything about this place away that you've not let yourself know it yet. I know that if you let yourself know before the time comes, it's over, you won't choose yourself, and once you go to Fæðme, you won't be able to help yourself knowing. And then what?

You forced me into a promise I didn't want to make, and They forced me into a calling I don't want, and one contradicts the other —I can't do both. And now I see I may have to force something on you I know you wouldn't want, but there's no alternative that I can see, and I can't trust any one of these people enough to help me see another way.

Fucking hell, I've been trying so hard not to take your choices away, but this one's mine, and I don't know how to make it without betraying everything.

Angry, *furious*, Dallin abruptly pulled rein, then waited for Wil and the others to do the same. Dallin couldn't explain it all, not even half of it, but they all deserved to know at least some. He was going to need every single person who was capable of fighting, after all, and he did truly believe that people fought harder when they knew what it was they were fighting for.

"The Brethren are here in Lind," he told them bluntly, watching all their reactions closely. Shaw looked surprised and wary but not disbelieving. Both Calders seemed more enraged and offended than anything else. Wil looked... angry. Fear and trepidation, but with an implicit accusation of perfidy beneath the bristling, and pointed directly at Dallin.

"How long?" Wil's tone even but peculiarly soft.

It was new, this cold, quiet anger. Wil usually got loud and heated when he was pissed off, and this calm fury was novel and unnerving.

The question would have seemed ambiguous, perhaps even nonsensical, if Dallin hadn't spent the last thirty minutes steeped in conjecture and self-rebuke. He knew exactly what Wil meant, but he looked at Wil straight and answered the question only obliquely.

"I didn't know when I chose this path. I can't do anything until we get down to the Bounds, and we can't go any faster over this terrain than we're going. The *Weardas* can sound the horns and send runners when we get there."

"Hunter should ride ahead," Shaw volunteered. "They could be—"

"No, I need him here—I need *all* of you right here—and they won't dare move until they know where Wil is."

Wil's jaw tightened. "How *long?*"

Dallin made his expression as blank as he could. "About an hour ago." *So at least I haven't been lying to you for very long.*

"Where?"

"I don't know. I felt the land... I suppose you might say it protested when they crossed in, but I don't know where."

"It is impossible!" Hunter said sharply. "Every entrance into Lind is guarded—every *Weardas*, even the eldest and those who have not yet earned their Marks, are recalled to stand their watches. The Border is too thick with Linders. No one could have got through."

"And you are welcome to go on believing that until one of them skulks up behind you."

Calder was shaking his head. "The lad is right. Lind is nearly barren but for the infirm and the too young. Every able body is patrolling. They *can't* have got through."

"Then we'd best get some of them back from their patrols to

protect the rest, because it's too late to worry about the borders now—they're here."

Calder looked first at Hunter, then Shaw, finding no help on either front. He looked strangely helpless in a way that surprisingly didn't please Dallin. "But *how?*"

Wil was staring over Dallin's left shoulder, gaze gone slightly hazy. "There are passageways honeycombed beneath the Temple. Two of them join a network of tunnels that lead directly into Ríocht. Another three are dead-ended with cave-ins. One crosses beneath the Flównysse and ends where Éaspring won the border from Áthlone." He pinked, shifting a slight shrug when they all stared at him openmouthed. He shot an uneasy glance at Dallin, then pointed it to the ground. "People aren't the only ones who dream."

You didn't even know you knew that. Wait 'til you figure out what else you know.

Dallin scrubbed a hand through his hair. "Right." He looked at the others. "They're waiting, but they won't for long. Their Cleric is on the way, but if they can get their hands on Wil before he gets here, if they think they can secure him and get him out of Lind, they'll give it a go. There's a lot of them this time—one of them once told me there were hundreds, and I don't think he was lying —and they're all here. I can feel them."

He took a deep breath and turned to Wil.

"This is it, this is where it all happens, whatever it turns out to be. We'll be down at the Bounds within the hour, and if I play all this right, we'll have the protection of the soldiers, at least until Wheeler gets here and court-martials the captain. But they *are* coming, and they *are* going to try an attack." He leaned in his saddle and pierced Wil with a hard stare. "I won't argue with you about this. If I tell you to run, you'll run. If I tell you to shoot, you'll shoot. If I tell you to dig a hole and climb into it until all the shooting stops, that's what you'll do. Are we clear?"

He'd expected Wil to argue, at least bridle. Wil did neither, merely stared for a moment, mouth thin, then tore his gaze away and stared at the ground. He nodded.

Dallin watched Wil distractedly slipping his fingers through Miri's rough mane, watched his mouth twitch, holding back the things he wanted to say, but he remained tense and silent. The badger was nosing about but not yet ready to bite. In this one thing, at least, Dallin wasn't sure how to feel about that. Either he'd been worrying needlessly about Wil's survival instinct dulling, or Wil was working up to an explosion that would throw a spanner into everything anyway.

Dallin shook it away and turned to Hunter. "You want to be his bodyguard. Now's your chance." Hunter blinked, peered closely at Wil for a moment, then sat straighter in his saddle and lifted his chin.

"Don't I get a say in this?" Wil wanted to know.

"No." Dallin kept a solid gaze on Hunter. "He will not leave your sight except for when he's with me. You will remain armed at all times, and you will shoot anyone who tries to take him from your side." He jerked his chin at Calder. "Even him." He waited, watching closely as Hunter turned a startled gaze on his uncle.

"Dallin," Wil said, quietly and through his teeth, "I don't think—"

"I wasn't asking you to."

Testing the boundaries, seeing how far Wil would let Dallin push them. As far as he liked, it seemed, or at least giving him enough rope to hang himself. Wil went silent again, and again refrained from arguing. Seething—Dallin could see it beneath the ice. When Wil blew, it was likely going to be an almighty big one.

Dallin waited again, keeping his stare fixed to Hunter,

watching as Hunter weighed family against faith and chose the latter. He sucked in a long breath and turned back to Dallin.

"As you will, Guardian."

Wil let out a small growl. "Hunter, I'm sorry. This isn't what—"

"To do else would be an insult to my uncle and all he has ever believed." Hunter's gaze was going defiant as he held Dallin's, more steel in those bright blue eyes than Dallin had seen before. Hunter dipped his head. "At your command."

"I'll remember that." Dallin shifted his glance to Shaw. *One last chance to do this yourself, shaman.* "When was the last time you held a gun?"

Shaw didn't take the opportunity. "A shaman doesn't generally—"

"Unless he's former military. Please don't fuck with me. We haven't the time and I haven't the tolerance."

Wil glanced sharply at Shaw, who in turn shot a speaking look at Calder. Calder merely shook his head and sighed. Shaw echoed it, dipping his head on a small half bow, acknowledging a point scored.

"I had not realized your skills had grown so quickly, Shaman."

Dallin snorted without humor. "It's nothing to do with anything but the fact that you ride like cavalry and bear yourself like someone who keeps forgetting to try not to look like a general." Dallin's mouth quirked at the corner. "I admit the connection took me a little while, but I fought in the Shaw Campaign, you understand. It was pure chance my regiment didn't fall under your command at the northern border."

"Chance, was it?" Shaw slanted a rather chilly little half smile. "If memory serves, it was the Fifth Regiment that cleared our way into Ríocht, led by a young lieutenant who earned his captain's rank by blowing past my men and almost to the Guild's doors." He tilted his head. "I might not have remembered the young lieu-tenant at all, seeing as how I never actually met the lad, but for the rumors going about the troops at the time." He turned a dry glance toward Wil. "Something about a legend come to life, a giant sent by the Mother Herself to lead Cynewísan to victory over the Dominion, and who coerced his men to follow him down into the Beast's very throat by using only the magic of his voice." Shaw turned back to Dallin, gaze measuring. "Do you know what they call you in Ríocht?"

Whatever reaction Shaw was looking for, Dallin refused to give it to him. "I'm aware of one or two epithets."

"*Diabhal Mháthair. Aithnidiúil Bás.*"

Wil obviously didn't need a translation, staring at Shaw now with a strange intense curiosity.

Shaw translated for the others as much as for effect. "Mother's Devil. Death's Familiar." He waved a hand. "My own troops would have marched under that banner, if they hadn't half believed you were a myth altogether."

Dallin ignored Wil's critical gaze and forced a smirk. "Military men are ever a puzzling mix of superstition and practicality—both of which I found useful and so useable."

"I've no doubt." Shaw's expression was thoughtful and not entirely approving. "I believe I now see your strategy for Lind more clearly."

"Then we understand each other."

"Perhaps *you* do." Wil's tone was challenging. "But I would prefer it if you didn't keep it a secret from the rest of us."

He stared Dallin down—*How long have you known? And why didn't you tell me?*—until Dallin shrugged, perhaps somewhat repentant but not even a little apologetic. Just one more secret Dallin didn't necessarily want to keep, and he was beginning to resent having been put into the position in the first place.

It's for the best. I swear it's for the best.

So why did Síofra's voice keep encroaching?—*I kept you safe.
It was too big for you, too much... I took it all away for you. For you,
Chosen, always for you....*

The guilt, born from the accusation in Wil's eyes, sideswiped
Dallin—which was stupid, because he'd known it was coming, and
he knew what he was doing. He *hoped* he knew what he
was doing.

With massive effort, Dallin kept himself from answering the
silent indictment and turned his gaze to Shaw. He kept his face
blank and waited. Shaw's return stare was a mix of hard reprimand and grudging approval until he turned it toward Wil, softened it.

"Rank speaks to rank." Shaw's voice and gaze were both kinder
than they'd been since Dallin had spilled his little secret. "Your
Guardian does not wish my presence as a healer, but as a general
in the Commonwealth's service." He shot a sharp glance back to
Dallin. "A *former* general. I am a shaman now, and have been since
my calling rang louder than the war horns."

"Which is why you left your Temple with all its initiates and
apprentices when you understood that the Commonwealth was
being misled. Old loyalties never die. This one perhaps betrayed
you, but it was a happy betrayal—for me, at least. I need you."
Dallin waved his hand. "I appreciate that you were weary of war—
so was I—but one is on its way, if we don't use every tool we can
lay our hands on to stop it. A person can have more than one
calling."

And Dallin should know.

Shaw's mouth twisted. "My religion—"

"It was not your religious sentiments you followed when you
decided to join us in Chester. You left your Temple because you
saw what Síofra's presence among those Commonwealth troops

meant to Cynewísan, and your loyalties bit you on the arse. You knew you might prove useful."

"Useful." Shaw sighed. "So I am a tool." He didn't look insulted, but he also didn't look entirely pleased. "I am a healer now. I left the Temple when I saw Wil collapse in the street, when I saw the power that he—"

"*Bollocks*, did you. You did it because a strategist never stops strategizing." Dallin paused and deliberately softened his voice. "And that power may well find its way into the hands of men who really shouldn't have it, unless you do what's necessary."

Shaw was clearly unsettled, struck to a standstill between whatever he saw as his current duty and his former loyalty— neither of which had come so close to clashing before, Dallin guessed. And why should they?

Dallin held up his hand. "I'm not asking you to lead a charge against Commonwealth troops—quite the contrary. I'm not even asking you to carry a weapon, though I'd much prefer it if you did. I'm merely asking you to lend your influence when Wheeler gets here. He's a general—a career general at that—and if his ego has grown any more since my last experience with him, though granted it was a peripheral one, my paltry former captain's rank will be seen as an insult. He may not deign to talk to me at all. In fact, it's debatable whether he should even know that I was in the military. He might see all this as more treasonous than walking away from the constabulary."

Shaw was shaking his head, but it didn't look like refusal; more like skepticism and disquiet. "If I didn't know Wheeler, I would say it wasn't possible for his ego to have grown, but I'm afraid it's not only possible but likely."

"You fear him," Wil put in quietly.

Dallin had been getting the same impression, but he kept silent and let it come from Wil.

"You don't have to do it, you know," Wil went on. "You've already done a lot for us. We've no right to ask more." He shot a reproachful glance at Dallin.

Dallin refused to even twitch beneath it.

Funny, Dallin had worried that Wil might see Shaw's secrecy as a betrayal and avoid Shaw after it was exposed. Ha. Instead it seemed Wil was sympathizing with Shaw and blaming Dallin.

Dallin made a mental note. *Lesson Six: Nothing draws empathy out of Wil like witnessing someone else with his back to the wall.* Maybe it was Lesson Seven. Or Lesson Six Hundred and Forty-Two. Who could keep track?

"I realize it's a difficult position." Dallin was speaking to Shaw, but he kept his eyes locked to Wil's. "I'm not trying to be callous about it, and if it weren't as important as it is, we'd drop it right here. In fact, I never would have brought it up."

Wil stared at him, scowling a bit, before he shrugged minute concession and looked away. Dallin turned back to Shaw.

"Is he right? *Do* you fear him?"

And if so, why?

"Brother Shaw." Calder's voice dipped down to tones vaguely threatening, but somehow Dallin didn't think the threat was directed at Shaw. "You do not have to answer. You are my guest in Lind, and if—"

"No." Shaw slanted a weary smile at Calder. "No reason for secrets, and Brayden is right." Frowning, Shaw turned back to Dallin. "I wouldn't say 'fear.' I am... wary of him. He has always had his own agenda, one that I long suspected did not quite coincide with Cynewísan's welfare, but he was always terribly clever and...." He shrugged, discomfited. "If I could explain it, I would have done so to the elders in Penley and had him dismissed years ago. But he had this... charm about him, this...." He turned to Wil, frown deepening. "I was minded of him when I saw Síofra."

Dallin stared down at his fist on the reins. The beat of Lind's heart was abruptly hammering in his ears, a rising crescendo. Síofra; soldiers at the Bounds; Wheeler on his way; the Brethren prowling even now; the faceless Cleric catching up, with every intention of inviting a nightmare to... to—

The Cleric must commune with the Aisling. Unite his mind and soul to the Dreamer, then annex him....

Fæðme—just sitting there, waiting.

Something was there. Some kind of fulcrum Dallin couldn't see yet was turning but still driving everything inexorably, and all of it gaining speed, building toward that final pivot of convergence.

"...everything theoretically right," Shaw was saying, "but there was something *not right* about it all, and I could never lay my finger on it. His strategies were mechanically flawless, their successes predictable, the reasons for their failures beyond suspicion, but...." He shook his head, frustrated. "His victories were many, but never strategically important. His failures were few but massive, the loss of life staggering."

If someone wanted to get close to the opposition, have the most influence possible, without having to go through the bother of spying or the constrictions of state formalities, what profession do you think would be most convenient?

And if someone wanted to lose a war, to what level of incompetence would he have to rise? All the compromises Cynewísan had made toward the end of the war, all the concessions, placing the Commonwealth in a position that was both finely balanced and potentially strategically weak should more hostilities boil up. Stacking the hierarchy of the military with men inexperienced and unprincipled. Drawing back troops at the borders and sending them into retirement while Ríocht's presence thickened like smoky shadows at every guard post and picket. And all of it a slow-rolling chain of policy negotiated by Wheeler himself. And written into the formal treaties by—

I've become quite... familiar with the High Seat, Channing, Síofra had said, all smug confidence.

A cold fist locked around Dallin's chest, constricting air. Dim connection, perhaps, but now that it had been made....

Reason? Logical deduction? Or screaming paranoia? Was Wil's proclivity for dreaming up conspiracies around every corner rubbing off on Dallin, or had Wil been right all along?

Dallin had been assuming the Brethren was a Dominion brotherhood, but there were plenty of Dallin's own countrymen who would be susceptible to the sort of mission those men followed. Payton back in Putnam had the right sort of smarminess about him. In fact, that might explain how Wheeler had known to drag Manning and Ramsford in for questioning, how he knew which of the staff to imprison and which to keep. And Payton certainly wasn't the only one Dallin knew who might fit that particular bill. No stolen marks, but Wheeler couldn't possibly have them either, so that didn't necessarily mean anything.

How did that joke go?—*Just because I'm paranoid doesn't mean everyone's not out to get me.*

"If compared to any other general's record," Shaw was saying, "the losses would have been glaring, but the elders saw only the victories stacking up. I suppose they considered all those young lives necessary sacrifices." His jaw tightened. "Not a military man among them, so I don't know why I was continually surprised by it."

Dallin had heard much the same, but it hadn't had a lot to do with him at the time. Wheeler had come in during the last year of the official declaration, assigned to the eastern border, and Dallin's regiment had never fallen under Wheeler's command. By the time the discontent had started to reach up north, truce had been declared and Dallin had seen enough. He retired when his commission was up and went home, vaguely angry and empty and having no idea why.

"But." Hunter had been silent for quite a while, so much so that Dallin had nearly forgotten his presence. Now Hunter noted all the gazes turned toward him, and he flushed a bit but plowed on. "But war demands sacrifice." Dallin suspected the puffing of Hunter's chest was entirely unconscious. "Surely there are some who enlist for reasons other than the honor of their country"—his lip curled, again unconsciously, if Dallin didn't miss his guess —"but to die for one's country is to die for the glory of the Mother, surely. It is dishonor to imply that sacrifice is anything other than necessary, or that any who make it have gone as sheep to a charnel house."

Dallin sighed. He'd seen so many like Hunter over the years— bright-eyed and eager to die for their cause. Until they realized that sacrificing oneself to one's country or beliefs often meant slogging through hip-deep mud and blood toward a grisly, lonely end that meant no more than another finger-length on a map to the men who had sent them there. Ask ten soldiers what they were fighting for, and you'd be liable to get ten different answers, all of them likely more noble than the goals of those men with their maps in their clean, marble-floored spaces, with their cozy fires and their hot baths and their hot meals waiting for them in the next room.

"And what about dying for the honor of the Father?" Wil asked softly, his face unreadable as he peered at Hunter. "Is that any less honorable? You believe the Mother grants Her favor to those who die fighting against men who believe just as strongly that they fight in the Father's name. He is Her beloved; They fought side by side, or so the story goes. Do you really think She looks upon war between our countries and approves?"

Oh, well *done*. If it wasn't so obviously damned inappropriate, Dallin might have applauded.

"The Dominion has abandoned the Father," Hunter argued. "Every day they stumble further from His grace and gird themselves with the lies of the Guild. They reject the Mother and hate those who do not."

"So they should be punished." Wil tilted his head, his face blank. "They should be hated in return for being tricked and lied to."

Dallin winced. This could go horribly, terribly wrong, and very quickly, if he didn't stop it before it got started. He turned to Wil and laid a hand on his arm, the tension running beneath Dallin's palm hard and trembling, sharply contradicting the cool calm of Wil's expression.

Dallin tried to make his voice soft and commanding at the same time. "We haven't the time for this, and I don't think—"

"I'll have an answer." Wil roughly shrugged Dallin off, his gaze cold enough to snap-freeze a raging inferno. "I *will* have an answer!"

Hunter stared, wide-eyed and clearly beyond his depth, cheeks flushed bright red, mouth moving but nothing coming out of it. He wasn't capable of answering, but that didn't stop Wil from driving daggers into him with his eyes.

Calder dismounted and went to stand beside his nephew, placing a hand on Hunter's knee. "You must forgive his ignorance, Aisling." He dipped a small bow. "He does not know, he cannot understand—"

"Lack of knowledge should not preclude understanding. Or at least the attempt to understand." Wil set his jaw, narrow-eyed and dangerous. "Is this what Lind teaches its youth?" His voice was softly poisonous. His gaze, if possible, intensified as it shifted to Calder. "Will Lind accept an Aisling who has been tricked and lied to? An Aisling who has rejected the Mother and cursed her name?"

Hunter gasped, short and sharp.

Wil ignored him and kept his eyes on Calder. "I expect it would've been easier for you after all to get Dallin to kill me, though I suppose I should be grateful you didn't quite have the courage to do it yourself. But I wonder—what sort of excuse d'you think you'd give Her when you stood before Her at the end? That I was stupid and weak?" He watched, cold satisfaction, as Calder colored and just kept staring at him, speechless. Wil's gaze slid over to Dallin, still hard but not quite as cold. "That I believed too blindly?"

It wasn't meant to skewer, merely to cut a little. All the same, it drove into Dallin with the impact of a punch to the chest. Bloody hell, had Dallin really been thinking only moments ago that Wil had lost his edge? Apology leaped to Dallin's tongue, desperate and mildly unnerving for its urgency.

"Wil—"

"No." Wil shook his head, even smiled, though it was somewhat frosty. "I won't hear defense while you have secrets behind your eyes." His eyebrows went up when Dallin twitched. "Did you think I wouldn't know? Or were you just hoping?" He lowered his voice. "You despise blind faith, and yet you expect it from me under the guise of trust. I told you before I wouldn't trust you blindly."

Except for when he *did*. Wil was hardly consistent, was he? How the hell was Dallin supposed to know when Wil would trust and when he wouldn't?

Dallin's heart was thumping, his temples throbbing with dull, heavy heat. "You also told me you'd choose yourself."

Wil's eyes changed, the cold anger slipping down into reluctant understanding, perhaps a bit of resentment. "All right." He nodded, lips pursed. "All right, yeah. I expect that's fair, if looked at from a certain point of view."

Not really a concession, and certainly not forgiveness. Dallin's throat was tight. He shouldn't want either concession *or* forgiveness, and the fact that he wanted both only drove home further the words of the Old Ones :

Your Guardian owns the priorities of a lover....

...you must think about it as the Shaman now....

Dallin shook his head, teeth set tight to hold back whatever anxious denials might be lurking behind them. "I'm sorry." He didn't even care that the others might hear. "I can't think about this as the Shaman, I can't... can't make myself not care, and it's mucking up everything. I can't—"

"You can do anything you truly want to do. I've seen you."

That seemed like an awful lot of unnerving faith, considering the current conversation, though Dallin didn't miss the implication of the remark.

"Somehow I don't think that's quite the vote of confidence it sounded like." Wil opened his mouth, but Dallin shook his head. "We don't have time for this. Later, you have my word. Right now, our first priority is to get to the Bounds and put Lind on alert. We'll pick this up when we've more privacy."

"And what good will that do me," Wil asked slowly, "if you've already made up your mind what's best?"

It stung. And the cool, calm delivery of it made it burn.

Dallin all but scoffed. "How the hell would I know what's best?" The acidic sincerity of the question was a bit... surprising. Dallin glanced about at the others. "We're wasting time we don't have. Let's go."

It was growing dark enough by the time they neared the Bounds that Dallin had begun to wish he'd thought to commandeer a lantern from somewhere. He'd chosen the path along the river because he'd thought it would please Wil, and because there had been little reason at the time for speed. That had changed a little more than halfway through the trip, and the sometimes-treacherous sloping terrain—alternately mud-slick with the recent rains and moss-slick as a general rule—quickly became a serious impediment beneath the horses' hoofs. Had the mild urgency never arisen, it would have been nothing more than a slight annoyance and reason for caution. Now, with the drive to give warning gnawing at him, it was maddening.

The sun was low behind the trees, its orange-gold haze thick above them, but here, inside the cover of overhanging pines that lined the river's edge, it might as well have been nightfall already. Still, by the time Dallin's ears had started to pick up the telltale voices and sporadic animal sounds, alerting him that they were nearing a campsite, it was still light enough that Dallin couldn't mistake the nine tall figures—alternately straight and somewhat hunched, thin and wide—standing on the path ahead of them.

Relief took Dallin, and he turned to Wil, riding just behind.

"The Old Ones have come to welcome you." Dallin nodded up the path. "I can hear nothing alarming coming from the *Weardas* at the Bounds, and they wouldn't be here if anything had happened. Or at least they wouldn't be standing there calmly waiting for you. We're all right, for now."

He couldn't see Wil's expression in the gloom, but he made out a nod.

"Thank you." Wil's voice was soft. "That's good to know."

They'd hardly spoken since the bit of palaver upriver, except for a brief exchange when Wil had led his mare too close to the river's edge and onto a stretch of slippery-smooth granite—he'd seen fish leaping, he'd said, and wanted to have a closer look—and Dallin had warned him off. As politely and kindly as he could, and in direct contrast to the surge of alarm that had washed through him as he'd watched Miri's hoofs slip-slide briefly before she reasserted her balance. Wil had accepted the caution with nothing more than a short nod and a conciliatory "Sorry. You're right, of course" as he'd patted the mare's neck and led her back onto surer ground.

Now he jogged the horse a few steps until he caught even with Dallin, snatched at his sleeve, and halted, waiting for Dallin to do the same. Dallin reined in and waited for the others to pass them by before turning his horse. He brought her up close so he could see Wil's face in the gathering dusk. He waited.

Wil watched the others until they were out of hearing, then turned to Dallin and looked at him straight. "I don't want to be angry. I don't want you to be angry."

Dallin shook his head. "I'm not—"

"There is a very fine line between doing something *for* another and doing something *to* another." Wil paused, then went on more cautiously, "Síofra managed to genuinely convince himself at the end that what he did, he did for me."

It was so close to Dallin's own thoughts earlier. He was glad for the thick shadows, so Wil couldn't see the flush that heated Dallin's cheeks. Dallin had to be imagining the luminescence of Wil's green eyes in the dark.

"I trust you." There was no diffidence in Wil's steady voice. "I have trusted you with my life, more than once, and I can't imagine anything that might change that in future." Again the relief, and Dallin tried not to sag beneath it. "You are a good man, Dallin, I've never doubted that, and I have put you into a position I know you hate and resent, and I know you hate and resent it *because* you're a good man."

Dallin's teeth clenched—he couldn't help it. "Wil, it isn't to do with—"

"Let me finish. Please." Wil waited while Dallin sighed, shifted his position in the saddle, and steadied his gaze. "I know you know things you're keeping from me, I know you're seeing things I can't see. Every time I trust you with something, I am trusting you as blindly as any one of these people you so despise for their faith in you. I am walking behind you with my eyes closed, holding on to your arm and trusting you not to let me fall into the rapids, but... but you have to *warn* me of what's beneath my feet! I can't—" He ran a hand through his hair and stared up at the sky for a moment before dropping his gaze back down to Dallin. "I can't keep going if you're going to hide the path from me, if you're not even going to warn me of a sudden drop because you're afraid I'll—I don't even *know*—whatever you're afraid I'll do. Can you understand?"

Of course Dallin understood. He even managed not to rage at the searing shame that swamped him. But it didn't allay a single fear nor damp a single warning, however oblique and dream-symbolic.

And *still* Dallin was going to have to say it. He was going to have to tell Wil everything. And all because Dallin couldn't bear that look of suspicion and reproach in Wil's eyes.

He couldn't stop fucking this up.

He shot his glance down the path. The Old Ones were waiting patiently. Hunter and Calder and Shaw had dismounted and now stood among the shamans, also waiting.

Dallin loosed a shaky breath and gripped the reins hard in his fist. He turned back to Wil.

"And am I allowed to prevent you from jumping off a cliff?" It came out too soft, and with too much pleading warbling beneath it.

Wil was silent for a long moment before he shook his head. "I expect that would depend upon whether or not it was something I truly needed to do." He leaned in, the leather of his saddle creaking. "But I can't really answer that unless I know why, can I?" His tone was gentle and far too knowing. "You'll have to answer my question before I can answer yours, I think."

Dallin shut his eyes. His head was bloody *killing* him.

"As with everything, Wil, you give me no choice." Dallin opened his eyes and peered at Wil as calmly as he could. "But I would ask one thing of you." He waited, watching Wil's eyebrows draw slightly in and down, watching a new flare of suspicion catch and hold in his gaze. Dallin put every bit of sincerity he had in him into his voice. "Think about it. Think about it hard."

"Think about what?"

"Think about whether or not you really want to know. Think about it very carefully, because it would be a lot easier on both of us if you didn't."

To Wil's credit, he peered closely at Dallin, probably looking for prevarication. Dallin had to assume he didn't find any, because for one thing, there wasn't any—Dallin was dead serious about this one—and for another, Wil sat back in his saddle, looking thoughtful and somber, all the previous suspicion sliding into honest concern and, to Dallin's inadequate relief, a new bit of dread. Wil stared for a long time, considering, before sinking Dallin's heart right down to the ground by nodding slowly. Dallin already knew what Wil was going to say, but that didn't stop the words from grinding into Dallin's chest.

"I want to know."

All Dallin could do was nod, dip his head, and close his eyes. "If it's what you really want." He sucked in a long breath. "I already gave you my word. Tonight."

Wil was silent for a long time, just looking at Dallin, measuring. Finally he nodded, even smiled, the bastard—a quick flash of teeth in the dark—then leaned in and kissed him, soft and sweet.

"Tonight, then." Wil reached out and squeezed Dallin's hand around the reins. "C'mon." A quick nod toward the waiting crowd down the path. "Let's get this part over with."

CHAPTER 3

Meeting the rest of the Old Ones was not quite as daunting as it had been back up at the caves. For one, Wil supposed, he was tired and sore and rather anxious, thinking the Brethren might be behind any bush or rock, and his attention was spread too thinly to concentrate on worrying about whether or not the Old Ones were judging him. For another, the altered circumstances lent them a normalcy Thorne, Siddell, and Marden seemed to have lacked. It probably helped that Dallin paused more or less impatiently to let them make their introductions while he had words with the commander of the *Weardas* who'd apparently escorted them and then whisked Wil off before the Old Ones could do much more than present more gifts.

Something called a blessing bowl from Singréne, who looked to Wil to be barely older than Dallin—the effects of Fæðme, as Wil understood them, because there were no men in Lind Dallin's age. Singréne had keen hazel eyes that reminded Wil of Brother Millard, and he'd handed Wil the blessing bowl with a soft look and a wide grin.

A tear bottle from Heofon—a thick vial of cut amethyst,

hollowed out and stoppered with moss-lined cork—which Wil thought odd at first, until Heofon told Wil it held the tears he'd wept when he learned the Aisling was safe and on his way "home." Then Wil thought it *very* odd but smiled and murmured his thanks as he hunted for an empty pocket in which to keep the strange little thing. Anyway, Heofon was a thin, arid husk of a man who didn't look like he could spare a drop of moisture, so Wil appreciated the gesture, if nothing else.

"Different tears hold different sorts of magic," Dallin told Wil as they collected their gear and surrendered their horses to the squires looking after the Old Ones. They struck downhill toward the camp, the *Weardgeréfan* moving on ahead, the others following at a discreet distance behind Wil and Dallin. For what it was worth, Dallin seemed less tense since he'd spoken to the commander. "Tears of joy are supposed to be the most precious, because they're meant to lend the recipient peace and well-being in times of hardship."

Wil frowned, his hand going unconsciously to his coat pocket, fingers outlining the vial's shape. "I'm not meant to drink them, am I?" Because that would be just a little *too* strange.

"No." Wil could hear the smile in Dallin's voice. "You're meant to keep them, that's all."

Good. Wil had eaten weevil-infested bread when it was all he could get, and once he'd hacked off the maggot-encrusted head and hide of a rabbit and roasted the rest of it, but somehow the idea of drinking a withered old man's tears gave Wil's stomach a twist. He peered down at the silver bowl still in his hand, swung his pack around, and stuffed it in along with a bottle of wine from.... Seofian, or something like that.

"What's the bowl for?" he asked Dallin.

"Well, in other places, where reading and writing are permitted, you're meant to write down all of the things in your life for which you feel blessed. Then you put them in the bowl and burn them, along with something special to you. Here in Lind, you'd take something like a leaf or the like and whisper those things to it, then burn it."

Wil thought about that. "Why burn them?"

Burning bits of paper or leaves only made his eyebrows rise a bit, but burning something special to you seemed somewhat stupid and wasteful. He clutched his pack more tightly and slipped his fingers along the rifle's strap over his shoulder.

Dallin shrugged. "Burning releases them." He waved his big hand. "Their essence joins with the essence of the Mother. She'll know you love and appreciate those things, so She'll see to it they're not taken from you. That's supposing you're a decent person and deserve the things you have, of course."

"Huh." Wil reslung his pack and peered up at Dallin through the dusky light. "So what if you're not a good person and don't deserve the things you have?"

Dallin snorted. "Then you'd be wise not to offer them to a burning. Then again, if you don't burn them, She'll just assume you're ungrateful and perhaps take them from you anyway." He peered sideways at Wil. "Rather gets you coming and going."

Most things did, in Wil's experience. "And what about the wine?"

"Now, *that* you're meant to drink."

"It doesn't mean anything?"

"Only that Whatshisname probably thought you could use one."

Too right. "Seofian, I think. I sort of lost track." Wil looked down. "So...." He cleared his throat. The truce between them seemed... not fragile, really, but shakeable, and he truly didn't want to argue or be angry. But he also didn't want to feel like he had to pick his words as though he was trying to step carefully through a nest of sleeping hornets. "So, how d'you know all this?"

"Hm." Dallin squeezed Wil's shoulder. "That's a good question," he said, and then didn't answer it. He jerked his chin downhill. "I can see the fires through the trees now."

So could Wil, now that he looked. Dozens and dozens of them. And he'd been hearing sporadic music and the steady hum of voices and various animal noises since they'd dismounted.

"Don't shoot anyone," Dallin said, the smirk plain in his voice. "There should be a sentry melting out of the dark any second." He let go of Wil's shoulder and raised his hand. "Hullo out there! Step out, please. We could do with some light."

Perhaps it was all the talk of magic, or just the fact that magic seemed to define this place—wound into the soil itself, pulsing from it—but it seemed to Wil as though the wide figure formed itself from shadows on the path and became whole from nothing in the blink of an eye. A woman, Wil guessed by the shape, and armed. He could see the shape of the bow silhouetted on her shoulder and the long barrel of the rifle slung across her middle.

"Cawle!" she shouted. "Torches! Step quick!" And then she went silent, bowed her head, and stood with spine straight and shoulders squared.

Dallin stepped forward, slowly and with a tilt to his head Wil recognized—measuring and calculating. Wil didn't even need to see Dallin's narrowed eyes or the slight curl of his mouth.

"Greetings," Dallin said. "I am—"

"We know who you are," the woman blurted, then gasped at her own audacity and dipped her head lower. "Forgive me, Shaman." Her voice was subdued now, and wobbling. "I meant no disrespect. It's only—" Her head bobbed up, gaze flicking to Wil and then back down to the ground. "With your permission...?"

Torchlight flickered through the trees, resolving itself into a middle-aged man. His broad face didn't need the fire to light it, bright with expectancy and something that was, if not actual joy, at least close to it. Wil could see the woman more clearly now, the torchlight glimmering over her fair, plaited hair and sharding over her clear, hopeful face. Now that Wil could see her better, he realized she was no more than a girl, probably not even in her twenties yet.

"Um." Dallin shot a quick glance at Wil.

Wil didn't know why—he had even less of a clue about what was going on than Dallin likely did. He shrugged.

Dallin turned back to the young woman. "As you will."

Having been granted whatever permission she'd been seeking, the girl's face turned nearly beatific. She bowed low to Dallin, her long braid flopping over her shoulder and swinging down like a pendulum.

Nervously she mumbled, "*Thank* you, Shaman. We've waited for you for so long."

She straightened, and stepped cautiously over to Wil. Again she bowed, then reached out with her wide hand and hesitantly took up one of Wil's... kissed it. It was all Wil could do not to snatch it back in alarm.

"Aisling." The woman's voice was breathless. There were actual tears tracking down her smooth cheeks. "Welcome *home*."

Wil... stared. He couldn't do anything else. A vague bit of something that felt like mild horror was curling in his gut, and he couldn't make his mouth work. He dragged his gaze up and over to Dallin, slack-jawed.

Dallin didn't look quite as poleaxed, but it had clearly caught him off guard too. "Hunter!" He yelled it without looking away, gaze still pinging between Wil and the girl, brow drawn down and mouth tightening by the second. "I think you'd best get down here and handle this."

84

Yes. Hunter. These were Hunter's people. He'd know how to... to... to make them *stop* it.

As gently as he could, Wil withdrew his hand, resisting the impulse to wipe it on his trousers. There was nothing repulsive about it, after all, and the girl clearly meant nothing but good, but.... Wil couldn't explain it, even to himself. He'd never been welcomed *anywhere, never,* and this was just too... something.

Wil took an unconscious step back and waited for Dallin to quickstep over to him. He didn't care even a little bit that he was still supposed to be annoyed with Dallin, and he cared even less that he probably looked like a terrified five-year-old as he sank into Dallin's arm around his shoulders, almost cowering from people who had been kinder to him in these first few seconds than anyone before—*ever.*

"What the hell?" he croaked.

No answer but a tightening of Dallin's arm and then a low near-reprimand from Hunter, striding down the path as if he owned it. "Andette! Cawle!"

They both straightened. Andette dropped one more quick double-bow to both Dallin and Wil, then turned to Hunter.

"All is ready, brother." Her shoulders were straight and her chin jutted proud, for the first time since Wil had seen her materializing like a ghost from the dark.

Brother? Wil peered between Hunter and this Andette. In truth, all Linders rather resembled each other to his eye, but these two.... Yes. It wasn't merely some kind of honorific—these two were kin. Perhaps even twins, if Wil was judging their ages correctly. He shot a quick glance at Dallin, noting the reluctant realization, the reflexive roll of Dallin's eyes. Wil almost snorted. Poor Dallin—he couldn't seem to get away from Calders.

"The *Weardas* are alerted, and the captain of the Commonwealth agreed to come across this afternoon." Andette glanced quickly at Dallin, then blushed, turning her eyes back to the ground. "After your message came back, he agreed to meet with you here, unarmed, with only a small entourage. The bulk of his party waits across the river on the other side of the Bounds. Your...." She frowned, seeming to hunt for the proper word. "Your companions from Putnam joined us in camp several days ago. We saw no need to disarm them."

"I see." Dallin smiled, smirky and knowing in the flickering light. "I assume just about everyone's met Corliss, then."

Andette smiled, her expression fond and light, some of the awe leaking from it and making her seem more... real. More like the young girl she was and not the abject devotee she'd seemed a moment ago.

"Constable Stierne has been... busy," Andette agreed. "We thank the Mother that she was sent to us, and we thank the Shaman for guiding her words."

She peered up at Dallin, that same look back again, the obsequious devotion and fervor Wil had seen when Hunter had spoken of his Lost Shaman. Complete and utter adoration. The tension in Dallin's grip on Wil was telling, and Wil knew Dallin saw it too. Wil had never in his life expected to see that same look directed at him, but every time Andette's glance skimmed shyly to his, a new spike of sympathy for Dallin struck Wil. It *was* unnerving, perhaps even a bit obscene. These people knew nothing about Wil, after all—how could they even pretend to love him? And why did they just assume they had the right?

The rest of their party had dropped back, heads bent together, and appeared to be deep in conversation farther up the path. Wil should want to know what they were talking about, but he didn't. Instead he only wondered why the lack of their buffering presence was making him like them more than he had ten minutes ago. Hunter was familiar, and so his presence somewhat comforting, but just thinking about those dozens of fires down there through the thin screen of the trees separating him from them, and the no doubt dozens of people to whom they belonged....

Not caring anymore what it might look like, Wil pushed back more into Dallin. It felt stupid to fear these people, any of them, but it *was* fear—*burned at the stake or crammed on a makeshift throne*, Dallin had snarked at the Old Ones just that morning. Right now, both seemed too possible.

Wil leaned up. "Are they all going to be like this?" he whispered to Dallin.

Dallin sighed. "I'm afraid that's all too possible. It's best we get it over with, I think."

Wil wasn't entirely sure he agreed, but he let Dallin push him past Andette and urge him once more down the path. Hunter silently took up a position to Wil's other side, nodding to Andette as they passed. Wil watched it all with growing trepidation.

"This," he told Dallin, voice thin and strained, "is not at all what I thought it would be."

"It rarely is." Dallin drew Wil in close. "Just *don't* shoot anyone." He snatched the torch from Cawle as they passed, then nodded at Hunter. "You first. Make sure they're not scraping and kneeling when we get there, yeah?"

Hunter shot Wil an apologetic glance before he dipped his head at Dallin. "I'll do what I can." He looked rather dubious, but he nonetheless turned and sprinted off ahead.

Dallin watched him go and then twisted to glance over his shoulder, presumably at Andette, who was neglecting her watch and instead staring after them with a look of blatant longing. Dallin turned back, looked down at Wil, and rolled his eyes.

"Fucking Calders."

"Huh," Wil breathed, overwhelmed and a bit shock-stupid as they paused on the ridge, staring out over the camp. "I thought I smelt cows."

There had to be more than a hundred of them—people, not cows—spread out in various clusters below, campfires set in front of tents that fanned out along the riverside in small constellations. It was lighter down there than where they now stood, still screened inside the cover of the trees. Dusk was only beginning to snatch at the fringes of the lingering gold of failing daylight, and shadowed only slightly the various faces of the people below. Torches were only now being lit, a loose circle around the knots of tents and fires.

It wasn't like up at the caves. These people looked settled in, as if they'd been here for a while and planned to stay for a while more. Chickens clucked and scratched down by the strand, several goats wandering among them and bleating irritation at their fusty complaints.

On a brighter note, maybe that meant there'd be eggs and milk for breakfast.

Dogs roamed through clots of people, sniffing at campfires, then agreeably wagging their tails and scuttling off when they were shooed away. Another fenced pasture was set farther down-river, scores of horses and several cows nosing at winter grass and bundles of hay set at intervals around the wooden fencing. Three great fire pits smoldered beside what Wil guessed was some sort of small barracks or guardhouse, the smell of roasting meat singing its usual siren call to his stomach. Cauldrons steamed nearby, barrels and casks piled and propped against the outer wall of the short stone building.

It didn't look anything like a campsite. It looked like a village.

Children rammed around the place in various stages of play, squeezing through clumps of adults and laughing as they scampered away from half-hearted chiding. They shot at each other with guns made of grubby fingers, then clutched at small chests and crumpled in heaps of giggles as imaginary bullets struck them down.

It gave Wil an eerie shudder—echoes of violence he hadn't seen, had refused to see, but that Dallin had escaped only through... what?

Wil frowned. For the first time, he wondered how Dallin's mother had known, how she'd managed to smuggle her son out before the Brethren found the one child they'd wasted so many other young lives looking for. They'd been thorough, wiping out an entire generation of males, so how did the one male who might as well have had a target painted on his back manage to waft through their crosshairs like so much smoke?

The thought was abruptly troubling. Dallin's dark eyes scanned the scene below, assessing and measuring, and not even seeming to register the children or their macabre sport as they teased death and innocently mocked its reality. Ignoring it deliberately, Wil wondered, or genuinely not seeing because he was so used to looking away?

"What did that commander say to you?" Wil asked quietly. "That *Weard... Weardger...?*"

"*Weardgeréfan.*" Dallin squinted against the gloom as he marked a squad of armed men and women striking off away from the river and heading west into the treebrake. "He said the Old Ones had already alerted them. They've sent runners uphill to warn everyone, and hunting parties to flush out as many as they can. They didn't know which path we'd take down, or they would've sent pickets up to meet us."

Wil watched the fires, thinking. "So they knew."

"Good thing, yeah? One thing that went right today, at least."

Wil didn't reply, somehow disturbed and surprised that there was nothing in Dallin's gaze that marked the significance.

They knew.

He dragged his gaze away and pointed it over his shoulder, watching the old men hobble ever closer, still chattering among themselves about... whatever old men chattered about. Except *these* old men.... Somehow, and all at once, they didn't seem quite as friendly and benevolent as Wil had been thinking them, and Dallin's withholding of trust seemed much more reasonable.

They knew.

Wil turned back to the camp. "Why are there children here?"

"Whole families. They follow along when the *Weardas* have extended patrols. This is their camp—the sentries are billeted farther downriver, broken up into squads and scattered along the Bounds throughout Cildtrog. They're allowed to come to camp when they're not on post." Dallin swiveled his glance up and down the strand with a shrug. "It makes long posts easier on the *Weardas*, and it makes sense, so far as the children. Some of them have both parents on watch at the same time, so the rest of the adults look out for them. Defense is something of a family business here."

Wil watched two children—a boy and a girl, it looked like from here, but since they all wore their hair long, he couldn't tell for sure. They were scrapping over something between them Wil couldn't see, but by the aggression of the encounter, it must be something valuable. Those were some serious punches being thrown. One of the dogs yipped and danced around them, anxiously wagging its tail and sticking its nose into the mix, then leaping back again.

As Wil watched a young man drag the two apart, speaking harshly and shaking them each by the shoulder until they dipped their heads on something approximating apology, he wondered if

Dallin had ever camped here with his mother, playing with mates and waiting for his father to come off patrol. He didn't ask. He didn't want to have to see Dallin's pain as another memory was resurrected and reburied. And then Wil wouldn't be able to help himself asking, pushing, and prodding, and he didn't think he could bear it if Dallin lied to him again, even if Dallin didn't realize he was doing it—it didn't suit him, and he was quite bad at it.

Wil thought of Hunter, the light of righteous violence shining in his eager eyes, and couldn't help seeing its reflection in the features he could make out from this distance.

"I imagine Linders make good soldiers."

"When they're allowed." Dallin caught Wil's curious look, and grimaced. "It's against Lind's laws for its people to leave the Bounds unless so ordered by the Old Ones. And even then, sometimes they won't be allowed back in. Depends on whether or not the Old Ones judge them—" He paused, searching for the right word, his mouth pinching slightly as he found it. "—contaminated." He rolled his eyes. "If they're conscripted, they have to go. Lind is a part of Cynewísan, and they abide by the Commonwealth's laws as much as they have to. So those called up are given provisional dispensation. But there hasn't been a draft since before I retired, so...." He waved a hand over the camp.

All these frustrated warriors with no one against whom to exorcise their pent-up aggressions. Wil almost snorted—the Brethren couldn't *possibly* know what they were getting into, skulking into a place like this.

"Does all meet your satisfaction?" It was a loose, craggy voice attached to a man just as craggy, though he seemed nearly as fit as Dallin, considering his apparent age. The Old Ones had caught up. Walde, Wil thought this one's name was, but he couldn't be sure—he really had lost track after the first few.

Wil turned, and looked them all over more carefully than he'd done before. Gracious and open to the casual glance, all of them, but... now Wil wasn't so sure. Nothing but kind to him, every single one of them, but now he couldn't help wondering what those soft gazes concealed. He caught Calder's eye and remembered Dallin's wariness of him from the very beginning, speculating that Calder's opinions were likely slightly more vigorous than the Old Ones to whom he'd once belonged but perhaps not too far astray. Wil hadn't really had cause to think about it before, but now, seeing how easily Calder fit in with the others, how anyone might have guessed Calder just another of them, were it not for the scars where his Marks used to be and the fact that Wil knew better....

If it hadn't been for Shaw, Wil thought he likely would have allowed Dallin to chase Calder off—that was, assuming Calder would have gone. But Wil liked Shaw, trusted him for the most part, and Shaw seemed to think Calder worthy of an apparently long friendship. Something didn't fit, and Wil couldn't help looking at the group of elders with new caution.

Dallin was right to be suspicious of them. If asked, Wil wouldn't have been able to prove it, but he knew it anyway. The Old Ones were lying to Dallin, every one of them, and if not lying outright, then at least not saying everything.

Dallin said he'd heard the land protest when the Brethren stepped onto it. Was it so unreasonable to assume the Old Ones possessed at least a faint echo of that same connection?

They'd *known* all those years ago. Wil knew they had; they *had* to have.

"Everything appears adequate from up here," Dallin was saying. "Healdes tells me all of the patrols have been alerted, and we can't do much more until they start finding and turning over whatever dens they've managed to hole up in. I'd like to ride out in the morning and—"

"*Brayden!*"

Wil didn't know why he jumped as he did. Perhaps because he'd heard the voice before, and the circumstances under which he'd heard it had been rather unpleasant. The last time he'd heard it, after all, the barrel of a gun had been resting against the nape of Dallin's neck.

He turned to watch Corliss quickstep up the slope, footholds established carefully but confidently as she rushed at them, relief and reprimand both in the wide smile on her flushed face. Cleaner than Wil had seen her last, her blue and brown free of stains and road dust, and her bright hair twisted neatly into a knot at the back of her head.

It was stupid, childish, but Wil couldn't help it—he angled himself slightly behind Dallin and peered at Corliss warily from around Dallin's shoulder.

Dallin seemed to have no such reservations. His face lit up, and he started to move forward. Stupid and childish again, but again, Wil couldn't help it—he snatched at Dallin's sleeve and tugged him back. Dallin peered down at him with a bit of a frown, questioning, but Corliss was upon them before Wil could even try to form an excuse.

"Thank the Mother!" Corliss took hold of Dallin's arms, and shook him. "I've been talking myself blue in the face for bloody *days*. One more and my throat will start to bleed."

Dallin snorted good-naturedly. "And we all know how you hate to talk."

"And we all know how you love to dump your work on your peons."

It was like nothing had ever happened, Wil thought uncomfortably. Had he missed the forgive-and-forget part?

Corliss's pale blue eyes shifted, locking on to Wil and narrowing slightly, but unaccountably her smile modulated into something softer. She pushed Dallin aside—no easy thing—taking away Wil's barrier of wide shoulders. There was nothing Wil could do but either move with Dallin and make it obvious that he'd been hiding, or stand and meet Corliss's stare. He chose the latter and lifted his chin—which, again unaccountably, only made Corliss's smile widen into a grin.

She let go of Dallin, and extended her hand toward Wil. "We've not exactly met." There was perhaps a touch of apology in her tone, but Wil couldn't be certain. "Corliss Stierne, constable of Putnam and sometime-aide to your, um." She shot a smirky, knowing glance up at Dallin.

"Guardian." Dallin's tone was a stern warning inside a bit of affection.

Corliss arched an auburn eyebrow. "Is that what they call it here?"

"Corliss—"

"Yes, yes, I expect that's the new title you were talking about, and I must say it suits you." Corliss turned back to Wil, hand still extended. "A pleasure."

She wasn't going to drop her hand. Wil could keep ignoring it until the discomfort was apparent to all, or....

He grimaced, then reached out and took her hand. "Wil."

"Wil. It's a pleasure and an honor to meet you."

Corliss's grip was strong and sure as she pumped Wil's arm—only once, but firmly—then let him withdraw his hand. Oddly, she seemed sincere, and even more oddly, Wil believed her. Corliss tilted her head, eyeing Wil with a gaze that reminded him this woman was a constable, and it had been mere chance that Wil had ended up across a table from Dallin all those weeks ago. It could just as easily have been her. Wil couldn't help wondering how different things might have gone in the basement of the Putnam constabulary if he'd been sitting across from Corliss, and if her questions would have been easier to answer. Or even harder.

"You look hungry," Corliss informed him.

Wil blinked and shot a small frown up at Dallin.

Dallin puffed out a weary snort. "Don't look at *me*. You always look hungry." He nodded at Corliss. "Small word of advice— always follow a mum at suppertime. They know where to find all the best stuff, and no one complains when they cut the queue." He turned to the Old Ones and their squires. "Are we ready, then?"

It didn't sound like much of a question, but nonetheless, several answered with a negating shake of the head. "We must sound the horn," one of them said—this time Wil didn't even try to remember or guess his name—and prodded the young man next to him down the slope with a stern nod.

Dallin watched the boy go with a grimace.

Corliss's mouth tightened and she took a step closer to Wil, then flipped a dour look on the Old Ones. "Is this really necessary?"

The one who'd given Wil the bowl—Singréne—bristled somewhat. "We must welcome the Shaman back home. It is tradition."

"So is fucking in the fields on Planting Day, but we don't blow horns while we're doing it, do we?"

Wil couldn't help the surprised bit of a cackle—both at the question and the way every mouth but Shaw's pinched in tight upon its utterance. Shaw merely covered his mouth with his hand, laughter twinkling bright in his eyes. It only made Wil's own laughter burble more insistently, and he had to duck his head and hold his breath to stop it when all eyes turned on him.

"Corliss, it's fine." It didn't look like Dallin *quite* meant it, because he hardened his gaze and directed his next statement more to the Old Ones than to Corliss. "He's stronger than he looks."

Wil frowned, more surprise, and this one not terribly laughable. Defense again, and he hadn't even known he'd needed it. But now that he looked, he could see the worry on each wrinkled face, the vague suspicion that Wil might spasm any second and start shooting lightning bolts from his fingertips.

They had to have heard about Chester. Why hadn't he thought of that before?

"Of course he is," Corliss agreed, stout and serious. "Anyone can tell by looking, I should think—anyone with half a brain." She deliberately looked only at Dallin, but it was clear her words were meant for the Old Ones. The past few days at the Bounds must have been very interesting ones indeed, if Wil was interpreting the tension correctly. "I only meant that you've been riding all day, and Wil looks like he'd eat a side of beef if someone would only hand one over. So it seems to me—"

"Wait." Dallin's voice was shot through with realization and new urgency. He grabbed one of the boys by the elbow. "Go after him and stop him. No horns." When the boy looked wide-eyed to the Old Ones, Dallin's teeth clenched, and he shoved the boy toward the slope. "Now—*hurry!*"

The boy slid down the incline in his haste, then quickly caught his feet to sprint after the other boy, who was just now wading into the crowd.

Dallin turned back to the Old Ones. "You sound those horns and they'll know exactly where Wil is. We can't risk it."

Enlightenment flashed over each face, then chagrin, except for Corliss.

"That's why he's First Constable," she murmured aside to Wil. "You couldn't do better for a Guardian."

Wil couldn't help the small smile, the agreeable nod. "I know."

"Sorry," Dallin was saying to the others. "I don't mean to spoil your party, but I won't risk his safety."

"He couldn't be safer," one of them argued. "Where is safer in all of Cynewísan but in Lind itself, surrounded by *Weardas*?"

"How about *not* in Lind, where hundreds of nutters are prowling about looking for him?"

Wil was surprised Dallin didn't mention that the raid of his youth had been in Lind, and the *Weardas*, according to what he'd been able to glean from all of the Not Talking About It, had been thoroughly ineffective. It seemed increasingly apparent, however, that it was an event to which there was recurrent allusion but never actual vocalization—at least not by using actual descriptive words. Come to think of it, Wil had yet to hear anyone mention a single word about Dallin's mother, or even the fact that he'd had one.

"It isn't as though they don't know already." Corliss nodded down toward the camp. "Look at them. Word is already spreading."

She was right. Perhaps it was the commotion with the boys, or maybe Hunter's cautions under Dallin's earlier directive, or perhaps they'd simply been lingering up here for too long and it had only been a matter of time. Whatever it was, faces were turning up toward them and a hushed expectancy was leaking across the camp in swift waves of silence.

"Where are Creighton and Woodrow?" Dallin asked, his voice low and slightly edgy as he leaned in toward Corliss. He shot a narrow look down over the quieting crowd, then over his shoulder to sweep the Old Ones with a bit of a glare, before turning his dark gaze back on Corliss.

The silent message was clear: *I don't trust these people. Where are mine?*

Corliss patted Dallin's arm. "Creighton went on patrol with a squad of the Linders. Woodrow is waiting down by the kegs."

Wil and Dallin both followed the jerk of her chin. The surcoat was difficult to pick out in the falling dusk but still distinctive. Wil peered about, looking for Hunter, but there were too many blond heads and wide shoulders to pick out one set.

"Don't start jumping at shadows." Corliss slanted a smile at Dallin. "They love him already, and they bloody worship you. If there's trouble, it won't be from them."

"I didn't think it." But Dallin's discomfort was apparent, and he stepped closer to Wil. "Nevertheless."

He nodded at Corliss and waited. She twigged right away, stepping to Wil's other side and placing a hand at the small of Wil's back. Wil scowled and only just kept himself from twitching away, but he couldn't keep from being annoyed at the assumptions —from both of them. Regardless of the fact that the idea of walking down that slope and into that watching crowd was probably one of the most daunting things he'd ever contemplated.

"I doubt they're going to eat me." He shot Dallin an irritated glance but softened it when he marked the apparent unease. "There are nothing but good intentions down there. Can't you feel it?"

Wil could. Or, at least, it was nothing like the oppressive weight of too many *voicesmindseyes* drilling into him as it had been this morning. Granted, Dallin had taken most of that away for him, but he couldn't change what was in other people's hearts, and right now Wil felt nothing that alarmed him. Except perhaps an overfaced inner writhing at being stared at by so many sets of eyes. Then again, they were likely staring more at their Lost Shaman than they were at Wil, so perhaps Wil was overreacting.

Anyway, he *was* hungry, now that Corliss had mentioned it,

and whatever was roasting in those pits was making his mouth water.

"Good intentions are not always a promise of good behavior." Dallin's gaze continually swept the crowd, dark and watchful. He nodded. "Off with you, let's go."

Wil twitched his shoulders irritably as Corliss's hand pressed into his back, but he allowed her to prod him into a slow walk down the incline. Dallin led the way, staring down anyone who might even fleetingly consider blocking their path.

The silence was not complete, soft murmurs continually swiffing through, but it was unnerving even so. Wil fancied he could hear the horses chewing, and he was *sure* he could hear the chickens muttering at each other. The people seemed sufficiently cowed by their Shaman's stare, but there remained that light in their eyes that Wil had seen in all the other Linders when faced with Dallin—like he could tell them all to go drown themselves in the river and they'd bow deeply then leap in. No, they'd bow, then run, *then* leap. All of them dipped their heads as they passed, even the children. Some of the elders even wept, though quietly.

Wil could see the tension strung tight in the set of Dallin's spine, the stiffness of his shoulders, but he peered steadily back at all who met his eyes, his jaw set. Wil, on the other hand, watched his boots plant themselves in the pale trampled grass, watched Corliss's boots, watched Dallin's back, until the first hand came into his peripheral vision, and reached.

Smallish, a girl of perhaps fifteen. A whisper of "Aisling" leaked from her gently upturned lips as she plucked at Wil's sleeve, then snatched her hand back, curled it into a fist, and brought it up to cover her mouth. It seemed to open a floodgate. Two more, and another two, and then Wil was losing track, losing his calm, as one hand after another came at him. Never threatening, never grasping, merely touching once, quickly, then dropping away. And all the while "Aisling" flittered about him, and "Bless," and "Mother's Gift," and any number of unnerving descriptives that only served to drive Wil's heart up into this throat and constrict his chest. The closeness was making it difficult to breathe, the mass of bodies heating the very air and making sweat slide down between Wil's shoulder blades.

They weren't touching Dallin—almost as though they wouldn't dare—merely making a gap between them, then closing it loosely again behind him so that Wil had to actually push his way through. It took all his will not to snarl and snap at them as they smiled down at him, those fleeting tentative touches landing on arms and shoulders. Some even lightly brushed his hair, and Wil had to really try not to twitch and jolt.

"Dallin," he said, except his throat was too tight, and it came out a whisper, drowned out by the low murmur of voices surrounding him. He reached out, meaning to take hold of Dallin's sleeve, but bodies were coming between them, and hands came out, reaching for his own, so Wil snatched it back.

"Just breathe." Corliss was calm and soothing, and annoying as hell. "They won't hurt you. They only—"

"I know that." Wil couldn't help how it *snapped* out of him, peering up into blue eyes, then hazel, then blue again—all of them expressing some form of adoration and acceptance, and surely none of it for him, because they didn't know, they couldn't *know*—before he tore his gaze away and pointed it again to the ground. "I'm not a child." He would've wrenched away from Corliss's hand against his back, but he hardly had room to move. He was only just above eye level with broad chests and more bosoms than he'd ever seen in one place in his whole life, and they were cutting off his air, sucking it all up for themselves 'til he was nearly hyper-ventilating, and they wouldn't stop *touching* him.

"I know you're not a child." The tone of Corliss's voice, with its easy, soothing pitch, seemed to belie her words. "I've six of my own. Believe me, I can tell the difference."

"Wil?"

Dallin's voice, dark eyes peering back at him. Wil didn't know if he was relieved or embarrassed that his acute discomfort had been spotted, recognized, and the confusion only ramped up his agitation. He merely stared, letting Dallin read what he would, until it hit Wil—

This, right here... this was why Dallin thought it best to keep things from Wil. This was why an otherwise painfully honest man had stood in front of Wil just this morning, and again mere moments ago, looked him in the eye, and said it was "best" if Wil didn't ask about his own fate. Because if someone was perpetually asking you for rescue, how much faith could you have that they might dredge up the will to rescue themselves if they had to?

When had Wil crossed the line from accepting help when he really needed it to taking the easy way every time it was offered? And it *was* an offer, each and every time, Dallin *always* asked, he'd never forced rescue on Wil. Yet how many times had Wil actually refused? He couldn't remember a single instance.

...when you expect nothing but complete and total submission to your will from me.

Except was Wil submitting to Dallin's will, or was Dallin submitting to Wil's? If Wil twisted his mouth, furrowed his brow, Dallin would stalk through the crowding horde and whisk Wil away—because Wil asked him to. If Wil scowled and rolled his eyes, Dallin would leave Wil to it, and still be there, waiting, in case Wil changed his mind.

Wil *knew* these things—knew them because he'd lived both situations, and more than once. So who, in truth, was submitting to whom?

Blaming Dallin for a situation Wil himself had at least half helped to create.

Oh hell.

With effort, Wil lifted his chin. He even managed to dredge up a smile, though he wouldn't lay bets on how convincing it was. He told Dallin "I'm fine" with a look, then turned toward the next hand that reached for him—reached back.

His hand was immediately enclosed in a wide, rough grip, so Wil swallowed the lump of gravel in his throat and reached with the other too. He made himself look up and say "Hullo" to an old woman, then a young man without really seeing either of them, a rigid smile stretched across his mouth in a mask of what he hoped at least somewhat resembled warmth.

Dallin was still watching, concerned, so Wil took a deep breath, looked at Dallin straight, and gave him a real smile—meant for Dallin and only Dallin, small and private in this sea of people. Perhaps not wholly convinced but willing to take his word for it, Dallin half smiled back, lifted an eyebrow, and shrugged. He shot a mild warning glance over Wil's shoulder—presumably at Corliss —then started off again.

He really was a good man. And he really was an excellent Guardian.

And Wil really did want to have him by the river tonight.

"They've been waiting for you both."

Wil hadn't noticed until just that minute that Corliss's hand had moved from the gentle but commanding push at the small of his back to a more comforting grip on his shoulder—not as wide and warm and comforting as Dallin's, but....

Anyway, it wasn't like these people were impeding Wil in any way. They were just... touching. No grabbing, no trying to take from him, nothing sinister or even truly demanding—just touching. It made Wil's skin crawl, but it didn't actually hurt.

"The past four days have been very... enlightening," Corliss went on. "Most of them knew the legend, but none of them knew it was true. Word has been leaking back from your camp about how their Shaman was healing you, and then this morning—" She snorted. "Well, this morning for you—we didn't hear about it 'til this afternoon."

Wil grimaced. "The fires."

"Aye, the fires."

Wil nearly groaned. "The company that was with us—they hadn't been told. They didn't know what it meant." He turned a hopefully amiable smile on a young... girl, he thought; it was so hard to tell with the younger ones. Nods all around to whomever, a clasping of hands and a few mumbled greetings, and they all backed off and made room for the next. It was sort of orderly, now that Wil was paying attention.

"Ha." Corliss slanted a grin. "We didn't have that problem here. As soon as they heard, they—All right, that's a bit too close, lad, step back, there's a good boy."

This to a little boy who'd wrapped his arms briefly around Wil's torso before obediently dropping away and melting back into the gathering, but with a shy grin up at Wil as he retreated.

Corliss shook her head, but it was fond. "It was like they'd got proof they hadn't known they wanted. You've no idea how... hm." A small smirk lifted her mouth. "I was going to say you've no idea how popular you are here, but...." Her glance shifted over the crowd, then wryly back to Wil.

Wil couldn't help the snort. "'Popular' is—" He blew out a long breath. "'Popular' is new." And not wholly welcome.

"Mm, well, I think I'd prefer your version of it rather than Brayden's." Corliss watched Dallin make his way to the edges of the gathering, hailing the man he'd called Woodrow as he neared what Wil was sure now was a guardhouse—had to be, with that turret atop it. "Not much of a glad-hander," Corliss went on. "He'd much prefer they were all lined up and saluting, than... well, this. And at least they're not afraid to look you in the eye."

Wil kept nodding his head, kept smiling, kept touching and letting himself be touched as he followed Corliss's gaze, noting the bowed heads, the bit of a berth these people all gave Dallin as he bulled his way through. Yes, that *would* bother someone as straightforward as Dallin. He'd constantly be wondering what was behind the gazes they wouldn't let him see. Respect, Dallin knew what to do with; awe made him twitchy and angry.

Wil couldn't help but feel sorry for these people. They knew what they'd been taught, and they'd obviously been taught the Shaman was a man to be feared and obeyed, a man of great magic and skill to be revered and held apart from "normal" people. Obeyed blindly. Nothing to prove to these people, except perhaps that he wasn't a god, he wasn't all-knowing, he could be hurt, he could be killed.

"They expect him to be perfect." Wil frowned, surprised by the twist it gave him.

"Mm." Corliss pursed her mouth. "Doesn't leave much room for being a real person, does it?"

Wil peered back over his shoulder toward the slope where the Old Ones stood, apart from it all and watching. From here they all looked cold and remote—not at all the friendly old men who'd greeted Wil and given him gifts, but calculating and removed from the people they were supposed to guide and protect. The people gave the Old Ones as wide a berth as they were giving Dallin. Wil remembered his first impressions of Calder, how he'd seemed like a force of nature, swatting aside obstacles without prejudice or compassion only because they'd somehow managed to blunder onto a path that crossed his purpose. Now Wil could hardly pick

Calder out among them—Calder fit in as though he still belonged there.

How many of them had been here when Dallin was chosen? Some, most, all?

"Most" seemed the likeliest answer. They were extraordinarily long-lived, but Wil supposed it wasn't entirely logical to assume at least one or two hadn't popped off in the more than twenty years since Devon had called Dallin's name with his last breath. And now, for the first time, it occurred to Wil that it was quite conceivable that Calder had been one of them then.

It made Wil pause. People were still tugging at him, murmuring to him, but he no longer registered their existence.

He couldn't get it out of his head. They'd known the raid was coming. Just as they knew the Brethren were here before Dallin told them. They'd known Dallin as a boy, all of them, and Dallin didn't remember it, but *they did*, and yet they pretended otherwise. *Why?* What were they hiding from their Shaman?

"Wil?"

Wil peered over at Corliss, pensive. He opened his mouth before he realized he had nothing to say that would sound sane, at least not to her. Perhaps not even to Dallin, now that Wil considered, but Dallin would find the sanity in it eventually. He always did.

"Wil! Thank the Mother." Hunter was plowing through the thinning crowd, face so set with imperious authority that Wil almost snorted. "Back away, go on, give the man room to breathe. Léah, leave off, then, don't cling so."

Wil smiled at the young woman Hunter had apparently been chiding, because the light grip he hadn't even really noticed suddenly let go. She backed away a step or two, answering Wil's smile with one of her own, considerably less shy than most of the others. Not quite as stunningly beautiful as Thistle, but quite pretty and fit. For the first time, it occurred to Wil that, had he been paying attention, he might have caught more meaningful gazes during all the ruckus than Léah's, and he wondered how many of these people would let him bed them if he wanted to. Knowing what he was, not trying to dig into him to sate a hunger they didn't know they had, but trying instead to snatch a piece of what they knew him to be. All this want, all this belief, all this faith.

Her power depends on her people lending her the strength of their belief.

And what you do, take that want and use it....

Yes. Lind was a very powerful place indeed. Wil wondered if Dallin suspected just exactly how powerful.

Then again, of course he did. Why else would the idea of Fæðme and what it held frighten Dallin enough that he'd actually try lying his way around it?

"Apologies, Wil." Hunter dropped a small bow. "I warned them as the Shaman instructed, but by the time I—"

"Don't trouble yourself," Wil told him vaguely, eyes moving thoughtfully between the people still hovering and the Old Ones standing up on the rise and watching. He shook his head and turned to Hunter. "I expect you were given an impossible task, and you can't be blamed. Anyway, it isn't so bad."

Wil's skin was still crawling, and his heart was still rabbiting, but nothing more. He was whole and more or less unmolested, and he hadn't cowered and cringed within the circle of his Guardian's arm throughout, so all in all, it was rather a success. He tipped his head toward Corliss.

"This is a friend of the Shaman's. Corliss...." He paused.

"Stierne." Corliss finally released her hold on Wil's shoulder, and offered her hand. "Constable Corliss Stierne. And you are...?"

Hunter took Corliss's hand automatically, shook it, then

bowed over it before releasing it. "Hunter Calder. I am... uh." He frowned, obviously lost for a way to explain to an outlander exactly what he was—though clearly it involved some sort of possessiveness, because Hunter eyed Corliss with a guarded gaze and took a step in Wil's direction.

"Hunter has kindly agreed to babysit me." Wil smirked as Hunter sputtered. "Dallin has assigned him as my bodyguard for those times when he can't do it himself."

"Ah." Corliss smiled at Hunter. "And a fine bodyguard I'm sure you make." She nodded toward where Dallin appeared to be in the process of introductions with five men in the livery of Commonwealth soldiers. Wil realized with a bit of a start that these men must be the very ones who'd had their guns trained between Dallin's eyes as they'd stood in Chester's square. "Why don't you see if you can clear a path for us over there without snapping at these lovely folk who've come to honor their Aisling? I'm sure Wil would appreciate being included in the conversation, since I've no doubt it will have something to do with him."

The "*Yes, ma'am*" Hunter smartly snapped out almost made Wil laugh, but he merely kept smiling at those lingering around them, nodding his head and offering vague greetings when it seemed appropriate.

...she's got this... mother thing about her, Dallin had told Wil fondly. *People listen—they can't help themselves.*

Wil could see why. Corliss had laid a loaded gun at his Guardian's nape the last time Wil had encountered her and had appeared to have every intention of using it. And yet here Wil was, allowing her to prod him through the rest of the crowd toward a palaver he'd had no real intention of joining, and hoping she hadn't forgotten about the feeding-him part.

Good job she hadn't been the one assigned him back in Putnam, Wil thought as he followed in Hunter's wake. Wil likely would have spilled everything at the mere prospect of succumbing to her caretaking nature—seduction by mothering, *ha!*—and spilling everything to anyone but his Guardian would have been disastrous. No flight to Lind with Corliss—more like a quick trip back to the Guild with Síofra. She never would have believed Wil the way Dallin had done, regardless of any benevolent nature. Corliss would have thought Wil mad and sent him back "for his own good"—and lived the rest of her life believing she'd done right by him.

Wil shuddered. He couldn't quite help it.

"...did you end up in the infantry?" Dallin was saying when they reached him. He was smiling more broadly than Wil would have credited, considering who these men were and what their intentions had been only days ago. Apparently Dallin didn't carry grudges.

"It was made clear to me several years ago that the cavalry is now considered a young man's vocation," the captain said, civilly enough, Wil supposed, but Wil still couldn't help the way his mouth tightened. "When I reached my fifteen-year service mark, I was 'offered' either retirement or a commission training snipers, and, well." The captain shrugged. "The army is all I know." He shifted a bit. "I must say, when I was finally told what our assignment was and who we were meant to arrest—" The captain looked away quickly, then back up to Dallin again. "It didn't seem right from the beginning. And ordering us to take along Dominion scum—"

Corliss loudly cleared her throat, lifted her eyebrow at the captain, and shot a meaningful glance toward Wil. The captain reddened slightly but merely closed his mouth. If there were any apologies behind his teeth, Wil would never hear them. The captain had spent too many years fighting "Dominion scum," and it would take more than Wil's presence to dispel the epithet.

Dallin, smirking—because he just would—took up the sudden silence. "Captain Wisena, may I present to you my companion, Wil." He paused for a moment, flipping Wil an asking glance, then went on, "The Aisling. I know Corliss has informed you as to what that name means."

The captain nodded. "Indeed." The look he shot Wil was skeptical. He seemed caught between a bow and a salute, and not really wanting to offer either.

Wil decided to cut through both. He put out his hand. "Captain."

Wisena took Wil's offered hand and shook it, his grip almost reluctant. "Aisling." He was trying not to give anything away, but he wasn't quite as good at it as Dallin—even as Wisena said the word, his mouth turned down in a sour line.

"I'd prefer Wil, if you don't mind." With a smile he hoped was cool and confident, Wil withdrew his hand and peered between Wisena and Dallin. "Do you two know each other?"

"I served under Captain Brayden on the northern border." A different sort of awe was in Wisena's eyes and voice than those here in Lind, but Wil could tell Wisena had admired Dallin back then and had likely learned a lot from him. Good. This sort of respect Dallin didn't mind and knew what to do with. Wisena looked back at Wil, gaze going slightly tight again, skeptical and trying not to show it. "I was glad and relieved to hear there was a different reason for his... actions than what we'd been told."

Wil supposed he could substitute "treachery" for "actions" and be closer to what Wisena couldn't quite bring himself to say. And clearly Wisena blamed Wil for the besmirching of his former captain's character and reputation among those Commonwealth troops who'd been told the same story Wisena had been told by Síofra.

Wisena looked Wil over critically—not *quite* the way men

usually looked Wil over, but close enough—as though Wisena was trying to decide if what Wil apparently had to offer the noble former Captain Brayden could possibly be worth what Dallin had given up to become the little catamite's Guardian.

I know what I look like, Wil had told Brayden once. This was how he knew.

"You'll understand why I've asked Cap—" Wisena cut himself off. "You'll understand why I've asked Brayden if it might be possible to provide some sort of... proof of your claims." Wisena dipped his head, not even close to apology, and opened a hand. "Between Chester and Constable Stierne, I've seen and heard enough to make me believe it wise to hesitate before following my orders. But only hesitate." He smiled, and not terribly kindly. "Orders, after all, are orders."

Proof. Interesting. Just what exactly was Wisena expecting Wil to do? Wasn't Chester proof enough?

Dallin's mouth had gone tight. "As I've already told the captain," he said, speaking to Wil but burning holes in Wisena with his sharp gaze, "this is not a matter of performing magic tricks to satisfy his curiosity." He turned to Wil, gaze gone softer, with no small amount of warning inside it. "It's too dangerous. You've nothing to prove."

Perhaps not to Dallin, or even the whole of Lind. But to this man...?

Dallin needed Wisena, Lind needed him, and for all his prig-gish doubt about Wil himself, Wisena really was sincerely caught between faith and duty. More than Dallin had been all those weeks ago, because Dallin hadn't had much in the way of faith until it had walked up to him and bashed him upside his head. But Wisena stood on the border between risking his country and risking his soul—and he didn't have the consolation of direct orders from the Mother Herself, only the word of someone he used to love and respect but whom he'd been told was a traitor under the spell of a mad Dominionite who'd run away from home and caused a schism in delicate negotiations that could mean the difference between peace and war. And if even Corliss—who Dallin had apparently known for quite some time, and who seemed to genuinely love and respect him as well—if even she had believed what they'd told her, enough to put a gun on her friend....

"Too dangerous" didn't really seem to be the point.

Wil said nothing, merely sucked in a long breath, blew it out slowly, and nodded. He peered around at all the faces of those closest, watching and waiting, and all the faces of those farther away, also watching but not knowing why.

He dropped his pack to the ground, unslung the rifle, and shoved it at Wisena with a cold little half smile. "Hold this, please." Wil squared his shoulders and stepped away toward the river.

"*Wil!*" Dallin called and started after him. "Wil, you don't have to do this."

"Yes, I do." Wil looked over his shoulder as Dallin caught him up. "And you know why."

Dallin actually growled, clearly perturbed. "All right, then." He took hold of Wil's elbow, pulled him to a halt, and turned him to face him. "I don't *want* you to this. I'm asking you not to."

"You need him." Wil swept his arm to encompass the camp. "They need him. And this is the only way he'll do what you need him to do."

"Then I'll find another way. This isn't—"

"This is *exactly* the way, and you know it."

Dallin glowered darkly. "You don't know what could happen. What if—?"

"What if what I choose to do or not do right this second is the difference between peace for your country or another decade of war? I asked you once what would happen if you were given a choice between me and Cynewísan. This is it, Dallin, we're standing dead-center in the middle of that choice, and I've just decided it was wholly unfair of me to put it to you. It isn't even *your* choice."

"Strange, because it seems to me I've made it several times over already." Dallin was furious, frightened, and furious *because* he was frightened. "*Damn* it! All of what came at you this morning, it's still here, waiting for you and straining against its traces, and what you're proposing is tantamount to calling it down on yourself. I watched you bleed from your *eyes*, Wil. I watched you vomit blood into the dirt until I thought your guts were going to spill out into the mud."

Wil stared into the depth of pleading in Dallin's dark eyes, looked squarely at what was behind it all, and didn't allow himself to look away this time. He slipped his hand to Dallin's nape, pulled him down, and kissed him, hard and with more meaning inside it than Wil could ever speak. And then he pulled back, stepped away, and lifted his hand. He opened it, palm up.

"I have to."

He called the lightning.

Thunder boomed above their heads, but it didn't even come close to the thunder in Dallin's gaze, heavy and filled with wrath as he stared at Wil through the sizzling *pop* and too-bright flashes that danced over Wil's palm as lightning reached down from the sky in jagged teeth of dazzling light and then sputtered harmlessly as it splayed over his fingers. Wil could feel it all, what Dallin had warned him about—ramming against the boundaries of Wil's Self, looking for cracks in his defenses, trying to squeeze its way through —but by the set of Dallin's jaw, the tension in his face, and the pain lines beginning to etch themselves at the corners of his mouth, Wil knew Dallin was... what had he called it? Channeling.

Setting himself beneath it. Shoring Wil up, because it was what Dallin did—he couldn't help himself, because things like this... this was what you did for people you cared about.

"This is why you frighten me," Dallin said through his teeth. "These chances you take—" The spatter of light over his face made him look fierce and dangerous. "*This* is why I'm afraid to tell you what you want to know."

Even though they both knew he would.

Who is submitting to whom? Dallin wasn't saying it, but his eyes were.

Wil only shook his head, stepped in close, and kissed him again. Lightning spat all around them, a living column of raw power stretching from the sky to Wil's hand, through him, and into Dallin, tethering warp to weft and enclosing them inside itself. Ozone was sharp in the air, currents flaring between them and sharpening every touch, every breath, every reaction, until the need to have *more* was nearly unbearable.

Blatant intimacy for all eyes to see, and Wil truly didn't care. Let them look—they should see what their Shaman meant to their Aisling.

Slowly Wil drew away, said, "I'm pretty sure I love you," pleased by the way it gained depth with the power that bound them, pleased that it wasn't at all as difficult to say out loud as he'd imagined, pleased by the way Dallin's voice wavered and his eyes filled and his jaw clenched to stop it as he said it back. Words Wil had never expected to say, never expected to have said to him, and spoken through the blinding weave of everything that trussed them one to the other. "Warp and weft." Wil smiled at Dallin, said, "I'm sorry," because he knew Dallin would forgive him, then took a long breath, braced himself.

Pulled it back.

It wasn't nearly as wrenching as he'd been expecting. A

moment of pain and overwhelming heat, and his ears popped, but Wil didn't do much more than stagger, blinking into the darkness, the ropy shapes of the lightning still spiking his vision. A little dizzy, perhaps, but he hadn't swooned, as he'd almost been expecting to. His mouth tasted foul, full of copper, and he spat, noting without surprise the streak of red. He dragged his sleeve under his nose, again not at all surprised when Dallin shoved a handkerchief at him. Wil took it and blotted the blood dripping down over his lip, then obediently tipped his head back and allowed Dallin to guide him to sit in the grass. It was only another moment before Dallin settled beside Wil, draped his arm around Wil's shoulders, and pulled him in.

"You're a bloody idiot," Dallin growled, but there was no real anger inside it.

"Oh, I know." Wil dabbed at the blood seeping from his nose. "It's why you put up with me." He smirked around the handkerchief when Dallin gave him a bemused frown. "Because I make you look good. I mean, what good is a Guardian if he never has to rescue anyone?"

Dallin shook his head, exasperated but fond. "I only hope I live to see the day when you put me out of a job." He squeezed Wil in closer and roughly kissed the crown of his head.

"Captain Brayden." Wisena stood before them, holding Wil's rifle at parade rest, mien somber but more deferential than he'd been before. "Um. Guardian." He dipped a low nod to Wil, then turned his glance back on Dallin and lifted his chin. "I believe you have a strategy you would like to discuss."

Dallin's mouth pinched up tight as he stared at Wisena. He turned to Wil, noted the satisfied smirk beneath the handkerchief, and gave him a glare. "You're still an idiot."

Wil didn't participate in the discussion with Wisena. He didn't need to. Dallin would fill him in later. But Wil made sure Hunter was included in the party as they retired into the guardhouse for privacy. The problem of a bodyguard—Hunter's problem more than Dallin's—was solved by Wil commandeering Corliss. Hunter was clearly torn. Wil had to smirk at the jealous glances Hunter shot Corliss, but the Shaman was where Hunter's real loyalties lay, and he was obedient to a fault. So when Wil insisted, Hunter less than graciously ceded the charge of him.

Corliss certainly didn't mind. She seemed to know her way around quite well, and Wil hadn't forgotten that she knew where all the good food was. Anyway, despite the fact that Wil couldn't quite get past the gun to Dallin's head, Corliss was very personable and provided a comfortable buffer between Wil and the people who'd stood in line to touch him before and now gave him more room than necessary. The adoring looks of before had modulated into something quite a bit more chary, but it didn't seem like it was enough to put them off, just enough that they gave Wil some distance—which was what he preferred.

"That was a hell of a show you put on." Corliss said it casually as they sat in the grass, trenchers overflowing with slabs of beef, blackened potatoes, and more green vegetables than Wil had a name for.

He pulled apart the still smoldering potato jacket to expose the tender, steaming mounds of white pulp inside. "Yow, *ow*." He sucked on his fingers. "Seemed the best way to dispel all the doubts at once."

"I've no doubt it did that. Damn, I forgot beer." Corliss turned her head, scanning. "Ah. Ryne, dear, would you be a love and fetch us two beers? There's a good girl."

Amused despite himself, Wil watched the girl—Ryne, apparently—scamper off.

"You seem to know a lot of people here." He took a healthy bite of something that looked like a tiny cabbage and immediately regretted it—it was bitter and foul, and he leaned to the side and spat it into the grass.

Corliss watched it all with a smirk. "Try the beets. They've got a different way of pickling here, and they're quite good." She paused. "That's the red."

"I know what beets are."

Corliss only shrugged. "You didn't know what the sprouts were, that's all."

"Well, I know what *beets* are." Wil couldn't help the way it curled defensive. "And I know what meat is, and I know what green beans are, and I know what—" Shit. He slumped, cheeks warming. "All right, I don't know what this other green thing is."

"Mustard greens." Corliss pointed a bright smile over Wil's shoulder. "Ah, Ryne, lovie, you're a wonderful girl." She held out her hand. "Here we are, then."

Ryne came forward, lanky and tall, though she couldn't have been more than twelve or so. She smiled shyly at Corliss as she handed over a wooden flagon, amber beer slopping over the side, then more nervously at Wil.

Dropping the mustard greens back onto his plate and licking the buttery juice off his fingers, Wil smiled as unalarmingly as he could and held out his hand for the other mug.

"I won't bite, I promise."

Biting was probably not what she was worried about.

"He won't shoot you with lightning either," Corliss put in bluntly.

For all its lack of tact, it seemed the right thing to say, because Ryne snorted as though the idea had never even occurred to her and took a step toward Wil. She held the beer out to him and didn't even flinch when he took it from her.

Wil gave her a broad smile. "Thank you, Ryne."

"You're very welcome...." She faltered, eyes widening in dismay.

"You may call me Wil, if you like."

She had quite a lovely smile. "You're very welcome, Wil."

She blushed prettily, shot a glance at Corliss, and then escaped with several backward grins as a small horde of her peers immediately closed around her, apparently wanting every detail. Wil watched them as they bolted off, shaking his head. He took a sip from the cup, eyebrows rising. The beer was hearty and full-bodied and so concentrated Wil could taste the rich, warm flavor of the hops.

Corliss smirked out the side of her mouth as she gnawed at a hunk of beef. "You can be quite charming when you want to be."

"I might say the same of you."

She washed down her mouthful with a sip of beer. "So tell me, Wil-the-Aisling—how does a man get to be—" She peered at him closely. "—I'm going to guess twenty-five." Her head cocked slightly to the side. "How does a man get to be your age and not know what a cabbage sprout is?"

Wil frowned. "Didn't Dallin tell you?"

"We didn't have time for much but the necessities." She picked up a beet, gave it a pensive look, then turned her gaze on Wil. "The only things I know about you are what was in that little book he made me read and what I saw and heard in Chester." She took a bite of the beet, by all appearances merely making casual small talk. "And how he feels about you."

Ah, so that was it—protecting her friend, or trying to.

Somehow it didn't tweak Wil as he would've thought. He merely took a bite of his own beef—*oh* holy *fuck*, that was good—and chewed it slowly, both to savor it and to think about how he wanted to answer. In the end he decided she'd appreciate bluntness, so he gave it to her.

"I was kept prisoner by Síofra my whole life until a little over three years ago. Most of that time, I was drugged, and if I ever had a cabbage sprout during that time, I wouldn't remember it."

Strange. Something so big—huge—that had overpowered his entire life, and just speaking it straight out like that seemed to take away at least some of its power. Maybe if Wil went through the whole camp and told every one of them one at a time, the last of the sting would fade by the time he got to the end of the line.

Corliss was staring at him. "Not your *whole* life, surely?"

Wil made her wait until he'd had another bite of the fabulous, tender, juicy, amazing-bloody-delicious beef, then shrugged and took a slurp of beer. "As I understand it, I was taken by him from my mother's womb and directly to the Guild. So, yes, my whole life."

"That's—he—" Corliss was next to speechless. It should have embarrassed Wil, but it was so genuine he couldn't find it in him. "I knew he was a piece of work, but... the bloody *bastard*, the—the ruthless, spineless *fuck!*"

Motherly indignation—had to be. Wil was absurdly warmed.

"If you didn't know," he ventured, genuinely curious, "why have you done what you've done?" Corliss peered at Wil with a frown. Wil gestured around them. "You disobeyed orders from your constabulary, and from what I understand, you've been doing everything but actual backflips to get these people to listen to you, despite obvious resistance from the Old Ones."

"Feh." Corliss waved a green bean in front of her nose, dismissive. "The Old Ones are just that—*old*—and too set in their ways. The good thing about them is they expect obedience, even from 'outlanders'"—she said the word with a roll of her eyes—"so when they 'requested' I keep my mouth shut, they obviously thought I would listen." Her chuckle was low and a little bit evil. "Anyway, I have Woodrow with me, and all you have to do is set that one loose and not rein in his tongue. A bigger bloody gossip you've never seen, but in this case, it's been more than useful."

"But why did you do it? I mean, if you didn't know."

Corliss shrugged. "Because Brayden knew."

Blind belief. Wil muffled a snort. Dallin would be so pleased.

"And he told me I didn't owe him anything." Corliss's smile was tight, somewhat rueful, and discomfited. "So, naturally, I had to repay him."

Wil grinned. He might like this woman after all.

He was enjoying himself. After dragooning a small group of boys into taking supper to the men conferring in the guardhouse, Corliss chivvied Wil into making a circuit of the camp, stopping to greet those she'd met and introduce Wil in a less overwhelming way than had been done earlier. This time he met eyes and marked faces, though he doubted he'd remember names—there were so many of them. All of them friendly but quiet at first, until they—like Ryne before—were assured by Corliss in various humorous ways that the light show was finished and there was no danger of it starting up again.

The Old Ones watched it all, and Wil watched them back, wondering, until eventually—between one glance over his shoulder and the next—they had gone. No one seemed to mark their absence but him.

Wil and Corliss were invited by families to share their fires, their food, their drinks, and were graciously welcomed to Lind by almost every person they met. By some unspoken consensus, musicians drifted from various parts of the camp toward a clearing backed by the river, where they spread out and started to play. The fire nearest them was built up to blazing, and everyone who wasn't standing a watch or doing something else necessary gathered 'round it.

Songs first, in the First Tongue. Wil only understood the language in dreams, but the accentuated chanting rhythms still pierced him, almost wrapping around him like a warm, soft blanket. Dancing next, graceful gamboling and fluid shifts of bodies and limbs, like watching music itself come to life in the primal-but-elegant steps and dips reflected beneath the flickering light of torch and fire. It was nearly hypnotic.

Wil wasn't sorry when Hunter came to collect him, but there was a touch of regret as he hauled himself up from the grass and left the warmth of the fire, the beauty of the music, and the dancing. Several called out to him as he walked the green, and though he couldn't make out faces, Wil lifted his hand each time and smiled more genuinely than he had earlier. To Wil's amusement, Hunter escorted him to the door of the guardhouse then took up a post outside, looking serious and as intense as his young face could manage as Wil entered. Wil thought about telling Hunter he might be taking all this a little *too* seriously, but... well, that Wil would happily leave up to Dallin. Hunter was bound to get on Dallin's nerves eventually, and he would learn to keep a more discreet distance then.

Wil found Dallin hunched over the room's single table, scrutinizing a large leather map beneath the light of several smoking oil lamps and tracing routes intently with a stick of charcoal. The ruins of several suppers were stacked over to the side. Rough maps on stained, crumpled paper were scattered everywhere, and Dallin irritably shoved several out of the way as he worked on the larger one. A small pot of a woodstove squatted in the middle of the room, grate open, with several more half-charred maps leaking from its belly. Quite a sparse little barracks, this. A bed, a table, a few chairs, two shelves each on two of the walls, and the stove. Likely meant for the... *Weardger-whateverthefuck*—the commander of the *Weardas*—when they were on drills by the Bounds.

Strange, how natural Dallin looked here, poring over maps and plans, with an entire camp waiting on his orders. He didn't look up until Wil shut the door behind him. With a tired smile, Dallin leaned back in his chair and stretched.

"Well, we've reached an accord and agreed on tactics." Dallin yawned, absently rubbing the smudges from his fingertips. "Wisena agreed to leave his men under my command. He'll take Shaw and strike out in the morning to try to intercept Wheeler. I don't put much faith in talking reason to the man, but it might buy us some time, at least."

Wil dropped his pack on the floor, propping the rifle in the corner by the door. "That's good. Congratulations." He ambled over to the table, slipped around in front of Dallin, and leaned back. "Time for what?"

Dallin shook his head and rubbed at his eyes. "Time for Fæðme, and then...." He gave a vague wave.

"Hm." Wil reached out and picked up the stick of charcoal, absently running the tip of it along the edge of a crumpled map in the only shapes he knew. "I expect we should probably talk about *and then*, shouldn't we."

Not a question, and Dallin knew it. "Unless there's been a miracle and you've changed your mind." He smiled to soften it, though it was sour and somewhat bitter, and they both knew he really meant it.

Wil didn't answer, just crimped a thin smile back at him. He turned his gaze back down to the shapes the charcoal was making beneath his hand.

"Are you...?" Dallin sat up, leaning in with a frown. Brow twisted with interest, he scanned the table, lifted up a dish to slide a stained, discarded map from beneath it. Marks and runes that made no sense to Wil covered all of one side and half of the other. Dallin shoved the map at Wil. "Do that again."

Dallin watched, eyes losing a bit of their gravity as Wil merely frowned briefly, then shrugged and did it again. Dallin stared at what Wil had done for a long moment before looking up, bemused but pleased.

"D'you know you've just written your name?"

"Well, in a sense, I suppose." A soft smile tilted Wil's mouth. "I can write all of Wilfred Calder. It's like the Marks, in a way—I know the shapes, and I know what they mean, but I can't read them. I don't know why these shapes mean what they do—I just know that they do."

"Huh." Dallin sat back again, mind obviously wandering already, no doubt speculating on the discussion he didn't want to have. Wil traced the name again, waiting, while Dallin stared at Wil's fingers, silent. Brooding. And apparently willing to sit in silence until Wil got 'round to forcing the conversation.

Wil decided not to prolong the obvious unease. "Tell me what Calder says in the dream."

Dallin didn't move, didn't even sigh. "He says you've been weaned on betrayal." He was still staring at Wil's hand. "Says you know me and trust me, and asks me if I plan to betray you now."

Wil looked up from his fingers. "And do you?"

Dallin's mouth pinched down tight. "I should probably take insult with that." He scrubbed a hand over his face. "Then again, I expect it depends on your definition. And whose orders you're following, come to that."

"Hm." Wil balled up the paper, dropping both it and the charcoal into his coat pocket, and looked at Dallin straight. "I wouldn't have thought there was more than one." Dallin didn't answer, just rolled his eyes and waved a hand, as though that by itself was supposed to mean something. Since Wil had no idea what, he decided to get to the point. "I'd prefer it if we stopped dancing around the subject."

"And I'd prefer it if—" Dallin cut himself off, fists clenching all at once into concentrated knots of anger and then uncurling just as quickly. He pulled in a long, deep breath, sighed it out quietly, and looked at Wil. "One of Wisena's men—Merrod, I think, a lieutenant—he hails from Caerdydd, a few leagues from the eastern border. Fairly war-torn, being one of those points of strategy Ríocht generally aims for when things get hot."

A brief pause, ruminating, and Wil wondered if Dallin had spent time there defending the border, but he held back his questions. Dallin would get to the point in his own way.

After a moment Dallin shook himself. "Anyway, his parents saw enough over the years to want something other than the military for their bonny lad, so they tried to make a teacher out of him. Sent him to study in Penley." He peered up from beneath his eyebrows. "Spent time at the Temple there. Religious studies."

The pause this time was longer, Dallin just looking at Wil, expectant, clearly waiting for some kind of reaction, except Wil didn't have one yet. Dallin's tone and demeanor were giving everything an ominous edge, but—considering his reluctance to just spit it out—that could very well be deliberate, designed to put Wil off. Wil waited him out.

Eventually Dallin's expression went tight, very obviously stifling a growl, and he looked away. "There's more to the old gods than just the songs. There's more to—" Again he stopped, hands fisting, but this time they didn't uncurl. "Possession, Wil. That Æled—" It was like he was choking on it, his face screwing up, teeth clenching tight. "Fuck, I don't even want to say his name."

His breath whooped into his chest as if he'd just run a league, and he scrubbed at his face. "Æledfýres. Soul-eater. You get the pushing from Síofra because Síofra got it from him. So do the Brethren. Only he didn't just push people, he pushed them *out*. Everything a person is, he could take away and make a part of himself. He took magicians, priests, shamans. All that power, one atop the other, and he just kept eating it up, making himself more powerful, until They finally locked him away so he couldn't do it anymore." Dallin looked at Wil gravely. "Do you see where this goes?"

Wil frowned. "Of course. But what's it to do—?"

"He took their souls and kept them, used a person until he'd worn them out and then moved on to another. But he *kept* the souls. They—"

"I *know* all this," Wil cut in, shorter and sharper than he'd meant. "Or at least most of it, the important parts. And it still doesn't—"

"Just—"

Dallin shut his eyes tight, raised his fists as though he meant to pound them to the table, but willfully lowered them again. He was sweating, the hair at his temples curling with it. "Agitation" didn't quite seem to cover it, forcibly subdued though it was.

"Just... let me finish. Please." He took several long, strained moments before he opened his eyes, and looked at Wil. "He's doing the same to the Father. And you're the key to finishing it. He told Síofra where to find you because Síofra promised him he'd give him your name in return and bring you to him. That's why Síofra needed you to find him the next Aisling—because he couldn't do it himself. Æledfýres did it for him in exchange for *you*. Except Síofra didn't know your name—he lied—so he couldn't keep his promise, could he? I doubt he ever meant to—I'm betting he never had any intention of handing you over. Men like him always think they're smarter and stronger than they are, and I'd lay down just about anything that he thought he could take your power from you and become even stronger than Æledfýres. Betrayal, right from the beginning—rather seems his style, dunnit? I can't imagine what the penalty would be for betraying someone like that, but I *can* imagine it wouldn't've been pretty.

"So Síofra kept you and hid you, and I can't believe I'm actually saying this, but it's a good job he did, because if he'd handed you over like he was supposed to, I doubt any of us would be here to argue about it now. Æledfýres *wanted* you to kill Síofra—he was done with him, and Síofra had been living on borrowed time since the day you were born. But the Brethren are loyal to Æledfýres, and they know your name, they know about the dreamleaf, they hold all the keys, and they're here. They've been two steps behind you all these years because he's been telling them how to find you —every time you use your magic, he feels it. Blood to blood. The only reason they didn't catch up with you sooner is because you weren't using your magic—you didn't even know you *had* it.

"The thing is... Wil."

Dallin ran a hand through his hair, breathed "*Fuck!*" and stood to pace the small quarters in tight little circles. Wil backed away until he was leaning against the wall, unsure if he was giving Dallin space or merely getting out of the way.

"He's too strong. He's been leaching power from the Father for years, and he's stronger than you. You said you don't think you can beat him. I don't think you can either."

Wil's heart took a dive down into his stomach. Of all the things he might've expected Dallin to say....

"But you said... *you're* the one—"

"I said *we* could beat him, and we can. And I said you would come out the other side, and you will. But not... *shit*, Wil, not unless we do it my way, and I'm bloody terrified that you *won't*."

Dallin stepped over to Wil and took hold of his arms in a grip that made Wil gasp. Wil didn't think Dallin even realized he was practically shoving Wil into the wall. Dallin's eyes were nearly on fire, almost frenzied, with dark panic lurking behind them.

"You need to go to Fæðme—you need the power of Lind to beat him—but if you *do* go to Fæðme and he wins anyway, he'll take it all. D'you know what that means? This isn't just you and me we're talking about anymore—this is *everything*. D'you know what the Father told me?"

Wil's own fear was rising in answer to Dallin's and turning to a too-familiar defensive anger. "How would I? You never told me, did you?"

"Just one more thing you never *asked*."

"It wasn't my business. It was between the two of you, and I didn't think—"

"Everything about this is your business—even those things you don't want to know."

That one made heat bloom up Wil's spine. "Don't you mean those things you don't want to tell me?"

"Call it whatever makes you feel better. It hardly matters now. It's just one more piece of the puzzle, and now they're all fitting together a little too neatly.

"He told me it wasn't your fate to save Him. He told me—"

"You don't even *believe* in fate!"

"No, but *you* do, and apparently it bloody matters. He told me I have more than one calling, and that part of my job was to make sure you keep choosing yourself. What d'you think that means, *Aisling*?"

Wil shook his head. "I don't *know* what—"

"You *do*." Dallin tightened his grip on Wil's arms until Wil had to hold back a yip. "You know exactly what it means. Guardian, Watcher, Guide, and whatever other names are mine—

what's the other, Wil? What's the one name that fits here? You *know* it—it's the first name you ever called me by."

"What...?" Wil's heart was racing. Somewhere he knew exactly the answer Dallin was looking for, but it wouldn't travel from wherever it was hiding and out his mouth. He tried to twist out of Dallin's grip—couldn't. He glared up into dark, furious eyes, burning nearly black, and hoped his own were flaring at least as much. "Do you know," he said slowly, "you have an alarming habit of putting my back to the wall."

"Yeah?" The muscle in Dallin's jaw twitched, mouth quivering. "Well, maybe I should do it more often. It seems that's the only time you'll bloody well stand up for yourself. Except for when you don't want to know things and then blame me for not telling them to you."

"I never—"

"*Gníomhaire*, Wil. Intermediary. Middleman. Except d'you want to know what the translation into the First Tongue is? *Wæterþéotan*. Sorta pretty, innit? D'you want to know what else it means? Floodgate. Conduit. Doorway."

"What the hell does *any* of this—?"

"Through me and out to you, Wil. From you, to me, then away. It has to come through *me*."

Wil narrowed his eyes. "And then what?"

Dallin looked down, his grip on Wil's arms loosening slowly until he finally let go altogether. He pushed back and turned away. Slowly, as if he'd been weighted down with lead, Dallin paced back over to the table and slumped into the chair. He looked up at Wil, steady but strangely removed.

"The Brethren fancy themselves the new Guardians. The Cleric—"

"No." Like he'd been hit with ice water, Wil all at once *knew*. Dazed, he shook his head, said it again. "No."

Dallin gave him a cheerless little smile, which only served to chill Wil further. "It's what they were trying to do in Old Bridge—testing, making sure you really were what you were supposed to be, making sure it could be done before bringing you to their Cleric. Except they didn't know about the leaf then. *The Cleric must commune with the Aisling*, right? Follow you into dreams, let Æledfýres in so he can push you out, take everything you are and everything you have." He paused, dark eyes drilling right into Wil, relentless. "I call your name and summon him. *I* am the Vessel. You can beat him if you push it all at me before he can come at you. Once you've Lind behind you... you push it all at me, and you crush him. If he gets to you first, it's all lost. Everything."

Wil was still shaking his head, somehow expecting every word but nevertheless sideswiped by it. He shut his eyes tight, fighting back a knot of bile wedging in his throat. When he opened his eyes again, dark spots were spiraling at the fringes of his vision.

"And what...?" He almost couldn't speak. "What happens to you?"

Dallin's expression didn't change; his gaze didn't waver. "I don't know."

Liar.

Wil couldn't say it. Could barely even acknowledge it. "It can't be the only way."

"If there's another, I've not been able to figure it, and no one's bothered to pop by to help me find it."

Dallin was suddenly so calm, so infuriatingly composed, that Wil wanted to stalk across the small room and punch him in the mouth.

"The heart of the world, Wil." Dallin's voice had gone achingly soft. "You can't let him have it."

"I never intended to." It was vague and raspy and altogether too weak to support the arrogance of the statement. It was wrong, all of it just *wrong*, as though the skin of the world had just been snapped out from under Wil, shaken thoroughly, then slipped back on, backward and upside down. "There *has* to be another way."

Dallin sighed, nodding like he'd expected it. "All right, then. Let me know when you think of one, yeah?"

Rage flared through Wil, bright-hot and blinding white, and he let a growl burn up from his chest. "You're going to be bloody *glib*? You're sitting there and seriously telling me that the only way out of this is if I do something that will very likely kill you, and if I—"

He choked, the words clogging acidic in his throat like great chunks of poison, gagging him.

"I assure you," Dallin said, so tender and compassionate it was almost galling, "the irony is purely unintentional."

You will come out the other side, Dallin had told him—*you*, not *we*—and Wil hadn't even noticed the deviously deliberate wording until just this second. And all this time—

"You *fuck!*" Wil forced it through a throat tight and burning, not caring, more like refusing to care, that Dallin could very well give him another *Now you know how I feel*. Except Dallin wouldn't—Wil knew he wouldn't—and somehow that only made the rage burn hotter. "You weren't going to tell me."

Dallin shook his head slowly. "No."

And that was it. No apology, no justification, not even the satisfaction of watching the frank gaze waver.

"And how did you intend to get me to do it?"

Dallin propped his elbows to the table, and rubbed at his temples like he was trying to keep his brain from beating its way out. "That, I hadn't quite figured yet." He sighed. "The best plan thus far involved a lot of begging. Maybe a bit of weeping. Definitely some groveling. Probably an attempt at bullying mixed with reason." He puffed out a snort that sounded anything but humorous, then cradled his head in his hands and closed his eyes. "Surprise you with it when it was too late to back out. I hadn't got that far in the plan."

It didn't look like a lie, didn't feel like one, but suspicion flared and twisted a shard of bitter-sharp doubt through Wil's chest.

"No?" Wil's voice was shaky, too high-pitched. "You've all the keys as well, haven't you? The First Constable of Putnam, *the* Shaman of Lind, and the most obvious answer never once crossed your mind?"

Dallin went utterly still, so still that Wil thought Dallin might have stopped breathing. Tension wound between them, thick and choking—the hiss and shiver of the oil lamps, the low mutter of the fire in the stove nearly deafening in the silence. The drums still coming from outside throbbed into Wil's skull, set it pounding.

You think I'd drug someone all unsuspecting? What d'you think I am?

It was a mistake, an accusation made from fear and desperate denial and too much time spent around people who snapped their teeth the moment you exposed your jugular. And now Wil was drowning in it.

He couldn't move as Dallin slowly stood, hands planted on the table as though he had to hold himself up, and took several long, deep breaths, eyes shut tight and jaw clenched.

"Right." It was thick, flat, and heavy as an anvil. Dallin took another long breath and said it again—"*Right*"—and then he nodded, straightened, and without casting so much as a fleeting glance at Wil, turned and walked out. Wil was expecting the door to slam behind him, prepared himself for a mild jolt, and nearly jumped out of his skin when it merely shut with a quiet *click*.

Wil just stood there, staring at the door, tracing the whorls and loops of the grain, not thinking anything at all, his mind buzzing white and too loud, his body far away and numb.

You've just compared the most honorable man you know to Síofra and the Brethren.

He shut his eyes, started counting to ten, lost track around four, had to back up and start again twice before he let that go too.

You've just made the biggest mistake of your life kept wanting to jumble its way into understandable shapes in his head, but Wil wouldn't let it, too busy not thinking. His legs started moving, and he didn't think about that either, just followed them to the door. He watched his hand reach out, open it, and heard his voice ask Hunter "Which way?" and then his legs were in charge again, picking up pace until he was running in the direction Hunter pointed.

Dallin didn't believe in Fate. All right, Wil could understand that, because Fate was too often unkind and had shown Dallin the back of her hand more than was fair. But Wil *did* believe, he had no choice, and if the Father said it wasn't Wil's fate to save Him—

No. Fate, chance, or Divine command—Wil didn't care. There were only so many sacrifices a man could make, and Wil didn't think anyone could argue that he hadn't already made more than his share. He wasn't about to sacrifice Dallin too, or let Dallin sacrifice himself. Dallin had shown Wil hope, had made him believe he could change his own fate. He could damn well change *this*.

Catching up wasn't easy—Dallin had a stride on him, and he was angry, so he'd likely be walking fast. It was dark, which didn't help, and he'd taken a path down to the river, which didn't help either. Too-smooth rock interleaved too-soft sweetgrass, neither of which lent much by way of traction beneath Wil's boots on the path that didn't look like much of a slope until he tried navigating it in the dark and in a hurry. He slid to his arse twice, only keeping himself from sliding to his arse another four or five times by sheer determination, before he reached the bottom and stopped to catch his breath.

He'd seen Dallin standing just that way before, in just that spot, but that time the sun had been bright and the air had been sweet with spring, and Dallin's spirit had been bared and reaching. This was it, the bend in the river where Dallin had brought Wil that first night, when he'd shown Wil he wasn't as alone as he'd always thought he was, and then again when Wil had taken a chance he hadn't known he was taking and kissed him, and again when he'd been lost and Dallin had waited for him here, waited and searched and poured himself out. Now the posture was the same but everything else was wrong—closed in, pulling away—and Wil couldn't stand it. It was just *wrong*.

You didn't approach a person with an arsenal strapped all over him from behind, but Wil was still too busy not thinking to care. He stalked toward Dallin, kept coming when Dallin cocked his head to the side and then spun, kept coming when Dallin's mouth set firm and his fists clenched tight in the thin light of stars and moon. And when Dallin started to say something, to warn Wil off, perhaps, Wil kept coming until he was planted right in front of him. Reached out, took hold of Dallin's coat, dragged him in, and kissed him. Kept kissing him until Dallin stopped trying to pull away, stopped trying to protest, stopped resisting altogether, wrapped Wil in a death grip that made it hard to breathe, and kissed him back.

After that it was easy. Easy to fall to the cold grass. Easy to bare skin to the chill brilliance of the stars and heat it with hands and mouth. Easy to beg and plead and demand, and easy to rock into the rhythm of soft words spoken to the distant heady beat of earthbound drums and the immortal songs of stars and river. Easy to gasp things that were real and things he meant into sweated skin and damp hair that smelled of smoke and pine and the sharp-spicy scent of dreams that didn't hurt.

Easy to lie there after, panting and shaking, whispering apologies and promises, listening as they were whispered back, and realize that he'd just made real, honest love for the first time in his life.

They'd been given the little guardhouse—the perks of privilege, Dallin had joked as they'd made their way back up the path. Wil had to admit he was rather pleased. It would be nice to have an actual bed, and this one was built for Linders and so quite big enough. Still, he made himself stay awake until well after Dallin had dropped heavily into sleep. With any luck, the dreams would leave Dallin alone tonight, and if they didn't, Wil wouldn't be long behind him.

Dallin was snoring lightly, arm heavy across Wil's chest, when the drums finally stopped and the night went quiet. Wil waited until his own eyelids were drooping dangerously, then slid carefully from out Dallin's loose grip and stood over the bed for a few moments, holding his breath. Dallin slept so lightly, and Wil wanted to make sure this little jaunt would be private. Dallin was exhausted, so Wil wasn't terribly surprised when he stirred just a little and then slept on. Satisfied, Wil dressed quickly, slipped the knife into his belt, snatched up his pack, slung the rifle over his shoulder, and started for the—

Matches. It would be stupid to risk calling fire. Wil poked about on the sparse-covered shelves, found a nice bundle in a small crock on the second, and nicked several.

He took stock, ticked down his mental list, then stole outside, shutting the door as softly as possible. Quickly he sat down on the step to put his boots on and drop the knife—*can't forget the knife*—into the left, surprised when he noted no sentry at the door. Dallin had told Hunter to have Corliss and Woodrow take shifts, and it was unusual that Hunter would leave before he was relieved. Well, Wil wasn't about to rat Hunter out, and this way there wouldn't be the bother of arguing someone into a moment of privacy. Smirking, Wil stood, and made his way down to the river again.

It was easier going this time. It helped that he wasn't scrambling to make up for the nearly unforgivable, wasn't shocked clumsy by his own stupidity and callousness. He really could be an idiot sometimes.

The grass was still tamped down in a wide swath, and he couldn't help the ridiculous grin that stretched his mouth, the hot flush that moved from his toes all the way up to the tips of his ears. It really had been quite.... Wil sighed. There wasn't a word for it, and if there was, he didn't know it.

"It was what it was," he told himself, letting the smile curl as big and stupid as it wanted. "Just let it be what it was."

He swung his pack around, folded himself down, laid the gun aside, and pulled out the bowl. Setting it in the grass, he dug the charcoal and paper from his coat pocket and the knife from his boot. The moon was just bright enough, made a touch brighter by its reflection from the water. Tilting the knife slightly away, Wil could see the runes well enough to copy their shapes onto the crumpled paper.

It took him several tries, even going slowly and carefully. It seemed colder than it had been only a short time ago, and his fingers were clumsy with the chill. He was running out of clean spots on the paper when he finally got it right, tore what he'd written in a strip from the rest, and set it in the bowl.

Just to be certain, Wil dug into his pack, found the leaves by feel, and slid one out. Rather battered and torn, going dry and crumbly, but Dallin hadn't said the condition of the leaves mattered. Anyway, he'd said you were supposed to burn something special to you, and the leaf was special. Three of them—perfectly shaped—had been lying on his chest the morning he'd woken in a serene little wood to a doe, framed in morning sunlight and staring down at him, soft-eyed and wildly beautiful. He'd kept the leaves because he'd wanted to remember how those dark, liquid eyes looked, and how free and at peace he'd felt in that moment before she'd bolted off, tail twitching. Perhaps not worth anything to anyone else, but special to Wil, and it would have to do. He stroked the veins of the leaf with a fingertip, whispered to it what he'd hopefully written on the paper, and placed it in the bowl as well. Just to be safe, he dug out the remains of the other leaves and dropped them in too.

The match sparked to life immediately beneath his thumbnail, blinding him for several seconds. He touched it to both ends of the paper and then several spots on the leaves, slipped it beneath it all, and sat back to watch it burn.

It was... anticlimactic. He'd been hoping for some sort of... something—a sudden wind out of nowhere, a slight tremor, an owl hooting.

Nothing but the quiet and the sweet smell of burning leaves.

Ah well. He'd taken a chance. He'd done it. He'd swallowed the last of his anger and resentment, bowed to the Mother in his own way, and asked for Her favor. Well, asked for it for Dallin, but... sometimes it was one and the same. Just to be sure, Wil waited until the last of the ash was dead and black, then blew into the bowl, scattering it on the bit of breeze.

For what it was worth.

Satisfied, Wil collected the bowl and the knife, stuffed them in his pack and boot respectively, and turned—

Someone grabbed his hair. His head was yanked back so far he thought his neck might snap. His shocked yelp was drowned by a cup at his mouth and tepid brew washing over his tongue, down his throat.

Wil gagged, choked, reflex kicking in and trying to spew out what was going in. But an arm was around his throat now, and a wide hand clamped over Wil's mouth, his nose, and *fuck*, he couldn't *breathe*, couldn't... couldn't.

He fought. Kicking, punching, twisting and scratching and gouging.

The arm was like an iron band around him. The hand blocked the brew from going out and air from going in.

White sparks hazed Wil's vision. Reflex once again took over, his body taking the only option that was available to it—Wil swallowed.

"You do not understand how... precarious a position you've put your Guardian in, young Wil." Calder's voice, right next to Wil's ear, so serious, so concerned. "A link has been forged. Every weakness of yours, he uses his strength to shield. Your pain is his tenfold. I don't think you know just how much of himself he is using up to keep you from falling beneath the weight of what bombards his defenses."

The hand over Wil's nose and mouth let go. The grip around him didn't. It shifted, though, Calder's wide arm going around Wil's chest, pinning his arms, squeezing so tight he couldn't catch his breath, couldn't scream, couldn't *move*.

"He loves too well and too deeply," Calder said gently. "It is not meant, what you have between you. It can do no good—to you, to him, or to Lind."

"What...?" Wil couldn't pull in enough breath to make his voice come out above a wheeze. "What did you do? What—"

The taste on his tongue was flowery. Familiar.

Wil's mind stumbled, a slight haze covering his perceptions, making everything thick and sticky. The chain of his thoughts broke apart, the links flying out in every direction.

The arms around Wil let him go. He was on his knees a second later, propping himself up on his hands in the wet grass.

A tiny snort leaked from his mouth.

What had he been saying? What had he been doing?

"Bowl. I was... the burning bowl, and it...."

Slurred and syrupy, as though his tongue had just outgrown his mouth. He goggled at the ground, at Calder's boots, at the divot in the grass he'd clawed up earlier when Dallin had sunk his teeth into Wil's shoulder and made him beg, and then at the dirt still crusted lightly under his fingernails... at the cup smudging out of focus on the ground....

He knew this feeling. If his mind were working, it would be screaming.

"I am sorry, Aisling," Calder said gravely. "But even in this, I serve you."

"Serve...?" As though his hand belonged to someone else, Wil picked up the cup, and lifted it toward Calder. "What... what have you...?"

Calder knelt, and gently took the cup from Wil. Mouth pressed, eyes sad, Calder stroked Wil's cheek with a broad, callused hand.

"Someone has to be the Guardian, lad. I do the Mother's will, as I always have done."

Oh fuck. Somebody... help.

Clumsy and slow, his limbs too far away from his body, Wil groped blindly for the rifle, only to watch it slide across the grass at the end of Calder's hand then sail into the darkness as he pitched it aside. Out of reach. *Gone.*

Purge, Wil thought, sense and thought too slippery, but he latched on to that one—*puke it up*—and he raised his hand to his mouth—

Calder's wide hands closed over Wil's wrists. The grip was like iron.

Shackled.

Caught.

An oily little cackle warbled out from Wil's throat, and he shut his mouth tight. He snorted anyway, except nothing was funny.

"Sonuva*bitch*." Wil giggled, sloppy and garbled, snagging at one thought and one thought only, concentrating with everything in him until he shoved it out his mouth.

"Fuckin' hatechoo." It came out a hooting snort.

His mind was full of cotton, and he couldn't stop laughing about it. Euphoria closed him in a gentle hand, lifted him up, and he was floating, flying, and it was really fucking funny, except his brain wouldn't stop shrieking at him—*Run! Get up and bloody* run! *Scream, do* some*thing!*—except he couldn't, and that was pretty fucking funny too.

"Fæðme," Calder was telling him. "The Vessel is too weak, and your Guardian cannot know the risks he takes."

The Vessel is too weak.

Wil had heard that somewhere before.

"And I...." Calder's voice dipped down into something like wistfulness. "I would hear Her voice again."

You're mad, Wil wanted to say, but whatever came out was mangled and shoved out between sobbing little chuckles. Even Wil couldn't really understand it.

He was... so, *so* fucked.

Sense was slipping away, all but the keening knowledge that this was wrong, very very *wrong*, which couldn't be right, because whooping giggles were leaking from Wil like steam from a kettle. The peace was gentling him, so familiar, sliding its sinuous tethers around his mind, calling to him, and he knew it, wanted it, *needed* it, the need almost eating him up, and he didn't care, and *oh*, he'd missed it.

Boneless, Wil fell forward, careening into Calder's chest. It was nice, wide and hard, except not as hard as Dallin's, where Wil had rested his head forever ago and listened to Dallin's heartbeat —*ka-thump ka-thump ka-thump*—and Wil had slid his hand over a light sheen of sweat in the moonlight and kept it there so he could feel the muscles flex and slide beneath his palm.

Calder's arms were around Wil, lifting him up, and it shouldn't be Calder, it should be Síofra, crooning to him and carrying him to the chamber to slide dream into nightmare and nightmare into pain and—

No. *No.* Gone, dead, a soul crushed in his fist—Síofra was gone, and it should be Dallin here with Wil, because it should *always* be Dallin, because it always was. Dallin's arms around him, Dallin's voice in his ear, Dallin's heartbeat against his cheek —*DallinDallinDallinDallin*....

Wil latched on to the name, sang it in a loop in his head, and with his last shard of sanity, gathered it into a fist in his mind —*screamed* it.

CHAPTER 4

Dallin was already in his trousers, shoving an arm into his shirt, when he snapped awake, a heavy sense of urgent dread clogging in his chest and the echo of a phantom scream drumming in his head. He didn't take the time to strap on his guns, merely snatched them up by their holsters and slung them over his shoulder as he slammed across the little room and out the door.

"Hunter! Go and get—*Fuck!*"

No Hunter, which wasn't surprising—no Wil, no Hunter. It almost would have made Dallin feel better, knowing Hunter was likely wherever Wil was, if Dallin's gut weren't twisting and his mind weren't racing through all the possible tragedies that might be taking place right this second. Because that *scream*....

It wasn't a dream, it wasn't anything but Wil very definitely in trouble, and what the *fuck* was he doing out in the first place, and how the *fuck* did Dallin not hear him leave, and what the *fuck* had Wil been thinking, and why the *fuck* was Dallin wasting time wondering, when he could just as easily be dreaming up all the creative ways he was going to kill Wil when he found him, and then Hunter for not stopping him?

Dallin boiled around the north side of the guardhouse, meaning to rouse... *somebody*—Corliss, Woodrow, the whole bloody camp if necessary. The quick-fire thumping of his heart just made it lurch more painfully and land in a sick lump in his throat when he spotted a limp figure, limned in moonlight, half sitting and half sprawling against the outer wall of the guardhouse. It was the boots—buckskin, fringed at the tops, trousers tucked loosely inside them.

"Hunter," Dallin breathed, "you'd better be dead."

Because if he wasn't, and someone had managed to take Wil right out from under him....

Not dead, Dallin saw as he crouched down, but... not all right, just the same. No marks, no lumps to the skull, no blood, but too limp and unresponsive to be asleep. Not drunk—Hunter didn't smell of liquor or even beer, and so far as Dallin had seen tonight, Hunter hadn't touched anything but a cup of very mild mead, eschewing the heavy beer Wisena and his men had indulged in while they all talked strategy.

Hunter didn't even flutter his eyelids when Dallin slapped his cheeks hard enough to bruise, and if he'd drunk enough for that kind of nonreaction, he *would* be dead, or at least on his way. So. Not drunk. Drugged, perhaps, but how? Hunter might be naïve, but he wasn't stupid. If someone from the Brethren had managed to prowl through the perimeter—and after Wil's stunt with the lightning more or less blaring his location to any who happened to look up, that wasn't entirely out of the question—Dallin couldn't imagine Hunter giving anyone the opportunity to slip him something. It would've had to have been someone here, someone from camp, someone he knew, someone who—

"Son of a *bitch*." Snarled through teeth clenched tight.

Dallin stood, rubbed roughly at his mouth, and stared down at the crumpled figure. His mind was running around in circles, shrieking incoherently. His body was already on its way toward the chill composure of combat—heart slowing its rhythm, low tremors calming and stilling, stomach unclenching—and he waited while his mind caught up. Composed thought was necessary here. It wouldn't do Wil any good if Dallin allowed panic. Or rage. Or murderous bloody *fury*.

Dallin took a long, slow breath... pushed it back out of his chest.

All right.

Calder was probably better than the Brethren. Probably. He was almost as fanatical in his way, but—

Dallin shook his head with a low growl.

But nothing. Calder wasn't "almost" *anything*. He was just as fanatical in his beliefs as any one of those wild-eyed madmen, maybe more, and though he didn't have a little copper capsule tucked away in his cheek, his willingness to die for his cause—whatever it might be—was no less fervent. Calder had to know Dallin would happily kill him for even laying a finger on Wil—quickly if Wil wasn't harmed; slowly and painfully and with the proper amount of screaming if he was. So whatever Calder was up to, he believed he was following his calling, whatever that might mean to him now, since he'd foresworn it and followed after his dead son. He couldn't expect to live through this, whatever it was. In point of fact, he might be looking forward to being martyred—he had the right kind of suicidal insanity behind his eyes.

Reluctant understanding rolled over Dallin like a slow-sliding avalanche.

Calder might really mean to kill Wil. And only the knowledge that Wil wasn't dead already—the land hadn't cried out, hadn't screamed along with him—prevented Dallin from howling off in whatever direction he happened to be facing, hunting Calder down, and tearing out his heart with his bare hands. If he could find him.

Dallin let his hands curl into tight, solid fists. "Oh, I'll find him." He jerked a sharp little nod, stepped away from Hunter's limp form, and stalked toward the center of the camp, strapping his guns on along the way. One of the sentries spotted him, only a star-silvered man-shape in the darkness. Dallin merely waved a hand, ordered "Get a torch and come on," and kept walking.

Wisena and his men were camped just at the fringes of the Linders, those from Putnam only slightly more toward the river, close enough to share a campfire. Dallin lumbered through them all, kicking at limbs, and snapping, "Up, I need you," as he went. He didn't wait for them to blink and ask him why, just stalked on ahead, long strides eating the ground so the man with the torch had to sprint to catch up by the time Dallin had reached a clear spot toward the camp's center.

He stood, back straight, feet planted apart, and surveyed the camp with a critical eye. They wanted the Shaman; the Shaman they would get. Out the corner of his eye, Dallin spotted Corliss and Woodrow hurrying toward him, sliding on surcoats and holsters as they jogged. He ignored them, took a long breath, then shrilled a sharp whistle through his teeth.

Called "*Weardas*—to me!" and watched, satisfied, as the camp leaped to life.

It was the rifle that did it, seeing it lying there in the grass. That was when the reality of it all truly sank in. Wil wouldn't have left it like that if he could help it, which meant Wil *couldn't* help it, which meant... an endless array of very dark possibilities.

Andette had been the one to find it and Wil's pack down by the river, at the spot where Wil and Dallin had—

Dallin pushed that away and focused on *right now*.

He'd roused the camp, told them their Aisling had been stolen, told them they'd be hunting one of their own, and watched with cold satisfaction as their eyes turned hard and their faces set. Next he'd sent runners to every known picket and post with the same message, gave Healdes the charge of coordinating the search, then stood back and watched the wheels begin to turn.

He kept watching as the war horns blew, kept listening as they were answered in a slow-rolling chain from every part of Lind, farther and farther and deeper and deeper, until he could no longer hear the resonance. Ordered every able body to saddle up and be ready to move, and then ordered a sweep of the area just in case.

He'd known it was useless—Wil and Calder were long gone, and Dallin knew where Calder would be heading—but no possibility, however slim, would go untried. And even though Dallin had known, his heart still took a hopeful leap when Andette arrowed through the bustle of the breaking camp right toward Dallin and told him she'd found something.

Luckily she'd only been scouting with Shaw, and they'd been careful, so there wasn't much trampling. Not that the tracks and signs told Dallin much he didn't already know. He crouched down to examine the grass and waved at whoever that was with the torch to come closer... closed his eyes and rubbed at them. Choking back a growl, Dallin picked up the cup, sniffed it, then held it up over his shoulder, staring straight ahead—because if he looked at Shaw, Dallin might take out some of his wrath toward Calder on the wrong target, and Dallin didn't have the time to indulge himself.

"Does that smell like anything to you?" It was barely even a question, Dallin's tone was so hard and flat. And anyway, he already knew the answer.

There was a pause as Shaw took the cup from Dallin's hand, another as he gave it a sniff. "I can't tell," he finally said. "Too much spice."

Dallin nodded, stood, picked up the pack and the rifle, then stared unseeing at the flow of the river, thinking.

Something to put Wil out, surely. Likely the same stuff Hunter was currently sleeping off. Which was good, in a way—if Hunter was still out, so was Wil, and if Calder was heading where Dallin was almost certain he was heading, he might catch Calder up before Wil woke. Because Wil frightened and angry and confused, trying to throw off the dregs of a drug, and in the heart of Lind—

Dallin pushed that away too. He'd just have to get to Wil first, was all.

There'd been a fight. It was all over the flat crimp of the grass, the divots in the dirt. The badger had shown its teeth, but it hadn't done any good.

There was no reason to assume it had been mæting. There were plenty of opiates and soporifics that could put a person out quickly and thoroughly, and lots of them grew in these hills. Calder was a shaman, a healer, and he'd know more of them than Dallin did. There was no reason in the world to be so bone-deep *sure* that Calder had forced on Wil the one drug that would mean disaster—not just under the circumstances, but for Wil himself. No reason in the world except for the fact that it was Calder, and Calder *knew*, and it would be just the sort of thing in which someone like him would find some sort of twisted, serendipitous meaning. He'd take it as a sign or portent and think himself following the Mother's will, even as he—

"Son of a fucking *bitch!*"

One outburst, one moment of surrender to his rage, and that

was all Dallin allowed himself. He turned to the small crowd behind him, jaw set.

"You've all got your orders. Let's move."

Without waiting for any of them, Dallin turned toward the path up to camp, fingers literally *itching* for want of wrapping them around Calder's throat. If what Calder had already done to Wil—his bloody *Aisling*, to whom he'd sworn service—wasn't bad enough, the Brethren were still out there. Dallin didn't want to even think about what would happen if Calder ran into them with Wil unconscious, unarmed, utterly defenseless.

Dallin's grip tightened around the rifle.

"Brayden."

Shaw was behind him, hurrying to make up for Dallin's longer stride. Dallin ignored him, turning instead to one of the *Weardas* coming up alongside him.

"I want the fastest horse you can lay your hands on. I don't care who it belongs to. I've a mare to offer on a not-quite-even trade until this business is through."

"*Brayden.*"

Dallin kept ignoring it, kept walking. His head was already pounding, the power of this place beating at him, *screaming* at him, and it was all he could do to shove it to the edge of his consciousness and concentrate on more immediate matters. He didn't need Shaw distracting him when his mind was already in fifteen different places at once.

When he reached the lip of the rise, Dallin spotted Wisena, called to him, and hooked a thumb over his shoulder in Shaw's general direction.

"Get him ready. We're stretched thin here, but take five or so with you, your choice—not trackers or sharpshooters, though. I want every one of them with me. When you get across the Bounds, tell your men to go to Healdes for orders. And tell them to *hurry*."

"Brayden," Shaw rumbled, "you can't possibly still think to send me to intercept Wheeler? I know Calder. I can—"

"No, you can't. No one can, not now. He's used up his last chance."

"You mean to just kill him, then?"

Dallin stopped, fisted his hands, and turned on Shaw. He saw Andette watching, listening, and didn't care.

"Yes. I mean to just kill him."

Shaw stared. "Just like that."

"Just like that." Dallin tilted his head. "Did Calder ever tell you about what Síofra did to Wil? Did he ever tell you what Wil did at the Guild? How they *got* him to do what he did at the Guild?"

"*You* told me what he did at the Guild."

"True." Dallin's lip curled up on a cold little sneer. "But I didn't tell you everything. Discretion, you know. Wil doesn't like to talk about it, doesn't like to think about it, so I kept the things he'd prefer not everyone knew to myself." Dallin's teeth were clenching again—he couldn't help it. "Except, see, I told Calder, back in the cellars of your Temple. I had to, after all, didn't I? We needed him, and Wil had given his permission, so I told Calder how Síofra had kept Wil sotted on mæting from the time he was six years old until the Brethren finally kidnapped him some three years ago. I told him how Wil had been forcibly addicted to the stuff and then forcibly withdrawn from it, the Mother only knows how many times." He paused, cheek and jaw twitching with the effort of keeping his voice level and his expression under some kind of control. "And d'you know what Calder did with that knowledge, Shaw? C'mon, you're an intelligent man, a *healer*. Surely you can *guess*." That last emerged as a growling hiss.

Shaw was suitably disturbed by the revelation, suitably troubled by the implications. But not suitably daunted.

"The man gave up his *calling*. He grieved for the Mother's voice, and being back here, it... *did* something to him. He hasn't been himself. A temporary snap, perhaps, but he is not malicious." Shaw took a steadying breath. "You don't need me to go to Wheeler. You need me to help you find Calder. I can talk to him. I can—"

"No, the thing is, *General*, I *do* need you to go to Wheeler, and I need you to do everything in your power, even if that means killing him, to keep him away from Lind. Because Wheeler isn't just an incompetent, arrogant career officer who stumbled into a command he couldn't manage—he's the bloody *Cleric*."

Dallin hadn't really known how sure he was that it was true until the declaration had lurched up from the fear and anger seething in his gut and out his mouth.

Shaw reared back, eyes wide. He shook his head. "That isn't possible."

"Yeah?" Dallin snarled. "Well, I'll be sure to tell Wil it's not possible when Wheeler helps Æledfýres to shove him from out his own soul, because Calder has just done what the Guild and the Brethren have been failing at for the past three years—he's got Wil drugged stupid on leaf, and now Wil's wide open and helpless to stop it, and the place is bloody *crawling* with Wheeler's thugs."

Several people, hurrying about the business of getting ready to begin the search, had paused to stare. Dallin didn't know how many—if any—of them knew much about the Brethren or what their business with Wil was, other than that they meant to take him, nor did he care. In fact, Dallin thought it might be a good idea to address it to as many as he could. Perhaps that would make them search more vigorously.

Shaw was still shaking his head. "He wouldn't... *couldn't*. I...." He stared at Dallin, so stunned and grieved Dallin almost felt sorry for him. "He is... *was*... a good man, a *friend*."

"Not anymore." Dallin turned and started for the horses. "Now he's just another dead man."

"What about the Old Ones?" Shaw called. "They should be consulted, at least."

Dallin stopped. He turned on Shaw with a derisive snort. "Until they decide to pick up a weapon and stand a post, I haven't any use for the Old Ones at the moment."

Shaw peered around at those still watching and listening with their eyes wide and jaws suddenly slack. He stepped quickly over to Dallin, and lowered his voice.

"And what if I won't go?"

Dallin took a long, deep breath. "If you don't do this, I will have Wisena escort you across the Bounds, and what you do from there will be no concern of mine, because you will not step foot across them again. And if you try, I will shoot you down myself. This is the Father's Gift to the Mother we're talking about here, shaman. Just how deep is your faith, and what will you choose to do with it?"

"The Old Ones—"

"*I* am the Guardian." Dallin raised his voice for any who might hear. "I am the Shaman. I will do whatever it takes to find the Aisling and keep him safe. If you refuse your help, I've no use for you either." He stepped up close, and leaned in. "He trusted Calder. He trusted you. We know what Calder did with that trust. What will you do with it—*shaman*?"

Shaw bowed his head. "Wil would plead for him."

Dallin flashed a cold little twist of a smile. "Wil would also accept an oath of protection from him like it actually meant something." He turned, and started walking again. "Lucky for me, I've never had that problem."

"Guardian!" Shaw called after him. "You already toe the very edge of honor's line. Take care you don't trample it to ruination."

Dallin kept walking. Shaw said it as if he thought Dallin hadn't crossed that line too many years and lives ago and assumed he'd even know how to go back if he cared enough to want to. And did Shaw honestly imagine that it mattered? Perhaps he hadn't been paying attention. Then again, if he still thought it possible to save Calder, if he still thought Calder worth saving, Shaw obviously hadn't been.

The horses were all saddled, blowing in excitement and pawing at the ground impatiently as their various owners mounted and waited for the signal. Dallin was glad the man he'd ordered to find him a horse was watching for him, because Dallin hadn't been paying attention to whom he'd been barking the order. As it was, he found himself peering at a furry gray stallion, not terribly pretty, but with a feral glint to his eye that Dallin could appreciate.

"He's a bit wild," the man told him. "Never taken terribly kindly to the saddle. Or walking, for that matter—he'd much prefer to run. Sometimes I think he'd run himself off a cliff just to see if he can fly." The man shook his head, patting dotingly at the gray's neck. "He'll give you the business, if you let him, but he's clever and respects a horseman."

It was said with a fond grimace that told Dallin this was the man's very own mount, of whom he was terribly proud, and prouder still to hand the reins to his Shaman. Dallin accepted them with a steady look at the man and a nod.

"And he's fast?"

The man chuckled. "Just make sure you're seated well and you've a good hold before you prod him on." He scratched at the velvety nose, then gave the horse a swat when it took a nip at his fingers. "He's more than fast—he's unnatural."

Dallin cracked a small smile. "I thank you, and I'll take good care of him." He took hold of the gray's bridle, leaning in and looking straight into one dark eye. "Don't fuck with me and we'll get along just fine," he told it quietly, then nodded once more to the man and led the horse away.

Corliss and Woodrow were already mounted with a small group Dallin had to assume she'd picked out herself. Good. She knew them all better than he did, and she knew what to look for. He gave the horse an encouraging chirp and started over toward her.

It took Dallin a moment to realize he was being shadowed. He shot a look over his shoulder, expecting to see Shaw preparing more arguments. It was Andette, matching his stride, watching him and staring like she wanted to say something but couldn't quite manage the courage. Brilliant. One more thing Dallin didn't need, and he didn't have the time for it.

He stopped and looked at Andette. "His case has already been pled and heard. I haven't the patience to hear more. He made his choices. If you're looking to help your kin, I suggest you turn your heart toward your brother."

Andette shook her head, teeth set, and dipped a quick bow, considerably less deferential than she'd been yesterday. "Shaman," she said evenly, "I would ride with you. He has broken the laws of the Father and the Mother both. It is my right as kin to see justice done."

"He is your uncle."

"Hunter is my brother. Wil is my Aisling. You are my Shaman. Lind is my country. Barret Calder has betrayed it all, and defiled the names of all his kin with dishonor. It is my *right*."

She was shaking—with rage or fear, Dallin couldn't tell. Likely a bit of both.

"I haven't the time for the distraction of a blood feud." There might have been a bit more sympathy in Dallin's tone than he'd allowed before. "You would do best to stay here and look after your brother."

"Is blood not what you seek yourself?" Andette's retort was brash and held a touch of cheek Dallin hadn't expected from any of these people. She bowed her head, though with a smidge of irony that almost made Dallin smile. "I ask only for my right by the laws of Lind. Please, Shaman—I would ride with you."

Dallin rubbed at his aching brow. For pity's sake, why could he not seem to shake himself of Calders? He didn't trust her, but Dallin was not so full of bloodlust that he couldn't see it was because of her uncle, and he had no choice but to admit she had the right to make the demand.

"If you get in my way," he told her, low and serious, "I will put a bullet through you to get to him."

She raised her chin, nodded. "If I get in your way," she returned, just as serious, "it will be because my bullet has already hit its mark."

Dallin raised an eyebrow and waved her ahead. "Get your mount. I'm leaving now, and I'm not waiting for you."

He hadn't expected the grin—hadn't expected Andette to look so much like her brother when she did it—so it threw Dallin.

"*Yes*, Shaman!" was all she said, then turned and darted off.

Dallin shook his head, watching after her for a moment before he made his way over to Corliss and her party. He'd have to remember to be careful where he aimed these people.

It wasn't merely pain. It was consciousness, awareness, and it was driving into Dallin with an insistence that would not be denied for much longer. The land, the Mother—one and the same—trying to tell him something, and he'd damned well better stop to listen, and soon.

Corliss was riding beside him, the horses down to a walk. It was still dark, and the rocky path they were riding was steeper than most of the others that led to Fæðme. More of a footpath than a horse trail, and even if Calder hadn't taken this particular corridor—though Dallin knew he had, and the signs had borne it out thus far—they'd at least catch Calder up when they got there, or beat him to it.

It wasn't until Dallin had seen Shaw leaving with Wisena on the roan gelding Wil had... *liberated* from Chester that Dallin realized Calder must have taken Miri—Wil's own horse, the cheeky fuck. And though the fact that Dallin's party was traveling in a group might slow them down a bit, Miri still wasn't terribly fast or used to climbing these hills. With the added burden of two riders....

They'd catch up. Because the alternative was unthinkable.

Without giving himself much chance to think it over more thoroughly, Dallin shifted his calves to guide his horse closer to Corliss and held out his reins. "Hold these for a moment. And keep a tight hold. He's been aching to bolt since we started." More like dying for it and willing to throw Dallin off if he didn't leave him to it soon.

"Why?" Corliss looked chary, but she took the lead from Dallin's hand. "What are you going to do?"

"I'm a Watcher." Dallin rested his hands on the saddlebow and closed his eyes. "I'm going to Watch."

He didn't know what made him think he could do it—he just knew he could. He'd never tried it outside of dreams, but in those days when Wil had been wandering and Dallin had been searching for him, dream and reality had seemed to mesh more than once, one blending into the other, and actual sleep hadn't seemed necessary to the practice—a state somewhere in between. Dallin had needed dark and quiet to achieve it then, but if he couldn't have that....

I am the Shaman.

Three parts arrogant blustering, at the time, but now... maybe not so much. The Aisling needed the Guardian, so the Guardian Dallin would be.

He didn't think about the how of it. He stretched himself inside the channels Lind held ready just for him, butting up against his own barriers, but he didn't let those stop him. Too proud, perhaps, but Dallin had already known that as he cracked the locks on the floodgates and saw the might of the terrifying power straining behind them.

It was waiting for him, eager for him, so Dallin merely opened himself up and let it in.

The rush of relief nearly overwhelmed him. He hadn't realized just how bad the pain had been until he stopped resisting the call, let the power run through him, let it show him, guide him.

He saw his mistake with Shaw right away. Dallin hadn't needed to send Shaw to Wheeler, because Wheeler wasn't there anymore. Dallin had suspected as much, worried over it. He'd prevented the Old Ones from announcing Wil's location by blowing those damned welcome horns, only to have Wil announce it himself by trying to prove something he hadn't needed to prove. Certainly Wisena had needed the confirmation, and Wil was right when he'd argued it was the only way Wisena would believe with his whole heart and help in the way Dallin needed him to. But Wil hadn't done it for that, even if he truly thought he had. He'd been out to prove his own worth, his merit, to the people of Lind, and Dallin couldn't lay true blame, even though he'd wanted to choke Wil. Dallin knew Wil, knew how he thought, what was important to him, and he'd make himself a liability by trying to prove he wasn't one. Bloody apples and potatoes.

"He fought Calder hard," he heard himself whisper, and only

shook his head at Corliss's curious murmur. "He knew what.... Treacherous *bastard*."

Dallin could see it now, could feel it. The land had stood witness to it all, and it remembered, showed him. He couldn't hear words, but he could feel everything. The incomprehension, the murky awareness, the recognition, then the shock... the fight and the terrible, nauseating dismay—

Dallin pulled away from it before he lost his concentration. Instead he stretched himself further, trying to find the *now* and the *here*, but Calder was clever and talented. He hadn't lost all his magic when he'd lost his Marks. He might not hear the Mother's voice, but he could still manipulate Her land, as he'd manipulated Dallin that day in Chester. And Wil... wherever he was wandering, Dallin couldn't reach him, at least not yet. Either Wil was deliberately hiding from his Guardian, or the leaf made it impossible for him to reach out. Dallin was betting on the latter.

All right, then.

Magic untapped and unknown, Wil had told him. Dallin tapped it now. He put away every defense he'd clung to since this whole business started, let the magic in, and let it know him, let it twine itself into him with an awareness that nearly made him sick with its intimacy, its awful knowing. It was against everything Dallin had ever believed *right*. His mind was his own, and he'd had every intention of keeping it that way. Except now Wil was in trouble, more trouble than he'd ever been in before—which was almost incomprehensible in itself—and Dallin would knock down every barrier he'd ever held close and sacred to get Wil back out.

I will do whatever it takes, Dallin had told Wil, and even though he'd had no idea it would take *this*, still, he'd still meant it.

"This might take a bit," he murmured to Corliss. "Stop if you have to but don't interrupt."

Some part of him noted the absurdity of it, hunkering down to meditate while riding horseback on tricky terrain. Another part he didn't even know he had in him reached out with a mental hand, kept it firm on the horse's tether, warned him and instructed him, and sat back, satisfied by the compliance.

With one last deep breath, Dallin let down the blockades of everything he was, let it *all* in, let it wash over him, take him, *and it's so much less jarring and sickening than he'd thought it would be, so much less intrusive. More like a greeting, a reacquainting, than a conquest or invasion, and he almost laughs at the trepidation he felt just a second ago.*

Wæpenbora, it names him, and Ealdordéman, Foreládtéowes, and more names, too many, they flit by him too quickly. He snags them with mental grappling hooks, lets them tell him what he is, what he should be, the words themselves commands.

Soldier, Guide, Chief, Warrior, Doorway, Guardian....

On and on and on, it reaches down into those empty places he has inside him, and he lets it, lets it fill them up, only they're not as empty as he'd always thought them, rife with parts of himself he hadn't known he'd known, things tamped down and buried—

No, not buried... taken away.

"Bloody damn." It was a whisper, almost a laugh. "And here I'd thought—"

Do you put everything away like that? Do you bury everything that hurts?

Except Dallin hadn't put this away—it had been put away *for* him.

"What are you seeing?" someone asked, probably Corliss, but it was too far away, and Dallin couldn't make out the voice.

He shook his head and reached deeper. "Myself," *he thinks he answers, but he's not sure if the voice is inside his head or outside, and it doesn't matter.*

You knew your magic once whispers through him, and it may

be Her, or it may be Lind, it may even be him. He doesn't think it matters, because it's almost the same, and the words are truer than any half-believed bit of sacred rite he's ever bothered to look at from the corner of a wary eye. He'd known it, used it, and screamed and fought when they'd taken him from his bed, dragged him down into the glittering green throat of Fæðme, and stolen the memories of what he is.

"Green as the Mother's Womb," he muttered to... whomever, surprised by how much sense it made and how it had made none at all when he'd first read the words, scoffed at them. "That's where he gets his eyes."

He knows them all, all twelve. They've been his teachers, and he recognizes all but two now through a vertiginous sort of double vision, looking at them as they were and as they are now with eyes that are young and not so young at the same time.

Can't cross the Bounds, *they say with one voice,* not before he's Marked, not knowing what he knows. *Only no one speaks, and he understands it, thinks he approves, but Ríocht comes—he'd dreamed it, and they'd dreamed it with him, and they shouldn't be here, they should be blowing the horns, waking the countryside. Instead they surround him in the Mother's Womb and speak in silent circles, deciding his fate for him when his fate is not theirs to choose.*

Their minds dig into his, sorting and taking, and he fights with everything he has, and it's enough, or it will be, he's stronger than all of them put together. But there are too many of them, a concentrated assault, and he screams to his mother, and then to the Mother —They steal my calling—*and She's there, laying Her hand to his brow, cooling the fiery touch of too many minds inside his own.*

"We are all bound by those who believe in us." She draws up Her sleeve to reveal the iron that binds Her wrists, a clink of chains he hadn't heard before. He wants to weep, but She looks at him, reproachful, so he holds the tears back. "The magic of faith is great and strong," She says, "and We are its creatures." Her fingers slide beneath his chin, lift his face up until he meets Her depthless blue eyes. A wave of Her hand sweeps the Old Ones, and Dallin is surprised to note that none of them see Her, he's the only one, and he almost tells them to stop, this isn't what She wants, but She shakes Her head. "They do what they think they must. One day it will be yours to teach them, but today is not that day."

She leans down, and sets a kiss to his brow. Soft comfort moves through him, an immediate quelling of the minds inside his own, a lessening of the clamor. And then She's taking up the empty spaces where the Old Ones have just been, seeking, and Dallin doesn't fight Her as he had them—he merely closes his eyes, allows Her in, though he doesn't think he could stop Her even if he wanted to.

"They can take nothing you don't give them." She shows him the bars and locks, shows him how to use them. "Keep it safe. He will hold your keys as you hold his. How you each choose to use them...." She sighs and lifts Her shoulder in a graceful shrug, the chains at Her wrists chinking lightly, and the bone-deep outrage of it, the wrongness, makes him want to cry, but again he holds it back.

"You want me to hide," he whispers, offended and wounded and crushed right down to his soul.

"He needs you to live" is all She says. She kisses him again, slides Her fingertips across his unMarked cheek, and commands, "Lock it down where they cannot see it, and hold it close until you find him. I will come to you when he is ready."

And then She's gone, but he still feels Her watching him as he does what She'd commanded—buries what he is beneath what he will need to be in this place of Her making, with its walls of malachite that stagger and shift with the flicker of lamplight. They sigh, their weathered faces full of worry and sorrow as they lead him, weeping and confused, from Her embrace, and it's only when he is taken from them by his mother and hauled, resisting mindlessly, *through the fires and the screams and the clash of bone and metal, shoved into the back of the cart, that the horns blow. He grasps at what it should all mean, but he can't remember.*

It doesn't matter anymore. He is a different man now, he is what he's made of himself, and those things he was before are the building blocks he's used as foundations even when he didn't know it. He is the Shaman, he does have magic, and he almost thinks he feels Her smile in his mind as he reaches for it, takes it in his hand, directs it.

Like an old friend, it fits back into his grasp, and he knows it, and it knows him. He'd had true faith before, and he has it now again, and it's all he really needs.

He calls Shaw back first, calls Wisena and every man and woman in Lind who carries a weapon, shows them where the enemy hides, and shows them the enemy that waits. He calls to the land, warns it, and it whispers back to him, tells him of bootsteps beneath its skin and fires that burn hotter than suns and scrape moaning cries from deep in its heart.

Dallin opened his eyes and snatched the reins back from Corliss.

"He's waking up."

He kicked his heels into the horse's ribs and let him bolt, let him set the pace, only a short tug on the reins every now and then to keep him on surer footing. Dallin leaned down into the gather and release of thick muscle, winding his fingers through the rough gray mane, and dug in with his knees. His lips curled back, teeth bared and clenched together in a grin that felt hard and cruel but ripe with anticipatory satisfaction.

"You really can fly," he whispered to the gray and sank himself into the veil of fleeing night, guiding the horse's lurching strides by nothing more than Dallin's own forgotten bond with the land and the surety that the tie wouldn't fail him.

He understood now; he understood it all. Before, it might have angered him, might have paralyzed him with rage, but there wasn't time now for anything but the beat of hoofs to ground, the shortening of distance between him and what he knew to be happening farther up the trail. The physical was the only thing important right now—the rhythm of the uphill gallop, the silent urging for *more* and *faster,* and the horse's willing acquiescence to both, its mindless glee at opening its stride, pouring every bit of itself into the stretch and bunch of its thumping gait, hot blood racing through its veins and opening its heart, pumping air through its frothing mouth.

Dallin could be a part of it if he wanted to, could sink himself deep and watch it all from the inside, could feel the instinctive necessity to *run* and *go* with no knowledge of years of tricks and betrayals to complicate the pure power of speed. Not quite tempting enough, not now. The thin scent of smoke was wafting toward him, and he'd already lost too much time watching the past —the present was happening *right now.*

Miles stretched beneath them, then a league and more, the gray planting his hoofs on rock and paths still mud-slick from the rain three days ago, trusting the Guardian to guide him true. Dallin Watched and guided and trusted the horse in turn to carry them both on the wings of muscled flanks and pure, uncomplicated *heart.*

Thunder rumbled above at the same moment they rounded a slight bend and saw the first of the fires. Gnawing only at the tops of the trees for now, smoldering bits of leaf and branch fluttering down onto the path, the crackle and hiss only dimly reaching Dallin beneath the cacophony of wind in his ears and hoofs on rock. Dallin half-expected the horse to rear and shy, but he didn't, merely put his head down and barreled through the smoking rain of debris, eyes a bit wild and nostrils flaring but never losing speed.

"Almost there." Dallin dropped a reassuring pat to the thick neck as the booming report of splitting wood roiled from farther uphill, followed by the dull *whoosh* of new flame. The hard grin reasserted itself on Dallin's face, stretching and tugging at the new skin of the still-healing burn on his cheek. "Thought you knew better, did you, Calder?" He leaned to the side, guiding the gray around a tangle of burning brush and on up the path. "Thought you could control him, eh? Serves you right, you spineless fuck."

Dallin turned his head, spat in the dirt, and urged the horse on with a tightening of his calves and a shift in the saddle.

He could hear voices now, raised in anger and fear, a growling curse and an incongruous shriek of laughter before thunder boiled again and a streak of lightning split the sky, turning the heavy drape of darkness into bright daylight for the span of four of Dallin's thumping heartbeats. Two shapes seared themselves into his vision, locked in stumbling combat. He made out the wider shape of Calder holding Wil's smaller, struggling form against him with one arm. Wil's head was pulled back by a fistful of black hair. Calder held a flask to Wil's lips, trying to force whatever was in it down Wil's throat while Wil sputtered and snorted and twisted in a grip that was simply too strong and steady for someone who was already impaired and in the tight, grasping hold of a drug designed to make one helpless.

Fire leaped up again all around them, trees going up like giant candles and great, oozing gobs of it flying out in every direction, dripping flame like melting wax as it had been when they'd tried to crash the gates of Chester.

Dallin's horse reared this time, bawled a frightened protest, and tried to veer away. Dallin crouched down over its neck, wrenched the reins, and felt the tremor in the horse's hindquarters as it fought its own instincts and obeyed Dallin's command, gathering itself beneath Dallin and leaping to a driving run. It only shivered a small, frantic cry as they broached the barrier of flame and arrowed to its center, head-on to the men locked in lopsided skirmish.

Calder's arm was secured around Wil's throat now—Dallin saw it by the light of the fires. The shimmer of liquid flowed down Wil's chin as Calder poured the brew into Wil's mouth, letting up just long enough for Wil to get a gasping breath and choke, using that breath to try to spit the drug out. Calder knew Dallin was there, knew he was coming, and *still*, he kept trying to force the stuff down Wil's throat, Wil gasping and kicking, face going from red to blue to red again and pulled into an unsettling mixture of pain and rage and laughter as he fought with everything he had to keep the stuff from sliding down his throat.

The gray didn't balk or back down but kept driving on as Dallin fired a shot at Calder's head, missed and hit his shoulder instead. The force knocked Calder back, and he loosed his hold. The gray kept driving still as Dallin leaned in the saddle, reached out, and snatched firm hold of Wil's coat by the collar. Dallin clenched his teeth at the way his muscles wrenched, and his shoulder nearly slipped its socket as he threw Wil up and around, tried to sling him over the horse's rump—

They were going too fast, and Wil's reflexes weren't worth much of anything at the moment. He yelped and scrabbled momentarily at Dallin's back, trying to latch on to the strap of the rifle and failing. Desperately, Wil's hand found the crossbow wedged into the saddle's straps and took hold, but Dallin hadn't tied it down. Wil slithered out of Dallin's hold, hands still wrapped around the bow's tiller, and thumped to the ground, bow and all, before Dallin could rein in.

Three shots whizzed over Dallin's head, rapid-fire. He ducked and jerked the gray around for another pass at Wil, thankfully not trampled and not looking too terribly worse for the fall. Another shot, this one right past the gray's nose, and it reared again, a thick, heavy scream rolling up from its barrel as two more shots rang out. One was close enough to flick at the hair over Dallin's left ear. The other thumped into his right bicep.

Just the meat, not the bone. Dallin's mind automatically assessed the wound, almost not feeling the searing heat and quick-sliding pain of the bullet hammering through flesh, but it knocked his aim wild as he returned fire. His shot this time went harmlessly over Calder's head as the gray finally threw Dallin to the ground and took off through the small patch of surrounding forest that wasn't on fire.

Winded, Dallin rolled, anticipating more shots as he reached for the gun at his hip and tried to aim himself for nonexistent cover at the side of the rocky path. No shots followed him. Dallin lifted his head, found Calder reloading, so he hauled himself up and made a sprint toward Wil. It was farther than he'd thought. Damned horse must've thrown Dallin at least twenty paces.

He could hear shouts now from farther down the path and could feel the steady rumble of hoofbeats beneath his feet. He almost laughed. In truth, he'd forgotten about the rest of the party, hadn't thought of them once since he'd closed his eyes and opened himself up to magic.

You're not alone, Corliss, he warned. *Watch your back.*

Wil was grinning—Dallin could see the flash of teeth as he got closer, horribly savage and empty. Wil was sitting on the ground, eyes locked on to Calder as he planted his feet to the staves of the crossbow, yanked the whipcord with both hands, and seated it in its notch. He nocked a bolt like he'd been doing it all his life, pulled it up to his shoulder in the same way he aimed the rifle, and sighted down.

Good man, Dallin cheered silently, not terribly confident Wil could actually hit anything on his first go, but at the very least, it might be a distraction. Calder had finished reloading his own gun, eyes following as Dallin continued to run in a low crouch toward Wil. Calder raised the gun—

Dropped it in the dirt, eyes wide as he stared, amazed, at the fletching of the bolt sticking at an angle from one side of his wrist, the tip protruding from the other. Delayed reaction hit, and Calder screamed, something thwarted and enraged. He dove to the side as Dallin complemented Wil's shot with one of his own, aiming this time for the artery in the thigh that had caused so many problems back when Dallin had first stumbled into the chaos of Wil's life back in Dudley. There was no telling from here if the aim had been true, but Calder went down quickly and heavily, giving Dallin time to cover the remaining distance between himself and Wil.

Wil was still grinning, and chuckling quietly now, Dallin saw with both fury and unease. The soles of Wil's boots were once again planted to the crossbow staves, his hands loading another bolt. His face was filthy, scraped raw at the left temple and down his cheek from his fall, mud and leaves covering the left side of his coat and trousers and clinging to his hair. His green eyes were murky and somewhat crazed, a strange reflection of the euphoric savagery that had glinted from them when Wil had taken the butt of Locke's gun to a man's head.

Dallin reached out—tentatively, as he had that day—and laid his hand to Wil's arm, the light of the fire making Wil look feral and macabrely beautiful.

A blooming stain was spreading right between Wil's collarbone and right shoulder—Dallin could see it widening beneath Wil's coat. One of Calder's last shots, had to be. The fabric around the ragged hole in the coat was still smoking. Dallin bit back his alarm and unlaced Wil's shirt, slipping his hand inside to cover the wound with his palm. Not immediately fatal, but it could be if

Dallin didn't do something, and Wil would definitely feel it when the leaf wore off.

"All right?" Dallin asked, afraid for a moment as those wild eyes fixed on him, narrowed, that Wil wouldn't remember him. Afraid that whatever the leaf did to Wil's fiery core—damped beneath those terrible, cheery smiles, unreachable—would also keep Dallin from reaching Wil at all.

But Wil sobered, though the smile never left. He shook his head, tears Dallin hadn't noticed before tracking thick down Wil's dirty cheeks and glinting like stars in the firelight. With a low growl, Wil jerked out of Dallin's grip, dropped the bow, and turned on hands and knees. He jammed his fingers down his throat and retched everything he had in him into the leaves and spiny bracken.

Eventually Wil warbled "No," hoarse and heavy.

With a low curse, he spat, wiped his mouth on his dirty sleeve, then crawled away from the mess and toward Dallin. Dallin didn't know what to expect, but Wil only clutched hold of Dallin's coat, almost scaled his chest as if it were a particularly steep hill, and managed to drag himself up into a wobbly crouch. Somber and serious, Wil leaned in, said Dallin's name—slowly, like he was reacquainting himself with the shape of it—and took hold of Dallin's arms like he meant to say something terribly important. Dallin flinched when Wil's fingers closed over his right arm. He couldn't help it.

Wil pulled his hands back, movements slow and jerky. He blinked down at his fingers, red with the blood seeping through Dallin's coat.

"Oh." Soft and far away. Wil's eyes drifted shut, his head tilted. He lifted his hand and drew his fingertips along his right cheekbone. A trail of Dallin's blood streaked unevenly and mixed with the tears on Wil's cheek.

"Blood to blood." Wil snorted, then opened his eyes slowly and tilted in. Dallin thought for a moment Wil was going to kiss him, but instead Wil dipped his mouth to Dallin's ear. "It isn't finished yet."

He quavered something like a tortured little giggle that made the hairs at Dallin's nape stand up and chills skitter up his spine.

No, not finished, not by any stretch of the imagination.

"No," Dallin agreed. "There are more coming."

Eyes closed, Dallin let the land gather at him, let it push its power through him and seep into Wil, let it swamp his body and directed it back out through his hand, asking. Confident for the first time in forever, Dallin reached for the Mother's blessings to the Shaman and accepted them all, then altered the balance. Joyful, the land sang its songs of healing. Dallin silently added his own voice until he heard Wil hum a happy little sigh and felt him go boneless against Dallin's chest.

Not healed completely—they'd need more time for that—but not life-threatening, and not bleeding now, at least.

The leaf was another matter altogether. The stuff worked incredibly quickly, and whatever Calder had managed to get down Wil had set to its purpose before Wil had managed to purge the rest. Dallin couldn't get past it. Its tendrils were wound too inextricably with Wil's core, incipient and clinging, and if Dallin tried to unwind it, he might end up unwinding Wil. Instinct wouldn't take Dallin through this one, and he certainly hadn't practiced enough to know what he was doing with something this apparently intricate. He clenched his teeth and did as much as he dared, which wasn't much. It wasn't fair. What good was healing if Dallin couldn't touch the one thing that might prove more lethal to Wil than a bullet to the brain?

Mother—a low interior growl—*if this is some kind of test, I'm going to be really fucking pissed.*

Shots were ringing down the path. Dallin could almost see the configurations of the crude battle line by the echoes of the reports and the shouts that rose above the steady chuckle of the fires. Perhaps six or eight of the enemy versus the twelve in the party following after Dallin. Corliss and the others would take care of them, but they wouldn't be the only ones, and they wouldn't stop coming, not 'til they got what they'd come for.

Dallin pushed Wil back gently, told him "Stay here," and got to his feet. He wiped his sticky hand on his coat and waved it vaguely at the fire and the sky still grumbling threats. "Can you defend yourself if you have to? I mean...." Dallin ran a hand through his hair. "Are you still coming down, or did he...?"

Wil smiled, sly and wicked, almost enough to make Dallin take a quick step back and away. Until Wil spoiled the effect by whiffing out another deranged little giggle. He flicked a hand up over his shoulder, grinning as the fire leaped, spat, and climbed its way too quickly up a sagging pine.

"Aim's a little off." Wil snickered. "Meant to get Calder with the lightning, but—" He rolled his eyes with a lopsided grin. "Missed."

Dallin merely nodded, watching the fire for a moment, then turned back to Wil. "Only if you have to, all right? There are others closing in, and we're rather stuck here with no horses for the moment." He raised his eyebrows, not terribly hopefully. "Unless you know where Miri got off to?"

Wil drew his knees up to his chest, and laid his head atop them. "Told her to run." It was sticky and slurred with exhaustion. "Pretty sure she listened."

Dallin said, "Stay here," again, then walked slowly and cautiously toward Calder.

Calder was on his back, wrenching in slowing breaths, grasping weakly for the gun just out of reach. By the looks of it,

Dallin's shot to Calder's shoulder had splintered the bone—it slanted down at an odd angle, and it was lumpier than it should have been. Calder's other hand twitched uselessly below the wrist shattered by the crossbow bolt; he gasped when the bolt's tip hitched against the ground every time he so much as breathed. And still, he kept reaching for the gun. Bleeding out into the Mother's Heart, the land he professed to love and serve drinking up his life as he poured it out.

Dallin kicked the gun out of Calder's reach with the toe of his boot. There were so many things he wanted to ask Calder, so many things he wanted to say. In the end all Dallin managed was "How could you?" through a snarl that would do no one any good now.

Calder grimaced, somehow still defiant. "Your love weighs more profoundly than your calling. It is not meant and does the Aisling no good." He swallowed thickly. "I die now knowing I have done the Mother's will."

He looked... satisfied. Almost exalted. Wrong, too wrong, and it twisted in Dallin's gut, then *clenched*.

Eyes narrow, heart cold and quiet, Dallin crouched down next to Calder. Calmly he reached out and laid his hand to the small, neat wound on Calder's thigh.

"Since Wil called to me when you took him"—Dallin's voice was cool and even, and he tightened his fingers until Calder let slip a weak yelp—"I have been wondering what punishment would suit you best for your crimes against the Aisling, the Mother, the Father, Lind. Up until thirty seconds ago, wrapping my hands around your throat and tearing it open was topping the list." Dallin leaned in, voice low, Calder's faded blue eyes going wild and fearful in the dying wash of flame. "Now I've decided that the best sentence one could hand a would-be martyr would be life, so you can watch with your own eyes as the Mother's voice whispers to her Shaman, guiding my hand in Her true will." Again

Dallin reached for the power. "You stole my calling once." He watched with icy satisfaction as Calder's eyes squeezed shut. "You tried to steal it twice." He spoke silently to the land and listened as it answered him back. He smiled, cold and cruel. "How very painful it will be for you to have your miserable life saved by that calling—false prophet."

Power rushed to his call, and Dallin let it slide up from the ground beneath his feet, shard through him—

Nearly fell back as it ricocheted back into him, and slammed into his chest with a heavy fist, shock-blunt and solid.

Dallin reeled to his feet, staggering, reaching blind, until his hand latched on to the first solid object it found. Disoriented, ears ringing, he blinked.

Calder's blue eyes were wide, staring sightlessly up into the still-blazing treetops. A thin trickle of blood leaked from the corner of his open mouth, the white fletching of a quivering arrow jutting from his throat.

Dallin realized he was propping himself on Andette and let go abruptly.

Andette was staring down at her uncle, her mouth set hard, eyes bright and glistening in the uncertain light. She lowered her longbow and turned slowly to Dallin. She dipped her head.

"It was my right."

It was, Dallin couldn't deny it, though so much for his "suitable punishment."

Dallin decided not to comment, just turned and watched as Wil shambled up behind them. Dallin reached out to steady him, but Wil shook him off. Eyes too obviously unfocused, Wil goggled closely at Andette as though he was trying to decide if he'd seen her before. Apparently satisfied that yes, he had, he nodded to himself and walked a bit unsteadily over to Calder. Dallin wanted to reach again when Wil listed, but he didn't, only watched as Wil righted himself, then bent to retrieve Andette's arrow, grinding it through cartilage and bone as he pulled it loose. He stared for a long moment, drew in a deep breath, and... spat.

Muttering lightly to himself, Wil paced slowly and carefully back over to them. "H'llo, Andette." He handed her the arrow. He didn't wait for her to respond, merely shifted his murky gaze back to Dallin. "We've company."

Obviously, Dallin didn't say. He shot a quick look at Andette, wondering what she was making of her Aisling now, but she was staring at the gory arrow in her hands and didn't even seem to register their existence at the moment, so he decided to leave her to herself.

Thunder still muttered above, like it was just sitting there waiting, and Dallin supposed that wasn't too far off the mark.

"Look at me." He took hold of Wil and turned him to face him, peering intently into eyes that were faraway and hazed. Wil's gaze kept wanting to wander further, but Dallin could tell Wil was willfully holding to the present, trying with everything in him to concentrate. Filthy and tear-streaked and wearing Dallin's blood on his cheek like a Mark. "How much, d'you think?" he asked bluntly. And how much was the last dose still working on him?

A helpless, watery snort knocked loose from Wil. He shut his eyes tight, collapsed forward, and laid his head on Dallin's shoulder.

"I'm so fucked." He took hold of Dallin's coat, holding himself up. "I'm sorry."

"It's not your fault." Dallin's fingers were once again itching, wanting to throttle a dead man—and anyone else who'd ever forced a cup to Wil's lips, while he was at it. He wrapped his good arm about Wil instead. *"How much?"*

"Dunno." Wil's legs kept loosening, his body leaning more heavily into Dallin with each passing second. "Too much, even a little is far too much, but it's so *nice*, I've missed it, 'm sorry, and 'm so tired."

Thick and slurred, but Dallin couldn't tell how much of it was the drug and how much of it was the circumstances. And it mattered.

"Brayden!"

Corliss. Good. Dallin looked over Wil's shoulder, freed a hand, and waved her back. He pushed Wil carefully upright and waited 'til the fuzzy gaze latched on to his.

"Listen to me. Are you listening?" Dallin waited for Wil to nod. "We're going to finish this. Right now. Everyone wants so badly for us to go to Fæðme, so that's where we go. We can't do this by ourselves—we need the Mother."

Wil stiffened. He tried to draw back but couldn't quite make it by himself, so Dallin helped him. He pushed Wil back until Dallin could see the expected agitation flaring in Wil's eyes. Wil's mouth was twitching, fighting the vacant smile that kept trying to stretch across his dirty, bloody face.

"Not like this, I... not.... Please." Helpless pleading that nearly broke Dallin's heart.

Dallin held Wil's panicked gaze steadily. "Do you think for one minute She hasn't seen you in worse shape?" Wil's eyes squeezed shut. Dallin shook Wil's shoulders lightly 'til Wil looked at him again. "We go to Her, you take what She has to give you, and no one can ever do this to you again."

"The Brethren—"

"Are surrounding us as we speak. They think they're herding us toward Fæðme, and we're going to let them keep thinking that. I've got squads of *Weardas* flanking them—none of them will get out of Lind alive—but they can't know that until we've done what we came here to do." Dallin took a long breath. He wasn't sure how much sense Wil was making of all this, but he seemed to be following, feeble little chuckles leaking from him now and then that Dallin was finding it harder and harder to ignore. "The Cleric. He's here. He's down in the tunnels."

Wil stared. Then... laughed. He backed away, stumbling until he hit a tree. It looked like he had no choice but to lean against it, until he just slithered halfway down the trunk, propped precariously.

"So fucked." Wil's snorts were harsh and wild as he bowed his head and closed his eyes. "So fucked, so fucked, so *fucked!*"

"Maybe so." Dallin was surer now that he was trying to have a life-and-death discussion with someone who was only very tentatively hanging on to reality. "But if we go out, we do it our way."

They could still get out. They could still run. It wouldn't be too terribly hard. Call to the *Weardas* shadowing the Brethren, tell them to ambush, and Dallin could grab Wil and flee across the Bounds, hole up somewhere, and hide, rebuild strength and sense. Perhaps they could even find a way to assassinate Wheeler, put off the inevitable for a while.

Except that would be all they'd be doing—putting it off—and it wouldn't take long for Æledfýres to build up a new cabal, find a new conduit for himself. Only this time they wouldn't know ahead of time. They'd both be living as Wil had done for the past three years, constantly looking over their shoulders—not sitting by a river all night long just to hear its songs change when the stars gave way to the dawn. Dallin wanted to give Wil something better than a life of running away, or at least make it so Wil could get those things for himself.

All that, and the Father weakening steadily, holding Æledfýres back with all the strength He still had left. And what would happen to Wil when that strength finally gave? Perhaps Æledfýres wouldn't even need a false Guardian anymore to blaze his trail for him. Perhaps he could simply find Wil and... take him.

Dallin shook his head. No. Now. If there was such a thing as fate, if anything was truly meant, events and circumstances were converging right now to force them on the path toward Fæðme. And considering what waited there for Wil, Dallin had to believe Her hand was guiding them at least a little. Perhaps even Calder had served Her purpose in that respect, because Dallin couldn't deny that the trip down to the Bounds had been more than a bit of stalling, and if things hadn't happened the way they did, he might have even come up with a few more excuses to delay. And he couldn't imagine another, gentler circumstance that would have caused him to reach for his past, his Self, Lind, the way he'd done, and come to understand the power of it all, his own ability to use it.

Dallin doubted, as a rule. He always had done, and the Father approved. From the moment twelve old men had tried to take Dallin's Self from him, he'd doubted, and now he knew why. Knew why the idea of letting another into his mind so offended him. Why he'd never quite believed that any one priest or shaman or cleric knew all the answers, and if they did, that they were interpreting them correctly. Why street magicians and petty conjurers had never impressed him, because he'd seen real magic once, had wielded it himself, and all else paled beneath the power of true gods.

He will hold your keys as you hold his.

And that was pretty much that.

Wil was watching him, slumped against the tree. That soft, impractical smile curved his mouth, but his eyes were bordering on blind delirium.

"You can make me, y'know." He chuckled and waved a hand, the fires that had been settling into smoke and smoldering ash now reawakening with a crackling little growl. A murmur of thunder and a small flash of lightning slipped through the sky. "Oops."

Wil tucked his hands beneath his arms and squinted, his gaze trying to sharpen as it took in Andette crouching over her uncle's body, then Corliss and the others splitting their wary stares between the darkness surrounding them and the newly bolstered flames. Wil set his muzzy gaze back on Dallin with a lopsided grin and a tilt of his head.

"Could never seem to refuse you anyway, but now I *really* couldn't."

It had the feel of confession—Wil really believed it. Dallin resisted the temptation to point out that Wil certainly *could* refuse him, and often did, to Dallin's very sincere dismay, most of the time. Wil's hazy gaze narrowed.

"He'll be able to make me too. What shall we do about that, Guardian?"

Dallin had thought about that. Ever since Wil had made the accusation an eternity ago, Dallin had thought about it.

The leaf would make it so that Dallin could follow Wil even if Wil didn't want him to, and according to the things Wil had said about the Guild, he'd *have* to listen, would *have* to do what Dallin told him to do, even if it was against everything Wil wanted. And if Dallin were the same person he'd been only a few hours ago, he might have thought about it more seriously. In the most objective sense, it was probably the smartest thing he could do—drag Wil down the throat of Fæðme, order him to accept what the Mother gave him, order him to stand aside while Dallin spoke his name and called Æledfýres, and then order Wil to push everything he had at him. Dallin could die knowing he'd fulfilled his calling, walked the path the Old Ones and Calder had been so sure had been set before him. And not have to put a bullet through Wil's head if they didn't win this thing.

Except Dallin would be doing to Wil exactly what Síofra had done—taking away choices, using strength and power over someone who was too vulnerable to fight back, and forcing Wil to places he didn't want to go. He'd be doing what Calder had been trying to do—assuming he knew better, making Wil watch help-lessly as his fate was decided for him.

He'd be doing what everyone else seemed to think the Shaman *ought* to be doing—putting legend and purpose higher than a man's right to self-direction.

And yes, the stakes were extraordinarily high, and the wrong decision could mean the difference between Wil walking away from this with at least half his mind left or life as they now knew it reverting back to the savagery and slavery of a time before men had raised their gods above them and chained them to divinity. Perhaps the sacrifice of one or two souls was not so much to ask, considering.

But.

The funny thing was, Dallin was pretty sure that was exactly what the others meant when they insisted he had to think about it as the Shaman. And he was fairly certain that if he didn't care so much, he just might've done. Ironically, he'd been more prepared to think and act like the Shaman the Old Ones seemed to want way back in Putnam—before he'd seen the fierce life in Wil, the simple desire to *have* a life and to own himself, to shatter the control under which he'd existed for so long. Before Dallin had begun to realize he cared.

Shaman or not, Guardian or not, Dallin was only one man. He was no god, he wasn't bound to any beliefs but his own, and Wil's fate was not his to choose. And if that meant he would have to keep his promise....

Your love weighs more profoundly than your calling.

And that was pretty much that as well.

"I could." Dallin took the few paces over to Wil slowly, and stood in front of him. He looked at Wil straight. "But I won't."

Somewhere in that sharp mind, right now being dismantled piece by piece and subsumed beneath a cottony haze of euphoria, sense tried to work its way through the sticky clouds of leaf, tried to bare itself on the razor-edge inside the murky gaze, and couldn't quite make it.

"He'll be there to try to take from you," Dallin said evenly. "I'll be there to help you keep it. You tell me what you want, and I'll make sure you do it. I can, you know—I'm stronger than Wheeler, at least. He won't get past me."

Wil snorted. "You'll order me to follow my own orders?"

"I am servant to the Aisling." Dallin held out his hands, open and offering. "I always have been." Slowly, making sure Wil watched him all the way, he went down to one knee. He kept his hands out before him and bowed his head. "I am at your command."

He could feel the eyes of the others on him and nodded to himself with satisfaction. Andette and nine others from Lind watching their Shaman bend his neck and knee before their Aisling, and Dallin had no doubt word would spread once this was over. If he didn't live through it, and Wil did, Wil would need the support of people who'd been set their example by the one figure they placed above all mortals, even above the Old Ones. Perhaps Dallin had never felt entirely comfortable with the deference the people of Lind showed him, but in this case it was useful and so therefore usable.

Wil had stopped laughing, his smile now weary and lopsided and still twitching as if he were trying to wipe it off and couldn't. But his soft gaze throttled screams behind it. His eyes drifted down, caught on the bloodstain purled over one side of his shirt, and he stared at it like he'd never seen it before, then dismissed it like it didn't matter. He slid all the way down the rough trunk of the tree, a bit of a chuckling *whoof* puffing from him when his arse hit the ground, and he blinked and squinted as a light drizzle began to fall.

"At my command." He nodded, like he was trying to push the sense of it through the wooziness. Clumsy, he flicked Dallin's fringe from his brow with dirty, blood-stained fingers, then leaned in until his head was flopped once again on Dallin's shoulder. "Don't leave me alone. I want... please... so *tired*." Fading quickly now, and what had it been costing him to remain even this aware? And would he even remember any of what they'd just said?

Dallin tried not to let the worry gnaw at him, telling himself he was borrowing trouble. He dragged Wil in close, mindful of the wound on Wil's chest.

"I'm not going anywhere." He squeezed as hard as he dared as Wil's body crumpled against him, going limp and too bendy. Dallin let himself feel it for as long as he needed to, let himself know the warmth and contact until he was sure he would remember it even if everything else was taken from him. Then he shook himself, dragged Wil to his feet, and slid one of Wil's lanky arms across his own shoulders to hold him up.

"C'mon, then." He reached out, sent a mental call to Miri and the gray, and started steering Wil, leaning heavier and drooping more by the second, toward the others waiting for them in a loose ring around Calder's body. "We've still got a ways to go, and now you've gone and made it rain."

"'S 'cause 'm sad," Wil mumbled into his shoulder.

And somehow that made all the sense in the world to Dallin. He dipped in and dropped a kiss to Wil's dirty hair.

"So am I."

They gnawed on jerky and hardtack while they waited for the

horses, Corliss and Woodrow somewhat skeptical when Dallin told them laconically that they'd show up shortly. Andette and the others merely folded down around one of the smaller fires and broke out travel sustenance from their saddlebags to share about. All of them shot surreptitious glances at Wil, though—out cold again, head propped on the pack Corliss had retrieved from where they'd left their horses farther down the path where the fires wouldn't spook them, and covered with a coat from one of the young men. Seaf, if Dallin was remembering right.

Nine of them were sat in the loose circle, two keeping watch around the temporary perimeter, one watching the horses. And all of them shifting glances at Wil that looked remarkably alike—awe and sympathy and a hard little glint beneath it all that Dallin couldn't quite put his finger on, but if he had to guess, he'd name it possessive protectiveness. Which would make Wil twitch and snarl, probably, but which made Dallin nod to himself in newfound satisfaction.

"How many did you get back there?" Dallin directed the question at Woodrow while looking the entire party over for injuries, but apparently, besides a quickly bruising gouge—bullet graze, it wasn't hard to determine—angling up over the wide forehead of a taciturn young woman who'd guardedly introduced herself as Setenne when Dallin had a look at it, everyone appeared relatively unscathed. Mud and sweat and the lingering nibble of fear and adrenaline didn't count.

"There were eight, by my reckoning." Woodrow shook his head with a puzzled frown, following as Dallin retrieved the rifle and the crossbow from where they'd been dropped in the brush. "We got five of them, and the rest scattered." Woodrow chewed his lip. "It was easy. Too easy. Either they were trying to get shot, or they've little enough training so as not to count."

Dallin nodded, said, "Mm," and sat down with the others. "A

little of both, I expect. They're priests, mostly, or at least they think they are, though what they worship—" His mouth tightened, and he shook his head. "Their god poses as the Father, and they have a calling of sorts, but I think...." He paused, pondered. "I think he can only reach those who... who already have a weakness toward him, if that makes any sense. The rest, he has to rely on those like Wheeler to charm for him, but I don't think they would be so willing to die as the Brethren are. He seeks out those most easily used and uses them, speaks to them with the voice of a god, and hands them a calling. And it doesn't matter if they die for him, because all he has to do is find a hundred more to take their places, and he doesn't seem to have a lot of problem with that bit of it."

"This is that Æledfýres you've been talking about," Corliss put in.

Dallin merely nodded, staring at Wil's rifle in his hands. He hadn't been talking about it, in point of fact. He'd called to the land and everyone in it, showed them the enemy as he'd sat and meditated on a horse that he was now sitting here waiting for so he could stand at Wil's back while they faced another monster. But Dallin supposed he couldn't blame Corliss for trying to bend it all into practical shapes in her mind.

She was silent for a while, staring at him, then looked away. "Seems a big thing to tangle with." She was trying to make it an idle observation but not quite succeeding.

Dallin shrugged. "We'll find out, I expect."

Corliss wasn't done, working herself up to saying something else, Dallin had no doubt. He waited her out until she tilted her head, frowning. "Brayden—"

"It's real." Dallin made it sharp and steady, because he really wasn't in the mood to argue with Corliss's stubborn pragmatism. "I know it's difficult to imagine me as... as anything other than how you've known me, but the Guardian is real, and I'm it. Wil and I... we can do this. We haven't any choice."

Corliss looked away again. "'Tisn't difficult to imagine at all." She looked like she was trying to smile. "I'm afraid it suits you."

That seemed to quash any chatter for the moment.

The rain was still coming in a light drizzle, just enough to add a low hiss to the sound of the dying fires and slick skin and hair, but not enough to seep through coats yet. Anyway, the trees blocked most of it, and they were as comfortable as they could be for this short respite with no one shooting at them.

"You're bleeding." Corliss was scowling at the stiffening stain on Dallin's coat.

Dallin peered down at his arm, surprised when he remembered there was a bullet stuck in there somewhere and it had better come out soon. And now that his attention had been called to it—fucking *ow*.

He'd never been shot before, and he sat back for a moment, pondering his luck in that respect. Eight years in the military, more of that time spent on the front lines than not, and he'd been grazed twice by arrows, wrenched his ankle once leaping from the saddle in the thick of things, and had suffered a few bruised ribs when a particularly messy skirmish had ended in hand-to-hand that had quickly degenerated into hand-to-axe-handle. Almost ten years as a constable—in all that time, he'd had a gun turned on him three times but never a shot fired, and as far as assault... well, the criminals in Putnam tended to rather stand down when they saw Dallin coming at them. Either that or run.

Never shot, not even scarred, really, but for where he'd healed too fast after the stabbing in Chester, and the healing skin had more or less absorbed the black sutures. Now it was only a lumpy little line of vaguely pink-blue-black on his lower back.

Strange. All that time spent more or less wearing a target on his back, and the two times Dallin had actually been hurt—*really hurt*, in a life-threatening sort of way—Calder had been, if not precisely aiming at him, at least not in Chester, then at least present. Dallin thought about examining the oddity of it but dismissed it instead. Too many other directions in which to focus his attention, and suspecting the Old Ones, or someone who used to be one, had the power to hurt him didn't exactly surprise him. The other possibility—that his defenses, his instinct toward self-preservation, diminished when Wil needed his Guardian—was dismissed before Dallin had even allowed it to form fully in his mind.

He angled his arm out of his coat sleeve and tore the little hole in his shirt until he could see the wound. Still bleeding, but slow and thick now, beginning to congeal. Wash it out and bandage it for now, and worry about it later, if there was a later.

"Have you got anything for bandages?" he asked Corliss, poking at the jagged edges of the wound and wincing absently.

"Well, I do, but...." She let her gaze wander over to Wil, his head resting on her pack—where, presumably, the bandages were.

Dallin just had to laugh. Here Corliss was, watching one of her oldest friends oozing blood down his arm, and she didn't want to get a bandage out of her pack because it might disturb Wil.

Smirking, Dallin tore away the already bloodied sleeve of his shirt and held it out. "Tie that about it, can you?"

Corliss's eyebrow went up. "I thought you could—" She waved her hand. "You know."

"I... could. But it takes a bit of strength, and I think I'm going to need all of it soon." Dallin ignored the way Corliss's mouth tightened in worry. He nodded toward Wil. "He's got one in him too." Again, Dallin had to laugh when Corliss voiced a startled little noise of alarm. "I've taken care of it as much as necessary," he assured her. "Should probably tend to it more thoroughly before I get him up on a horse, but we'll get him fixed up when this business is through." He smirked at Corliss, deliberately cheerful. "Think you can be moved to dig up a bandage for *him*?"

Corliss scowled, snatched the sleeve out of Dallin's hand, and began tearing it in long strips, setting aside the bits that were soaked through and draping the cleaner ones over her bent knee. "You always were a smartarse."

"What do you mean to do?" Andette asked quietly.

Dallin had been wondering how he was going to address what happened with her, or if he even should, and he thought perhaps addressing it, making sure she was all right, was his responsibility somehow. Still, he was glad when he was saved from further conversation with her by a low whistle from the direction of the man watching the horses.

Miri was back.

Dallin got to his feet, made a vague apology to Andette, and took himself over in time to greet the mare and then grin at the young man who held her bridle when they heard another set of hoofbeats in the distance.

"Corliss! Un-squirrel those bandages, yeah? We're leaving in five minutes."

It took more like twenty. Wil's dead weight was floppier and harder to manage than Dallin had thought. It took concentration for Dallin to maneuver Wil semi-upright and hold him in place while Corliss focused on winding the bandage around Wil's shoulder and chest. The dressing was sloppy and temporary, but better than nothing. Dallin had managed to stop the bleeding altogether before, but he hadn't dared to begin the actual healing process until the bullet could be removed. Hopefully, between his and Corliss's efforts, the provisional fix would hold until....

Well. Until.

Dawn was trying to bully its way through the gathered cloud cover by the time they'd wrangled Wil back into his coat and up into the saddle with Dallin, but so far all it had managed to do was turn the black to a grudging gray. The thunder had subsided, but the rain seemed to be digging in to stay, and considering what Wil had said, Dallin wasn't much surprised. Depressingly fitting, in a way. It would make the last stretch of uphill travel more difficult, though. Dallin hadn't realized it while they'd been beneath the shelter of the trees, and what with the fires still sputtering and all, but once they got back out on the trail and in the relative open, the drizzle had already resolved into sharp little spicules of sleet. Not ideal for hoofs. Especially not hoofs belonging to a poxy gray stallion who thought walking was beneath him.

"You carry the Aisling," Dallin told it—stern, but under his breath, since he saw no reason to share his bit of vagary with the others. "Watch your step, or I'll have your hide for gloves."

He was suddenly sorry he hadn't asked the horse's master its name so he could address it more directly. It always seemed to work for Wil, after all.

The warning was unnecessary, as it turned out. Miri, trailing on her lead behind Woodrow, seemed determined to keep the gray in line with the occasional cross snort and nip to his neck. Dallin had no illusions that she was doing it as a personal favor to him, of course. In fact, it was more likely that she was merely pissed off and jealous that her own saddle was exhibiting a severe lack of Wil.

There were three more skirmishes, rather rote exchanges of gunfire in which no one was truly threatened, and the hollow sounds of misses and ricochets were more annoying than worrying.

Dallin felt them coming each time and drew the small party into a tighter knot around him and Wil just in case. But knowing what the Brethren thought they were doing made it so Dallin's heart didn't even bother skipping beats except in irritation. It was tempting to call out to the land, see if Dallin could try Wil's trick of making the ground move and swallow them up, but that would give away the game.

Dallin wouldn't exactly have the element of surprise on his side when they reached Fæðme, but it might be at least a small surprise to Wheeler that Dallin and his party were in truth aiming for it and knew what to do once they got there. Wheeler would've looked into Dallin's history back in Putnam—likely the reason Ramsford and Manning had been so extensively questioned; Dallin would have to ask Woodrow or Corliss if the same was true of the Tanners. It wouldn't have been difficult for a man of Wheeler's experience and motives to deduce that Dallin had spent more than twenty years ignorant of what he was, untrained and unpracticed. Now Wheeler was doing everything he could to keep it that way. He couldn't possibly know it wasn't entirely true anymore, and pretending their drive to Fæðme was flight instead of purposeful design was the best way to perpetuate the error.

So Dallin allowed the Brethren to keep pace, allowed them to "drive" the course. If what Wil said was correct—and Dallin had no doubt it was—Wheeler would have had to detour into the tunnels all the way back at Éaspring, and he'd have to be on foot. Even if the tunnels ran in straight lines and were clear of cave-ins or debris, it was at least twelve leagues from there to the Temple.

Dallin closed his eyes and skimmed a light reach outward. Wheeler and his men were only just now under the river, and the way ahead was all uphill and not exactly uncomplicated. Time was ticking steadily and relentlessly, but it hadn't run out yet.

It was getting easier to see, gray day finally winning over grayer dawn, by the time they broke through the heavier foliage and out onto a slim corridor of mud and wintergrass that formed the final leg of the trail to the Temple. Dallin could see the white curve of the dome and pediments nudging through the evergreens behind which it thrust its peak at the sky.

"Almost there," he whispered to Wil, who'd been slumped against Dallin's chest, unresponsive, since they'd left Calder's body behind.

White and gray striated marble, Dallin remembered now, with moss- and ivy-covered pillars presenting before somewhat redundant pilasters. Quarters for the Old Ones were niched into a long, narrow corridor that ran the length of the Temple's west-facing side behind the altar, which—as in all Temples—faced the east so as to stand witness when the Mother awoke each morning and brought the sun as She smiled a greeting to Her beloved.

And beneath the altar, where supplicants whispered their orisons and laid offerings, and initiates humbly and silently accepted them in the Mother's and Father's names, lay a single incongruous slab of granite, cut from the Stairs before time was time. It barred the entry to Fæðme—the Mother's Womb, from which all life sprang—to all but the Old Ones and those they deemed worthy. Dallin remembered the scrape and grate of the stone as a young boy, weeping and demanding the call of the horns, watching it levered aside, his anger and resentment temporarily forgotten beneath the new apprehension of being compelled down the dark earthen throat of Lind.

Now, all these years later, he wasn't at all surprised to see the twelve figures standing before the steps in the cold rain, watching the path and waiting for them as they negotiated through the last of the trees that looped the clearing in which the Temple stood.

Dallin halted, the rest of the party following his lead without comment as he nodded to Woodrow and Setenne to take Wil. He waited until they had Wil's limp form propped safely between them, Wil upright but not exactly standing, arms across their shoulders. When he was sure they held Wil securely, Dallin dismounted, taking the time to stretch his spine and readjust to having his feet on the ground.

He paused, looking from the Old Ones—pristine in their formal robes, standing tall and waiting patiently—and back again to his own party, disheveled and dirty and exhausted but gazes bright and alert, more sanguine than Dallin might have given them credit for a few days ago. Then, he might have been surprised that the expressions on Corliss and Woodrow matched those on the Linders; now, it seemed a logical consequence of the chain of events that had brought them all here.

He thought about taking Wil himself, carrying him up the Temple steps and formally presenting him to the Mother before they made the descent into Fæðme. In the end, Dallin decided it would seem too much like laying a prize from a hunt across the altar, a helpless offering, so he let Woodrow and Setenne keep Wil between them instead.

Sucking in a long breath, Dallin gave them all a nod and gestured for them to follow as he turned and started across the pale, sleet-coated grass toward the waiting picket of priests. He eyed every one of them as he approached, staring evenly into each set of eyes before moving on to the next, giving away nothing in his gaze or mien before fetching up before Thorne. Thorne merely looked back, wearing the same kind half smile he always wore, his iron-blond hair plastered to his skull and slicked with ice, robes heavy and frozen-wet. They must have been waiting here for hours, probably making their way up last night after they'd disappeared from camp.

"You remember now," Thorne said quietly.

Dallin lifted his chin. "She showed me."

"Ah," said Thorne, a small ripple of approval wrinkling through the line of old men from the center outward. Thorne's smile widened, genuinely pleased. "We knew your powers were vast, but we could not tell how deep. It has been so very long since any of us heard Their voices."

"So Calder told me."

Thorne merely sighed sadly. "An unfortunate loss. One cannot be healed unless he recognizes the necessity." He opened a hand. "We could not interfere. The Mother's will, you see—in all things. Even when we might prefer a different... course."

"But you didn't know Her will."

Thorne tilted his head in acknowledgment. "It has become difficult to interpret the signs, yes."

"And you second-guessed it."

"Did we?" Soft challenge.

Dallin had to concentrate fairly hard to keep his teeth from clenching. "You tried to take my calling from me. You might well have succeeded, had She not stepped in."

"Never 'take,'" Thorne said, sincere and grave. "We could not allow you to remember. Not out among outlanders, not without the Old Ones to guide you. The enemy could not know you'd lived, and we could not keep you here, not when we realized it would be...."—his mouth twisted, and he lowered his gaze—"unsafe." Quite an admission, coming from a Linder, and it hadn't come easily. Thorne sighed again. "We would have come for you, but your mother was killed before she could tell us—"

"Oh, I understand. It even makes sense." Dallin let his gaze drift up and down the line again, hard. "Except for the part where you—*all* of you—continued to try to keep it from me once I returned." He tilted his head. "You doubted the Aisling, you second-guessed the Guardian, and through me, you second-guessed the Mother. All of you did. How very... cheeky of you."

"Not second-guessed," Singréne put in, the first of them besides Thorne to speak, seeming a bit put out by the accusation. "Say rather, we waited for our Shaman to guide us." He smiled, sardonic, then waved a wide hand toward Wil. "He is as no other before him. And not all his gifts come from the Mother or the Father." He shrugged when Dallin narrowed his eyes. "Thorne tells us you guessed right from the very beginning. He also tells us the Aisling has never shied from what he knows to be his task. You, however...." He and opened a hand. "You place him above his task. Perhaps it is the Mother's will, perhaps it is not, but the risk is great and terrifying. You must forgive old men their fears."

"No," Dallin said stonily, "I mustn't."

"As you will." Singréne's half smile was remarkably like Thorne's. "But the Shaman has claimed the land now, and the land has claimed him back. Our calling has been fulfilled. We must now trust in the choices of the Mother and the Father and stand back while our fates are decided." He bowed his head, the others following suit. "Guardian. Your will."

Dallin raised his eyebrows, then turned to cut a look over his shoulder to Corliss, who was standing at a casual form of attention, face intent, gaze going from the Old Ones to Wil and then to Dallin. She met Dallin's eyes steadily, staring at him good and hard for a long moment before she tipped her head, a slight nod. Dallin had no idea what it was meant to convey, but somehow it laid any doubts he might have had to rest.

Not betrayal from these men—merely placing faith above any single life or soul, no matter the importance of that life or soul. None of it was personal, which wasn't necessarily all right with Dallin, but... more all right than the alternative.

He turned back to the Old Ones, addressing his next statement to Thorne. "We go to Fæðme now. Once the Aisling has laid himself before the Mother, we wait for the Cleric and what he brings." He shook his head at the way the plain, simple words joined to form a statement that sent a chill down his spine that had nothing to do with the sleet. He raised his voice and waved toward those before and behind him. "Any who would champion the Aisling, I would have at my back."

"Outlanders have never been permitted into Fæðme," Marden pointed out mildly.

"Do you defy me?"

Marden's mouth curled into something that looked annoyingly like a satisfied smirk. "Never defy. I merely remind."

Dallin grunted, then turned to the small party behind him.

"I don't ask any of you to come with us. I don't know exactly what's going to happen down there. It may all end very badly." He shifted his gaze to meet each set of eyes, somber and serious. "Then again, I can't imagine your faith could do anything but good." He pointed at Wil. "He goes to stand before the enemy, to face the beast, and to free the Father. I go to stand at his back and to guard him as I can—as he wills. If you would do less, you'd do best to stay here and wait until your fate is handed to you."

No one averted their eyes. A few blinked a bit against the sleet, a few lifted their chins and straightened their shoulders, but none of them looked away. Silence but for the steady wintry chime of sleet falling and bouncing off the thin layer of ice that coated the sward. Steadfast and stolid, all of them, and Dallin didn't know why he'd ever thought they might do differently, any of them.

Finally Woodrow shuffled. When all eyes turned his way, he adjusted his grip on Wil and cleared his throat.

"You'll forgive me, Bray—er, Guardian, but I'm thinking we're all agreed, and it was rather a daft question. P'raps we could get out of the rain now?"

Dallin remembered it. He remembered it all, and he looked at it now with that same strange double vision—the fear of the child he'd been calling to the fear of the man he'd become. He'd feared death then, and he'd feared for his people, feared the Old Ones and the relentless force of their combined power. There were so many other things to be afraid of now.

The way was dark and steep, narrow passageways and slick steps chiseled intermittently into the stone of particularly treacherous stretches. Cold at first, and growing steadily warmer as they descended. The ceaseless, faraway trickle of water eventually resolved itself into the song of the river as they neared the vert glimmer bleeding out into the tunnels from the mouth of Fæðme.

Thorne entered the chamber ahead of them. They waited as he lit the lamps, then called for them to enter. The sheer power of the place was only half-remembered and somewhat daunting, thrumming against Dallin's skin and into his head. No pushing it away this time, no locking himself down. He couldn't help wondering what might be happening inside Wil's head right this minute—was the place assaulting him as it had done before, and was he in pain?

Dallin allowed himself to think about it for exactly ten seconds before making himself stop. He'd find out very shortly, and then... well. He'd do what he could, whatever it took.

He was prepared for the murmurs of awe when they crossed the threshold into the vast cavern, but he still smiled and wished Wil was awake to see it. Things like this, things of beauty... these were the things that made Wil's eyes go soft and bright at the same time, made his face smooth out and his mouth curve up into a smile that was completely his.

"The mouth of the Flównysse." Dallin's voice resonated over walls of green striated in every shade of the color. "Mother's Blood. It flows down from the mountains from several different paths and collects here to form the river. The malachite in its bed has been polished smooth since time began."

All but the Old Ones stepped closer to the water to look down and then shake their heads at the beauty. The light of their torches and the lamps ringing the chamber caught all the different shades of green and sparked like sage fire against the stone beneath the water. Dallin took Wil from Woodrow and Setenne, and carefully laid him out beside the water's edge, running gentle fingers over the scrapes and gouges on Wil's temple and the browning streak of Dallin's own blood on Wil's cheekbone.

"It really is just like his eyes," he heard Corliss murmur.

"Yes," Dallin answered, though he didn't think she was addressing him directly. "First thing I noticed about him." He brushed wet black hair from Wil's pale brow. "I recognized it even then. I just didn't know it."

"Brayden," Corliss said gently, watching him. "Can't you—?"

"I don't know what to tell you to expect." Dallin kept looking down at Wil because it was safer. "I can only tell you to be ready." He sat on the stone by Wil's side, took up a cold hand in his, and closed his eyes.

"What are you going to do?"

Dallin sucked in a long breath and twined his fingers tight with Wil's limp ones. "I'm going to follow him." He set his jaw. "Wait here. I'll call you if I need you."

And then he reached for what power was his with one hand, reached for Wil with the other, and followed.

"You're here."

Dallin manages a smile. "I'm here."

He hasn't realized how worried he's been that Wil wouldn't want him to follow, would resent him for it, until Dallin finds himself standing here in front of Wil.

Not the river, the spot that has come to mean so many things, has become almost expected, has become theirs. The same star-clotted nothing where Dallin first saw Wil tending his threads, working his fingers raw. Only Wil isn't weaving now, isn't doing anything except standing there and looking at Dallin. Waiting.

It's strange, because Dallin is still dressed in muddy trousers and blood-caked coat, still wet, still has his weapons strapped in place. His hair is still dripping from melting ice, a nagging itch as the miniscule trickles wander down his scalp.

Wil is clad in the clothes he was wearing the first time Dallin saw him, fresh and dry, his hair neat and clean, shining blue-black in the light that isn't really light. There are no bruises on his face, no scrapes, no bloodstain flowering over his clean white shirt, though the streak of Dallin's blood still sweeps over his cheekbone—his own Mark. He wears the boots he fought for back in Dudley—his own, he said. And maybe that's why he's dressed as he is: none of it given to him, none of it borrowed from another, all of it his in whatever way he'd managed to procure it. Dallin wonders if Wil even notices what he's wearing, and if he knows why. Wonders if Wil did it deliberately, if he decided he wanted to die on his own terms and wearing his own boots.

Dallin pushes that away, because yes, of course that's it.

No leaf-smiles here, no vacant gazes.

Wil looks so calm, so strong as he stands tall in his own element, chin up and back straight, stretched to the full height he usually tries to hide, usually afraid of notice. He doesn't look like he's afraid of anything right now. He looks like he's daring the world.

Until he meets Dallin's eyes, tries to smile, and can't. He shakes his head slowly, says, "Not lost," and it isn't spoken like a question, but it has the feel of one anyway.

"No," Dallin tells him softly, "not this time."

Wil nods. "I trust you," he whispers, says it again, louder, "I trust you," like he's trying to convince himself. And in this one thing, perhaps he is.

"I'm right here," Dallin says. "I'm not going anywhere." He pauses, says the only thing that truly matters now: "She loves you."

Wil looks down at his boots for a few long—too long—moments before he straightens. Bracing.

"All right."

Wil holds out his hand, wraps his fingers hard around Dallin's when he takes it. Dallin can feel the tremors running though Wil but only squeezes Wil's hand tighter in answer.

"All right," Wil repeats. "I'm ready."

Dallin smiles, as encouraging as he can be, takes a long breath, and sends out his call.

CHAPTER 5

A place of his own choosing, because it's as close to safety as Wil has ever known. Before he even was Wil, Father would come to him in this place, speak to him like he was real and worth something more than what he could do, what was in him. He couldn't always understand the things Father said to him, but he's known since he could know anything that the warmth he felt inside the words was love. The eventual comparison was what made him understand that what came from Síofra—captor, gaoler, tormenter—was nothing more than a cheap, transparent mockery. A perversion. Father taught Wil how to love, even though Wil hadn't recognized it for that for far too long, and that helped him to see it in his Guardian's eyes, recognize it, and for that... for that, even if there were nothing else, Wil would still love Father.

So many more reasons, though, and he wishes he hadn't so stubbornly failed to see them. He's wasted so much time on anger.

But this place, Father had given to him—a place to be still, a place to be quiet, a place to dream dreams that were his own and no one else's, where he could pick apart the insanity and fit it into shapes that turned it sane. Smiles he'd always thought sleepy and *dreamy but that he now knows to have been weary and drained. Handing him the language of the stars and letting him listen, letting him join his small voice to their songs, letting him wrap himself inside it all until the next time he was wrenched from dream and into nightmare.*

No idiotic smiles here, no leaf seeps through the cracks of his mind. He is something other than what is confined to his body on the other side. There he is vulnerable, small, weak. People can trick him and have done, can overpower him and have done, can bind him to their own courses, and he can struggle and kick and bite, but he doesn't always win. Not here. A place of safety inside his own mind, and it's more Father's than his, but that's never really mattered. Here he is strong. Here he is sane. Here he is himself, or as close to it as he ever can be.

Here he can meet Her on his own terms.

She loves Father. Wil's not sure he ever believed that before, but he does now, just as much as he believes his Guardian's stalwart assertions that She hadn't forgotten Wil, hadn't left him alone and in pain because She'd chosen it. She loves Him just as Wil does, She wants to help Him, and if nothing else, it gives Wil a common ground on which to rest hope.

He's calmer than he thought he'd be. Ready as he never would have believed, but he's got his Guardian—more, he's got Dallin— and Dallin won't let this go wrong.

Strangely, Wil's more anxious about this than he is about what must come after.

His Guardian will be the end of him, he's known it for always, and it used to fill him with fear and loathing and dread. Now it's a comfort, though he's sorry to put the burden on Dallin. Still, knowing it was coming has more or less prepared Wil for it, and he mourns uselessly, because he does love life, what he's come to know as life, but Dallin will make the end as painless as he can, because *he loves Wil. That used to be quite terrifying, but now... now it gives Wil an odd sort of fatalistic hope.*

He's hated Her forever. With every breath, every beat of his heart, he's hated Her, resented Her, feared Her, and hated himself because he still loved Her. Abandoned, used, tormented, and broken, time and again, and yet he's never been able to make himself scream for Her, never let himself reach out. The fear of real, tangible rejection has always loomed larger than the pain of knowing himself to be the nameless hostage of a man he once loved with a little boy's naïve, trusting heart. The fear of crying out, asking, and hearing only "No" in return, or worse, silence.

He understands Calder's pain; he always has done, because it's been his own fear for time without end—reaching out, searching, grasping, and your hand comes back with the knuckles bloodied. Or empty. It horrifies him, and still it's a risk. His Guardian insists it won't happen, can't happen, but Wil knows the heart of the Divine can be fickle and hard, and he knows gods are not infallible.

Still, he has to know. Finally. And even if She refuses him....

No, he won't fool himself—it will crush him. But it won't defeat him. Perhaps that's why he can do this now. Dallin has taught him it's all right to reach out; you won't always draw back a stump, and if you do, well... there's always the other hand.

"All right?" Dallin is staring at him, anxiety and concern in those dark eyes, and he gives Wil's hand a squeeze.

Wil swallows and drops a slow nod, though part of him still wants to back away, tell Dallin this is a mistake, he's not ready. But that hard bit of steel in Wil's backbone won't let him.

"All right." Wil says it too softly, but he lifts his chin.

Dallin smiles, gives Wil's hand another squeeze, then leans in and kisses him, soft and warm. He takes Wil's hand, slips his fingers over the crystal on its silver chain that wasn't hanging around Wil's neck only a second ago.

"I'm right here," he whispers, draws back, and shuts his eyes.

Wil can hear the call—not with his ears but with something inside him, a low vibration that winds up through his hand linked with Dallin's and into Wil's chest, stuttering through the crystal in his palm. Like the healing, but only peripherally. This isn't for Wil, doesn't move through him, doesn't seek his core and touch it. This is for Her, and Wil merely stands inside the echo of it. Waiting.

The response is immediate and nearly overwhelming. A strange euphoria moves through Wil, but it isn't nonsensical and frightening like the leaf. It's heat like a thousand suns, but it doesn't burn; it's strength ensconcing him in a relentless embrace, but it doesn't hurt; it's a devastating presence inside his mind, his heart, his soul, but it doesn't invade, merely asks.

Dallin has gone still, head bowed, eyes closed, and his grip on Wil's hand is loose but there. This is yours, Dallin tells Wil, except his mouth doesn't move and he doesn't stir. I'm here, I won't leave you alone, but this is yours.

Wil takes a long breath, closes his eyes, and withdraws his hand. Dallin steps back, retreating but not, here if Wil wants him, and oh, Wil loves him for it. Wil straightens his spine, squares his shoulders, and lifts his chin. He grips the crystal tighter.

"Mother" is all he says.

And She's there. Blue eyes kind and calm but filled with tears, and it's strange because it never occurred to Wil that a goddess might weep, which is stupid because he's seen the tears on Father's cheeks more than once.

She's beautiful—strangely plain, almost ordinary, but every ordinary feature combines with every other and comes together into something extraordinary and beyond any beauty he's ever seen but encompassing it all too. He sees echoes of Miri, of Mistress Sunny, of Thistle and Andette, and though none of them look like Her, they all have Her within. He sees Dallin and Ramsford, and even

Wisena, the Old Ones, and if Wil looks hard enough, he might even see Siofra, so he doesn't.

She only looks at him, steady and expectant. Wil can't help feeling measured, and he wants to look back, keep his head up, meet the blue gaze with confidence and perhaps even defiance, accusation. He dips his head instead and looks down, unable to do anything but stare at the toes of his battered boots.

Overfaced and overmatched.

What had he been thinking? How could he have ever thought this was anything but a new opportunity for disappointment and humiliation, pain and disillusionment? How could he have ever believed he might, just might, be good enough?

"It is not in my eyes you must seek your measure," She says softly, Her voice kinder and more musical than Wil had imagined, "nor in your Guardian's." He knows it's the First Tongue, Her own language, but in dreams he can always understand.

Wil shakes his head, says, "No," and his voice cracks, so he clears his throat. "Not in my Guardian's," he agrees, because his Guardian has never judged him, sees only the good in him, though Wil can't make himself believe the same could be true of Her. Isn't it Her place, after all?

A small metallic chink catches his ear, and he shunts his glance toward it, watching as a link is added to the chain dangling from the shackle around Her wrist that he knows wasn't there a moment ago. The sight startles him, sliding a sick lump into his chest, nauseating, and he can't help how his gaze skims to the scar on his own wrist, hangs there.

"Servant to faith," She tells him, "hostage to belief. Bound by the certainties of others." She holds Her hand out, palm up. "Would you strengthen my bonds?"

Wil shakes his head and takes a step back, horrified. "No, I—" He looks to Dallin for help, but Dallin is the Watcher now, head bowed, eyes shut, waiting and Watching. Leaving this to Wil, because this is his.

Wil shudders and turns back to the Mother. It's absurd, he doesn't even really know what he did, but he wants to throw himself down and beg forgiveness for it.

"I would never" is all he can manage to whisper.

"No?"

She smiles, gently takes up his hand, and strokes the lumpy scar on his wrist. Wil allows it, trying not to let his knees loosen at the soft sensations winding through him with Her touch. She guides his fingers over the chain one link at a time.

"These are those times when your keepers told you you'd been forsaken and you believed them." The links slide over Wil's palm, too many to count, and so heavy. "These are those times when you were in pain and called out your curses." More links, more weight, and Wil can't hold it up.

"No." He tries to pull his hand from Hers, tries to back away, but She won't let him go.

"I have no mother, and yours is dead!" His own voice, but it comes out of Her mouth, and more links pile into Wil's hand.

"Dallin." Wil sends a desperate glance over his shoulder, and Dallin is there, still Watching, waiting, but he doesn't react to Wil's plea.

"Why can't he hear me?" Wil can't help how his tone bends accusing.

"He can always hear you" is the soft reply. "When you want him to." She tilts Her head, blue eyes narrowing slightly. "Do you want him to?"

"I don't...." He can't finish. Because he really doesn't know.

She nods as though She'd expected it. "He is more than Watcher, indeed more than Guardian. He is Witness, he is Historian. He will sing the Aisling's dirge, add it to the songs of his coun-

try, wound through with his tears and cries of loss. He will carry on and teach because you have asked it of him. He will wait, alone, for the call of the next, and when he has fulfilled the duties of the Guardian, he will die, still alone, still reaching for you in dreams he won't allow himself to know he dreams, still feeling his finger on the trigger and trying to call back the bullet with his last breath."

Wil flinches, shakes his head, but She doesn't give him time to respond, even if he could.

"Is that not what you wanted?" She asks him softly. "Is that not what you have demanded of him?"

It's soft but razor-edged, dangerous, and Wil is once again reminded of Calder, of the Old Ones—real caring, real concern and compassion, but placing purpose above all else. She loves him—all right, he can believe that—but She'll sacrifice him if She has to, She'll sacrifice Dallin, She'll hurt to help, and strangely, Wil can't find it in him to blame Her.

"I want to live," he argues without even thinking about it, without even knowing it was coming. "I never... I don't want to die. I don't want to cause him pain, but I want—"

"But you want him to live more, and that is well. It is, after all, what he wants for you." She steps in close, pulling Wil's hand in, the chains weighing it down clinking gently. "Tell me, Aisling— Wil That Was and Redeemed That Would Be—when will your pain be enough? What will be enough to purge your imagined sins?" She dips down, whispers, "You or him. Have you already made your choice?"

It's unfair and terribly cruel.

"Is there one?" he rasps back, the question choking him, aching in his throat.

"You have all the pieces of your puzzle," She tells him, Her voice harder now, commanding. "You possess all your keys. Accept your gifts. Wield them. All of them." Her eyes flick over to Dallin, still waiting in the dark, removed and excluded. "Hand him your keys, if you dare, for he knows the locks all too well. There are more choices than either of you can know."

Riddles, more riddles, and She doesn't even have the excuse of malady and weakness as the Father does. Puzzle pieces and questions to answer questions, and only more questions to follow, and Wil is bloody weary of it all.

"What does that mean?" he barks. "Why can't you just say it?" He's unheeding of his blaspheming tone, the bit of a glare he can't help.

"Ah." A satisfied smile curls maddeningly at Her mouth. "You ask me to take away your choices, then?"

He can't answer. Because he thinks maybe the answer would be "yes," and he couldn't stand the shame if it tripped off his tongue.

Playing with him, testing him, and he's failing and doesn't even know how, couldn't help it if he did. Perhaps, if he'd not allowed himself to be so tricked, She wouldn't mock him so. Perhaps, if he'd been stronger, let down his walls and allowed that other Watcher in, he wouldn't need redemption, wouldn't be begging for it now from one who has every reason to withhold it. Perhaps, if he'd never refused Her....

He was right to fear Her, right to be afraid of reaching out, right to fear that he'd angered Her, and right to bow his head in shame for what he's done. She's kind, surely, but wise and too knowing. She can be ruthless and relentless to a supplicant who has been fool enough to want so badly. Warrior-goddess with a great, tender heart armored in adamant, and it's his own fault for allowing hope when he knew better.

"This is right now," She tells him gently, holding up a single oval link between Her fingers. It catches the not-light and glints sharp into his eyes. "This is shame and doubt and fear of one who loves you above all others." For a moment Wil starts to protest, *thinks She means Dallin, and he doesn't fear Dallin, not anymore, the accusation is unfair.... But then She places the link in his palm, closes his fingers over it. "You fight shackles like a wild animal," Dallin's words but Her voice, "but you accept a cage like you belong in one." She squeezes his fingers around the link. "Would you expect less from me?"*

"Cage," he whispers and shakes his head, because he should understand, but he doesn't.

"We build our own cages. And we make our own keys. Sometimes, if we're very lucky, there is another who will hold that key for us until we're ready to unlock the door and step out into the light. And sometimes that other will, unknowingly and with all love and good intent—or even with hatred at perceived betrayal—add links to the chains that bind us."

She's talking about Wil, though it makes no sense, no sense at all.

Wil tries to speak several times before he finally manages. "I've made you—"

"Weak" is the word that hovers on his tongue, but he can't bring himself to speak it. Surely someone as small as he could not have the implied effect on one like Her?

"So much stronger than you think you are." She kisses his brow, a soft, warm tingle striating out from the touch and into his chest. "So willing to lock yourself inside your cage of self-doubt, self-rebuke, when there is another that would free and not confine." She draws back and places Her hands to his cheeks, holding his gaze to Hers. "I am what I am, you cannot unmake that. I am bound only by what you believe of me, the links you add to the chains, and that, even I cannot unmake." She peers at him closely, a soft smile curling at Her mouth. "What do you believe, beautiful Gift?"

He shakes his head against Her palms, shuts his eyes, and bows his head, tears burning behind his brow, searing at the backs of his eyes. "I'm so sorry," he whispers, dismayed and revolted when he hears the unmistakable sound of another link being added to the chain at Her wrist. He snaps his head up and stares into Her eyes.

"No. I didn't mean it. I mean, I did, but—" He swallows, clenches his teeth, and tries to collect himself, calm himself. "Please. I don't know what to... how I should...." Damn it, why can't he twist the confusion ramming around his head into something that at least sounds like sense? And why can't She just look inside and see it so he doesn't have to? "I would never bind another," he tells Her, earnest and open. "I would never bind You. I don't know what to believe. I've been lied to for so long, I can't... please, can't You see, can't You—?"

He stops there because he has no idea what to ask for, or if he even should ask. She's still looking at him with that soft smile, Her hands still warm against his cheeks, wet with the tears he hadn't realized were falling, but he can't bring himself to be ashamed of them. Invitation, he's just handed it to Her, and he's not sorry for it, he meant it, and he knows if he lets Her, She'll take it.

You must empty yourself to the Mother and accept what She gives back to you.

Empty himself. Bare himself. Let go of who he is and let Her see it, let Her measure and judge it, and bend his neck while She does it.

He's wondered before if it would be liberating to confess his secrets to all those in Lind, pour out what he is and accept their respect or rebuke with no regrets. What would it be to do the same with Her? Would She cleanse his soul, or would She flay it?

He's amazed that he wants it, amazed that She'd care to see, so he does it—opens himself wide and lets Her in.

She looks, and he lets Her. Gives her everything, all the power he's been holding inside him since before he even knew there was anything there, every bit of Self he kept from the pretender who would call himself "Father" and all those whose hunger and greed made them monsters even against their own wills. He gives it all to Her, and She takes it in, binds it to Her own Self, empties him, and he doesn't even worry if She'll fill him back up again.

Gentle and timeless, forever, and he shows Her all the things he showed Síofra, shows Her yet more. All his secrets, such as they are, all the things he wants and dares to want. He shows Her everything, and if She wants to censure him for it, strip him of this last irrational hope... it still won't take away what he is, who *he is, and that makes it all right. She sees it all, and like the Guardian of Her making, She doesn't look away.*

"Yes," She tells him, just that one word, but it's so full of everything that there's no need for more, and it fills him with such stunning possibility he almost can't breathe.

Yes to every question he's ever asked.

Yes to every plea he's ever made.

Yes to all things, and all things are possible.

Yes, he was tricked and used and lied to, and Yes, *he can be a person despite it.*

Yes, he can love and be loved, and Yes, *he is worthy.*

Yes, She loves him, and Yes, *he wants it, and* Yes, *he loves Her back and is not ashamed.*

"There, now." She kisses him again, this time over the streak of Dallin's blood on his cheekbone. "Now you see."

He does. She hasn't left him empty. He poured himself out, offered Her everything, and instead of hating him for it, She has shown him his cage, shown him he owns the keys, and that accepting this one perhaps isn't something for which he should feel shame.

Caught and caged.

No more hostage to it than Dallin is to his. Their cages might ruin or save them, but neither has been truly imprisoned by the other. Not meant, Calder had told him, and perhaps that's true, but She seems to approve nonetheless. Not all cages are prisons, after all.

A link breaks in the endless chain that binds Her, and Wil smiles because he understands. One lie put to rest, another's truth he can disbelieve, and he would no more bind Her than he would allow another to place shackles around his own wrists. Never again.

Her smile widens, and She takes Her hands from his face, prying open his fingers to reveal a tiny key shining silver in his palm where the link used to be. Without a word, She lifts up Her wrist and holds it out to him.

The key slides easily into the lock, turns without even slight resistance. A soft click and the iron band is gone, the chains are gone, and with them, tremendous weight lifts from Wil's chest as though he's been buried beneath a mountain for so long he's grown used to it, and someone has come along and moved it for him. He can breathe. He can probably fly. He doesn't know what to do with himself. He's weightless and free, filled with grace, and it's nothing at all like the euphoria of the leaf, nothing at all like even Dallin's touch of healing. It's softer but stronger, real and corporeal but ephemeral and fey.

"Mother" slides from his tongue, soft and asking, and She smiles. She closes Her eyes, tears sliding out from the corners as She reaches out, pulls him against Her, guides his head to Her breast, and strokes his hair. Wil shuts his eyes, clenches his teeth against the tears for as long as he can, then gives in, lets them come, long and harsh and cleansing. Says it again, "Mother," and folds into the embrace—reaches back.

He could stay here for always, and he thinks maybe She'd let him.

Time doesn't seem to have anything to do with reality at the moment—reality doesn't seem to have anything to do with reality— but this is real, it's really happening. A lifetime of pretending not to wish for it, pretending he didn't want it, was revolted by the very idea of it, and here he is, living it, and he doesn't ever want to stop. It's almost more than his mind can take.

It's strange, because he'd never thought of Her as so corporeal, but Her heart beats steadily, Her embrace is warm, Her tears damp in his hair, and She's real.

He's exhausted, spent. He could close his eyes and sleep forever, his cheek pressed against Her breast.

He used to see children just so, in their mothers' embraces, and it used to confuse him, make him vaguely uncomfortable and oddly irritated. He thinks now perhaps it had been jealousy, thinks perhaps he'd been wishing for it and didn't know it. Or knew it and wouldn't admit it, which is all the same in the end.

His eyes feel swollen, the lids heavy and gritty, and his nose is so clogged he can't breathe. He's reduced to mortifying snuffles. Her robes are just as real as She is, and Wil doesn't fancy embarrassing himself by leaking all over Her. Where the hell is Dallin with his bloody handkerchiefs now?

As if he'd spoken aloud, She pushes him back gently and slips Her fingers beneath his chin so he has no choice but to look up into Her soft gaze. She sighs, smiles, and lays another kiss to his brow.

"There is much still ahead of you. It is time to call for your Guardian now."

Wil swallows. He's afraid, but it doesn't paralyze him, though he thinks if he weren't here with Her, it just might.

"He's a good man," he tells Her. Flushes, because of course She'd know that—She'd chosen him, after all. "I should—You—" The warmth at his cheeks burns hotter, and he wants to dip his

head, but he can't, not on this. "Thank you," he whispers. "I don't think any other would've done, and I... I wish...."

She brushes his hair from his eyes, tender and dear. "You do not yet know of what you are capable. You do not yet know all of your gifts." She nods toward Dallin, then peers at Wil closely. "It is his task to guide you, but it is yours to choose."

"It isn't much of a choice," Wil mutters. Now he does dip his head, because the tears are threatening again, and he's already shown himself weak before Her.

"There is a very fine line," She tells him, tone clear and some-what amused, "between doing something for another and doing something to another."

His head snaps up. A scowl sets his jaw tight. She's using his own words against him, and this is different. It isn't fair—one of them has to meet his end, and he knows who it has to be, he's seen it—

"Have you, then?" She asks, eyebrow arched. She gives his hair a light tug. "Such a stubborn boy," She says fondly and pats his cheek. "Tell me, then—what exactly did you see?"

He frowns, opens his mouth... hesitates. No one's ever asked him that before, not even Dallin.

Dark eyes, boring into his, the Mark almost blazing, hurting his eyes. He closes them against it, then... nothing. Nothing and more nothing, the end of everything—just gone, all of him, and... and Síofra told him....

She's nodding now, Her mouth curled into a smile that's too knowing and perhaps even a touch patronizing. "Shall I show you the links to your own chains?" She asks him gently. "The bonds your not-father forged himself?"

"No." He shakes his head, almost slips his hands behind his back, but he makes himself stand still. He doesn't want to see, doesn't think he could bear to look.

"You know them for travesties, and yet they nevertheless weigh you down." Her voice hardens, that touch of command Wil had heard in it before. *"I cannot break them for you, for they are not of my making."* Her eyes flick over to Dallin, and Her eyebrow rises again as She turns Her gaze back to Wil. *"Your Guardian cannot touch them, for you choose not to show them to him and thus limit the choices for him, as well."*

Wil clenches his teeth, angering slowly but steadily. *"That isn't fair,"* he tells Her boldly. *"There are two choices, both of them terrible, and not—"*

"Are there?" She shrugs and nods once again at Dallin. *"It is time to call for your Guardian."*

Wil's anger rises. *"If there are more, why won't you just tell me?"*

"Perhaps because you believe so very stubbornly that there are only two." She lifts Her hand, the shackle back again, but with only one link dangling from it this time.

Fury rises at the sight, bald and choking. *"You're not being fair,"* Wil grates, not caring anymore that he is addressing a being who could squash him beneath Her foot like an annoying insect.

Maddeningly, She smiles. *"And is fairness a link with which you have ever burdened me?"*

She lifts Her hand and flicks at the lone link; it tinkles musically as it swings. Her smile disappears, Her face going hard, that of the warrior-goddess, and he is reminded that She may love him, but She will also use him, hurt him if She has to, like any other mother who would punish a child *"for his own good."*

"What is your name, Aisling?" She demands.

For the first time, real fear spikes into Wil's chest. He takes a small, involuntary step back. *"I don't—"*

"But you do." A flash of light at Her fingertips, and before Wil can even register what it is, what's happening, it's sailing toward

him. *He doesn't even have the wit to flinch before Dallin's knife is thudding into nothing at Wil's feet, its hilt vibrating with the force of the impact.* "Your true design remains hidden until you are ready to see it, and yet you persist in blindness."

He's heard that before, but he can't remember where or when or from whom. He takes another step back, trying to swallow down the fear and the anger, but he keeps choking on them, and it just pisses him off more.

"You tore a man from his own mind to have it," *She goes on, ruthless,* "and yet when your Guardian tried to hand it to you—"

"You think I don't want it!" *Wil realizes too late that he's just interrupted a goddess, but he couldn't stop himself—it felt too much like accusation, and surely She can't mean what he did wasn't justified?* "It's all I've ever *wanted*, but—" *His teeth clench, and so do his fists.* "If he gets it, if I give it to him—" *He can't finish, and damn it, why should he have to?—She knows.*

"Then perhaps it is best in the hands of one who does not fear it," *She tells him coldly. She seems to grow in front of him, almost threatening, and all kindness has been wiped from Her expression as She merely lifts Her hand and points to Dallin, a wordless directive.*

Ashamed as he hadn't been before, Wil swallows his fury and his fear, swallows his questions and accusations, and does as She has commanded. He is no equal, he'd almost forgotten that for a moment in his anger, but he's reminded of it now, and he bends his neck beneath the clear rebuke.

He steps over to Dallin, takes up his hand, and calls his name. Dallin peers at him closely, all cagey concern.

"All right?"

Wil almost laughs, but... it isn't really funny. He shakes his head instead. "Not really," *he answers honestly.* "But better than I'd thought." *He tugs at Dallin's hand.* "C'mon, She wants you."

Dallin follows, eyes gone a bit hard, and Wil can't help but take an odd sort of warmth from it. His Guardian would protect him even from a goddess, and it still boggles Wil that it's all real.

They stand before Her together, hands linked. Dallin's shoulders and back are ramrod straight, like he's standing at attention, and his eyes meet Hers boldly.

"Guardian," She says, Her voice more stern than it had been, Her mien grim and unyielding.

She waves a hand, and Dallin lets go of Wil's, steps forward, places his hands at the small of his back, plants his feet apart, and lifts his chin.

"You have accepted your calling," She says, blue gaze leveled at Dallin. "The Aisling has acknowledged you as his champion. The land has called to you and heard your answer. You have waded through much adversity to stand here before me, and yet you are not yet through." She tilts Her head, appraising. "What would you ask of me?"

Dallin's shoulders twitch and his head jerks back, the surprise obvious. He frowns, hesitant, then cuts a quick look at Wil, a light flush blooming on his cheeks.

"I would ask only for the strength to serve the Aisling as he wills it."

She shakes Her head, the disappointment obvious. "You forget— your heart is plain in your eyes."

Dallin bows his head. "I would ask too many things to count, Mother," he says more quietly. "More than I've a right to ask." He sucks in a long breath, squares his jaw, and won't look at Wil. "I would ask that You take this from him. I would ask that You give me the power to bear the burden alone. I would ask that You see to it that he survives."

She turns a small, sad smile on Wil. "You would take away his choices?"

"*If I thought it would....*" Dallin looks down and shakes his head. "*I don't know.*" His voice is too soft, cheeks hinting at shame, and he closes his eyes. "*I expect that's why he's been given the choice and not I.*"

Wil should be angry at the revelation, but it won't come. Dallin has been handing Wil choices since the very beginning, and Wil's given Dallin none. How could Wil possibly find anger for the want of a wish?

This time She nods, satisfied. She slips her fingers beneath Dallin's chin and lifts his gaze to Hers as She did to Wil forever ago.

"*You have more than one calling, Guardian.*" Her voice is soft this time, compassion that nearly makes Wil's throat clog.

"*So I've been told,*" Dallin answers, voice hushed, a quiet defeat inside the tone that Wil has never heard before. "*I will do my duty to You and Lind, the Father and the Aisling, as You so will.*"

"*So many fates to carry upon your shoulders.*" She tsks. "*Have you no duty to yourself?*"

Wil can see Dallin's teeth clench, can see his eyes harden, resentful.

"*Does it matter?*"

She takes Her hand away. "*All things matter, in their ways. A single flap of a butterfly's wing can reshape the world.*"

Wil frowns, and by the way Dallin too obviously holds back a growl, it's clear he doesn't understand it any more than Wil does. More bloody riddles. Wil's had more than he can stand, and he knows Dallin has too.

"*I have more than one calling, and one contradicts the other.*" Dallin's expression is stony, and he meets Her gaze with unveiled anger. "*Either way, I will fail You and the Father. Perhaps You'd like to tell me which failure would displease You less.*"

"*I will suffer no failure,*" She returns, hard and cold. "*If your choices are cruel and few, it is your task to find another. You were* not made for this, Guardian, but chosen. The fates of those I love above all rest in your hands, and you will not fail me."

Wil stares, almost can't believe this is the same being who held him and rocked him against Her breast only a short while ago, comforted him and made him believe he wasn't broken. Now She is harsh, pitiless, cruel, and commanding, demanding a hopeless solution to a nonexistent choice, Dallin's broad shoulders bending beneath the weight of impossibility. Wil has often wondered how the goddess of healing, childbirth, and comfort could also be the goddess of war. Now he knows.

"We take what the Mother gives us and do our best with it," Wil answers, though he thinks he really shouldn't—this is Dallin's, not his—but he can't help himself. It's unfair, all of it, and She doesn't even seem to care. So many times Dallin has come to Wil's defense, and Wil owes him at least this. "My Guardian could do no less—it isn't in him. You can't ask more."

"No?" She doesn't look at Wil, her hard blue gaze locked on to Dallin. She lifts Her hand, shows him the shackle again with its one lone link, then lifts the other, bare and devoid of any kind of bond. "I am bound by no beliefs, Guardian, for you have none. A man of vast and great magic, yet so little faith. You believe in the power of the land because you have touched it, but it will not be enough to save all you wish to save. You believe in your gods because you have seen them, but we cannot go where you must lead, for we are bound in other ways that are not yours to unfetter." She steps in close, looms over Dallin, but Dallin keeps his gaze steady and doesn't flinch. "What else do you believe, Guardian?"

An echo of the same question put to Wil before, but Dallin doesn't bow his head as Wil did, doesn't look away, his gaze steady and devoid of the pleading Wil suspects had reflected in his own.

"You ask for blind faith," Dallin says steadily.

Wil's heart sinks, and he has no idea why—whether because

he's sure Dallin won't give it, or because he's equally sure She will take his Guardian away from him if Dallin doesn't. And yet Wil wouldn't ask Dallin to give something it's so against his nature to give, even at the risk of losing Dallin's presence when Wil goes to face the monster.

"No?" She asks. Wil is surprised and all at once painfully uneasy when he sees that Her gaze has shifted to him. "And yet you have."

Answering the question Wil didn't ask, instead of the one Dallin did.

Wil flinches, but Dallin frowns, bewildered, and turns a quick asking glance on him. Wil can't do a single thing but shake his head and take a small step back.

Her gaze slides once again to Dallin. "I ask for the trust you demand of others. Can you give it?"

Dallin stares for a long time, hands fisting behind his back, jaw twitching. And then he blinks, his eyes filling just the smallest bit, and he bends his neck.

"I don't know, Mother. I love him, and gods must—" He swallows and shuts his eyes tight. "—gods must sometimes be dispassionate, for They see more than we mortals. We are sometimes crushed beneath Your greater purpose, and I would not see him crushed." He shrugs helplessly, then looks up. "I'm sorry. I love him."

Wil's eyes burn again, and his chest goes tight. A test, and this the cruelest. It nearly breaks his heart to watch Dallin try to be what She demands of him and still be what he is—choosing between the Guardian and Dallin, the man who loves Wil and the Shaman who must ensure the Aisling does not become the next meal for the soul-eater. Dallin shakes beneath it, splitting right down the middle.

"As do I," She replies, voice softening. "Love can often hand us the magic of faith, if only we reach for it. I ask for no more than that." She waves a hand. "What do you see?"

Dallin frowns, peering about before shifting his gaze back to the Mother. "I see stars. Stars inside clouds."

Wil frowns too. He sees the threads as he's always done— threads and patterns, all winding into their places in the weave, color upon color and strand upon strand.

But She's smiling as if She's expected it. She turns to Wil. "What does the Father's song tell you of stars?"

"...Fate." Wil slides a quick glance at Dallin, but Dallin isn't looking at him. "Handing... giving yourself to fate."

His voice is quieter at the end than it was at the beginning. Anger crawls through Wil's chest, resentment that She's trying to make Her point through him when She could just as easily have told Dallin Herself.

Her eyebrow arches as if She knows what Wil's thinking, because of course She does. She's proven that more than once, hasn't She? She seems amused more than anything else, and that annoys Wil too, but She only turns Her gaze back at Dallin, hardens it once again.

"Can you give it?"

Relentless. Implacable.

Dallin won't look at Wil, his head still down, his eyes shut again. His hands clench and unclench rhythmically behind his back as he nods slowly.

"Yes, I can give You that, if it's what You demand of me." He says it in a voice that's hollow, that same note of defeat ringing at its edges. "Though I will not thank You for it."

"And can you give it to the Aisling? For it is he who will need your light in the darkness."

Dallin's hands and jaw both tighten. "Then this is a test wasted. Wil already has it—he never had to ask."

Despite Dallin's obvious anger, She smiles. "Ah, but does the Aisling?"

Dallin frowns, blinks, then looks at Wil as though Wil's got some kind of answer for him, and... maybe he does. Dallin is splitting himself in two, his love of Wil in conflict with his duty to the Aisling.

"Wil is only a name I borrowed," he tells Dallin softly. "Aisling is what I've always been. If you would choose one of the two...." He shrugs helplessly. "I'm afraid only one is real."

Dallin stares at him for quite a while, bemused. "I choose you," he finally says. "I always have done."

Wil hasn't realized how tense he's gone, waiting for that answer, or that his breath has been clogged tight in his chest until it whooshes out of him in a long, audible sigh.

Dallin gives Wil a look that's impossible to interpret. "How could you have thought else?" He doesn't wait for Wil to answer, and good job he doesn't, because Wil doesn't think he can. Dallin turns his gaze back to the Mother. "I have sworn service to the Aisling, and I meant it. He holds my faith and my fate, and I hold all of what he chooses to give me."

She shrugs, her smile bordering on smug. "Then all is well, is it not?" Dallin's fists clench tighter, but Her expression turns soft and as loving as it was when She held Wil inside her forever-embrace. "What is your name?"

Dallin sighs, lifts his chin, and looks at Her straight. "I am Dallin Brayden, son of Ailen and Aldercy, Guardian to the Aisling."

"And where is home?"

Wil is expecting to hear "Lind," but Dallin steps closer and takes Wil's hand. "Home is where the Aisling leads. I follow by his will."

And Wil... has absolutely nothing to say to that. He doesn't think he could speak now if he wanted to, and he really doesn't want to.

"*Ah, you have remembered your name,*" She tells him, satisfied, and without so much as a flick of Her eye in warning, She reaches out and swipes a thumb over Dallin's right cheek.

He gasps—shock and pain both—and jerks back with a growling curse rumbling behind his clenched teeth. He snatches his hand from Wil's and presses it to where She's just touched, wincing.

"*Take up your task, Guardian,*" She commands. "*Lind awaits, the Father awaits, and the enemy will not. Remember who you are, remember what you believe, and where you lay your faith. You cannot fail, for so very much depends on you.*"

Right, *Wil thinks bleakly,* no pressure.

She smiles at Wil. "*Hand him your keys, and with them, your belief. If it is strong enough to bind, it is strong enough to free. Not all cages are prisons.*"

She reaches out, both hands extended, palms up, toward Wil. He doesn't even have time to reach back, think about what it means, before it all hits him, a hammerblow to the soul.

Pressure builds, like a low growl rumbling in a giant's chest, except he can't hear it with his ears. He feels it in his chest, in his head, pulsing against his skull. Everything he gave Her before is now shoved back at him, wound through and boosted a thousand-fold with Her own power, too big for him, too huge for his small mind and body to take in. Mind-bending, soul-tearing, and unbearably crushing. Pain—blinding, overwhelming, and all at once—grinds into every inch of him, inside and out, and he doesn't know if it's going to mash him to pulp or make him explode. It doesn't really matter, because it'll all work out the same.

He screams—he thinks he screams, he can't tell, maybe not, because he has no breath, so how could he?—then goes to his knees. He's never felt torment so pure and piercing, an ecstasy of agony, and he twists inside it like a worm on a hook, helpless.

Voices resonate from the threads themselves, set them vibrating, *and it only adds to the shrilling in Wil's head. It's like the land gathering at him, but worse, so much worse, because this isn't only the land but the world. Every voice shouting at him, every thought pounding into his mind like it's his or it should be, like he knows everything—all of it, and all at once—and it's too much, he can't take it all. He can feel it shattering into him, crushing him from the inside out, and he screams again, means to beg Her to take it away, it's killing him—*

And then Dallin is there, taking Wil's hands, stilling it all between one breath and the next. Stunned and shocky, dizzy and weak, as though he's just been drowning and now suddenly isn't anymore. Dallin's hands lift Wil up, drag him close, keeping a firm hold and waiting patiently until Wil opens his eyes and meets Dallin's steady gaze.

The new Mark on Dallin's cheek is already scarred over, but red and angry-looking. His eye is red-rimmed and watery, like the Mark hurts but not badly, just enough pain so he doesn't forget it's there.

The look is so familiar, it nearly takes Wil's breath again. Like in his vision, and he thinks dazedly, Is this my end, then? *except he knows better. Dark eyes boring into his, the Mark bright and burning. Before, he thought the look somewhat savage, angry and dangerous, but now he sees it for the worry it is, and there's anger, but it isn't for him.*

You know them for travesties, *She'd told him. Only days ago, Wil might not have been sure. Now he is.*

"Reborn." Wil thinks he whispers it, but he can't tell, and he doesn't feel reborn, *so maybe he's wrong. He tries to decide if he cares, but he feels hazy and still a bit stunned, so he stops thinking altogether.*

"I've got it," Dallin tells him calmly. "Do you trust me?"

Wil sends a woozy glance around, notes they're alone, She's gone, and he feels a strange mix of relief and sorrow. "Yes," he says faintly, doesn't even stop to try to think about it. "Yes, I trust you."

"Close your eyes."

Wil does.

It's so very different this time, so much less suffocating but no less overwhelming. Dallin was right—it's been waiting for this, and it's insistent. It batters at Wil's defenses, and it takes everything in him to listen to Dallin's voice in his mind—It's all right, trust me, it won't hurt this time—trust him as Wil had just said he did and lower the walls, let it in.

He's buffeted inside it like a leaf on the wind, and it winnows into his every crevice, fills him up 'til he thinks he'll burst. And still it pours itself into him.

He sees the Mother, only She was called Ælíf back when time began, and he sees the Father, who was Brionglóid when He caught sight of His beloved for the first time. Mœting, She calls Him, because She'd dreamed of Him, and Wil almost flinches, watching as She plaits a silky strand of sable through with the spiny green stem of the delicate little white flower that had kept Wil captive for so very long.

"'Tis a mark of ownership in my country," He teases Her, grinning, so charming and beguiling as He steals a kiss and then another. "Now I must do as you say."

He's telling tales, teasing and seducing, Wil knows He is. It wasn't true then, but He spoke it, and so made it true ever after.

"Then I say kiss me again," She demands, and He grins again and obeys.

The tales are wrong—all the legends, they're all wrong. They didn't wage war on their kin but gathered them to Them and joined against Æledfýres.

Soul-eater, dearg-dur, daeva, stealing the magic of others, and if they didn't have magic and he was bored, sometimes he'd merely drink their blood or eat their hearts, and those were the lucky ones. Slowly he walked across the infant land, herded the clans, took the souls of those who had magic and used the minds of those who didn't. Built himself an army while Ælíf and Brionglóid fell into each other and bided for a time in newborn bliss.

For ages They heeded only each other and the budding lands, built Their mountains, and forged Their waters with Their kin until Célnes cried her death song on the wind, and They knew what Æledfýres had done. They called Their kin to them, called all men whose minds were still free, and marched on the corrupt god.

One after another, the old gods fell to him. Eorðbúgigend first, His brother, then Diepe, Her sister, until all but Brionglóid and Ælíf were gone—He with His sword, She with Her bow and quiver —and they hunted down Æledfýres. Together They cut the captive souls from out his heart, took his fire from him, and imprisoned him forever within the bole of a great evergreen, spoke Their spells to keep it strong and secret, and gave to it eternal life. The souls of the captive men They set free, and the men thanked Them, named Them Mother and Father, bowed to Them, and bound Them to Their thrones.

But with the souls of Their kin They could not part, so the Father dreamed into life a son for His beloved and placed the souls of Their fallen kin into his heart, where their essence would live on in the one They loved best. The Father named his son Aisling, for he was a dream—a vision He sang into poem and then into life—a wish He made Their own. But the Mother gave to him his true name, breathed it into his heart with a kiss to his brow, and made of it the last lock to Æledfýres's prison. Kept it secret even from Her beloved so the Aisling alone held all the keys to his bondage.

Keeper, Coimeádaí, of all the Kin.

And then the Mother took Her beloved back to Lind, the first place of Her making, the birthplace of the world and Their love.

Peopled it with great warriors, Marked them, and chose its finest to stand guard over Her beloved Gift.

"You have a name." Dallin strokes Wil's cheek with *callused* fingers. "You've held it in your hand. All you have to do is see it."

Wil nods, turns his face into the caress, links his fingers through his Guardian's, and keeps watching, keeps feeling, keeps accepting as power keeps pouring into him, as the land keeps up its songs. And every time he thinks he can't take any more, Dallin tightens his grip and he can, soaking it up like parched soil beneath a spring rain. He watches the earth move as new mountains are made and old ones are swallowed up, as streams turn into rivers into seas. And all the power inside them, all their strength, pulsates through him, drives down into his bones, and he sees their patterns, touches them, and knows them.

The land, its people, and everything they've ever seen or been. He sees every Aisling who has ever come before him—brothers of a sort, he supposes—and every Guardian who has taken his place at the Aisling's back. Sees the land as one, clans interbreeding and wandering borders, burning their offerings to the Mother and the Father and singing their orisons with one voice.

Until Ríocht-that-will-be, fosterer of Aislingí, betrays Lind-that-is, begetter of Guardians.

Wars at the borders and defenders at the Bounds. The people of Lind have been warriors since the place was birthed, and its soil has taken in the blood of native and ally and enemy alike. Calders and Portwaras and Braydens—they've lived and died, spent themselves and left their bones beneath its skin. It's ancient, and it holds the memories of long years, from the infancy of the world, and it doesn't forget.

"Are you seeing all this?" Wil asks. He knows Dallin answers, but he doesn't really need to, because yes, of course he is. The very soul of the land and all its power—its history, its magic, its people—

flows through the Guardian. It's what he's for. Gníomhaire,
Wæterþéotan.

It's hard to imagine that Dallin has been holding it back all this
time, keeping it from crushing Wil beneath the onslaught for... how
long now? It doesn't matter—he can feel the release of pain and
tension from Dallin as Wil accepts its weight, doled out carefully
and slowly and only as Wil's mind can take it, adjust to it, before
Dallin sends him more.

Lind's power depends on her people lending her the strength
of their belief—*someone had told him that, except he can't
remember who, and it doesn't matter.* It's so profoundly true it's
almost strange he had to be told at all. *Bound by belief*—he knows
what it means now, knows the power of faith, because he can feel it
all coursing through him, winding its way into heart and spirit,
blood and bone. From them to Dallin and then to Wil, channeling
through his Guardian so he doesn't fall beneath its weight. It keeps
amazing Wil that it doesn't overwhelm him, that he knows it
because Dallin knows it, can grasp it and wield it because Dallin
knows how, and it doesn't occur to Wil that he might fail, because
Dallin knows Wil won't.

The strength of faith. It almost makes him laugh, bizarrely
elated, because Dallin is so sure he hasn't any.

Oh, Dallin, *he thinks,* you'll be the very last to know the things
you can do. You'll be my savior yet.

And again a strange euphoric delight moves through him,
because he can actually feel Dallin smile—his spirit to Wil's—and
it's small, just a smile, but it's almost more intimate than anything
they've shared between them before.

"I'll be anything you'll let me be," Dallin answers, and Wil has
no idea if he's doing it with his mind or his body, but he reaches out,
wraps Dallin in a firm embrace, and hangs on. Wil's mind and soul
may be buffeted and battered inside something almost too vast and

*wide to comprehend, but his heart is right here, wide open, and he's
never been so glad to be so exposed.*

*"Nearly there," Dallin tells him, and it's strange, because it
feels boundless, as if it couldn't possibly have an end, and then Wil
realizes it doesn't. Dallin isn't merely pulling in the last of it but
securing the tether—from the land to Dallin to Wil—bolstering the
connection, protecting it, propping himself beneath it all like a stan-
chion, sliding it into shapes that aren't devastating but manageable,
understandable, and usable. Wil can see the threads, wonders what
Dallin sees in them, if he realizes he's weaving patterns of his own,
and decides not to ask.*

Warp and weft, and surely this is what it all means?

"Have we got it?" Dallin asks.

*It takes a moment for Wil to realize he's heard it with his ears.
He nods, dares to open his eyes—*

—and the murky residue of the leaf hit him all at once. It was
as though he'd been flying all alone through a vast, wide-open sky,
serenaded by sun and stars, and suddenly he was caught in a sticky
web, nearly blind and halfway deaf, his own body sucking him
down 'til he almost couldn't breathe. Cold, he *hated* the cold, and
wet and fucking-*ow*-sore, every bone in his body radiating a throbbing pain that bloomed outward from his chest and shoulder, his
head thudding sick and heavy. *Everything* was heavy, as if he'd
been weighted down and halfway buried, his limbs laden and slow
and altogether too far away from his body.

"...the *fuck?*" He tried to focus but only managed a blurred
image of blond hair and dark eyes hovering a few inches
above him.

"Can you hear me?" Dallin's voice was soft and concerned.

"'Course I c'n hear you." Wil blinked and squinted but still
couldn't quite focus. "'M not deaf."

A bit more snappish than was probably warranted, but to go

from all that freedom and beauty and power, and then drop without warning back into... *this*. He almost wanted to weep. He was slumped in Dallin's lap again, Wil realized, his head drooping against the hard muscle of Dallin's chest—hair wet, cheek damp against Dallin's sopping shirt.

"Oh." Wil shivered. "We're back."

Dallin's fingers ran through Wil's tangled hair, slicking it back off his brow. "I'm afraid so. How d'you feel?"

Wil thought about it, then snorted, rough and weak. "Like I've just been trampled by a herd of Linders." Which was coarse and oversimplified, but not too far off the mark.

"I can't do anything about the bullet until we can get it out, and I don't think it's a good idea to give you anything for the pain right now."

It had started out soft but progressed to throttled anger by the end. Wil turned it over in his head a few times, trying not to chuckle as he pressed his face into Dallin's soggy shirt, where it was wet and uncomfortable but still warm, before the words tripped into sense. He frowned, opened his eyes, and blinked Dallin into cleaner focus.

"Bullet?" Well, that would explain a few things, at least. "I'm shot?"

Wil tried to sit up, but Dallin tightened his grip, keeping him down, and anyway, it hadn't been such a good idea in the first place—everything but just sitting still and breathing seemed to shoot daggers through Wil's chest, and breathing wasn't all that great either. Which wasn't funny at all, but Wil couldn't help snickering. Which was even less funny, now that he thought about it.

"Bloody *hurts*."

The leaf was wearing off. And Wil didn't quite know how to feel about that. He was already shaking, and though that was likely all in his mind, or maybe it was just that he was wet and cold, each twitch and shiver brought back a remembrance he didn't want. Too many horrible memories of his time at the Guild, and prominent among them himself, broken and begging and offering anything, everything.

"I want to go back," he heard himself whisper, and he was appalled that he wasn't quite sure if he meant back to the Mother, where some things hurt but in a different way, or to the Guild, where they'd give him what he loathed and needed.

"I *don't* need it," he said through his teeth, clenched tight to keep them from chattering. Wil hated this part the worst—how everything in his head just spilled out his mouth. And *fuck*, he didn't want Dallin to see him like this, but Dallin wouldn't look away, it wasn't the sort of person Dallin *was*, and that just made it... rather awful, really.

"I don't *need* it." Wil said it again as if he were trying to convince himself, and Dallin would know that. No point in trying to make it sound better, because it wouldn't disguise the fact that Wil *wanted* it. Before, forever ago, when Calder had shoved a second dose down his throat, Wil had fought it, mindlessly defiant. Now all he wanted was more. He clutched tight to the damp wad of linen in his fist. "Dallin—"

"I know," Dallin told him calmly.

"No, I don't think you do."

Dallin didn't answer that one. "I can't touch the leaf," he said instead. "I already tried, but maybe—?"

"*Yes.*"

It didn't even matter what Dallin might be offering; it had to be better than this. Wil tried to stay still as a shudder racked him up and down, but pain exploded through his chest and shoulder again, and he couldn't help the flinch, which only made things worse.

"Fuck, yes, anything, just... *now*."

"Perhaps some valerian, Brayden?" another voice asked softly.

Wil jolted—a very bad idea—but he managed to tilt his head back and turn it.

"Oh fucking *hell*."

He hadn't realized he had an audience. At least a score of people stood in a loose picket above him—two in the blue and brown, which meant Corliss was here, witnessing, *looking*—all of them staring, some shifting nervously, and it wasn't at all difficult to imagine what they were seeing, what they were thinking. At least everything was still blurry, so Wil didn't have to see their expressions.

Slowly Wil turned away. He didn't care what it looked like this time, just shoved his face into Dallin's shirt.

"What's going on?"

"We're here," Dallin told him, quietly and just for Wil, "in Fæðme, and you...." He dipped his mouth close to Wil's ear. "You are the Heart of the World."

It should have been humbling, heavy. All Wil could do was snort tiredly and sag a bit more against Dallin's chest.

"Then why do I feel like the arse-end of it?"

Dallin started rapping out orders to... someone else. "Get me a waterskin, and if anyone's got a dry coat or something he can use to keep warm, hand it over, please, he's freezing." Dallin shifted and, by the feel of it, looked over his shoulder. "Not valerian—it's too strong, and he doesn't like to lose his wits."

Do I have any of those left to lose? Wil wondered bleakly.

"There are other ways to overcome such things," another voice said—it sounded like Thorne. Which probably meant that at least half of those standing over Wil, watching him shudder and twitch, were the Old Ones. Brilliant.

Damn it, if he'd been "reborn" as the Heart of the World, why did it still take only a dose or two of leaf to turn him into nothing more than a pathetic addict all over again?

Her with Her links and Her cages—surely this cage was all too real, and no help at all in what She wanted from Wil. More tests, perhaps, but Wil couldn't quite believe that, not when so much was on the line. Healing his soul, soothing his conscience, reconciling him to his own nature—so why hadn't She healed *this*?

"It can't be withdrawal," Dallin was saying. "It's not been long enough for that, and he's not been dependent for years."

Oh, and Wil wanted to believe that more than anything.

"There is more to addiction than the body's needs," someone else put in, though Wil didn't recognize this voice right off. "The mind can do many—"

"And assumptions can do many more," Dallin cut in. "He's fevered and shaking, which I expect has more to do with the fact that he's been outside since last night and exposed to freezing rain all morning. It's more likely a simple case of the ague. The man's been shot and thrown from a horse, for pity's sake. Let's take care of the things we know are real before we start worrying about things that may not be."

Huh. Wil frowned. He'd been assuming right along with them, but now that he really examined the aches and injuries... maybe Dallin was right. Wil wanted more leaf, he couldn't deny it—always with him, that want, singing in a low hum he usually managed to keep buried in some little pocket of his subconscious he never let himself look at—and stronger now, he couldn't deny that either. If one of these people made an offer, Wil would very likely take it and thank them for it. But the *need* wasn't burning at him, wasn't gnawing away his sanity, wasn't making him twist and beg and offer his soul for one more sip. No uncontrollable giggling, and his thoughts weren't spilling out his head like messy confessions. His guts weren't cramping, and his mind, though fuzzy and somewhat sluggish at the moment, was his own.

And more—Dallin believed it. If She was bound by Wil's beliefs... was he bound by Dallin's? Tethered by the faith of one who believed everything good about him. Wil could do a lot worse.

"He makes a good point." That one had to be Marden—the thick baritone was unmistakable. "Perhaps Singréne would do best here."

"Mm," Dallin grunted. "I can very well—"

"If it's what you think it is, Singréne's songs of healing are best," Thorne said, soft but with a tinge of severity that almost made Wil snort. "Shaman"—quieter now, asking—"your magic is great, but your skills are rough, unpracticed. We all want what's best, and the best for this is Singréne. Lend him your magic and let him guide you."

There was a pause. Wil could almost see the thoughtful frown he knew had to be creasing Dallin's brow.

"The leaf makes him vulnerable," Dallin finally said, soft but direct. "He won't be—"

"Don't talk about me like I'm not here," Wil muttered. Which was a little stupid, since he was currently doing his very best to hide and pretend he wasn't. Which was a lot stupid. Because he could cower here like the pathetic leaf freak they seemed to think he was and let them debate for another hour, or he could grow some stones and act like he'd just stood before the Mother and accepted all the power She chose to give him. Either way, what they thought of Wil was his own to guide, and it was going to matter soon.

He pushed himself up from the damp warmth of Dallin's chest but couldn't help the wince and hiss as pain shot out from his shoulder, wound through his ribs, and momentarily took his breath. Dallin held on to him, but only to steady him.

Wil managed a weak smile in thanks and ran his fingertips just below the new Mark, careful not to touch. "I'd almost forgotten. I expect it's official now."

Corliss handed Dallin a waterskin over his shoulder. Dallin nodded his thanks and passed the skin to Wil.

"Official. Sure." Dallin's return smile was tired. "For what it's worth."

"Everything, of course." Wil took a long drink, craning his neck to squint up at... everyone.

Everything.

He was here, in Fæðme, the *Cliabhán*, and it was nothing at all what Wil had feared it would be. Then again, nothing about this had ever proven even close to his fears, so he wasn't terribly surprised.

It was beautiful. Ancient and primitive, the vast caverns arching up so far above that the flicker of the lamps didn't even reach its highest recesses. The rock was like nothing he'd ever seen —he'd never imagined there could be so many hues of one color, but there were more shades of green here than he thought perhaps had names. *Like Father's eyes*, he thought, and a sharp stab of worry and remorse churned his heart.

Water flowed past just to his right, the very mouth of the river, catching the lamps and torches and sparking bright gold-emerald. Something about it warmed the chill that had settled in Wil's bones.

Flównysse. Mother's Blood.

Maybe it was as simple as that.

He let his gaze wander over the various faces—some he knew, some he didn't—and stopped at Singréne. He nodded.

"If you can help, I'd appreciate it if you would." He caught Dallin's look of worry, so he offered another smile and dipped in close. "You can't do everything yourself. You have to start trusting them sometime. If they had any corrupt intent, you'd know it. You knew all along with Calder." Wil flushed lightly and looked down. "Dallin... I'm sorry about—"

"Don't." Dallin shook his head. "Just... don't."

He really meant it. Not just *I don't want to talk about it*, but *I don't blame you. Let it go.*

Wil nodded. "All right. You're right—I won't. Only don't let him get in the way of what we have to do here. We need them, or we will. Right now *I* need them." He tried to flex and fist his right hand, couldn't quite make it, and brought his left up to rest lightly over the wound on his shoulder. A light shudder swept him, and he winced. "If it's the ague, and I sneeze, I think it might kill me." And naturally, since he'd gone and said it, Wil's nose started to tingle and itch. He dared a sniffle and wiped his filthy sleeve across it.

"Here," Corliss piped up, behind Wil now, crouching just at his left shoulder. He caught a bit of worry in her eyes as well, so gave her a smile and let her carefully angle his arm out of his wet coat. "This is Léaf's." She nodded at the shirt draped over her knee. "It'll be big on you. He's gone up to fetch another from his saddlebags. Andette's donated her coat. For pity's sake, Brayden, get out of the way, can't you?"

Wil might've snorted at the way Dallin immediately and unquestioningly did as Corliss said, but even the small amount of shifting set the pain humming.

"Here, lad." Corliss tugged at the sleeve of Wil's wet coat. "Lift your arm if you can."

Wil tried, but—fucking *ow*. "I don't think I can."

Corliss and Dallin were both being exquisitely gentle—Dallin trying to drag his legs out from under Wil's and get out of the way without too much jostling, and Corliss trying to remove the coat with as little movement as possible—but there was apparently no way around the fact that every slight shuffle made the pain flare out and remind Wil that... bloody damn.

Wil blinked, near-disbelief.

He'd been shot. He'd actually been *shot*.

"I was *shot*."

"And thrown from a horse," Dallin reminded him grimly as he finally extracted himself and stood. "And... other things. Don't put the shirt on yet, Corliss, I'll want to check the bandage."

He watched Corliss work for a moment, watched Wil try not to flinch every time he moved, then sighed and turned his attention to Singréne. A low conversation between the two ensued above Wil's head, during which Wil hoped threats were not exchanged.

Corliss's mouth pinched as she dropped Wil's soggy coat and began working the shirt off his left arm. She stopped, thoughtful, then shook her head.

"No point in making it worse."

She slipped a long knife from her belt and proceeded to cut the shirt, careful to draw the knife down and away from Wil's chest. Too bad. That shirt was nice and soft, almost as green as the cavern, and he didn't even know who'd given it to him. Corliss shot a quick look up at Wil, strangely pointed, then turned her glance up and over Wil's shoulder.

"Andette, come give me a hand, won't you?"

Wil didn't turn around—it hurt too much to move, and the process of just getting the coat and shirt off was almost more than he could take. His head was throbbing, his gut was beginning to curl in on itself, and his nose was starting to clog and itch maddeningly. And more than anything else in the world right now, he desperately *did not* want to sneeze. Or cough. Or even breathe, really, but he hardly had a choice in that one. He waited until

Andette crouched down to his eye level, then raised his gaze to meet hers, a polite smile at the ready.

He ended up frowning instead.

Andette was subdued and pale. Her mark had gone stark and vivid over her wan complexion, and her long braid was now a short stump at the back of her neck. She kept her eyes on her hands as she fumbled at Wil's sleeve, fingers very carefully not touching him, head bowed.

Wil didn't mean to blurt "What happened to your hair?" but it just kind of... fell out.

Andette's jaw worked for a moment, and her eyes welled at the corners. "It will be buried with Barret Calder's body." It was short and clipped. "So that his ghost may remember who he was and what he's done."

"Barret Calder" and not "my uncle." This was not at all the girl who'd greeted Wil so happily and sincerely on the path down to the *Weardas'* camp just yesterday. From the tight look of... shame—he was sure it was shame—Wil wouldn't have been surprised if Andette had smeared her face with ash.

He turned his frown up at Corliss. Corliss dropped a slight shrug and waved her hand in a gesture Wil was fairly certain translated into *It's up to you.*

He was tempted to ask her exactly *what* was up to him, but... he was pretty sure he knew. He waited until Andette gently pulled the sleeve of his tunic free, then reached out with his good hand as she made to pull away and stopped her.

"Andette, I... I'm sorry about your uncle."

Andette flinched. She tried to cover it with a quick shake of her head, but she still wouldn't look at Wil.

"Contrition is mine." Her voice was shaky and small. She looked squarely at the bandage wrapped around Wil's chest and shoulder, then at the colorful bruising that was blooming out from beneath it. "That he would *dare*—" Andette bit her lip and looked away.

"It was your arrow," Wil said quietly. "Wasn't it?" His fingers tightened automatically on Andette's arm as she nodded.

Wil only half remembered it, and what he did remember slipped from reality to dream, so he couldn't be entirely sure of exactly what had happened. But he remembered the blood on the arrow, on his hand, scarlet drops on white fletching, and he remembered placing the gruesome thing over Andette's palms like some sort of trophy.

Perhaps that hadn't been the smartest thing he'd ever done.

Andette lifted her head, chin set, but she still wouldn't meet Wil's gaze. "It was my *right.*"

Wil looked over at Corliss for help, but her face remained impassive. Wil shot her back a look that was definitely *not.*

What was he supposed to say to this girl? Andette had spilled the blood of her kin in Wil's defense. Did that make this his responsibility? Was Calder's blood just as much on Wil's hands as Andette's? Was Wil expected to mourn the man or absolve his executioner? Wil didn't know the traditions here—he had no idea how to even begin to soothe Andette's conscience, or if it was even his place to try.

"I'm sorry" was all he could say.

By the way Andette flinched again and gasped, bowed her head, and quickly jerked herself up and away, Wil guessed it was the wrong sentiment to offer. He stared after her as she slipped around the Old Ones before he turned back to Corliss, nonplussed.

Corliss merely shrugged and draped the thick coat carefully over Wil's bare shoulders. It was still warm from Andette's heat, and Wil couldn't help the slight shiver. He also couldn't help the scowl he arrowed at Corliss.

"Was that really necessary?"

"Yes." Corliss nodded and patted Wil's good shoulder through the coat. "I think it was."

He didn't have an opportunity to pursue it, which was just as well, since he wasn't even sure he wanted to. Instead he turned his glance gratefully—for more than one reason—to Dallin and Singréne as they broke away from the others and sat to either side of Wil. *Finally*. Leaf or no, he *hurt* everywhere, and the need for relief was becoming more necessary than any need for leaf, whether it was ingrained habit and expectation, addiction to the craving in his own mind, or blunt reality. Wil didn't even think he cared which anymore.

Except they'd only just settled in and got themselves as comfortable as possible on the cold stone, when they both started and exchanged alarmed glances. A hush fell over the others, and every weapon in the room came up followed by the grinding, metallic slide of bolts cocking and the thin whisper of arrows being drawn from quivers, bowstrings tightening.

Wil tensed too, though he had no idea why until a tight few seconds passed and he heard the sound of quick, light footfalls approaching. Fuck, he'd forgotten where he was for a few minutes there, forgotten why he was here. Now it all rushed back at him, all the fear, all the... everything.

Anxiety wasted, it seemed, at least for the moment—Dallin and Singréne both relaxed for reasons Wil couldn't share until Dallin gave Wil a small smile, then turned and addressed the others.

"It's only Léaf."

Who? Wil almost asked, but then he remembered the shirt Corliss hadn't handed over yet.

Dallin blew out a long breath and shook his head ruefully.

"He wouldn't be coming from that way, anyway. Gave myself a start for nothing."

He jerked his chin over Singréne's shoulder. Wil followed Dallin's gaze to the darkness on the far side of the chamber, the opposite side to where Léaf was now emerging, red-faced and breathing hard, eyes scudding over the others before landing squarely on Dallin. Dallin saw him but merely indicated the other side of the cavern again and went on with what he'd been saying.

"He'll be coming from those tunnels over there."

Wil was determined not to shudder. "You know where Wheeler is?"

"He'll be here shortly, so let's get you as ready as we can, all right?"

"Skirmishes," Léaf panted as he bulled his way over to Dallin. He dropped a quick, cursory bow and absently swatted the long wet waves that had come loose from his messy braid from out his eyes. "Bealde's squadron lost a few, but she managed to secure the Temple. She's sent for Gebyld to fortify the perimeter but fears the runner may not have made it across the line. Your Creighton is there with two squadrons, so Bealde is up to almost a full battery now. She sends word to the Shaman —*The enemy has reconnoitered and is trying to concentrate its attack here, but the* Weardas *followed as they drew upward and inward. The battle lines are many and holding, but all of the enemy now aim for the Temple. Healdes and Wisena hold the Bounds against a full battalion of Commonwealth soldiers, though no word has come back yet as to whether any shots have been fired.*"

Léaf paused to catch his breath.

"She also said Wisena says to tell you their orders from Wheeler were to invade and subdue by any means necessary, and to arrest Ríocht's Chosen for his personal interrogation. You,

Shaman—" Léaf's teeth set tight, and he lifted his chin. "You are to be executed on sight."

Wil's head was spinning with all the dismaying information, but Dallin merely nodded as though he was already fully aware.

"The runner made it and Gebyld is on her way, not to worry. Thank you, Léaf. Sit down before you fall. It'll all be over shortly."

It was surreal. The quiet here was like a soft, soothing blanket, and Wil had been so worried about his own aches and what they might or might not mean, when all the while there were actual battles going on who knew how far above. People dying.

"How many is a battalion?" Wil asked faintly.

"A thousand men."

Dallin's reply was calm and even, but that didn't make it any less shocking. Wil's heart took a jolt in his chest.

"A *thousand?* Plus all the Brethren?" He shut his eyes tight before looking back into Dallin's unruffled gaze. "Surely there aren't enough of the *Weardas* to hold them *all* back? Lind will be overrun."

Unaccountably, Dallin smiled. "They're outnumbered at least ten to one, if it comes to it. The *Weardas* are not the only ones who carry weapons. No Linder forewarned is defenseless. Anyway, Wisena's already got Wheeler's men convinced they arrived just in time to stop an invasion, and he's ceded command to Shaw. A soldier wants a general, and Shaw's reputation will do what no direct order from Wheeler ever could. Unless Æledfýres prevails"—there was only the barest hint of an angry grimace —"which he *won't*, Lind and its people are safe from Cynewísan's guns for the moment."

"Did you know all this before?" Thorne asked from behind.

Dallin looked over his shoulder. "I knew Shaw would be necessary. I've been... keeping track." And that was all he would say, it seemed. He looked again to Wil, took careful hold of his arm, and pushed him lightly back. "Let's get you ready, shall we?" He nodded at Singréne.

Wil's eyes narrowed, but he let Dallin and Singréne guide him until he was stretched out on his back on the stone floor, Andette's heavy coat cushioning Wil's bare skin from the chill that was still seeping in through his damp trousers.

"You said Wheeler will be here shortly." Wil couldn't help how his eyes darted over toward the pocket of darkness that concealed the tunnel Dallin had indicated. "How shortly?"

"I'd say within the hour."

Wil took as deep a breath as he could, then blew it out slowly, trying to calm the thumping of his heart. He watched with only half interest as Singréne slid a small charm between his palms, the way Calder had done that first day in Chester when he and Shaw had prayed over Dallin. Wil's hand unconsciously wandered to his trouser pocket, outlining the shape of his little Sun and Moon charm within. Singréne delicately pulled the crystal pendant from where it had slid on its chain down to the floor by Wil's shoulder and laid it in its place on Wil's breastbone. Eyes closed, Singréne centered his big hands over Wil's chest and began to sing, low and gorgeously deep. The words were indistinct, but Wil recognized the familiar cadence of the First Tongue.

"You know—" Dallin slipped his hand around Wil's; instantly Wil felt the soothing magic of Singréne's song redouble, felt the unconscious power leaching from Dallin's hand into his own. "I know where they are." Dallin's tone was steady and low. "He's only got one squad with him. I could...." He met Wil's curious gaze with one that was even but hard. "I could collapse the tunnel."

He could. Wil didn't doubt Dallin had the power. He could feel a tiny fraction of it running through him, after all. And Dallin wanted to, Wil could see it. Dallin had likely been thinking about it since they'd arrived down here, but he'd waited—waited for Wil.

Everything about this is your business, Dallin had growled at Wil last night, even as he'd been trying so desperately to withhold his suicidal plan from Wil, trying to keep things from him to protect him, and not quite managing the lying part of it. *Servant to the Aisling*—Dallin down on his knee before him, that Wil remembered all too clearly, and though the interpretation of "servant" seemed to vary from one person to the next, Wil thought Dallin's definition the most definitive. It warmed Wil, but still... he didn't want it. He didn't want a servant at all, any more than he wanted to be one.

"Is that what you want to do?" Wil's muscles were relaxing without him even having to work at it, Singréne's song and Dallin's magic winding into Wil's bones, soothing the aches despite everything else.

Dallin rubbed at his face with his free hand, rough fingers scratching over at least a day's growth of thick red-gold beard. "Part of me, yes. Part of me still wants to get rid of Wheeler while I can and get you out of here, go into hiding until we're stronger."

Singréne's song didn't pause or hitch, but his eyebrows rose and his gaze flicked to Wil's, hung for but a moment before he shut his eyes again. Wil kept looking at him, wondering, before he too closed his eyes on a relaxed sigh. The pounding in his head was receding, and the pain that radiated from his chest and all down his arm was edging back. Dallin had been right—it really wasn't the leaf. Wil's relief was pure and perfect.

"I'm not sure we can get any stronger."

"Maybe not, but...." Dallin shifted, his hand tightening around Wil's. "We could stay ahead of them, at least for a while. And perhaps when a new Cleric is chosen.... I mean, I can feel Wheeler, so it stands to reason—"

"Dallin." Wil kept his eyes closed and his voice soft. "What do you want to do? I mean, what do you *really* want to do? What's the best strategy, Shaman?" Dallin didn't answer, but then, he didn't really have to. "You don't want to run and hide." Wil made it as gentle as he could. "You don't want to leave Lind to itself. You can't. It isn't in you."

Again Dallin's fingers tightened around Wil's, this time almost painfully. He was silent for quite a while, the power seeping from his hand to Wil's keeping pulsing time to the rhythm of Dallin's slow breathing, like it was an extension of his body.

"I want you to live, Wil. I want us both to live."

Wil nodded. "So do I. I know you don't really believe that, but I—"

"It isn't—"

"—but I promise you that I would like nothing better than to live a very long life, learning as slowly as I possibly can all the ways there are that will make you smile at me like you did by the Stair." Wil's mouth turned up gently at the corners. "You've a beautiful smile. Has anyone ever told you that?"

"No. I don't think so."

What a horrible pity.

"I'm not afraid of Wheeler." Wil opened his eyes. "You're stronger than him—you said it yourself. He's trying to take from you, he's trying to take from your people. And you can't stand that someone like him has control of the Commonwealth's military. You want him, and you want to see his eyes when he realizes you have him. You only want to collapse the tunnel because if I let you, that means I'm afraid enough that I'll let you talk me out of the other."

"Wil—"

"I want to live." Fierce now, because he really meant this, every bit of it. "I want to know everything about you, even those things you don't want to remember. I want to learn your every thought, your every feeling. I want to get to know the ten thousand nuances of your every kiss. I want to watch Lind learn and grow beneath your hand, and I want to find out all the things I can do, find my place, and stretch myself into it." He paused, dismayed and warmed both at the slight glimmer in Dallin's dark gaze. "If I have anything to say about it, Dallin, I promise you this one thing —I want us both to come out the other side of this."

Dallin nodded, sincere agreement, but his sigh was sad and resigned. "And how do we do that, d'you suppose?"

Wil closed his eyes again, Singréne's song and Dallin's warmth pouring into his every crevice now, soothing everything that hurt, even his heart.

"She told me to give you my keys. Said we've more than two choices, but She wouldn't tell me what the others were. She also said I've all the pieces of my puzzle, which pissed me off a little, because *you're* the one obsessed with puzzles. Told me to use my gifts—*all* of them, She said, like I wouldn't use everything anyway, or something—and then She said I don't even know all of my gifts, so...." He frowned and squinted up at Dallin through drooping eyelids. Amazingly, Wil thought he could fall asleep here on the cold stone floor of Fæðme, waiting for the Cleric. "I don't know what that means, really, but if I find any keys, I'll be sure to hand them over."

"More riddles." Dallin almost growled but too obviously held it back. "I suppose that's where the Old Ones get it from, but it would surely—" He stopped, staring down at Wil with a deep, thoughtful frown. "You mean She implied you've more gifts than the ones we know about?"

"I... guess?" Wil shut his eyes again and let himself drift on the gently flowing brume of consoling healing. "Implied lots of things, in fact, but you know how that goes. Or...." He frowned. "Well, no. She said I already knew, although I beg to differ, but that doesn't seem to make a difference." He sank deeper into the thick coat.

"All in all, it was more than I'd expected it to be, but... maybe it's ungrateful, but I still wish They'd just *say* things."

"Huh. I think maybe—" Dallin went silent for a moment before Wil felt him shift. "Not all your gifts come from the Mother or the Father." It sounded like Dallin was talking to himself, musing. "But if not Them, then...?" Singréne's song stuttered somewhat, grew slightly louder, and the power pulsing from Dallin's hand intensified. "You get the pushing from Síofra, because Síofra got it from him." The cadence of his words had gone slow and deliberate. "That man," he said, almost reluctantly, "in Dudley."

That man in Dudley. Fírinne. The man they'd questioned. The man Wil had pushed until he couldn't stop, and then... and then he'd pulled it back. The man Wil had refused to look at after, because he didn't want to see what was left in those blank eyes, afraid to know, afraid he might understand the emptiness, the void where a man used to be.

Soulless.

You do not yet know of what you are capable. You do not yet know all of your gifts.

Dearg-dur.

Soul-eater.

Blood to blood.

Wil's eyes snapped open and stared, sightless, up into shadow. "Oh," he wheezed, shocked and sickened and altogether too certain. "Oh... *fuck.*"

CHAPTER 6

D allin watched Wil's expression slide from blankly stunned to revolted to pissed, then settle back slowly into blank. All but his eyes—burning, outshining the polished stone in the river's bed, boring tight and tense into Dallin's. And Dallin knew exactly what it all meant.

"Right." Dallin gave a short, sharp nod. "Can you get up?"

He barely even waited for Wil to nod back before Dallin hauled them both to their feet, pausing only for a second or two to make sure Wil had his balance before calling for Corliss and Thorne. Because if Dallin faffed about, if he let himself stop and consider it all, he might end up balking altogether.

"I'll want everyone armed and watching that entrance," he told Corliss as she helped Wil into Léaf's overlarge tunic. "He knows Wil and I are here, but he doesn't know you are. You'll have surprise on your side, plus a half-dozen Linders who can move like cats. Have them flank them from the shadows, disarm them, and we'll deal with what comes after. The arrogant pillock only brought ten men with him, so you should be able to do it without firing a shot."

"And what will you be doing?" Corliss shot a look of blatant concern between Dallin and Wil. Wil merely shrugged and opened a hand toward Dallin.

"Other things," Dallin said.

"But what about...?" Corliss frowned, her fingers unconsciously brushing the grip of her sidearm in its holster. "He's got magic, hasn't he?"

"He's no match for Fæðme. Or for me." Dallin made it deliberately cocky and added a sly wink that made Corliss grimace and roll her eyes, but it seemed to soothe any nerves that might've been building.

Dallin waited for her to get about her business, obviously glad to have something to do, someone to direct, before he turned to Thorne.

"Protection spells. You're right, I'm not practiced, and I don't want to take chances. Can you—?"

"Runes." Wil's voice was quiet but curiously resonant. His eyes were locked on Thorne's, somber. "Made of the stone of Fæðme and the water of the Flównysse." He sent a sharp, steady look up at Dallin. "And the blood of the Shaman."

And just how d'you propose to get that? Dallin almost protested but only groused, "Not all of it, I hope," and flattened his mouth into a scowl he didn't really mean. If Wil said it must be so, then it must be so.

Wil turned his gaze back to Thorne. "All should be Marked."

"I agree most heartily," Thorne answered, gravely approving. "Any particular charms you would urge?"

Wil shrugged. "I expect you'd know that better than I."

Thorne gave him a look that said *I wouldn't be so sure*, but he nodded and accepted the charge. He clapped his hands as he bustled away, called, "Incense!" to the other elders, and confiscated two of the Linders to start the business of gathering chips and dust from the stone that laced the floors of the cavern and pounding it into powder. Dallin supposed they'd come and find him when it was time to make his own ghoulish contribution.

"Blood?" he murmured to Wil under his breath. "Really?"

"Baby," Wil murmured back.

Dallin tried to keep the scowl but couldn't. "Just thinking it's a bit on the dramatic side. Then again, it *is* you."

Wil returned just enough of a smile to make it clear that the jab was accepted in its spirit, then abruptly sobered. "I wouldn't ask anything of you that wasn't necessary."

It was heartfelt and filled with things that any other time would have warmed Dallin to his toes. Now it chilled him.

"Ask it all, Wil. You understand that, don't you?"

A weary sigh and a quick, gentle squeeze of his hand was all he got for an answer.

"How much longer?"

"Listen...." Dallin trailed off, gathering as much calm composure as he could. "You know my way is safer. Wheeler... he's an unknown, unpredictable. If you try, just for one minute, to come at this from an objective angle, you have to see that—"

"How much longer?" Implacable and just on the edge of hard.

Dallin kept his jaw from clenching. He pulled his hand away and scrubbed at his stubbly chin with a bitter sigh.

"Not much." His arm throbbed, hot and dull. He stretched it straight and flexed his fingers. "And here I am, going into battle with my good arm gone stupid."

"Don't think you'll be needing your guns." Wil held own right arm stiffly across his torso. "It's fine for now," he said when he caught Dallin's glance. "I'm fine for now. Well." He looked down. "Relatively speaking, anyway."

"Wil—"

"No."

Dallin's mouth tightened. "You don't even know what I was going to say."

"It doesn't matter. It all amounts to the same thing. He's dying, and She doesn't want Him to. I don't know why She can't help Him, but I do know She would if She could. We're all there is, and it's down to us. Maybe this was the only way from the beginning, and we were just fooling ourselves with choices that weren't real."

"Torturing ourselves, more like. And it isn't as though this is a perfect solution to all our problems." Dallin's hands fisted, a pulsing spark of aching heat sliding up his right arm. It felt good, it felt *real*, so he did it again. "If we had more time, maybe... maybe we could learn how to direct it better. No commander would lead his troops into a battle with these kinds of odds, Wil. No commander would march on the enemy without first collecting all the intelligence there was to gather and drilling his troops until they were sharp and ready. We're *not ready* for this."

Wil shook his head, mouth tight. "If we tried to get out of it now, something else would happen to force us to it. Time's running out—don't you feel it?"

Dallin pinched at the bridge of his nose. "You think She's set all this up? You think She's pushing us about on some other-worldly chess board?"

Because Dallin didn't believe that for a second. If She had that kind of power, She could have taken care of all this Herself. Dallin had seen Her urgency, had felt its unmistakable tension, and he didn't think any of this was some kind of test of Her Aisling or Her Guardian set up by Her own hand to prove their strength or faith. She needed them, and so did He.

"No." Wil's brow twisted as he pulled his gaze up and turned it to the quiet bustle around them. "I think gods have no more control over our choices than we do over each other's. If They did —" He didn't finish the thought. "A gift and a curse to Their beloved children, and I don't necessarily damn or thank Them for it. This is my choice, and I've made it. They can't touch Æled-fýres, and I don't know why, but I can. I know my name now, and I won't dishonor it."

Dallin's eyebrows twitched up. "Oh?"

"It's funny." Wil turned his eyes slowly to Dallin, that small smile going soft and warm. "The Brethren forced it on me, wrote it into my very skin. If I'd known what it was, I likely would've cut it away then." He chewed his lip, but he didn't look away. "You handed it to me, kept it for me until I could understand it and be glad it's mine. You've been handing me keys since the moment I met you." Wil's head dipped down, a small deferential bow. "Thank you, Guardian."

Sentiment again, crowding Dallin's eyes, clogging his throat, only this time he didn't curse it. He swallowed, then cleared his throat. "You can't read."

Wil smiled this time, a real smile, and pulled the knife from his boot, the flicker of the lamps and torches sharding green-gold fire over the etching on its blade. "No. I can't." He slicked his fingers over the runes. "And it's a shame that the first time I hear it in the language She spoke it, it'll be from the mouth of the Cleric. But I know what it means, and I believe it. That's all that matters."

Wil squared his shoulders and ran the tip of his finger gently over the last words of the verse engraved on the blade.

"I am the Mother's Beloved Son." His voice was calm, even, and deeper than Dallin had ever heard it. "And you are my Guardian. *This* is my end, Dallin, and it *is* you who's brought me to it. I'm not Wil, I'm not Aisling, I'm what you've shown me I always was. I can't ever repay you such a debt." He held out his hand. "If Fate is at all kind, this will be the last blood you'll spill on my account."

Warm as he'd never been before, and calm, though he

shouldn't be, Dallin placed his hand in Wil's and turned it palm up. "Take all that you need," he said hoarsely, and by the way Wil's smile turned sad, Dallin knew every meaning packed into the statement was understood.

Wil neither nodded agreement nor blanched. He merely rested the blade across Dallin's bicep, tilted it, then slicked a long diagonal slice, the edge so keen Dallin didn't even feel it until the skin split slightly and blood welled in the wound. Wil didn't let go of Dallin's hand, but dipped two fingers across the neat wound, then swept a new Mark over the one that had gone brown and flaky on his cheek, mostly washed away beneath rain, sweat, and tears.

He smiled, hand curled tight around Dallin's.

"Let's get this part done."

Taking Wheeler and his men was almost disappointingly easy.

Wheeler's arrogance contributed to the ambush, which was no more strategic than Dallin's party skulking in the shadows with weapons drawn and flanking them. The "great general" had obviously been expecting to just stroll in, and take the Aisling, probably execute Dallin in the bargain, and the look of anger and embarrassment on his broad face when he found himself surrounded was fairly amusing. But the familiar chittering buzz that slipped up Dallin's backbone, Wheeler's attempt to push him and take control of the situation, was not.

"Can't we just kill him?" Dallin muttered to Wil, only half-joking, because this man was lower than those he led, more contemptible. At least the Brethren truly believed they served the Father, even if they'd completely lost sight of what that might once have meant. Wheeler had no delusions about whom he served.

Wil snorted, the negating shake of his head tellingly reluctant. "Only if you'd like to volunteer to call Æledfýres yourself."

"I think I've already done as much." Dallin's tone *might* have been a bit more acidic and aggressive than he'd intended.

Wil shot him a look that, another time, might have made Dallin step back. "I won't discuss it again."

"We've barely discussed it the once!"

"Which was once more than I can stand!" Wil took a long breath, then softened his bearing and his voice. "I know what I'm doing, Guardian. Can you give it or not?"

Using the Mother's challenge against him. Dallin could have choked him. Instead he merely set his jaw, hardened his gaze, and turned back to Wheeler and his men. Grunting out a surly "Mm," Dallin stepped through the circle of armed victors and into the cluster of disarmed captives, Wheeler at their center.

Shaw had been right—Wheeler didn't look anything like Síofra. Wide where Síofra had been thin; fair-haired and tan where Síofra had been dark and pale. But he had the same look to him, like he was certain what was coming and knew exactly how to twist it all to the outcome he wanted. The confidence of a senior officer, a man who gave an order with never a question that it would be followed. A man who commanded the respect of the army because he had the rank that made it a given. Power he could wield in service to all, and yet Wheeler had *chosen* to back a monster.

Ten years ago, Dallin would have followed this man. It would have been his duty. The thought made him want to vomit.

Wil had been right too—Dallin wanted this. Wanted to see Wheeler's arrogant gaze go wide and frightened. Wanted to watch as Wheeler realized he couldn't win, and wanted to keep watching as the superior light behind the arrogant sneer was snuffed, hopefully by Dallin's own hand. Vengeance burned in Dallin's chest, seared up his spine. This man had threatened Dallin's friends, taken control of the law of his country, arrested Jagger—likely put him in shackles, because this sort of man just would. Dallin knew what that felt like, and the empathy was just too vivid. Wheeler had been responsible for Kenley, for uncounted deaths of Commonwealth soldiers, for battles raging even now above their heads, for dragging Dallin's own country to the brink of war and the world ever closer to intended near-slavery.

Oh, Dallin wanted this.

For commanding that the Aisling be chained and broken, then leaving him alone to die with his laughing ghosts. For hunting the son of gods nearly to ground, trying to use him and take from him and make him no more than another sacrificial tool to claim whatever reward Wheeler thought his due. For having the bleeding *audacity* to think he had the *right.*

For Wil. Dallin wanted this for *Wil.*

"Dallin." Wil's touch was soft on Dallin's arm.

Dallin blinked, realizing only then that he'd drawn his revolver and had the barrel pressed to Wheeler's temple, finger twitching at the trigger. Well. At least he'd got his first wish—Wheeler looked satisfyingly worried. Dallin took a long breath, forcibly unclenching his teeth, but didn't draw the weapon away until he'd savored the look of fear in eyes as dark as his own.

"...Right." Dallin cleared his throat. "Sorry."

He took a step back and peered around at his own small company, gauged their eyes and found no blame in any of them, not even the Old Ones. Alert and intent, certainly, beneath the runes of protection drawn on each of their brows, but there was neither accusation nor approval in any of them, merely interest in what Dallin would do and faith that whatever it was, it would be the right thing. Dallin wished he could be as confident.

He set his gaze on Andette. "Find something to bind these

men with. A soldier's first duty when captured is escape, and I don't want any of them getting loose and mucking things up."

He took hold of Wheeler's sleeve where the gold leaves of rank were embroidered, then Wheeler's collar where the star insignia shone mocking-bright in the flickering light.

"Make sure they're paying attention," he murmured quietly to Andette, flipping a tight little nod to the captive soldiers. "I want them to hear this, if they'll listen."

A shove he couldn't quite resist, and a growl he didn't bother trying to—Dallin pushed Wheeler ahead of him, out of the circle and toward the flow of the river, and didn't stop until they'd reached the edge, where Dallin turned Wheeler so his back was to his men. Wil followed silently, his rifle slung over his shoulder, a look of dry amusement tracing his otherwise somber expression.

"This changes nothing," Wheeler said as Dallin reluctantly released his hold, giving one last bit of a shove before he stepped back and away because he really was *aching* to throttle or shoot. Wheeler turned his avid glance to Wil. "Aisling." He dipped his proud head, by all appearances earnestly beseeching, but there was an oiliness beneath it he couldn't quite hide. "You must know by now that your transgressions against the Father cannot continue. He will forgive you, but only if you let me help you now."

"Don't," Wil said, deadly quiet, "call him that."

That buzzing was all around them now, ramping into a steady hum. Wheeler was trying to pull power from Fæðme, the cheeky fuck, like it belonged to him and he had the right. There was power there, certainly, and stronger than what Dallin had felt from Síofra, but it couldn't compete. Dallin reached out and slammed a protection down, adding it to the magic of the Old Ones and Fæðme itself.

Wheeler's mouth pressed tight, but he only shook his head

sadly. "You have been taken in by the false Guardian, but there's no blame to you. The whole of renegade Lind shall pay for the lies it perpetrates—fools for the Mother, who seeks only to put down the Father and take all power to Herself." He shot a wrathful glance over his shoulder, flipping a hand out to indicate the Old Ones, who'd moved as one into a loose semicircle behind them, hands held out and palms up, singing softly in one voice. Wheeler sneered. "Priests of the daemon-goddess, the whore who seeks to usurp the Father, and *this* one"—he pointed at Dallin, face flushing choleric in his pretense at righteous anger—"is their soldier, Her mack, peddler of lies and trader in your flesh and magic." He held his hands out to Wil. "It's not too late. He will forgive you, if you'll only...."

Wheeler trailed off as Wil's knife slowly rose, the tip of the blade coming to rest just below Wheeler's flapping jaw. Its edge was still scarlet and shining red-gold in the torchlight.

"I think it's time we all stopped pretending now," Wil told him softly. "You'll get what you want, though I doubt you'll truly want it when you get it, and I won't hear any more of your rot in the meantime. Save your wheedling for when you finally meet your hungry god. He feeds quite well on the small, stupid minds of men like you." Wil tilted his head, genuinely curious. "Tell me—did you know Síofra?"

Wheeler smiled, trying to make his glance down at the blade casual and not nervous. "A man who grew arrogant and too settled in his own lies through his long stolen years."

Dallin couldn't help but roll his eyes. "Said General Pot to Mister Kettle."

The corner of Wil's mouth quirked up, and he shot Dallin a sharp but nonetheless amused glare.

Wheeler ignored it, morphing his expression into something that tried very hard for sympathy but only achieved poorly hidden anger. "He used you very badly." He said it in a soft voice that almost made Dallin shiver with its similarity to the man about whom Wheeler was now speaking. "And you allowed it, a sin for which you must realize you cannot escape all punishment." Wheeler sighed. "But I must admit, he did have his uses, such as they were."

"I imagine between him and High Seat Channing, you didn't have much trouble manipulating both countries into rattling swords." Dallin smiled at the reluctant surprise on Wheeler's face when Dallin named his accomplice. "Síofra's desperation toward the end must have seemed like a gift from...." Dallin grimaced, unwilling to complete the adage. "All that flapping about Síofra did at the end—all you had to do was let him go and follow after. Probably should've put more men on the Bounds, though. It was pretty easy crossing over." Dallin's smile came back when Wheeler bristled at the critique. "In fact, what you *should* have done was train the Brethren better. Or even *at all*. They're far too easy to kill. Especially since they're so willing to kill themselves."

Wheeler lifted a hand, conceding the point. "One does what one can with what one is given. I do prefer the discipline of soldiers."

"And if Dominion soldiers had been caught across the border, you wouldn't have been able to stop a declaration of war before you were ready, before Æledfýres was ready—I see."

Dallin did. All laid out before him in plain contours that had finally taken on the shapes of facts, the last of the puzzle pieces. Use men from Ríocht, so if they'd been caught across the border, the Embassy could claim they were merely a fanatical sect and nothing whatever to do with their government, no threat to the treaty. Let them do all the searching and all the dying, and when they found the Aisling, Wheeler would be the authority called in to handle the negotiations with the Dominion. Síofra himself might have even demanded Wheeler handle it. He'd been arrogant enough to insist upon Cynewísan's highest-ranking officer for any negotiations—after all, he'd demanded Wheeler take charge of the hunt, hadn't he? And once the Aisling was in Wheeler's hands... speak his name, bring Æledfýres into the world through Wheeler, and through Wheeler, push the Aisling out of his soul, possess the power of the kin, and finish the job that had been started before time was time. War, slavery, mothers murdering their children because their false god told them to—

Dallin shuddered, his finger once again twitching at the trigger of his gun.

"Wil," he said, because it was all he *could* say—a warning, a plea, a demand, a bone-deep scream hidden within the speaking of it, he didn't know.

It didn't matter, because Wil understood it, whatever it was. He nodded slowly and took a long, deep breath. "Yes. It's time." He looked again at Wheeler as he withdrew the knife, hand curled comfortably around the grip between the cross guards—like it belonged there and always had. "Speak your spells, fraud. My Guardian is impatient to watch your daemon-god reward you for your service."

Wheeler frowned, real curiosity, and tilted his head. "You really do intend to defy the Father."

"He is *not*," Wil seethed, razorsoft, "the Father."

"No?" Wheeler merely shrugged. "You shall see."

His hand rose too quickly, and Dallin's gun automatically came up, thumb chambering a round. Wheeler paused, smiling, mock-indulgent, and opened his surcoat slowly to withdraw a flask from its inside breast pocket. He held it out to Wil. Dallin only watched as Wil's gaze narrowed on it, hung there, unreadable.

"I expect you'll be wanting this." The soft tone of Wheeler's voice was belied by the hard little smirk crooking his mouth.

Dallin didn't think he'd ever hated anyone so much as he did Wheeler right that minute. He tensed, and it had nothing whatever to do with trust or confidence or faith. Dallin had seen addicts —he'd seen the want, however reluctant, the need, unbearable and entirely necessary, and Wil had been dependent on the stuff for almost as long as he'd been alive. The sensation of it must still linger, even if it hadn't been for Calder. As far as Dallin knew, it never truly went away, and it didn't matter how necessary the drug might be to what Wil—they—had to do, because Dallin still hated Wheeler for handing it over so smugly, for the self-satisfied assurance in his gaze as he watched Wil's face, waited eagerly for that first sip as Dallin waited with his gut curling in on itself.

Inscrutable, silent, Wil reached out slowly to settle his fingers around the slick silver of the flask, careful not to touch Wheeler.

"You expect a lot of things." Wil hesitated for only a moment before taking the flask. Eyes never leaving Wheeler, Wil removed the cork with his teeth and spat it aside, took a whiff from the slim neck of the flask before he shook his head. "But I expect not."

Wheeler wasn't the only one who was surprised when Wil tipped the flask's contents into the running veins of the Flównysse.

Dallin said nothing, confused though thoroughly impressed, but Wheeler's face twisted—anger, thwarted expectation, and a flicker of genuine fear he couldn't quite cover. He slid a quick glance over his shoulder—his men captive and guarded, bound, slouching in a dejected row against the cavern's far wall and no help at all. His dark eyes turned on Dallin, enraged and frustrated, before shifting back to Wil.

"Delay will do you no good. I am your doorway. If you would challenge the—"

Wil snapped the knife back up beneath Wheeler's chin.

Wheeler opened a hand. "If you would challenge him, you must allow me to follow. I am your key."

Wil only snorted as he drew back, flipped the knife in his palm, and shook his head. He slipped the knife back into his boot.

"I shrink to imagine the locks." He took hold of Wheeler's coat and leaned in. "You won't be following. You'll be leading." Wil shot a sharp look at Dallin, a tiny nod. "Don't take too long." He turned back to Wheeler, captured his gaze, and smiled. "Don't worry," he told Wheeler softly, "this is what you want."

Eyes gone bright and dark all at once, shifting and churning, almost their own source of darkling vert ghost-light. Dallin didn't have time to so much as blink, let alone react, before he felt the surge and shiver rattle inside him, the shift of power as Wil gathered strength from all around him and *pushed*.

They went still, Wil and Wheeler, locked in a gaze of mutual loathing, the empty flask dangling from Wil's lax fingers. Dallin only stared for a moment, wondering uncomfortably if this was what it had looked like before, when his and Wil's soulless bodies were entangled on the floor of the cave while their spirits had been standing before the Mother—empty, defenseless husks. He peered over at Corliss and Andette and Woodrow, looking back at him like they knew, and he supposed they did; they, after all, had seen it before.

"We watch the Watcher." Andette dipped her head on a confident nod, hands gripping her rifle and back straight, chin out.

Dallin eyed the Old Ones chanting their soft songs, all eyes slightly hazed as though watching something inside themselves, concentrating. Dallin blew out a long breath, let their song wind through him, let the magic of Fæðme slide into his blood to beat a pulsing tattoo through his heart and mind.

He shut his eyes and followed.

Not the star-pocked nothing, not the river, not anywhere Dallin has seen before. Clean and stark, soft prismed planes that nevertheless gyrate and spasm now and then, landscapes curling into vistas. From great swaths of emerald grasses, bowing and shuddering in a breeze he can't feel, to a panorama of pristine snowscape, the clear ice-blue of a frosted lake spiderwebbed with fairy lace, then sand, then the blasted nothing of solitary nightmare, tinged indigo and burned at the edges in the twisting colors of flame. The dreamscapes of one who has seen them only inside the minds of others, found beauty in each one that he could keep and make his own. Like picking up a stone or leaf that appeals to a singular sense of beauty and stowing it in a battered pack. The facets lash out in every direction as far as the eye can see, and Dallin thinks there are probably more he can't see, scope beyond scope, and it seems so extraordinarily fitting that he has to smile. This, after all, is the creation of a mind that's vast and flung wide, open and seeking, and if Dallin loved Wil for nothing else, he would love him for this.

Solid ground beneath his feet, and it's like Dallin is only halfway here. If he tries, he can see both at once: his body standing stock-still and rigid inside a pitiless embrace of malachite, breathing the thick spice of the incense Thorne splashed into the lamps, Dallin's own hand resting heavy on Wil's shoulder; the rest of him right here in this place of bewitching impracticalities, actually watching Wil's mind work all around him. It's slightly vertiginous, but not alarmingly so.

It's impossibly full of horizons—horizons with dazzling, jagged edges, skies boiling obsidian, heavy and hung with silver, the blinding patina of it carving its way into his retinas, imprinting itself behind his eyes, strobing through his head and stretching the boundaries of his mind. Borders washed black with shadows that move like ghosts, hunched and crooked and creeping with goblin stealth, forming and reforming like the ebb and flow of an empty sea.

With anyone else, it would be frightening. With Wil, it's merely strange and beautiful, somewhat telling.

"Dreaming awake," Wil had told Dallin once, as Wil had stood in Chester's stables and nearly wept because it didn't hurt. Dallin thinks perhaps this was where Wil had been wandering then, thinks this is the place Wil's spirit reaches for when it's not being battered and abused, when he can finally dream dreams that are his, and Dallin can't help but smile that he's found it.

Wil has changed himself again. Not the sprung boots and threadbare tunic he'd worn for Her, but a plain white shirt that drapes soft from straight shoulders, tails tracing loosely over dark trousers that flare to a slight crease over his bare feet. Unadorned but for the knife in his hand and the little crystal on its chain against his breastbone. His arm isn't held stiff and awkward against his torso, there is no edge of a makeshift bandage peeking out from the V of the half-laced shirt, and once again his face is unbruised and unmarred but for the bright stripe of his Mark. He is strong here, tall and powerful, eyes aglow, and his wounds are elsewhere, in another world, on a body that stands on mortal ground and feels pain for which there is no use here.

Dallin looks down at himself, strangely disappointed that he again wears his filthy shirt and damp coat, boots now coated in drying mud and the fine green dust of Fæðme, his arm still throbbing dully. He rubs at his chin, expecting to find at least a day's growth of scraggy, itchy beard, but he doesn't.

"You don't have it over there, y'know," Wil had whispered to him, that first kiss still humming at Dallin's lips, and Dallin thinks about that for a long moment before tucking it away—perhaps useful but not yet usable.

Wheeler is the same, only he looks somehow more craven here, smaller and slyer, as if the skin of the respected general had fit ill before and his true character has no choice but to show itself as the vile little thing it is. Dark eyes gone black and flat as coal, smile gone blatantly hungry. Dallin would almost not be surprised if Wheeler appeared as a misshapen little imp, gnashing razor teeth and cackling greedily because it couldn't help itself. *And he's got the bloody gall to wear marks here. Dallin could kill him for that alone.*

"Impressive," Wheeler tells Wil, gaze calculating and perhaps a touch uneasy.

Dallin doesn't even try to hide the smirk. Wheeler had been expecting to have the broken, frightened Chosen, leaf-stupid and at his command, and here he is, faced with the son of gods.

"Not really." Wil shrugs as though this world of marvels and curiosities he's built is nothing special. "There's more that you can't see—you haven't enough magic in you. There's more that even I can't see. There are other worlds than ours, and we're all bound by truths we don't even know about." He smiles at Wheeler, somewhat pitying. "I know you think you're quite powerful, chosen by your dog-god, but it's only that you're weak and vain. Shamans could do what you do, y'know. You're not terribly special. You're only just wicked and greedy enough to consent." He takes a step in and fixes Wheeler with a somber stare. "You don't have to do this. You haven't crossed your last line yet. You've a chance, still."

Dallin's heart slows down, genuinely unsure what he hopes Wheeler will answer. Dallin wants Wheeler dead, punished, something. "Go forth and do no more evil" no longer seems possible, and Dallin doesn't think Wheeler's vanity or fear of his god would permit it anyway. But to witness it happening holds an odd allure for Dallin, even with the need for vengeance knocking heavily in his chest. Wheeler is being handed one last chance by the one he would see owned, possessed, and displaced, and there's a strange sort of beauty in the offer that tugs at Dallin's soul—a plain and very definitive beauty in the one who extends it in an open hand. Certainly more generous than Dallin could be. Then again, Dallin has suspected, before he even realized he was suspecting, that Wil is a better man than he is, so he's not terribly surprised.

Wheeler doesn't hesitate, doesn't even think it over. He merely smiles, smug now, as if he's taken the very real offer of reprieve as a sign of weakness and fear. It's interesting to watch his mind work like this, and Dallin can see now how Wheeler had managed to manipulate his way to the mortal power he holds and the immortal power he craves. Always calculating, measuring, and he does get close to his mark, but he doesn't quite hit it. Dallin thinks it's because Wheeler sees things only through the shadow of his own lust and greed. It hardly matters now, but it's interesting.

"I do genuinely regret your fate, Aisling," Wheeler says, "but all rewards require sacrifice. My god does not fear you, and neither do I."

The anger that was almost receding in Dallin rises again. He thinks of all the young men who marched to their deaths beneath this man's command, believing right up 'til the last that their commander would not ask for unnecessary blood, never even suspecting that his strategies were driving toward a goal that would have surely meant mutiny had they known. Dallin can hear their ghosts crying out to him as clearly as he'd heard the previous Guardian call his name. The betrayal is profound, and there is not enough rage, Dallin thinks, to equal its enormity.

"Your god doesn't know him very well," Dallin says, deadly soft. He smiles; it feels like a blade across his mouth, sharp and lethal. "And neither do you." He turns his gaze to Wil. "You gave him his chance."

Wil nods sadly, but his back is straight and his face impassive as he snaps his wrist, the dagger landing with a soft hiss, hilt-up, *between Wheeler's boots. Wheeler directs a quick look down but doesn't move.*

"Call your spells," Wil tells him, "before my Guardian abandons his control and throttles you for your betrayal of his countrymen."

There are so many things in the command that make Dallin's heart heat and swell, "my Guardian" among them, which has a possessive pride inside it that Dallin thinks would make him strong even in his weakest moment. But more—Wil knows, Wil understands. He has spoken the betrayal and laid it as an accusation at the usurper's feet. And Dallin never had to explain it to him. Dallin feels ashamed that he wouldn't have done, even had Wil asked. He's kept too much of himself back, kept things locked away from a man who's offered him everything, and the dishonor is a hot red iron in his gut.

"Wil." Dallin pauses and shakes his head when Wil looks back at him, eyebrows raised, expectant. "I only... if we get out of this...." Dallin opens his hands. "I took too long, and I didn't give enough. I let the quickmud keep too tight a hold, and I'm sorry. I mean to do better."

Wil's smile is soft and private, just for Dallin, but Wheeler chuckles, derisive.

"A pretty sentiment, for what it's worth, but I fear you will not live long enough to do anything about it." He shrugs at Dallin, unconcerned. "There is no more use for you, boy. You are a ghost, and the true Guardian now claims his place."

It should drive the rage up, but Dallin only rolls his eyes.

"Come, lad," Wheeler tells Wil, and reaches for him. "Let us be along with our business."

The intent is clear, and Wil steps back, trepidation showing on his troubled face for the first time. His own hand rises, fingers no doubt grazing over the scars beneath his hair.

"*Just say it.*" It's a growl. A literal growl. "*I don't want you touching me.*"

Wheeler sighs, impatient. "*You killed the man who found it, don't you remember?*" His mouth pinches, mild disgust. "*A man of great magic and a martyr to my Deartháireacha. But he made sure the knowledge would remain for the Cleric, the true Guardian.*" He lifts his hands again. "*Come, then, no use delaying.*"

Wil peers at Dallin, mouth tight and gaze poignant. All Dallin can do is reach out, lay his hand on Wil's shoulder, and stand at his back as he is meant to do. Wil shifts ever so slightly into the touch, then sighs out a loose, shaky breath and submits. Wheeler grins, hungry, as he slides his fingers into Wil's hair, leaning in closer than he needs to. Dallin has to use all his will to restrain himself from knocking Wheeler away, breaking every bone in those grasping hands, saving the fingers for last to shatter slowly and one at a time.

"*Drút Hyse,*" Wheeler breathes.

Beloved Son.

Dallin's heart nearly breaks wide open as he watches Wil's eyes close, his brow twist, and his mouth trace the words in a silent echo. His name, spoken aloud, heard for the first time, and Wil had said it would likely hurt hearing it from this man's mouth, but Dallin hadn't expected it to pierce him as well, just watching the mingling of relief and new pain etch itself in acid furrows across Wil's face.

There is no time to ponder it or let the pain take hold, because the change is instant and undeniable. The air shifts, building pressure, and the rank smell of death and decay all at once encloses Dallin in a tight fist, cloying and heavy. He gags on it.

The horizons stretch and shatter, and in the moment before they rebuild themselves, there are clots of stars hemorrhaging through, screaming, and the shrieking blare of them makes Dallin wonder if his ears are bleeding. Everything shifts again, and then again— they're standing on the nothing of Wil's threads and Dallin's stars, *then there is grass beneath their feet, the solid ground of Lind sliding out from beneath them and shifting to brittle malachite, then the stone floor of the constabulary, the oily flicker of the lamps skidding behind Dallin's eyes and into his nose, then places he's never been, things he's never seen. The vertigo is nauseating.*

"What the fuck?" *Dallin wheezes, weak with the sensation of being thrown from one nonreality to another and another before he can blink his stinging eyes even once. He reaches out, unthinking, and slams Wheeler's hands away from Wil, drags Wil back and away with a frantic grip and a few stumbling steps on ground, then floor, then nothing.*

"He's trying to take it away," *Wil hisses, eyes shut tight, and he reaches for Dallin's hand, clutches it, panic-stricken. Says,* "Give it to me," *and that's all.*

Dallin doesn't have to ask what Wil wants. He lets whatever Wil needs flow from feet that are planted firmly in Fæðme, attached to some other body, up through Dallin, and out to Wil. Intermediary, *Dallin thinks wildly,* Doorway, *and opens the floodgates.*

The ground stops slipping and morphing, and Dallin stops feeling like he might spew any second, but it isn't done yet, and he wishes the ground were the worst of it.

Wheeler isn't Wheeler anymore—he isn't anyone, or even anything—a loose blot of man-shaped matter, face and form mutating in a constant flow of skin tone and hair color, contour and countenance. He screams, something wrenching and filled with pain, and Dallin can't help the wince, the way his hand tightens on Wil's, the horror and agony sliding through the shrieks so vivid Dallin thinks he can taste it—bitter and rotting and coppery on his tongue. The urge to vomit climbs again, but Dallin wills it back. He wished for this scant seconds ago, this vengeance that's so obviously torturous, and now that he has it, he wishes it would just stop.

Wil's hands come up over his ears, and he stoops as if he's in pain. "He's doing it already."

Dallin keeps the power flowing, reaches out and builds what stanchions he can. It's enough, but it won't be forever. This is more than Síofra's small attempts to influence his mind, more than Wheeler's blunt pushing. This is big, this can beat him if he's not very careful, or if he loses his hold for even a second. He pulls himself open, sends what Wil can take, and holds the rest, setting himself beneath it like a yoke across his shoulders.

Wil straightens, breathing easier, glancing about, and his gaze stops dead at what was Wheeler only a short while ago—still writhing and contorting but gathering shape to itself now, solidifying. Dallin doesn't expect it to resolve itself into Síofra, and apparently neither does Wil, because Wil gasps and jerks back into Dallin, stumbling in his bare feet and shaking. Síofra just stands there for a moment, smiling that arrogant smile, blue eyes over white teeth, before he tilts his head, extends his limbs, and sighs. It's as though he's stretching himself inside his body.

"That isn't Síofra," Dallin whispers to Wil.

Wil only shakes his head, trembling, rasps "No," and keeps staring.

Æledfýres broadens himself in Síofra's body as if it's a mask that doesn't altogether fit, though the smile remains, clever and charming but with something rotten and vile beneath it. "Ah, my lad." He speaks with Síofra's voice or something very near, holding out his arms as though he expects Wil to run right into them. "At last, here we are, you and I. Where we belong."

Wil's eyes are too wide and wild. "No" is all he says, and Dallin doesn't know if it's an answer to the statement or complete denial.

"Come to me, lad," not-Síofra says. "You loved me once. You love me still. You can't help yourself. Come to me. I can love you *now as you've always wanted, and you don't have to be ashamed anymore for wanting it."*

Wil shoots a quick, anxious look at Dallin, his face paling to wax, and he wrenches his gaze away, shuts his eyes. "Don't." It's raspy and small, and he jerks away from Dallin, snatches his hand back—not tall and strong now, but drawing himself in, reflexively making himself smaller. "I don't love you. I never did, I never could, and I don't—"

"Locks and chains, cages and shackles." The voice is smoother now, as though he's getting the feel for it.

Not-Síofra flicks his fingers, and a sound like screeching metal whines into Dallin's ears. Dallin doesn't know what it is until Wil gasps again, lifts his hand, and a rusted chain hangs from a shackle at his mangled wrist, the skin raw and scraped in a bloody flap that sloughs down over the back of his hand. Dallin makes a grab for him —to calm, to comfort, to tear it off—but Wil flinches away.

"Come now, Aisling, did you think I never knew your most secret wish? The shame that chokes you because you can't help wishing for it?" Not-Síofra tsks, blue eyes sad and somber. "I was as a father to you. I can be that father now."

"Stop it." Wil's eyes are locked on the iron at his wrist, and Dallin can tell it's taking everything in Wil not to try to pull his hand free as he'd done when the shackle was real.

Dallin steps closer. "Wil." He says it quietly as he reaches out, takes Wil's arm, and lifts it up between them, the blood running down Wil's forearm, over Dallin's fingers, and staining Wil's white shirt. "It isn't real."

"I didn't love him," Wil snarls.

"And d'you think it would be so terrible if you did?" Dallin takes another small step closer, dips his head, but Wil won't look at him, gaze nailed helplessly to the bloody metal.

The same tangled web of love mixed with hate Dallin has seen in any number of children whose fathers have a bit too much liking for a switch or a belt or even his fists—whose mothers have eyes that can go from soft and maternal to wrathful and hard between one breath and the next. Tears wept bitterly not for the physical pain, but for the small, trusting heart beneath it that breaks every time the pain comes—the cheated confusion, the inner cry at the perfidy of the one who is supposed to love and protect and instead turns on them, hurting them, and the constant litany of whywhywhy? *burning at the spirit. Loving them still, because there is love inside and it has nowhere else to go; wanting them to love back, because being alone and unloved is any child's constant nightmare.*

Does Wil think Dallin has never seen it before? He hasn't lived it, surely, but he's certainly seen it enough. Children with blackened eyes and swollen mouths eagerly grinning through split lips, eyes shining as the hand that had hurt them just the night before now lays itself tenderly on a shoulder. The unabashed basking in the tiniest show of love, the most miniscule validation. Does Wil really think Dallin so naïve? Or does he simply not understand that it was all part of the steady erosion of a child's spirit, and that Wil had stopped the slide himself with no help from anyone at all—no stern constable arriving when he heard the screaming, hauling those fists away, clamping them in shackles so they couldn't hurt anymore— that Wil chose his aloneness and his pain over the self-betrayal of handing over his soul and never gave the man who called himself Father the one thing with which he could have broken Wil for good?

There are no words, and if there are, they are too many to speak now. Dallin grips Wil's fingers, slippery with blood, says, "Look," and when Wil slowly lifts his gaze from his own hand, turns it to Dallin, Dallin shows him. Shows him it's all right, it's not shameful, doesn't make Wil depraved or mad or weak. Says, "Look," and shows him that Dallin knows, that he understands, that he's seen it before and it's painful but not appalling.

"I did," Wil admits, shaky and still a bit feeble. "I wanted—"

"We all do," Dallin tells him. "It doesn't make you weak. It makes you normal."

Wil nods and swipes, annoyed, at his eyes. "You told me that once before."

"Did I?" Dallin blinks. "Wiser than I'd thought. You should listen to me more often."

There is no sudden pop or clank of metal—the shackle is merely gone, the gruesome ragged wound and blood with it, the familiar pink puckered scar back as it's always been since Dallin spotted it in the ill-lit cellar room of the constabulary. Wil's shirt isn't even stained anymore. Dallin drops a kiss to Wil's hair, sighs relief. The first battle, and they've won it, and all it took was the truth. It gives him hope.

There's laughter now, easy and amused. Dallin knows it, has known it for years, and he pushes Wil away slowly, then turns, all at once crowded by dread.

"I fucked him, you know," Ramsford says, that laconic grin that used to make Dallin's stomach do tiny flips dropping amiably over his mouth. "He was better than you—at least he knows how to pretend he loves a man. But then, I expect you'd know." Ramsford winks, all sly conspiracy. "All he cost me was clean sheets and an extra blanket. I tossed in the sausages for free. The lad was so skinny!" Chestnut hair that's always been too long curls over his ears, flopping over that wide, clear brow with a familiarity that stings. *"Damn good, he was, but I didn't know until too late that he was eating my soul all the while."*

Wil has gone stiff and tense. "I didn't."

"I know" is all Dallin says, but he can't take his eyes away. Síofra had been strange, but this is... just wrong. *"He's got in my head."* He's sickened by the thought and shocked by the fact that he hadn't felt it, but the proof is in front of him, undeniable. *"I can't*

block him, not when I'm open like this." Dallin fists his hands and stares, revolted, at the glamour of his friend—handsome, kind, dependable Ramsford—as it mocks him in a voice that once skirled into Dallin's ear in heated whispers in the dark. "Fucking hell."

Ramsford chuckles, the scornful tone of it grating against the affable mien of his friendly face. "Is he better than me?" he croons to Dallin, all silk and treacle, then slants a crafty glance at Wil. "He doesn't know how to love, boy, though he'll fool you with his pretty talk. Strung me for three years, did 'honest' Constable Brayden." He tilts his head, sly sympathy. "Told me I impressed him." His smile crimps into a malicious imitation of rueful when Wil hisses a sharp breath in through his teeth. "I was just a green boy, easily flattered— how could I resist?"

It's lies, strung through with just enough truth to make it ache. Dallin wants to deny it all nonetheless, but he keeps his mouth clamped tight.

"He'll leave you when he's through with you too, boy. How could he love the man who killed his mother?"

Wil gasps as though he's been sucker punched. Dallin turns to Wil, reaches for him, means to deny it, but a woman's voice stops him cold.

"Dallin-love," it murmurs, soft and perplexed, "what have you done?"

All the air goes out of him, and his fragile grip on hope loosens and falls away.

"Mum" drags from his mouth before he can stop it. Dallin shuts his eyes, refuses to turn, reaches out blind for Wil, but no hand meets his, no long, slender fingers wrap comfort around his own.

"Tell me it isn't true," his mother's voice demands, just enough confused query in it to make it almost believable. "He told them where I was, Dallin, pointed the way, and they came with their swords and their torches."

"Shut up," he wheezes, hoarse and heavy.

"They burned *me*, Dallin, did he tell you that? And you would choose him?"

Burned alive—Dallin has always feared it, never wondered, pushed it away, and convinced himself her death was as clean as the runes on the notice that had listed her name among the dead, gentle as Mrs. Tanner's voice when she'd read it to him. Burned alive, a blackened skeleton, the very first of his ghosts, kept company by but set above the children of Lind, and he supposes he knows now why those of Ríocht and Kenley have haunted him so.

"No," Wil warbles, weak and watery. "It's not.... She didn't, Dallin, I swear. She... this isn't... it's... I...."

Dallin knows she didn't burn, he does. Wil doesn't lie, but—

He isn't just inside Dallin's head—he's inside nightmares Dallin has refused to know he had.

It's strange, now that Dallin thinks about it, now that it's slammed him in the chest, that he never asked Wil how she died when Wil confessed to having been there when she breathed her last. No, not strange, not really—one more thing Dallin had buried, refused to look at, though the horror of it has been waiting inside him, a malignant seed sprung to life by a daemon wearing his mother's face, speaking with his mother's voice, and this... this is low. This is obscene.

A chittering buzz leaks over his mind, spreading like the skittering legs of an army of spiders kicked from their nest and marching over his thoughts. An exploratory prod, seeking cracks, then a push that rocks him just enough to make him pay attention. He wants to slam down his defenses, clamp his barriers over everything he is, but he catches himself just in time. Instead he throws power at it, feels it like ropes of lightning in his hands, and spears it with whatever strength and magic is his.

A scream in his mother's voice, the pungent stink of burned

hair, the stench of charring meat. "Dallin-lad!" A pitiful shriek. "You know how he loves the burning. Would you let him murder me twice?"

Going for the soft underbelly, because he's in Dallin's head, pulling out all the things that are Dallin's and parading them in front of him, and all Dallin can do is look away. Driving the knife deep because he can—Dallin handed it to him, he knows, and there's nothing Dallin can do but endure it.

"It isn't real." He clenches his teeth and shakes his head, a light spring of clammy sweat threading his brow. "She isn't there. It isn't her." Then, a little desperate: "Wil?"

And he's there, taking Dallin's hand, telling him, "It isn't true, she didn't burn," in a wavering voice that's just this side of panicked. "I didn't tell them about her, Dallin, I swear. You don't—"

"I know." Dallin's whole body is heavy, weighted down, and he opens his eyes, looks first at Wil—notes the look of fear that just won't do, not here, not now, so he repeats, "I know," urgent, because Wil really needs to believe it. Wil's strength is huge and limitless but too fragile a thing, and he never believes its depth, and they need it now.

They're on the defensive, trying to hold their own, get their bearings, when the strategy is so obvious it makes Dallin's pride curl up in shame that he's allowing it. His focus is scattered and too driven by reacting—damn it, he's better at war than this. The monster is winning quietly but steadily, pushing so subtly and slyly, burying the real danger inside this cheap overt offensive, that it's slipping right past them both—and Dallin's just standing here and letting him do it.

"Push him back," he tells Wil, low and through his teeth. "Make him bleed."

Wil looks over Dallin's shoulder and shies away from whatever he sees, wild eyes skittering back to Dallin's. He shakes his head. "You... she's your—"

"That," Dallin snarls, "is not my mother." Another shriek, and now the sounds are getting to him, fire crackling and hissing, and he wants more than anything to just haul himself out of this place, shut down everything, and flee. He takes hold of Wil's arms. "I need you. I can't do this. I don't have the right magic. This isn't—" He blinks away the stinging behind his eyes. "You have to do it." Quiet and as composed as Dallin can make it. "For me, Wil. Please."

He doesn't know how much of it is for his benefit and how much of it is for Wil's, but he watches it ease Wil, watches Wil dig down and find his concentration and calm. That telltale lift of his chin, and Wil merely hardens his gaze and nods.

Dallin steadies himself on that strength, lets Wil see Dallin's belief in it, his reliance on it, before he straightens his back, and turns.

He was expecting something shocking and gruesome, but this... this is bad.

Beautiful, untouched, unmarred, just as he remembers her, young and vital and stronger than the mountains. Her smile is perfection, and Dallin wonders dazedly how Æledfýres has managed to mimic it so flawlessly, how he's managed to imitate the love and comfort and the bit of steel Dallin remembers so well it's like a cramp in his heart. And then he realizes it comes from his own mind, his most precious memories perverted and twisted to another's purpose, and the revulsion shatters through him again. A violation of the mind, the rape of a memory, and it both sickens and infuriates him. He's almost glad he's nailed to the spot, because if he tries to move, he thinks he'll stumble.

"Burn it," he breathes. Æledfýres, the god of bloody fire, and Dallin wants—oh, he wants—to see his own gift used against him, wants the poetic irony to hurt.

Wil only stares at him for a long moment, uncertain. "There are other—"

"Burn it!" Dallin snarls and makes himself watch as what pretends to be his mother watches him back knowingly, that soft look of love and strength twisting into a mask of mock fear and horror. And only now can Dallin truly remove himself, wholly convince himself that this is not his mother—a daughter of Lind, born and bred, she would never show fear so plainly, never open her sorrow like a gift in an open hand, not even when her land was burning around her and she was heaving her only son and the hope of the Mother into the back of a cart. Dallin can watch as white flame closes around her, as her screams wrench the air and split the sky, as her skin bubbles and blisters and burns, as her hair catches and makes a ghoulish halo of her melting face. He can watch as the remains of the mask shrink and blacken and mutate into the twisted form of a child, the Mark blazing fire on a cheek that's not there. He can watch and not feel, which he thinks is the best he can hope for.

Dallin can actually feel the push this time, the shove, the power of Lind coursing through every fiber of him, unfolding itself out to Wil, and Wil takes it in, uses it.

"He's too strong." Wil's voice shakes, but he doesn't give in, doesn't allow so much as a hitch or hiccup as he reels in power, turns it into strength, and hurls it. Æledfýres's chuckle comes from beneath the shrieks in a blackened throat, lurid and too deliberate, and Dallin's mind tells him none of it's real, but a disgusted shudder still walks up his spine.

Wil is panting, the strain all too evident, and Dallin can feel the conflict in the air as though it's the meeting of two storm fronts, a clash of wills that dredges all the oxygen from the air, all the color from the shifting vista. The shrieking of the cindered slag of bone and charred flesh sounds real enough, the pain and thwarted intent inside it adding to the weight that clutches at Dallin's chest and *drags the wind from his lungs. Power runs through him, but it slides into him and back out before he can snatch enough to let him breathe. Wil's hand is clenched tight around Dallin's fingers, sucking everything through him, throwing it all at Æledfýres, pushing as hard as he can and stretching it all around himself and Dallin like a barrier, a penumbra of strength.*

Dallin has a wild, giddy moment of satisfaction—I think he might really do this, then, ha, told 'em all—before there's a shudder in the air, a heavy whine, and Dallin realizes it's not enough. They're still merely holding their own, not gaining ground, and if this is all there is, it could go on forever—or until Wil wearies and can't hold his own anymore. Before Dallin has a chance to dig down and snatch for more, there's a thin pop *and the carcass is gone—just gone—as though it's folded into itself, winked out without prelude or drama.*

Wil stumbles back, shaking and sweating, his breath blowing in and out like he's been drowning. Dallin feels the sharp snap of recoil, that same wallop he'd felt when healing was snatched from his grasp by death at Andette's hands.

"Too easy." Wil shakes his head and cuts his glance everywhere. "He's playing with us."

Dallin doesn't even have time to agree. He's shoved, his hand torn from Wil's, pain like he's never known rupturing through him. Saw-toothed shards of himself rip loose and burst through his chest in breathless agony.

"The Guardian is no more," a deep silky voice whispers to him, and he thinks this is the true voice of the soul-eater, low and seductive as Dallin should have expected of a beguiler. Even inside the revulsion, as pieces of him are torn away, ripping great, gaping holes in his sanity, he hears the beauty inside the tone, the allure. "You are in my way, Mother's mule."

And he's flung, hurtling through nothing, agony chewing him up with gnashing teeth as he reaches out for his own Self, grips it in a mental fist. It only ramps up the torment, his bones liquefying inside muscles turned to broken glass, his mind bellowing in near paralyzing shock and pain, and the harder he hangs on, the more intense the torture becomes. Every nerve ending is lit up in glitter-sharp constellations. He's never even thought to consider what it might feel like for a mind to be ripped loose from a person. He thinks he knows now, thinks he understands what all those unfortu-nates felt just before the dearg-dur swallowed them down, thinks he knows what Wil suffered at the commands of Síofra all those times. Dallin wants to weep in outrage and pain and fury, but he has no eyes from which to squeeze the tears, no body with which to curl in on the pain. He is a formless mass of agony, and if he lets go of the pain, he lets go of his Self. It might almost be worth it, he thinks, screaming with a voice that isn't there, rigid splinters of himself breaking loose inside it.

There isn't enough of him to catch it all, pieces of him slipping through fingers he doesn't have, and he means to call out—to Wil, to the Mother, to anyone—if for nothing else than to do one last thing that's his before he slides into the forever-void that's sucking him down.

"What is your name?" curls through him, and he thinks it should be the Mother's voice, but it isn't. It's his father speaking to him from across time, drilling the lesson into his son so that even when he'd forgotten everything else, he always knew this one thing.

"Dallin Brayden," he answers back. "From the Valley," and "Brave," and he's always known what these things mean, even when he'd forgotten their purpose, but he's never truly understood the other, not 'til now. "Pride's people," he wheezes through the pain in his not-voice, thinks of Lind and its lineage of warriors, its centuries of secrets and unknowing, faithful defense of the Heart of the World.

And finally wonders what sort of power lies hidden in their belief. "If it is strong enough to bind, it is strong enough to free," She'd told Wil. Dallin thinks he knows what that means now.

He gathers himself inward, curls what he can around it, and cries out—

—in a voice that shattered all around him, a ringing bellow that bounded against the walls of the cavern as the shock of standing once again on solid ground recoiled through him, jolting up his legs and backbone. He blinked to clear his vision and found Wil still standing there, eyes liquid and shifting and locked on to Wheeler, who stared back, somehow lax and helpless-looking even in his thrall. Wil's nose was trickling a steady rivulet of blood, dripping down to a small puddle on the floor of the cavern between his boots.

Still there, still locked in some otherworld conflict with the monster. Dallin had somehow left Wil behind, and he didn't even know how.

He didn't take the time for guilt or horror, merely tightened his grip on Wil, eyes settling on the closest one available—Andette, staring at Dallin in something between fright and cool faith as Dallin reached out his hand to her, said "Hurry!" then *"Thorne!"* and waited the barest of moments for Andette's wide hand to lock on to his before he hurled himself—

—back into the nothing of agony, caught in midscream as it all slams back into him, the rip and tear of a soul being shredded from a Self. "Thorne!" he calls again and feels new power burning through him, setting whatever's left of him on fire. It hardly matters—he doesn't think anything could possibly hurt worse than this—so he pulls it all inside him, builds it like a wall around himself, a calm center of silence inside the nothing.

His mind is his, his soul remains, and he's standing once again beside Wil, here and whole, but with his feet planted firmly in the quickmud of Fæðme, his hand locked to Andette's and hers to Thorne's. He thought once that he'd have to be careful where he pointed these people, that their faith could be as dangerous as a loaded gun aimed at the world. He'd forgotten that a loaded gun can mean salvation too, if held in the right hand. He tightens the hand that hangs at the end of the body he left in Fæðme and reaches with the other for Wil.

"Dallin!" Wil cries, voice raw and weak, and he stumbles, sweat seeping through his shirt where Dallin grips his arm. Wil is shaking, not from fear but debility, his strength flowing out of him, and Dallin all at once knows why. It's not surprising to realize that the whole time he's been busy getting ripped apart, Wil has been reaching out for him, trying to keep him whole. Not surprising, no, but it makes Dallin want to scream in frustration, these chances Wil takes. They're always for the right reasons, but he's going to end up paying for it, if he isn't already.

"Take it," he tells Wil, only now notices that Wil bleeds here too, a hard knot of fear grinding in Dallin's gut as he watches the small stream leak scarlet-bright onto the clean white of Wil's shirt.

"The Vessel is too weak," says a voice that's too familiar, and only now does Dallin turn to see Calder—eyes with that same righteous exaltation, shoulder lumped and out of true, Wil's bolt still lodged in his broken wrist, and the blooded white fletching of his niece's arrow jutting from his throat. It bobs obscenely as he speaks. He raises his broken arm, bone grinding and crunching in the shoulder, and points at Wil. "I serve the Aisling, even in this. The Heart of the World sits too heavily on your soul. The Mother seeks to break you beneath it, take it to Herself. She weakens the Father."

"Liar," Wil grinds out, already standing taller, accepting everything flowing through Dallin and steadying himself on it. "You take truths and twist them into lies. You wear faces not your own."

Wil shoves again. Dallin can feel it buffeting through him and is heartened just the smallest bit that not-Calder seems to stagger.

"Show me your own face, fraud." Wil's tone is deeper now, more powerful than only a moment ago. "You hide behind masks and accuse deception. You steal from others and claim it your right."

Calder's form ripples, glimpses of other faces melting into and out of the scarred countenance, some faces Dallin knows and many more he doesn't. The echoes of souls consumed then cut free, he thinks, and shudders.

"It is my right," Calder hisses, the voice now raw and croaking, thick with the obstruction of the arrow. "Do you think yourself so far above me, boy? You've had the taste of it, have you not? You've taken the magic of another, fed on it, and grown stronger with the taking. Do you think your right more righteous than my own?"

The man in Dudley, Dallin thinks. He hadn't really thought it through before, but it's truth; it has to be. Wil's magic before that was weak and sporadic by his own testimony, and after that....

After that, Wil called storms, tamed fire. And Dallin explained it to both of them in ways that made sense, still make sense, but he wonders now if he's known what it all meant and just hasn't dared the knowing.

"Your Guardian knows it." Not-Calder chuckles and jerks his chin at Dallin, the arrow's fletching bobbling gruesomely. "Look at him. He can't help the disgust, can't help the revulsion at knowing that he's been the accomplice to daeva." A slippery little laugh, and Dallin is both shocked and repelled that the face that mocks so casually is now his own. "The things that happened, Wil... they offend me. I don't know how to say it any better. They offend me to my core."

It's Dallin's own voice, coming from Dallin's own mouth, like looking into some kind of noisome mirror. Dallin reaches instinc-

tively for the gun at his hip and wraps his fingers around its grip. Would it do any good here? Can bullets kill if their real shapes exist in another reality?

"I didn't know," he watches himself say. A sad shake of the head, and a hand that's Dallin's but not reaches out toward Wil. "I'm sorry, but you can't think I could countenance this."

Wil's frowning, shaking his head, and he glances helplessly between the two Guardians as though he's unsure which is the truth.

"You are dearg-dur," Dallin's other self says, low and trying for kind but with a hard edge beneath it that makes Dallin's teeth go tight—he's got the inflections down so well that even Dallin's not sure if he's here or there. "I can't love you, Wil. I can't even look at you." And to prove it, dark eyes turn away.

Wil stares, eyes narrowed, scrutinizing, trying to find the flaws and telltales. Dallin thinks to tell Wil not to bother, there won't be any, but he can't seem to bring himself to speak, too unsettled by hearing his voice coming out of... that. His words—Dallin can't deny them—he spoke them, and he'd meant them, he still means them, but not in the way they've been twisted.

"I saw your face." Wil drags his eyes up to Dallin's. "I saw the look on your face when you realized... when you saw what—" His frown deepens. "Why are you here?" He hesitates, lip quivering. "I won't be your task. I won't be your duty."

It nearly staggers Dallin, the doubt sliding through the question, the sudden ache that blooms in his chest, because it was so bloody easy to wake it. The insecurities Síofra planted are rooted too deep. Wil expects to be betrayed and abandoned, as though it's his lot in life.

Dallin tightens his hand around Wil's until he feels bones rubbing together. "Can you doubt me now?" is all Dallin can ask. He turns his gaze on the thing that pretends to be him. "I also told

*him I would do whatever it takes. I told him I want him to do what-
ever he has to do to survive. Did you forget that part, or did it just
not fit your plans?"*

*Wil's fingers twitch in Dallin's grip, but that's all the response
there is.*

*A red wave of rage that's not his pounds through Dallin, sharp
and blazing hot, an oozing, darkling touch from the monster's mind
directly into his. Seeking out Dallin's cracks and weaknesses again,
but only succeeding in revealing his own. He can't take from
Dallin, not this time, but he can impart, whether Dallin wants it
or not.*

*Insanity—oh, save him, the madness is almost a live thing.
Every base emotion there is—envy, fury, greed, hatred, lust—and
beneath that, a low seed of mewling, childish impudence.*

*A teacher of men once, wielder of fire. Æledfÿres was not
always the daemon with no face. Something gone wrong, some
fundamental bit of his being tweaked and twisted out of shape, and
the innovation of damnation tasted so much more delightful than
what his brothers pretended was life. Men were such stupid
animals, anyway—minds so easily bent by a whisper inside their
brittle skulls or a booming voice of authority from a rostrum—too
willing to be cattle, chattel, and so he'd given them their wish.*

*He sipped the first of his dark craft from the screams of the
daughters of men. Their flavor was sweet and piquant, so he moved
on to others, always wanting for More and Better, and when he
found his first sorceress... nectar like he'd never known. It almost
—almost—filled the blanks in his spirit.*

*He took and took some more—it was his to take, his right, for he
owned the strength and the will—they nearly begged him to take, for
weak minds leech the strength of others like ticks to deer.
Revenants, all of them. Corruptible children after his own black
heart. He only gave them what they thought they wanted, after all.*

They'd proved it when they took the Slattern and the Fool as their gods.

And neither envy nor vengeance would suffer the get of the Slattern and the Fool.

Dallin shoves the dark touch from out his mind and squeezes Wil's hand again. Could it really be so simple, so... normal? A jealous soul moved to gluttony, and with the power to take unchecked—finally checked and thwarted, and reeking of furious insanity. The simplicity—the grand mundanity—makes him want to vomit.

He grits his teeth. "You hide behind my face, you spout my words, but you can't seem to get them quite right." He's angry now, and it fills him up, pushes out some of the fear and uncertainty until the pulse that hammers through his head is his own heartbeat. He cocks his head to the side, an odd, slithering realization wending through him.

"He uses others," he tells Wil slowly, "because he can no longer tell which Self is his. I'm not so sure he even has one anymore. All he knows is his own hunger, his own greed, but he's fed on the greed of others for so long it's taken him over." Dallin smiles, for the first time on ground that's sure and real—he knows this, just as he knows when a suspect is lying. "I wouldn't be surprised if he forgets his own face."

The tension in the air notches up again, the push nearly crushing, but Wil pushes back, keeping the middle ground steady. Dallin's hand tightens around his gun, still wondering what would happen if he just leveled it at the not-him and pulled the trigger. It's what he promised to do for Wil, after all, and it seems Æledfýres is just as trapped in Wheeler's body as he would've been in Dallin's, had Dallin prevailed in his half-formed strategy. Dallin raises the gun just to see if there's a reaction, just to test, and it's flung from his grip before his thumb can even twitch toward the hammer.

Dallin's hand feels too light now as he watches the gun dissolve into nothing.

Æledfýres merely chuckles with Dallin's voice, but Wil sighs, contrite.

"I'm sorry," he tells Dallin. "I don't doubt you."

Perhaps not now, but he had. Then again, Dallin's own right-eousness has bitten him on the arse quite a lot since he met Wil, and it's only Wil's own nature that prevents it from killing them both. More, it's what Æledfýres wants, and they've very nearly just handed it to him—the power of belief even now bolsters the power of Lind, and if they don't stand together....

Dallin suppresses a shudder. The emptiness of his holster and his hand unnerves him more than he'd thought it would, but not nearly as much as what they've almost just let happen.

He turns to Wil. "You're right—you're not Wil, you're not Aisling, and you're sure as hell not dearg-dur. You're Drút Hyse, the Father's Gift to the Mother. And you give them what they think they want."

He watches Wil closely, watches the knowing depth of his eyes, as though Wil already guessed but is afraid of what it might make of him. There's sadness there, a bit of revulsion, but no balking. Wil pulls his hand from Dallin's, draws it to his chest, then closes it into a fist, opens it again to reveal the little charm—Sun and Moon, Mother and Father—he'd been so determined not to accept only days ago. He watches Dallin's eyebrows rise, then shrugs, his smile small but real.

The power running through Dallin intensifies. Wil's putting everything into it, building a wall of silence and protection around them, blocking Æledfýres out, even if it's only for a second.

"The rifle." Wil watches Dallin's eyes narrow, then shrugs again, a smartarse little smirk that's too characteristic flickering at the corner of his mouth. "It's a dream, innit?" He shivers, gritting

his teeth to keep the barrier for just another few seconds. "I'm blind to my design," *he goes on, a touch more urgent now.* "Find my key and you'll find his." *He stares long and hard into Dallin's eyes, waiting.*

And Dallin knows, all at once. He almost laughs, because he's surprised and he shouldn't be. This is Wil's element. Wil knows what he's doing, he has done all along; he's just been waiting for Dallin to catch up. Dallin curls his fingers around Wil's, closes the little charm back into Wil's palm, then—

—drew his hand from Andette's, reached out, and slid the rifle's strap from Wil's shoulder. One-handed, careful not to let his grasp slip from Wil's, Dallin placed the rifle into Wil's left hand and held on until the lax grip tightened. Energized and abruptly confident, Dallin reached once again for Andette and smiled when she wordlessly extended her hand and wrapped her fingers around his.

"Lind's power depends on her people lending her the strength of their belief." Dallin smiled again when Thorne and several of the Old Ones bowed their heads in what Dallin guessed was profound relief. Dallin couldn't really blame them. He pushed out a quick breath. "Drút Hyse stands now for the Father. And the power of Lind shall stand for him. Get ready." He didn't wait for reactions or questions, merely—

—*shoots a quick look at Wil, closes his eyes, and steps back. Lets go.*

Wil staggers with the loss of contact, the power ripping all around them suddenly shifting, a slight tremor rumbling beneath their feet, and a hole opens up in the sky above them. The stars leak through it, shrieking their songs, and Dallin watches them, listens for sense inside the chaos, thinks about Fate and threads and how it hurt Wil's soul when he changed them. Thinks about how Wil has never been able to find his own, tried and failed to find those of the ones who hunted him, how one does not make a being entrusted with such power invulnerable or all-powerful, and how Calder once told them that the Mother's wisdom in the making of the Guardian complemented the Father's.

Wil's hand goes almost immediately to his brow, and he shakes his head, swipes at his nose, and draws his hand back bright with blood. He sways, just a little, but Dallin sees it and frowns.

Too pale too quickly, gaze gone hazy, Wil shakes his head again as if to clear it, then levels a wobbly glare at Æledfýres. "Take off that face." His voice is tight and thin. He looks at his hand as though he's bewildered by the blood on his fingers, then clenches it into a tight fist. "Take it off!" A command this time, enraged and feral-eyed. Wil moves away from Dallin, lurching this time, and frowns again before he leans to the side and spits blood.

Dallin hadn't realized how quickly Wil would fade, how quickly he'd lose his footing when Dallin stopped sending him power. Now that Dallin sees it, new fear swarms through him and pushes out almost everything else. Time is almost as much of an enemy as Æledfýres is—Dallin can't waste a second of it.

"He can't remember his own," Dallin goads, the pain sliding into him again, dull agony creeping in, but he doesn't let his mind tear loose this time, just stands there and takes it and keeps gathering power—his hand to Andette's, to the Old Ones, to Lind. He bares his teeth at Æledfýres. "Show yourself, if you remember how. Take me on, if you've the nerve, but you won't use that face against him."

"Mm, so touching." Æledfýres chuckles. "My boy," he says, Dallin's own voice, strangely kind, "you demand as though you've a right or a choice or even a hope. Nevertheless." He waves a hand.

Dallin expected intense relief when his own eyes finally stopped looking back at him, but a new shock weaves through him when he finds himself looking into eyes too like Wil's. Bloody fuck, *he thinks, stomach sinking and new sweat springing to his brow,* one of *You might've mentioned at some point that he can do* that.

"*Father?*" *Wil breathes, eyes cloudy and dull, that constant green pulse down to no more than a murky spark. Terrible confusion crowding out everything else on his face and spiking Dallin's fear down his backbone, hard and fast. Wil reels, the blood not just dripping from his nose now but gushing, and this was an insane plan, a terrible plan, it's not working—a huge fucking mistake.* "*Father,*" *Wil whispers and steps toward the monster.*

No! *Dallin wants to shout. That isn't Him, can't you tell?* but he *can't, he's paralyzed, silenced, sent back into that in-between of Watching, put aside, and it isn't Æledfyres that's done it this time but Wil. And it matters. That blinding agony that's become too familiar is still ripping through Dallin, still trying to rend him from himself, compounded now by the strength of the Mother, of Lind, of her people, all pouring into him until he thinks his soul will burst. It isn't meant for him, only to go through him, and right now it's got nowhere else to go—he's a bloody dam for it. He concentrates on feeling the sweaty grip of Andette's hand around his in another where, concentrates on not letting go.*

"*Father,*" *Wil says again, his tone heartbreakingly sure now, and he extends a hand, says,* "*Help.*"

If Dallin could move, he'd reach out and snatch Wil back from the monster. He can't, he can only Watch, and he's not even sure Wil knows he's got Dallin pinned, not even sure if Wil did it on purpose or if he's so far gone he doesn't realize what he's done. It couldn't have been worse if Æledfyres had planned it himself. Then again, perhaps he did—how the fuck would Dallin know?

Æledfyres closes his hand around Wil's and draws him in until they're only inches apart. He smiles, all kindness and love, and Dallin is once again amazed and revolted that Æledfyres is so bloody good at imitation.

"I never stopped believing," Wil whispers, and it nearly breaks Dallin's heart because it's so sincere. Wil really believes this is the Father, and Dallin can't do a bloody thing about it. "You guided me even in Your weakness, and I never stopped believing You'd come back."

"Darling boy." Æledfýres runs his fingers through Wil's hair, brushing it gently from off his brow. "I would not forsake you like all the others. Síofra has been punished. All who have defied me will be punished." He spares a small, crafty smile for Dallin before turning it softer, lifting Wil's chin with a slender hand and swiping at some of the blood with a long white finger. "What lies in you was once mine. It's too much for you. Forgive me. I never meant to hurt you. Let me help you, lad, and we will go to the Mother together. All you need do is open to me, dear lovely Son."

"Together," Wil murmurs, too soft and distant, and Dallin wonders if it's some kind of spell. Wil had let his defenses down, trying to get up close, trying to deceive the deceiver, to let Dallin take a strike, and now Dallin thinks Wil's been caught in his own trap.

"Is it what you want, dear boy?" Æledfýres asks softly, borderline seductive. "Ah, but I can see it is. It's what you've always wanted, isn't it?"

"Yes." Wil takes Æledfýres's hand and slides it up and over his own smooth cheek. "We all want so badly."

Dallin could weep at the familiar turn of phrase, his gratitude is that deep, and he ignores all the pain, all the inner agony, as Wil's other hand slides behind his back and latches on to Dallin's. The paralysis breaks all at once, and all Dallin has been pulling into himself, all the power, bursts from him and into Wil in one great raging torrent of strength. Dallin's knees should weaken and buckle, but they don't—he's carried on it, in it, the connection to

Wil, to Lind and her people, so deep and profound Dallin thinks he can hear them all, see them all, and all at once.

Battles have gone silent, fingers have stilled on triggers as all hearts and minds look now to Fæðme, sending their strength in the form of faith to the Heart of the World, bolstering what runs through Dallin until Dallin thinks he'll split down the middle and burst himself wide. Wil just keeps taking it all, drawing it out of Dallin and throwing it at Æledfýres in unrelenting surges of brute force, teeth bared and hand clamped tight to the thing that would claim the Father's place. Dallin can feel the push, can feel it like a vise around his own chest, so strong and ruthless that fear for which he doesn't have the wit or time rolls through him.

"This is what you want." Wil's eyes are blazing again and wild.

Æledfýres tries to drag his hand away, surprise and rage plain on his beautiful face, but it's as though their hands are fused together.

Æledfýres is pushing back—Dallin can feel that too, like a solid wall butting up against Wil's offense—but Wil is at least as strong, and he's got the advantage, however small, and they all know it. It can't last, it'll rip the world apart, or take too much from the people of Lind, leave them just as dead behind the eyes as any Æledfýres has taken for himself. It occurs to Dallin only a split second before Wil snaps his head around and shouts, "Dallin!"

Blind to my design, Wil had said to him. Dallin sees him. Dallin has always seen him, has always recognized him, even when design was no more to him than another word.

Dallin reaches through the hole in the sky, doesn't even think about what he's doing and how impossible it is, just closes his eyes and wades through the sea of fates—voices, so many voices, and thoughts and minds and moments and eternities—captures stars right in his hand, testing each for the familiarity of Wil's spirit, seeking the darkling web that's wound around it. And the thread is there at the tips of Dallin's fingers—because it's a dream, innit, you can do anything in a dream, all you have to do is believe hard enough. Dallin does now, enough to take thin air and stardust and turn it into something he can't even really see, and he watches as Wil—

—cocked the rifle one-handed, eyes ablaze and jaw set hard as he set the barrel just beneath Wheeler's chin—

—sets a kiss to Æledfýres's mouth—

—and pulled the trigger—

—and plunges the dagger, still red with Dallin's blood, deep into Æledfýres's chest.

The reverberation was deafening as the shot echoed in the cavern, rolling over the walls of malachite and amplifying until only a slight ringing was left. The chanting continued, hands still linked as every eye turned with removed interest and watched Wheeler's head explode in a shower of blood and bone. Warm wet streaks of it striped Dallin's cheek and forehead and spattered Andette's face and tunic. Wheeler's hand spasmed once, twice, then—

—clenches in Wil's hair, pulling him in, and Dallin can feel the fight raging inside this perversion of a kiss. They've taken away one vessel—only one remains. It's down to this, as Wil has known all along, and nothing Dallin has done or said has changed it. "Don't leave me alive inside a cage," and Dallin promised, and the thread throbs in his hand like the living heart of a star. Fate, *he thinks and slants his gaze upward where the anger and arrogance of Æledfýres rent the sky. Threads and fate and stars and faith and belief and* It's a dream, innit? *and he doesn't need anything but the shrieking songs of the stars, the portents in their cadence, and the knowledge that Wil is just barely holding on—if Dallin is going to finish this, he'll need to be quick. He calls—*

—to Thorne, told Andette, "Don't let go!" then—

—grips the Thread in his fist—heaves.

He'd thought the pain before was mind-shattering. This is worse.

An agonized cry wrenches from Dallin's chest, and it takes everything he has to keep from losing his grip, keep pulling and tearing as he hears the screams curling up from the throat of Æledfýres, the sudden turn of his attention to Dallin and what he's doing. The agony doubles; Dallin almost can't believe someone can feel this much pain and still be alive, and then he almost wishes he wasn't. He understands fully now, the torture Wil endured for decades, and yes, pulling the trigger to prevent this would be a mercy, and Dallin would do it without hesitation. He wishes he could gather the breath to tell Wil so, but it's all Dallin can do to hold on, to keep his grip, and keep the power humming through him and into Wil.

Æledfýres is divided now, half his attention on holding on to Wil and the other half on trying to knock Dallin loose. He can't do both, he hasn't the strength or the magic, it's only a matter of time, and if Dallin can just hold out—

He feels the shift like a landslide beneath his feet, and he jolts, shouts, "No, Wil, don't!" even as he sends every bit of raw power to him, tries to reach for him—but it's too late, and why hadn't he realized, why hadn't he guessed? "Damn you, Wil, it's not yours, it's mine!"

Dallin is a helpless witness as Wil takes advantage of Æledfýres's diversion, gives one last great shove, before he gathers himself with a wild little grin, says, "I am Drút Hyse. And you are not my Father."

He wrenches the dagger, then twists.

Stops pushing and pulls it back. All of it.

Dallin is rocked, the thread ripping violently from out his hands and careening at Wil in an explosion of searing color and crude,

*feral power. Wil is sent hurtling backward as Æledfÿres screeches,
all hate and rage and thwarted intent, then crumples with that same
staring emptiness that Dallin had seen in a cell in Dudley.*

The songs of the stars alter, a rising screech that drives right
down into Dallin's spine, the shrieking din of an angry dirge, before
spiraling down into a soft, mourning cry of triumph. It's how Dallin
knows Æledfÿres is truly gone—the stars tell him so. It's over; the
pain is gone, except—

Wil is sprawled gracelessly, too still, face and tunic washed in
blood. It's Chester all over again, except this time his eyes are open
and aware. He watches as Dallin bounds over and crouches down
beside him, trying to wipe some of the blood away with his sleeve,
but there's too much of it. Even the whites of Wil's eyes are bloody,
but the irises still shift and whirl with light and color.

"What did you do?" Dallin's throat is thick and choked with too
much emotion. "Damn you, Wil—you pulled it back. I told you not
to pull it back!" It's accusing and angry but rife with a sorrow
Dallin won't allow himself to feel yet, not yet, it can't be over yet.

"You showed me how." Wil's voice is nothing but a thread-thin
wheeze. "Back in Dudley, remember?"

"No!" Except Dallin did. He'd told Wil to pull it back, but—"I
didn't know what I was doing then, Wil, I wouldn't've—"

"You always know what you're doing." Wil smiles, then coughs,
a thick spray of scarlet erupting from his bloody lips. "Guide is an...
another one of your names. It's Brídín in the North Tongue. Sorta...
sounds like Brayden, dunnit?" It's liquid, a little bit slurred, and
distant, as though Wil's already speaking from far away. He frowns,
bemused. "I've never seen you cry before."

Dallin hasn't realized he's weeping, but he isn't at all surprised.
"What did you do?" His voice is hoarse and rough and just on the
edge of cracking right down the center. Dallin is doubly dismayed
to see the wounds from before—the scrapes and gouges over Wil's

cheek and temple, the bloom of blood at his shoulder—like Wil's been holding on to his inner image of strength and wholeness and is now letting it go. Dallin clenches his teeth, reaches, and finds ruptures and bleeding in too many places, damage so terrible he almost can't see it all. "Wil... no." *He shakes his head helplessly.* "What did you do?"

Wil doesn't answer, just opens his hand, the little charm—Sun and Moon—pulsing to the faltering rhythm of his heart, and curls the other around the crystal at his breastbone.

"Changed my fate." *Wil reaches a shaking hand into nothing and pulls back the dagger he'd driven into Æledfýres. He cradles it against his breastbone.* "No cage. No bullet."

It sounds like a confession, or an absolution. It sounds like good-bye.

"Wil... don't." *Dallin is still trying frantically to heal what he won't admit can't be healed.* "Please. Please, Wil—"

"Do you trust me?" *Wil asks softly.*

Dallin doesn't know what it means, but Wil does, so Dallin just says, "Yes," *without giving himself a chance to think about it.*

"Apples and potatoes, Dallin." *Wil smiles.* "Are you impressed?"

No, *Dallin wants to answer,* I'm crushed and heartsore and angry and grieved, and how could you do this to me? *But before he can so much as force an answering smile, try to coerce some kind of response from his clogged throat, Wil closes his eyes, blood like tears sliding from the corners, stark on too-white skin. And doesn't open them again.*

"No!" *Dallin snarls, tears choking him, and when was the last time he's wept? He takes hold of Wil's arm, shakes him—*"Where's the bloody badger, Wil?"*—reaches again, but it's like Wil's been torn apart inside, fissures and breaches, and Dallin can't heal them all fast enough, there are too many, and it isn't fair, he won't stand* for it. "Mother" is all he can push out through his teeth, a sharp demand, and only at the last second does he curl it into a call, pleading. Asking for Her help and trying to believe She'll give it— grasping at faith and more than willing to bind Her to it.

A moment of vertigo, the slick shift of ground beneath him, and he's surrounded by stars, stars inside of clouds. She's there, waiting, and it's strange, because Dallin hasn't even thought of it before— how Wil did it all for the Father, for Her, and Dallin himself did it all for Wil. There should be shame there, or... something, but there isn't—only a growing sense of rage and betrayal and a deep-dark hole of loss opening wide in Dallin's chest. He can hardly see, his eyes are blurred and burning, and at the look he gives Her is full of censure and reproach.

"Have You got what You want now?" he asks Her, hand gripping Wil's arm, healing what he can as he can and praying it'll be enough when he knows it won't. "Has he endured enough yet?"

Maddeningly, She smiles, bends to Wil, Her hand wrapping around the fist in which the charm is curled. She looks up at Dallin and tilts Her head.

"Your calling has been fulfilled." She reaches out and brushes Her fingers over Dallin's cheek where the Mark still stings. "Do you believe, Guardian?"

Dallin chokes on a sob, nods before he even thinks about it. He doesn't even really know what She's asking, but he believes, he believes it all, he believes everything. He's just watched Wil tear away the soul of a god and eat the emptiness, and he cares about nothing but the fact that he can't help him.

"Please. Please."

The Father is there, pulling Dallin to his feet. He's not well, still weak, but not dying anymore. The stench of it has left Him—She's healed Him—and Dallin wants to rage at the unfairness. Hope stills his tongue, and he merely waits, because he promised Wil, told him *he trusted him, and Dallin will honor that promise at least, since Wil granted Dallin a terrible reprieve from the other.*

"Do you believe, Guardian?" He asks.

Dallin grinds his teeth, snarls, "Yes!" and what do They bloody want from him, and what does it matter now what he believes?

She holds up Her hand, turns it so the shackle with its one link catches the glimmer of the shifting stars that Dallin knows are threads and fates, but he can't care about it anymore. "A belief to which I am willingly bound," She says, reaches out—

—and pushed him away.

Dallin blinked against the smoky light of torch and lamp, nearly choking on the cloying scent of incense, hard rock beneath his knees and Wil's hand clenched so tight in his fist the tips of his fingers were white. The Old Ones had altered their songs, gathered in a circle around them. Corliss was swiping at Wil's face and ears, pinching at the bridge of his nose, trying to staunch the flow of blood, but her face gave away her hopelessness.

Wil was a mess, worse than he'd been in that other where, his face white as chalk and going to wax, his lips losing color, and his shirt clotted and soaked crimson. His chest rose in irregular small hitches, sluggish and weak, and his hand lay in Dallin's palm like a stone. He was cold. Wil hated the cold.

It took Dallin a moment to understand, and then another before the shock of it allowed anything at all besides choking rage. Banished. Sent away.

"*No.*" It came as a hiss through his teeth. Dallin shut his eyes tight and tried to follow, but—

Rebuff. Not harsh or jolting, not gentle. Just rebuff. Too plain; too simple. Rebuff, and Dallin didn't know if it was Wil keeping him away, trying to spare him those last precious moments, or if it was Them, for whatever reasons move gods. Nor did he care.

"*No.*" It sounded too much like a sob, and Dallin didn't care about that either.

"Shaman," someone murmured—Thorne, it sounded like Thorne—set a hand to Dallin's shoulder and tugged. "He is in Their care now. You've already made your plea. Come away and let us add our voices."

In Their care. And Dallin had promised he trusted. He'd promised he believed.

Had he pleaded enough? Had he pleaded at all? He did it now, with everything in him, curling Wil's fist around the charm and sending his own appeal, telling himself They would hear. It was the first time Dallin could recall ever having begged.

A sacrifice, Wil had called himself once, and why couldn't Dallin remember when and under what circumstances? Surely They couldn't be that cruel, not now, not after all *this*.

Spent, near broken, Dallin peered around himself, only now noting the gruesome corpse of Wheeler, the sad, compassionate gazes of those gathered 'round, the confusion on the faces of Wheeler's men, still bound and guarded.

"He saved the Father," Dallin said to no one in particular, and it sounded so hollow for such a weighty proclamation. There should have been horns blowing in celebration, shouts of triumph. There was nothing, only the sympathy of those who could meet his eyes.

He turned to Thorne, raw entreaty. "What will They do?" Shaky and too desperately brittle.

Thorne shook his head, reached down, and pushed black hair from Wil's clammy brow. "What They will."

CHAPTER 7

It was not, he decided, a test, nor was it a request or a demand. It was an offer—an offer with limitless caveats, it seemed, but he'd had a choice. They'd made sure of that.

Hardly a choice at all, Wil had thought when it had been presented to him, or not one he'd had trouble making, at least. He knew what he wanted—the same thing he'd always wanted. A chance to live an actual life. No chains, no walls, no locked doors, and the only cage would be one he made and chose for himself, if he chose one at all.

Furthermore, he knew what Dallin would want, and that... mattered. Likely more than it should, and that was a cage in itself, Wil supposed, but that was the pass to which he'd come, and he didn't think he could regret it, so he hadn't tried. He'd merely considered what They'd offered, considered what it might mean not to accept, then considered his heart. A little more selfish than he'd thought, that heart, and there was still the choice to be put to Dallin, but... the decision was, as had been made all too clear, his to make. So he'd made it.

Several forevers, though he knew it had only been hours. It

hadn't seemed so at the time, but neither had it seemed hours or minutes or years or decades—it just *was*. And now it wasn't anymore, but that....

That seemed right. He was sure.

Residual pain ached through him—hurts healed, or at least the ones that would have taken away *all* choice for good and all, but his mortal body still felt the echoes, still struggled for equilibrium, unsettled between divine curative and corporeal backlash. And that had been his choice as well. Better to accept the earthbound consequences than delay until there were none. Watching Dallin caught between hope and mourning—and Wil *had* watched, They'd seen to that—feeling every tear, hearing every prayer and song, the anger, the hope, the self-rebuke, the incredible, incomprehensible love... it had hurt so much worse. Wil would deal with the rest of the physical pain himself, or better, let Dallin deal with it for him. It would please him.

It was dark when he opened his eyes, the rolling orange-gold radiance of lamps and candles and fire scrimming across the high, flat ceiling. The heavy perfume of incense weighed in the air, and the distant chanting songs of the Old Ones that had been humming at the back of his consciousness for however long it had been now rose slightly in pitch, spiraling all around him.

The marble ringing the fire pit and the thick pillars supporting the ceiling to either side of the vent gave away where he was, though he could have guessed if he'd thought the energy worth it. The Temple. Probably priests' quarters, though done up in more luxury and comfort than Wil suspected any of the Old Ones ever indulged in, and certainly more than Wil had seen before. Shaw's rooms in Chester had been nothing like *this*. A fire stoked high in the pit in the center of the room, more thick furs beneath and above him than he'd ever seen at once in his life, and a mattress so soft it felt like he might sink right through it if he turned the wrong way.

Battles—he remembered there had been battles, and he remembered someone saying the enemy had concentrated their attack here, on the Temple. He listened more carefully. No shouts, no gunfire, no horns. If there were still battles going on, they were either very quiet or very far away. Safe. At least for now.

Sort of ironic, really, that Dallin was probably the best soldier out of anyone within leagues, and his part in the conflict had been miles beneath on an altogether different battlefield. And that he'd certainly done more good there than he could have done in the sorties for which he'd trained all his life. Wil didn't know how many would eventually know the full story, but he, for one, was grateful. Eternally.

A thin, continual hiss, nearly soundless but not quite, scattered over the flames of the fire, and a steady, rolling chime tapped at the closed shutters. It took a moment for the combination to work itself into a shape that made sense, and then another for Wil to place it as sleet. That, he half remembered. Rain, he'd wanted rain, because he'd been sad and he didn't think it fair that he should be the only one. Childish, puling self-indulgence, but it had made sense at the time. He should probably clean up that mess, at least, but he wasn't strong enough yet.

Very odd, this knowledge of events, of his own participation in them, and yet no real remembrance all the same. As though watching an actor who looked like him, spoke like him, ambling through a slice of life that looked like his, and yet there was no true memory of having lived it, just the sharp knowledge that he had. Bits and snatches that had welded for one reason or another onto his heart, and it seemed that was the best he was going to do, though it probably hurt less that way, so he was cautiously grateful.

He closed his eyes, reached out, and smiled when the song of the Old Ones changed once again—a slight pause, a hitch in the rhythm, then a brief prayer of wonder and thanksgiving before it slid down into silence. Wil waited, found the gloomed arch of the doorway, and watched it until Thorne's silhouette—or what Wil was fairly certain was Thorne's silhouette—appeared in the shadows like a specter, hovering for a moment before a hand lifted silently. Wil lifted his own in response, then Thorne bowed deeply and withdrew without a sound. Good. They would be left alone for a while.

Now he could turn his attention to the solid weight of a thick arm across his hips, the feel of a face snugged between his left side and the fur-covered mattress, the heat of breath released over his bare skin in the form of light snores. Dallin lay diagonally across the bed, his still-booted feet hanging off the corner and his arm slung over Wil as though he'd perhaps meant to adjust the furs and simply fell asleep halfway through it and now lay where he'd dropped. Not surprising, really—Dallin had barely slept for... well, quite a long time, anyway, and even now, in his sleep, he was still searching, calling.

Still fully dressed, filthy coat stiff with mud and blood. Wil had the presence of mind to hope the Old Ones had forced at least some measure of healing on their Shaman. Likely not, though, since the removal of the bullet would have necessitated the removal of the coat. Wil was willing to bet they'd tried like hell, though. He would have growled, maybe even smacked the stubborn fool in the head—that'd wake him up in a hurry—but the smile wouldn't go away yet, and there was just too much residual peace in his heart and spirit for it to have been convincing enough. Instead he gently slipped his fingers into the dirty, tangled mop of matte-gold. Lingered for just a moment. Not too long—cruelly unfair, when the seeking and misery went on behind those closed, deep-dark eyes—but just long enough to gather himself and let the miracle of reality take hold.

His fingers were on the edge of numb, quite clumsy, and even the small movement screamed protest through sinews locked to damaged muscle beneath the pristine bandage wrapped around his chest and shoulder. Small inconvenience, all things considered.

He was alive when he shouldn't be, loved when he couldn't be. Not meant, not wise, not chosen, unforeseen—*no one* could have seen Dallin coming—and yet here Wil was, love quite literally in his hands, pressed up against him, breathing it all into his bones like he deserved it.

Calder had called it dangerous and believed in it so hard it had sent his precariously balanced faith into madness. The Old Ones had shaken their heads in benevolent despair, their reservations writ clear on their weathered faces. She had called it unwise, yet Her eyes had sought His, and She'd smiled through the half-hearted rebuke.

Wil called it reality. Wil called it what it was. Wil called it incredible good fortune, and he'd made it a habit over the past few years not to look askance at the scarce occasions when he happened to be blessed with it. Wil called it rare and extraordinary and *his*.

Smile now more of a grin, he ignored the twinging pain and let his touch grow firm, let his fingers slide with intent through the tangles, trace the whorls of the shell of an ear, then slip down over a bristly cheek. A shift and a light snort as the pad of Wil's thumb swept along the firm jawline, slid purposefully up toward the lips—

Dallin's hand snapped up, lightning-fast, from where it rested on the blade of Wil's fur-covered hip. He'd already snatched and covered Wil's wandering fingers before Wil could so much as blink. Bloody *hell*, but the man had reflexes. The long, rough fingers closed over Wil's, squeezed so tight Wil thought the tips might pop off, and pressed them into warm, dry lips.

Stillness, silence—not even the warmth of breath on his hand —then: "Wil?"

Whisper-soft on a hot puff of breath, hoarse and full of disbelief and relief and pleading, and it was enough to make Wil want to kick himself for delaying it even for a second.

He swallowed, said, "I'm here," half expecting Dallin to jump up and lock him in one of those bone-crunching bear hugs he couldn't help sometimes. And Wil would let him, leftover aches and pains be damned.

Instead Dallin remained stone-still, not breathing, lips moving against Wil's rapidly numbing fingertips as though he was trying to speak and couldn't.

"Say it again."

Wil brought his other hand up and laid it between Dallin's shoulder blades.

"I'm *here*."

It cracked because Wil's throat had gone tight, and his voice shook quite a lot at the end. He shut his eyes and blinked them clear. "Dallin—"

"Are you *here* here?"

Still so quiet and full of caution—and the question, and all the questions behind it, made Wil catch his breath. His eyes misted over again.

"How did you—?"

"Just say it." Dallin's grip tightened impossibly, lips still moving silently against Wil's fingers like he'd forgotten how to stop praying. He sucked in one long, deep breath, hitching in his chest like it hurt, and then another. "Are you here to tell me good-bye?" His voice was so calm, that flat, even tone he used when something was choking him and he didn't want to show it, and it nearly made it impossible for Wil to speak at all.

Wil shook his head, mute, which wasn't helping Dallin whatsoever, but Wil almost couldn't breathe, the buried devastation in Dallin's level voice ringing through Wil like crystal, chiming at his bones and shrilling off-key. It vibrated at the back of his teeth, *painful* as nothing he'd ever heard, and he didn't think he'd ever get over the fact that an emotion of that much depth could be meant for him.

"No," he managed, *finally*, and slid his hand up from Dallin's back to his shoulder. "Not good-bye, not unless you want it."

The heavy burst of breath from Dallin that time could have been a laugh or a sob.

Both, Wil decided when Dallin finally lifted his head slowly, eyes too tired and full of ghosts, peering up at Wil with heartbreaking hope and relief. "Bloody idiot." Dallin wobbled a smile that kept tightening and crooking downward into a grimace before hooking back up, somehow catching sunshine in it and warming Wil right through to his heart. Dallin shook his head, said it again —"Bloody *idiot*"—then swarmed up the bed, slid his arms around Wil, and dragged him so close Wil thought he could have breathed for them both, if he could breathe at all.

Dallin's right arm was noticeably weaker, no doubt stiff and very painful by now, but he didn't seem to care much at the moment. One heavy leg swung over Wil's thighs, more or less pinning him. If the furs weren't in the way, Wil thought Dallin might've wrapped his legs around him too and hung on like a limpet. Which wouldn't necessarily be a bad thing, but Dallin was huge and heavy and apparently not thinking terribly clearly right now.

"Thank you," Dallin whispered, "*Thankyouthankyouthankyou*," rough and thick. Wil had no idea if it was intended for him or Them, but he didn't suppose it mattered much. Dallin's face was tucked down into the crook of Wil's shoulder, gasping breaths sliding down Wil's bare arm and neck.

"Dallin—"

"They wouldn't let me in, They shut me out, I couldn't —*couldn't*—"

"Dallin—"

"—They asked me if I believed, and I did, I *do*, but They didn't ask me *what* I believed, and They didn't say what They... if you— And then the Old Ones, they kept saying it was in Their hands, like I didn't know that already, and you were so... there was so *much*, and I couldn't fix it all, but They wouldn't let me in, and They wouldn't say—"

"*Dallin*."

Dallin stilled with another rasping intake of breath. "What?" It was low and wary.

Somehow it made Wil smile. And somehow the lingering pain couldn't get past the firmness of the grip.

"I'm here." Wil twisted his neck and laid a soft kiss on Dallin's hair, said it again, "I'm here," then added, "I'm not going anywhere," and wrapped his good arm awkwardly around Dallin's ribs. He swallowed, his throat clogged and aching, which wouldn't do at all. It was his turn to be the strong one. "Now stop your wibbling and listen, all right?"

Dallin snorted this time, rough and watery, and his hold tightened—thankfully briefly—before he relaxed. Finally, he jerked a tight nod.

Wil wished Dallin had at least taken off his filthy coat. It would be nice to feel more than caked mud and matted suede beneath his hand.

"Now, if I tell you something," Wil said quietly, "will you promise not to let go?"

This time Wil could feel the smile against his jawbone. "Not unless you want it," Dallin replied—muffled cheek, but cheek nonetheless.

Wil grinned. "All right, then." He braced himself, because promise or no, Dallin had some very predictable reflexes. "I didn't give Her the time to finish the job. There's some healing to be done yet, and I—hey, you promised!" He gripped Dallin's coat as firmly as he could and dragged him back down, though Dallin was stiff now and tense. "You said you wouldn't let go."

"I haven't let go. I've merely stopped crushing you."

Which was true, Wil supposed. But still. The wariness was back in Dallin's voice again, the inability to believe entirely, and it hurt that so much of Dallin rested on Wil's mere existence. But it took away a different sort of hurt too, so it was an even trade.

"All right." Wil sank his fingers back into Dallin's dirty hair. "But I have a few things I need you to do for me, more promises, and no weaseling out on technicalities. Agreed?"

Dallin must've been a bit drunk with relief, because he merely planted a firm kiss to Wil's ear—the only thing he could reach without letting go—and agreed.

Wil dragged in some much needed air and dipped his face down so he could whisper into Dallin's ear, take away any sting. "First thing—I want you to go and hunt down someone to get that bullet out of you before you end up with blood poisoning. And I want you to tell them to give you something that'll put you out for at least ten hours." Dallin stiffened, but Wil tightened his hold. "You promised." Gentle but ruthless. Wil waited until some of the stiffness leaked away, waited until Dallin nodded concession. "Second thing—I'm desperate for something to drink, lots of something to drink, and I'm sore and likely to become quite miserable and snappish if something isn't done. I want whichever of the Old Ones aren't helping you to come in here and help me."

Dallin lifted up on his elbow but couldn't quite control the wince and quickly tried to cover it by resting his weight on his other arm. "I can—"

"I know you can, and I've no doubt there'll be other things I'll be wanting you for, but you need your strength for yourself. All right?"

If he weren't such a practical man, Dallin would have argued. Wil could see the beginnings of denial on Dallin's face and in his eyes, so he kept quiet, only kept his gaze stern and hardened his mouth while the arguments springing to life behind Dallin's eyes died one by one, victims to helpless logic.

"You promised."

Dallin was silent for quite a while, his gaze drifting down to the sleeve of his coat, torn and dark with caked blood. Reluctantly he nodded. "I, um." His mouth flattened before he lifted his eyes back up to Wil's. "I'd like to sleep here, if that's all right."

Like he was expecting refusal or was embarrassed to be asking at all.

Wil rolled his eyes. "And *I'm* the bloody idiot." He pulled Dallin down and kissed him, long and slow, then ran his fingers over a stubbled cheek. "Have a bath first—you're getting ripe. And p'raps you might find it in your heart to shave?" He hadn't said it just to feel the vibration against his lips when Dallin chuckled, but it was a bonus.

Eventually Dallin sucked in a long, shaky breath. He laid his brow to Wil's, eyes shut tight, every line of his wide body tense and screaming silent anxiety.

"You came back."

Not *They sent you back*, not *They let you come back*—he knew.

"I did."

"You chose."

"I chose you," Wil answered immediately, because immediate

seemed terribly necessary right now. He slipped his hand to Dallin's cheek, brushing his thumb over the raised lines of the Mark. "How did you know?"

"There was a moment...." A heavy breath expanded Dallin's chest against Wil's. Dallin laid his head on the pillow, tucking his face back to Wil's shoulder. "There was *so much* damage. I can't even imagine the pain you must've... and you were so cold." Dallin shifted impossibly closer, hand coming up to rest lightly over Wil's freshly bandaged shoulder. "She loves you so much—She wouldn't've healed you, sent you back just because I asked Her to. She would have given you a choice, and I couldn't make myself—I mean, why *would* you, but I couldn't—couldn't stop hoping."

Wil slid his fingers through Dallin's longer callused ones, though his arm was still stiff and aching and his hand stupid and clumsy, so he couldn't grip as tightly as he wanted to.

"Yes, I chose it. And there are...." He paused. Did he really want to do this now? Hadn't he already put Dallin through enough? "And there are only so many delaying tactics I will abet." He smiled and poked clumsily until he hit a rib through the disgusting coat, and made Dallin jump. "Go on, then. Thorne's waiting for you. And I really am terribly thirsty."

"Right."

Dallin sat up, careful not to jostle Wil, though considering all the manhandling of a moment ago, it was a little late to be worrying about that. He gave Wil a tired grin and turned away to swipe not quite surreptitiously at his eyes. When he turned back, his gaze went reflexively toward the bandage, ghost-white against the furs in the darkness, and the little crystal that lay quiescent atop it.

"Are you in much pain?"

"Enough. Are you?"

Predictably, Dallin didn't answer. Instead he asked, "Are you hungry?"

Wil let it go. "Now, *that's* a stupid question." He wasn't—rather nauseated, in fact—but any other answer would have worried Dallin and delayed the necessaries even further.

Dallin dragged himself up from the wide bed. "I'll tell Thorne," he said as he started for the shadowed arch of the doorway. Wil couldn't tell if the slight limp in Dallin's gait was from injury or fatigue. Likely both. Dallin paused when he reached the door, then turned, half of him limned in fire, the other half drenched in shadow. "Wil—"

"I'm not going anywhere." Wil watched as Dallin opened his mouth, closed it, then merely nodded, looked down, and silently quit the room.

Wil settled back into the incredible softness ensconcing him, shifted his gaze to the ceiling, and watched the firelight ripple shadow-copper in lazy waves. He sighed and shut his eyes.

They'd have a talk when Dallin was healed and finally rested. Let him get some decent sleep for once, even if a drug-induced coma was the only way to do it, before springing his choices on him.

Not that Wil was putting it off. And not that he was afraid of what Dallin would choose. Not at all. After all, Dallin had been handing Wil the power of choice from the very beginning. Turnabout and all that.

Right?

Wil's good hand clenched in the furs, squeezed so tight he could hear the downy pelts squeaking between his fingers, and he gritted his teeth. He forced his grip to relax and wrapped his fingers instead around the crystal, making a concerted effort to breathe deeply and evenly.

Where the bloody hell was Thorne, anyway?

It was actually Siddell who came to him, hobbling on stick legs but with a sly bit of a smile that made him look amusingly mischievous, nearly youthful. Singréne followed with a wide tray in hand, a sweating pitcher balanced on its center, along with Heofon, who smiled at Wil with a beatific softness that made his skull-like face almost beautiful.

Wil pushed himself up to sit against the pillows and watched them come, peering somewhat blearily from one elated face to another as he accepted a cup of cool, clear water from Heofon and drank deeply. Already it seemed to soothe the slow empty churning of his gut.

"Drink it all, lad," Heofon told him in his craggy voice, and when Wil did, Singréne immediately refilled it from the pitcher.

"Drink as much as you can without upsetting your stomach." Singréne's rolling baritone was somehow muted and gentle. "You lost more blood than you should have survived. Rebuilding and replacing is needed now."

Wil remembered something like that from when Dallin had been stabbed. Now he supposed he had an idea of how exhausted Dallin had been, yet he'd carried on, got them out of Chester, and used up whatever was left to heal Wil.

"Your Guardian said you were hungry?" Singréne looked skeptical but willing as his gaze went to the steaming mug of what Wil suspected was broth next to the pitcher on the tray. It smelled good and rich, not nauseating as Wil had feared, but the clean taste of the water was what he craved right now, so he reluctantly shook his head.

"Dallin would have worried unduly if I'd answered any other way." He shrugged. "It seemed the most expedient way to get him to see to himself. Or to let someone else see to him." Wil smirked, small and weary. "The twelve of you couldn't've maybe tackled him and taken care of him, whether he wanted you to or not?"

As if on cue— "Hoy, watch what you're bloody doing!" Dallin's voice came from somewhere a few rooms away, edgy and too obviously through clenched teeth. There followed a muffled series of soft but stern chidings in what had to be Thorne's lowered voice before Dallin's voice rumbled again, quieter this time but in a very distinct growl— "P'raps in your world, but in my world, sharp pointy things are handled with a bit more care!"

Three very different grins curled up, and Heofon puffed a delicate snort. "To answer your question—I think I may speak for all of us when I say that we like our bones whole and just where they are."

"And," Siddell put in, still smiling but with a meaningful glance at Wil, "we are advisors to the Shaman, stewards in his absence. Whether or not he chooses to accept our advice...." He shrugged and took a pot of salve from Singréne's tray. Its scent was soft and fresh, like a pine forest after a rain. Siddell's smile crimped a bit. "I think *I* can speak for all of us when I say we would regret it sincerely if our Shaman's future choices were to cause him as much pain as those he's already made and those he continues to make."

Despite the cool soothing of the water, Wil's gut curled. Had they chosen this moment apurpose? Wil was exhausted and sleep-muzzy, and wanting nothing more than to drink a barrel of water and slide back into sleep. Surely these three astute old men knew what they were doing. Their pleasant, sympathetic smiles never quite concealed the shrewdness behind them.

Wil tried to brush away the cobwebs draping his mind, tried not to resent the calculation in their chosen moment. "You've heard Her voice," he said as Siddell dabbed at his temple and cheekbone with the salve.

They looked euphoric, as though the weight of the world had suddenly been lifted from off their shoulders.

"Indeed we have." Siddell bowed, still smiling, then replaced the small pot on the tray. He wiped his fingers on a wad of linen Wil suspected was replacement bandages. "And that of the Father." Siddell slipped his bony fingers around Wil's right hand and squeezed. There was sincerity in the grip, but with medical purpose beneath it as well. Siddell instructed Wil to squeeze back, frowning at the weakness of the return hold, and jerked his chin at Singréne. "They are so terribly proud of Their Beloved Son," Siddell went on as his fingers moved to Wil's wrist, timing the pulse beneath them and frowning again. "And there is no scale by which to measure our gratitude. What you did, my boy...." He took his hand away. "Courageous and selfless, if a bit"—his mouth turned up at the corner—"foolish."

He seemed to be expecting Wil's mouth to drop open, because Siddell's half smile flowered into an almost-grin. He watched Singréne finally lay the tray down on a wide table to the right of the bed before moving to sit on the furs to Wil's left.

"You have been told that what is between you and the Guardian is not meant." Singréne's tone was matter-of-fact and his movements coolly efficient as he retrieved a straight razor from Siddell and began to gently and carefully slice away the bandaging around Wil's chest and shoulder.

The statement brought back echoes of Calder and the strange euphoria-drenched rage that had swept through Wil when he'd realized—

He shook his head, jaw set. "So I have." Wil didn't care that it came out flat and tight. He took another sip from the cup.

"And so it is not," Singréne replied, "or *was* not, and yet...." He paused, his eyes on his hands as they worked carefully. "Had you been trained, had your Guardian been trained, had you honed your skills and used them as we would have instructed...." Singréne darted his glance to the others.

Siddell was nodding, solemn and thoughtful. Heofon still had his sly little smile, his eyes bright and intelligent inside their gaunt frame.

Singréne shook his head. "Sacrifice is too often the way of victory. Even your Guardian, his lack of instruction notwithstanding, knows that and was fully prepared to give himself to save us all." He pointed a sharp, narrow stare at Wil. "To save you."

Wil scowled, stung. "I know." It wasn't nearly as defiant as he'd hoped.

Heofon shifted, his smile finally slipping away. "The purpose of the Guardian always has been to protect and guide the Aisling but to serve the Mother in all things." His gaze turned pointed, though there was nothing unfriendly about it. "'Twas happy coincidence for us that one purpose happened to serve the other."

Anger prickled behind Wil's breastbone. "He was instructed by the Father as well, and the contradiction of his choices nearly split him in two. You can't blame him for not tendering a blood sacrifice, nor for not being one himself."

"Indeed we do not," Singréne assured him quickly. "Had he been any other Guardian, had you been any other Aisling—" He swept a glance to the others, then back at Wil. "—had we been consulted and our advice taken...." He sighed and set the razor across his knee. "Then the horns upon our ascent from Fæðme would have sung the songs of mourning, not those of joy, one way or another, and we would now be tending at least one corpse rather than two wounded. You found another way, changed fate, and yet... that other way...."

Wil looked away. He'd known this was coming, but he'd still hoped. "Your laws demand my death," he said baldly, refusing to shrink or shy. "I used the tools of the enemy, became like him, and your laws do not suffer dearg-dur to live."

Funny how there was fear skittering in Wil's chest but not fear of these men in particular. Whatever their verdict, it wasn't theirs to pass sentence, and they knew it—*Wil* knew it. He wondered vaguely, eyes drifting over the razor, what he'd do if they tried, then pushed the thought away. They wouldn't, he knew they wouldn't, and not because he could swat them all down with a mere thought. One way or another—either by their own deductions or instruction from the Mother—they were well aware of what Wil could do, though this was no judgment from them of what he'd truly done. Dallin, however....

"You did not merely become like him," Heofon put in, quietly somber as he took the cup from Wil's hand and set it on the tray. "You ate his soul. Blood to blood. What he was is now a part of you, what was his is now yours."

"I know that!" Wil snapped. "Did you think I didn't?"

Knew it with a dead certainty that had yet to truly reach his heart. Memories that weren't his and knowledge he shouldn't have, and yet it held a surreal quality Wil couldn't associate with reality. Perhaps it was because Dallin still looked at Wil the way he did, didn't pull away, his relief so very obvious and sincere.

"Does...." Wil stared at his fingers as they plucked at the silky furs. "Does Dallin...." He couldn't finish, couldn't ask this simplest of questions, and he wasn't at all surprised, because he'd barely been able to bring himself to form its outlines in his head before, when he'd lain willing in his Guardian's embrace.

"Of course." Singréne laid a wide hand on Wil's arm. "He knew it the moment before you did it and extended his hand in aid. A law has been not merely broken, but obliterated, and not by your hand, lad. He is our lawmaker—you have nothing to fear from Lind. But your Guardian...." He glanced at the others in appeal.

"Your Guardian is quite talented at not knowing the things he knows," Siddell said. "You have a choice you must present to him, so the Mother and the Father have told us, and our loyalties are left at cross-purposes. In this we cannot seek the Shaman's guidance, and so we must seek yours."

Wil narrowed his eyes. "Are you asking me if I want you to lie to him for me?"

"Oh, dear lad." Heofon shook his head. "The Mother recognizes the dangers in a Guardian whose heart lies so close to the Aisling." He raised a hand when Wil opened his mouth. "For all of Calder's zealousness and his unfortunate—" He paused, thin lips pursed. "—fall from grace—"

"You mean madness, Æweweard," Singréne cut in, tone sharp and gaze hard. "Call it what it was."

A moment of tense silence strung between them, heavy with things Wil could probably touch if he wanted to, but it seemed private, so he didn't. He'd never really thought about whatever internal politics must exist between the twelve of them. He'd more or less assumed that since they shared thoughts, they'd be inclined to share opinions, like bees in a hive, but it appeared he'd been mistaken.

Heofon stared at Singréne, his gaze moving quickly from anger to sadness to guilt and then, finally, to resignation. "As you will." He sighed. "For all of Calder's madness, there was sense and wisdom at the core of his objections." His gaze moved once again to Singréne, blazing this time. "The sense was the seed from which the madness sprang." He seemed to take no satisfaction from Singréne's acquiescent nod, only more sorrow. Heofon turned his gaze back to Wil, softened it. "And for all that sense," he went on gently, "he was wrong. We were wrong. And we would have guided you wrongly had the Shaman allowed it."

"We would have counseled remove," Singréne said. "We would have counseled retreat until his instruction and training were complete. We would have counseled that he keep his promise to you and put a gun to your head." He lifted his chin and looked at Wil straight. "We would have counseled execution."

He said it as though Wil didn't already know it, as though he was confessing, but there was no request for or expectation of absolution in his steady gaze.

"Why are you telling me this?" Wil asked quietly. *And did you really have to do it* now? Fuck, he was tired and growing more sore and achy by the second, a dull headache sliding behind his eyes and blooming steadily.

"Because our counsel would have been wrong," Siddell answered, blunt and even. "Our advice, if asked for and followed, would have led to quite a different outcome, and none of us would now be here to rue it."

"Provided we were fortunate enough to have been slated for mere execution," Singréne said.

"Mm." Siddell twisted a grimace that spoke volumes more than words could have done. He shook himself. "You are like no other Aisling before you, this you know, but the Shaman is like no other before him either. The combination, the binding of one to the other...." He shrugged. "We have been over the course of events, examined them and analyzed other likely outcomes, prayed over it, and the Mother has guided our reasoning. Yours was the only way, and his the only hand that could have guided you to it. The only hand that *would* have guided you to it and kept holding on after. 'Not meant' and 'not wise' do not necessarily mean 'not the way things should be.'"

Wil sat back, frowning. "Thank you" was all he could think to say. It meant something to him, though he wasn't quite sure what, yet, but he breathed easier, and his stomach stopped curling and uncurling.

"Gratitude is ours, surely," Heofon replied. "But that is not the reason for our concern."

Wil tilted his head. Exhaustion and creeping pain made him blunt. "You want to make sure I know how thoroughly we've allowed ourselves to be bound. You want to make sure I know his judgment is skewed by his heart, and that you still think it's dangerous." He didn't believe that one, though it seemed to be everyone else's point—though contrarily, all of them seemed to understand that if that bond didn't exist, they'd both be dead and Æledfýres would have won. It was like they were arguing with their own arguments. Wil sat back and eyed them all resentfully. "You want to make sure I make plain to him the things you say he knows before I present his choices to him." He looked between the three of them. "And you think I wouldn't?"

"We think your courage is unequaled when it comes to matters of the world," Singréne said gently. "When it comes to matters of your own heart...." He opened a hand.

"He *is* my heart," Wil retorted. Despite his very real surprise at the truth of the statement and the fact that he'd just blurted it like that, he managed to keep the insult and offense from his tone, but not the anger. "I would never—"

"You feared to tell him all of Síofra's hold on you, a hold that made you doubt and falter even as you stood before your enemy."

Wil stared, too weary to pretend he'd seen the bald statement coming. "How did you know that?"

Singréne smiled, soft and genuine. "The Mother's guidance has been a balm to sore hearts after so long. But the Father's wisdom is unmatched where it concerns His son."

A snarl curled Wil's lip. Telling his secrets, and he could

understand why, since he'd already tried and failed to broach the subject of choice with Dallin when he'd had a chance. Though he supposed he hadn't tried very hard, so failure wasn't exactly surprising. Still, it felt intrusive, and he resented the hell out of it.

"You have—" Siddell shook his head as though rethinking what he wanted to say. His gaze, when he turned it back to Wil, was sad. "We need not tell you the power that now resides in you. We need not tell you that the danger you presented to all when you first arrived here has now grown so vast, there is no scope by which it can be measured."

The anger rose, sharp and heated. "I will not sit here and defend myself against things I wouldn't do if my very soul were at risk, when I have already proven—or *should* have proven—that I would forfeit every bit of myself, *including* my soul."

"A soul which is now strange to you," Heofon said kindly. He rubbed at his brow and peered at the others. "We do this badly. Too many years of speaking in circles, as the Shaman would tell us." He turned back to Wil. "Your Guardian would have many opinions about our ineptitude in this, none of them good, and he would not be wrong." He placed both bony hands on the footboard of the bed and leaned into it. "To say it plainly, you are not as you were when you entered Fæðme. You are not as you were when you stepped from the Mother's presence. Wil That Was is no longer, and will never be again. You are Drút Hyse, but you are more as well. You have much ahead of you, and much now inside of you that you do not know. We can teach you how to learn it, learn from it, direct it, and use it. But we cannot teach you your own value—to the heart of another or, more importantly, to your own. We cannot teach you to accept an extended hand because you are worthy of it. Such a thing requires the patience and persistence of love.

"We know of the choice you mean to present to the Guardian, and it is his right—more, it is your duty by him. But you do not only need a Guardian, lad—you need *this* Guardian. Do not, we beg of you, allow doubt and insecurity to still your tongue when it comes to truths you'd prefer not to speak. Honesty is the only way with Dallin Brayden, and giving it the only way to ensure this Guardian remains *the* Guardian."

Wil studied them, one at a time, with sincere confusion and a healthy dose of suspicion. "The Mother didn't say as much," he said slowly. Not that Wil disagreed with them, but She truly hadn't. In fact, She'd as much as said outright that Dallin might well be better off—

No. No, actually, She hadn't. She'd deferred to the Father, and He'd told Wil that love might drive a person to extremes he wouldn't normally credit, and that sometimes it alone wasn't enough to save another. It had seemed like an answer at the time, but now....

"To the Mother and the Father," Heofon said, "our choices are Their most precious gifts to us. Ever is Their guidance for us presented in such a way as to keep those choices sacred." He shrugged, rueful. "We try to carry on Their example, but sometimes we falter into obscurity."

Wil accidentally snorted, thinking of Dallin's perpetually clenched teeth and his constant grousing about that very thing. He ducked his head and tried to cover the laugh with a cough, but he could tell by their rueful smirks that the old men weren't buying it.

"Sorry," he offered, though in the face of their own smiles, Wil still couldn't quite control his own. Perhaps he was growing giddy with fatigue.

Singréne patted Wil's arm, went back to ridding him of the last of the bandage, and gestured to Siddell for the pot of salve. "You understand our point, which our Shaman himself has made plain to us countless times." That got rid of Wil's smile. "He has a right to this choice, and though we may have leave to hope he makes the one we would prefer, neither we nor you have the right to prevent him from making it fully. Honesty, Aisling, in all things with your Guardian."

Wil looked down, noting rather absently that the bullet wound he hadn't even seen before now was nothing more than a small red pucker on his skin, somewhat impressive blue and brown bruising striating out from its center.

"And what do you...?" He forced his gaze up to each of the old men hovering around him. "What do you think he'll choose?"

He wasn't entirely sure why he'd asked the question, wasn't even entirely sure he wanted an answer. Perhaps he wouldn't get one, because they all looked away, shook their heads, and sighed as one.

"I fear," Singréne rumbled at him as he slathered salve over the healing wound and the bruises, "in this, we must remain annoyingly obscure." His hazel eyes were soft and kind. "I am sorry, lad, but this question is not ours to answer."

Wil let his head drop back, and stared at the ceiling, trying to let the gentle touch and the combined soft scents of the salve and incense soothe as they were meant to do. The hell of it was that, though they might be annoying, they weren't strictly wrong, not about any of it. Beyond all sense, Dallin loved Wil enough to die for him, to kill him if he had to, and to kill *for* him. More troubling, Dallin loved Wil enough to defy gods. He put Wil first, above any danger to himself, though Wil didn't quite believe Dallin would put him above a danger to the world. If it came to it, in the thick of things, Wil knew bone-deep that Dallin would have pulled that trigger. His honor would have demanded it, even if Wil hadn't been able to. He couldn't blame these old men for not knowing that. How could they, when they hadn't seen inside Dallin's heart the way Wil had done?

Ironically, that honor was now the thing that worried Wil the most. Because how could a man with so much of it countenance the things Wil was going to have to show him? And would that honor, by some twist, be the thing that in fact bound their courses together, but not in any way Wil would truly want?

...accept an extended hand because you are worthy of it.

Right. Sure. Worthy. Except how would he know if that hand was extended in love or mere duty? Because duty, when all was said and done, utterly defined Dallin.

There was so much more ahead, and Wil had chosen it freely. But he couldn't do it without Dallin, and if it wasn't for the right reasons, he couldn't do it *with* Dallin either. Not out of duty. Not out of obligation. Even Wil had more self-respect than that.

Bloody hell, they'd lived five lifetimes in the space of weeks and loved enough to fill a world. What if they found out they didn't even like each other? Exactly how far could love dragged from darkness, passion stolen from blind chance—how far could it carry a person?

To the very end, Wil supposed. One way or another.

"Shall we sing?" Heofon asked gently.

Wil shut his eyes and bit his lip to keep the burning behind them. "Yes," he whispered, dismayed that it came out thick and hoarse. He cleared his throat, said, "Yes, please," and shut everything else away. Just for now.

He lost himself in time again as the songs of the Old Ones wound through him. He was groggy and fuzzy when Dallin eventually stumbled back, shirtless and bandaged and blinking owl-eyed at Wil and the three shamans. He'd clearly already taken whatever sleep potion Thorne had given him, because when Singréne asked him if he wanted help with his trousers and boots, Dallin merely bobbled a nod, slogged over to the bed and stared down at Wil, frowned, and fell like a tree. Singréne and the others weren't quite able to cover their smiles, but they did manage to hold back any chuckles, and they rather came in handy for completing the disrobing and shoving Dallin into a position that wasn't sideways across Wil's torso. As soon as he'd been undressed and covered with the furs, he reached out in his sleep, glommed on to Wil, and didn't let go again. The shamans discreetly excused themselves without comment.

They slept.

And dreamed dreams all their own.

Three days, during which Wil slept and drank and slept and ate and slept and bathed and slept and slept and slept.

No more threads and fates for Wil. That was for the Father now, and Wil knew he was welcome if he chose, but he didn't choose for now. For now he accepted the strange normalcy of following his own wandering mind into whatever murk it led, and the only specters that spoke were those conjured from inside his own head. He dreamed his own dreams and only ventured a touch to Dallin's now and then. Dream-kisses that were his, meant for him alone, and no monsters chasing him through the cobwebbed corridors of someone else's insanity. The tender, sluggish pulse of healing running from Dallin's hands, still reaching even in his sleep. Mundane, ordinary paradise.

He hadn't yet returned the favor. So far he'd kept his own dreams to himself. He didn't want Dallin seeing things he shouldn't see, not yet. Or rather, things he *should* see, but not until Wil knew for sure.

Dallin had been up and about from the first morning, kept

away for most of the day every day, doing things he was too tired to tell Wil about when he'd plod to bed far too late every night, which was all right—Wil was too tired to hear about them. Trying to bring some order to the mess that had been made of Lind, which Wil only knew because the Old Ones had been keeping him informed when he thought to ask. The plain truth wasn't going to do it this time—there were politics involved, great, stonking, complicated politics, and a Council High Seat in Penley who would be all the more dangerous when he realized he was cornered. Which, apparently, Dallin was doing everything he could to prevent him from realizing. Wil could've helped with that —could've helped with all of it, really—but either Dallin hadn't thought of it, or he had and didn't want to.

Wil couldn't tell. He hardly ever saw Dallin. For once Wil could honestly say he wasn't avoiding a conversation he knew had to come; he just couldn't seem to get a chance to have it. Trips to the Bounds that took all day, or interviewing senior officers of the Commonwealth troops to see what their reports to Penley would reveal, with Dallin trying to tweak them to his own strategy. Rounding up those of the Brethren who hadn't died or killed themselves, or interrogating Wheeler's squadron who'd been present at Fæðme. It seemed there was always something to pull Dallin away.

They slept together, Dallin usually trudging in well into the night when Wil was already asleep—he couldn't seem to bloody *stop* sleeping—and then up and out again before Wil woke. Solicitous and tender when he happened to be around when Wil's eyes were open for a little while, but... distracted. Closed up. If he didn't have so many legitimate worries to keep him engaged, Wil would've wondered if Dallin was avoiding him on purpose.

Wounded streamed in and out of the Temple, and the Old Ones were kept bustling, though Wil hadn't even realized it at first. It wasn't until the second day that he noticed the steady hum of voices and horse sounds outside, and it wasn't until Marden woke him for his supper that night that Wil remembered to ask about it.

Twenty-six Linders dead, though Marden hadn't really wanted to tell Wil that part, and just under a hundred wounded so far, though they were still straggling in. Of the Commonwealth troops, only six had been killed, including Wheeler, since they hadn't engaged until the battles were already well underway or mostly won. Marden said that count might rise, and wouldn't say any more. They hadn't yet managed to get a good count of the Brethren's dead.

"Hundreds," Marden said heavily, shook his head in sincere mourning, and quietly quit the room.

Hunter found his way up to the Temple on the third day of Wil's stay there. Hunter's hair had been cut short like his sister's. His young face looked tired and not so young anymore—haunted, perhaps, though Wil would wager Andette had more bitter ghosts.

"Yes, I've seen her," Hunter answered when Wil asked, but he wouldn't look Wil in the eye. His voice was more subdued than it had been, his whole body set rigid with exhaustion. "She begs an audience with you as well, though I thought I might—" Hunter swallowed, his throat bobbing, then ducked his head even further. "My sister has redeemed... or has acted to... *tried* to redeem...."

They sat in a small antechamber off the room that Wil hadn't even known was there until one of the Old Ones—Déopþancol this time—ushered him to it and sat him in one of the three chairs to wait for Hunter. Wil had been given a thick, heavy robe, but no clothes yet. Seeing as how he couldn't seem to stay awake for more than an hour at a time, and that he still got dizzy every time he sat up or stood, he didn't complain. They made him flex out his arm, every time one of them got hold of him, and wiggle his fingers for them and grasp their own to test his grip, but he still kept his arm crooked protectively across his middle when no one was looking.

He'd been pleased when Déopþancol had told him he had a visitor, and even more pleased when he heard it was Hunter. Wil was annoyed with himself that Hunter hadn't even crossed his mind since he'd woken days ago. These people had put so much on the line because of him, and it had become terribly personal to Hunter and Andette. Wil should have made it his business to seek out Andette, at least. Now he sat and watched Hunter standing before him as one would stand before a tribunal, stumbling through what was sounding more and more like an apology with every lurching word, and wishing he'd put this off until his eyelids stopped weighing five stone each.

After the fifth "I cry your pardon, Aisling," Wil couldn't take it anymore.

"Hunter," he cut in as gently as he could, because he should have more patience—for this, of all things—and he simply didn't. "Do you know what happened down in Fæðme?"

Hunter hesitated, his mouth opening and closing soundlessly for a moment. "The Aisling and the Guardian stood against the enemy and prevailed."

"We stood against Æledfýres. Do you know who—?" Wil shook his head. "No, I'm not going to play games with words. You need to understand this, and you need to understand it the first time, because I don't think I've the energy for it more than the once." He leaned in. "Hunter, look at me." When Hunter did, blue gaze sad and unnervingly flat, Wil went on, "Do you blame me for what happened here? For what happened in Fæðme? Do you think I'm responsible for what Æledfýres did and what he tried to do?"

It seemed to shock Hunter. His jaw set tight, and the fixed gaze flared to life.

"Who has said such things?" *There* was the hot spark of the spirited youth Wil had met back up at the caves, finally blazing out to set color to Hunter's freckled cheeks. "It is blasphemy! That anyone would *dare* to—"

"*You* have said such things." Wil bent his voice stern this time, because it was suddenly extremely important to him that Hunter understand this, that the guilt and self-censure that, now that he was paying attention, Wil could see in the stiff angles of Hunter's stance died right here.

Hunter looked stunned. "I would never."

"Not intentionally. But Æledfýres was, in a way, just as much kin to me as Barret Calder was to you. If you insist upon taking responsibility for your uncle's actions, where d'you think that leaves me?"

A frown creased Hunter's clear brow, and his blue eyes went distant. "But—"

"But what? But your uncle's crimes were worse?" Wil softened his voice again. "They weren't even crimes, Hunter. Barret Calder was not an evil man. He wasn't even a bad man. He was a man who lost his way and was trying to do what he thought was right. Even as he prepared that cup, he truly believed he was saving me, saving the Mother." Bloody damn, Wil had hated the man—how was it that defense was coming so easily? "I don't condone what he did—in fact, I despise it—and I think that sort of faith is very dangerous, as your uncle proved. But perhaps, instead of punishing ourselves for things and people over which we had no control, we should remember what led them to it and not let ourselves get tangled in the same webs."

For fuck's sake, Wil was starting to sound like one of the Old Ones. At least Hunter was looking thoughtful now, like he was really listening, which was more than Wil had been expecting. Hunter reminded Wil so much of Dallin, or what Wil imagined

Dallin might have been had the raid never happened, and Wil often suspected that was the reason Hunter so annoyed Dallin. It wasn't hard to look into Hunter's clear blue gaze and see the righteous stubborn streak so very evident in Dallin's dark one.

Wil pinched the bridge of his nose. "I'm very tired, Hunter. I've *been* very tired, and now I won't sleep unless I know you understand this." He gave Hunter a level look. "I don't know about Lind's traditions and laws, but whatever they are, I don't blame you. I don't blame any Calder except—" He cut himself off. "I don't blame you, I don't blame Andette, and I don't want you to blame yourself. Please. I don't want to be tripping over you for the rest of my life with you trying to make it up to me somehow, and I don't want you flinching every time I look at you. If you truly honor your Aisling, then please—do as I say in this."

The flush was back, burning across Hunter's cheeks. "I spoke to the Shaman this morning."

Wil's eyebrow lifted—it was more than he'd done. "Did you?"

"When he sent for me, I thought—" Hunter's mouth tightened, and he blinked. "And then, when he commanded me to come to you...."

Wil slumped back into the cushions of the chair. "You thought you were coming here for some kind of sentence? Retribution?" He shook his head. "Well, I'm sorry to disappoint you, but you won't be getting any such thing. Sit down, will you? I'm tired of looking up." Wil waited until Hunter complied stiffly, then eyed him with a resigned frown. "Wilfred's not coming back, Hunter." The words clogged when Hunter's gaze flashed and narrowed, but Wil pushed on. "He died trying to find me, and apparently did find me, and got a blade to the throat for his trouble. I took his name when I took his papers from his corpse." He slouched deeper into the chair, weary of... this, of everything. "Your uncle knew, said he felt it when it happened, and it broke his heart. The fact that it also cracked his mind shouldn't be all that surprising. And not entirely unforgivable. And I don't want to talk about Barret Calder anymore."

There. Another secret out, more poison drained—from Wil's spirit and into another's. Quite the reverse of soul-eating, and the irony almost made him puff a bleak snort, but he managed to keep it in his throat.

Hunter was even more subdued than he'd been when he'd come, staring down at the rushes on the floor beneath his feet, the silence stretching, growing heavy.

Wil broke it with deliberate triviality. "What time of day is it, anyway? I've rather lost track." He thought he remembered lunch, but that could've been yesterday.

Hunter's gaze only rose as far as Wil's left shoulder. "It is late afternoon on the Eve of the Turning."

"Huh." Wil blinked blankly. He'd lost track of that, too. "Turning Night is tomorrow?"

The Turning, when the Father took the world in His hands, watching over it and the Mother while She slept, until He would wake Her with a kiss at Planting. At least according to the Commonwealth's beliefs. In the Dominion it had been something altogether different, with a sinister underpinning of struggle and oppression between the two gods. And even though they were both rather simplified, skewed versions of the same legend, Wil thought Cynewísan's version somewhat warmly romantic. Four years ago, if he'd found himself thinking something like that, he would've bashed his skull into a wall until he'd stopped thinking at all. Now he couldn't help the faint smile.

"What's it like outside?"

Hunter shrugged. "Cold. The sleet turned to snow three nights ago and made things worse. It's been snowing now and again ever since. There hasn't been snow for the Turning for...

well, at least as long as I've been alive. The Shaman calls it a gift, says there would have been more bloodshed had the weather not stopped...." He frowned. All boyishness leaked from his face as his expression turned thoughtful... perhaps even just a touch suspicious. "There was a moment," he said slowly, "a strange stretch of time uncountable, when it seemed as though... as though I was there, with you, when...." He opened his hand and looked down into his palm. "You held my hand, and there was blood and pain, but I didn't feel it. I just knew it was there. Someone asked me for my strength, and I thought... it seemed like the land itself was calling out and asking, but it was the Shaman's voice—I know it was. Andette says—" Hunter bit his lip. "All who have spoken on it have said the same." He stopped there, frowning at the floor.

"Whatever it was Andette told you, it was true. She was there."

Hunter merely nodded. There was no longer any doubt or question in his eyes. "I was down near the Bounds with Cáfne's squadron. We'd found a nest of the enemy, snipers who'd crammed themselves into a rock overhang above the river and were picking off runners. They'd got two already when we engaged." His gaze went confused and clouded. "They stopped too. If they hadn't, we all would have been dead, because I couldn't move, didn't *want* to move. But they did, and after—" He ran a hand through his short hair, then looked at his fingers as though they'd just touched a ghost. "Two of them simply fell dead, as though their brains had exploded inside their heads. One of them went to his knees, weeping, and surrendered. Him we took prisoner, but one ran, and we hunted him down. The one we took, we couldn't understand him—he was speaking the North Tongue, weeping as though his beloved had just died at his feet. I could not bring myself to hate him. He kept saying *Athair, maith do*. Over and over again." For the first time since Wil's revelation of his stolen name,

Hunter lifted his gaze and peered at Wil intently. "What does that mean?"

Wil rubbed at his face, only distantly noting that the left side of it was merely slightly sore now and not in fact painful. He'd been tired only a moment ago. Now he was exhausted again. He would've liked to ask if Hunter still thought war was noble and romantic, but he didn't quite have the heart right now.

"It means 'Father, forgive.'"

It was hollow. Maybe bitter. Wil wasn't really sure why tears burned at the backs of his eyes, but he didn't put forth the energy to figure it out. Something that had literally consumed his life since before it had even started, and now it was over, really *over*. Síofra was gone, Wheeler was gone, Æledfýres was gone and could never come back. So why didn't Wil feel... *something?* Something besides profoundly weary and vaguely sad.

He chanced a quick look at Hunter, saw the worry and concern, and quickly drew his glance away.

"Help me up, would you? I want to go back to bed."

On the fourth day, Wil was woken by a steady tapping at his nose and an annoyingly awake voice describing the breakfast that was apparently waiting for him.

"C'mon, then, I know you like porridge, and there's fish, if you want it. Bacon, some beans, and griddlecakes too, and spiced cider. It's getting cold—get up."

Wil supposed he should be pleased that Dallin was actually here for a change, but irritation crowded it out. "Gerroff." He swatted blind, then turned over and shoved a pillow over his head. "I'm *sleeping*."

"You've *been* sleeping."

"'S 'cause 'm *tired*."

"It's because you're stubborn and sulking."

Wil didn't even dignify that one with an answer. He wormed his hand from beneath the fur, rumbled a growl, and flipped Dallin off.

The pillow disappeared along with the top layer of furs. Wil snarled this time and sat up too quickly, the bright morning sun coming through the open shutters going to spangly gray. Dallin's voice dulled in Wil's ears for several moments before equilibrium reasserted itself.

"Fuck. Dizzy."

"That's because you're lying about too much." Apparently Dallin wasn't concerned enough to return the pillow and covers.

The room was warm, the fire high and hot, but Wil nonetheless balled himself over his knees, shivering. "Funny, everyone here keeps telling me it's because I lost a person's worth of blood."

"And now Thorne says you're sleeping for ten of them."

"I'm *recovering*."

"You're done recovering, or you should be. Now you're just hiding."

Wil glared, stung. "I was *shot*."

"So was I. And you moved pretty quick grabbing for those furs."

Wil only frowned, strangely out of balance, and he didn't know why. His shoulder and arm did feel pretty normal, the remaining twinges likely nothing more than residual stiffness due to his own refusal to move it. He'd healed very quickly, considering.

Still, Dallin's superior attitude, after his seeming scarcity for days, was tweaking at Wil's nerves.

"How would Thorne know, anyway?" Wil was still groggy and

so somewhat cranky and truculent. "I've not seen him for...." He paused and forced his mind to focus. "Days, I think."

"Yes, well, I imagine he's keeping an eye, one way or another. You're fine, Wil. You just need to start acting like it."

Unaccountably, that pissed Wil off. "And how would *you* know? I've not seen *you* for days either."

Dallin narrowed his eyes. "Not much of a morning person, are you?"

Right now Wil didn't think he was much of an anything person. He deflated and dropped his head to his knees. "Wait'll you get to know me."

"And you think I don't already?" When Wil only scowled and refused to answer, Dallin sighed, sat on the bed, and slipped a warm hand onto Wil's calf, which only made Wil feel more like a recalcitrant child than he had five seconds ago. "Wil, I'm sorry. I've been—"

"You've been busy trying to save Lind and Cynewísan, I know that. I don't even know why I said it." Thick and subdued now, appalled and mortified that tears were crowding.

"That's true, I have been doing." Dallin gave a light squeeze to Wil's leg. "But, as Thorne pointed out rather, um... astutely"— meaning *excruciatingly and sharply polite*, Wil had no doubt, knowing Thorne—"I've got Shaw and Wisena, who could be doing a great deal of what I've been doing, probably better, and my place is and should be here with you."

And why did that make Wil feel even worse? He decided he didn't want to know. Instead he slid a glance over Dallin. He did look rather fit, certainly not as pale and drawn as he'd been, and his arm didn't seem the least bit stiff. So why did Wil seem stuck in this relentless weariness?

"Where are your guns?" Dallin looked nearly naked without them. It took a second, but the question pinged something at the back of Wil's mind, and he shot a look 'round the room. "Where's the rifle?" Oh shit. "I didn't lose the knife, did I?"

"Everything's locked down in the vestry. Thorne won't allow them in the Temple proper." Dallin stared for a moment, measuring. "It's been three days. You've only just now noticed?"

"Well, if I'd noticed before, I would've *asked* before, wouldn't I?"

Not that Dallin would've been around *to* ask.

Dallin kept staring, his mouth set tight. "Thorne says you're depressed."

Wil scowled. What business was it of Thorne's? And whether Wil was or wasn't, what right did Thorne have to discuss Wil or his moods with Dallin?

"Only tired. I think I've a right."

"You have." Dallin watched Wil for quite a long time, annoyingly assessing, before he sighed and laid back crosswise on the bed by Wil's feet. He stared at the ceiling. "You've also a right to be depressed, though I wish you weren't, and I'm not sure I understand why you would be, but... we've both a right to a lot of incomprehensible things at the moment, I'm thinking. Shock, for instance. Although that's not exactly incomprehensible." Dallin's mouth went tight. "Anger."

Wil hadn't thought of shock. And didn't feel much like thinking about it now. He shook his head.

"I'm not angry."

"Ha!" Dallin lifted an eyebrow. "Yes. You are."

Wil opened his mouth... closed it. Was he? Maybe. Shocked and angry—it didn't seem as improbable as it should. He'd have to figure it out when his mind was working better.

"Well, if I am, it isn't with you."

"I didn't think it was."

Wil peered at Dallin closely, scrutinizing, as he hadn't done since he'd been bullied awake. Noted the tightness of Dallin's jaw, the crimp of his mouth, and the way he kept looking at the ceiling instead of at Wil.

"Pot, meet Kettle."

"Mm" was all Dallin said, and then he didn't say any more, just lay there, jaw winding tighter, the muscles in it twitching and jumping.

Wil stared for a long moment, sincerely bewildered, before it hit him, and a breathless little "Oh" slid out of him. The bewilderment vanished all at once.

"So you *have* been avoiding me."

"Not really." Dallin looked over at Wil, thoughtful. "Maybe. I'm not sure. No more than you've been avoiding me, I expect."

Honesty with Dallin Brayden, in all things, even when it came to things about himself he too obviously didn't want to dissect. He'd told Wil, as they'd stood looking down at the abyss, that he meant to do better. Wil wished Dallin hadn't picked this particular moment to start acting on his new resolution.

"I admit," Dallin went on quietly, "that it's been easier to sink myself inside a lot of other problems than to remember. Because when I do see you, when you're lying there asleep, so peaceful and whole and *here*—" His voice was gaining depth and timbre. He raised his hands above his face, looking at them like they were something entirely new to him as he turned them over and examined the palms. "I want to touch you and hold on to you, and keep touching you and holding on to you, and yet I want to wring your neck as well." He flexed his fingers, then folded his arms up to pillow his head, and looked at Wil again. Waiting.

Wil wanted to look away, but he didn't. "I had to. You know that."

"It could've worked. It *would've* worked, if you'd just waited, given it more of a chance. You didn't have to pull it back—I had his thread *in my hands*. You had nothing to prove."

"Didn't I?" Wil swallowed. This time he did look away. "It was killing you. I could feel bits of you tearing loose. I could *feel* how—" His teeth clenched, and his eyes stung. "It was the only thing—"

"You *swore* to me you'd choose yourself." Accusatory. Bitter. Outright angry now, the words shoved out and barbed.

"Actually, I didn't." The way he could almost feel Dallin's temper spike piqued Wil's own, and his jaw set. "You keep using this 'choice' thing against me like you're the only one who's got it. I had two choices—I could use you up and stay clean, or I could be what I am and—"

He shut his eyes tight. He hadn't meant to approach the subject like this. He hadn't even come 'round to planning an approach yet. Perhaps he really had been hiding. Wouldn't They be so proud?

"Be what you are." Dallin's voice was even, his expression unreadable. He scrubbed at his face, huffed a quiet "Bloody hell," and then went silent again.

And there it was. Wil supposed he *had* been hiding, even if he truly hadn't meant to and hadn't known he was doing it, but now that it was happening—

You are dearg-dur. I can't love you, Wil. I can't even look at you.

And Dallin apparently couldn't, that was the hell of it. He stared at the ceiling, his mien still flat and far too calm, and he—very deliberately—wasn't looking at Wil. It wasn't even truly Dallin who'd spoken the words, but they seemed as much his now as they had the first time Wil had heard them.

"You can—" Wil chewed on his lip, because it was abruptly quivering. He fisted his hands to keep the burning behind his eyes at bay. He shouldn't be doing this like this, sitting naked on a fur-covered bed where he'd been held and healed, and with Dallin lying so very near but oceans away. He shouldn't be shaking and close to weeping when he'd stood before the Mother and the Father just days ago and accepted Their charge like he was strong enough to take anything.

"I'm to relay to you a message." Wil was surprised his voice came out thick but steady enough.

Dallin grunted, mouth twisted. "I'd wondered. They haven't been speaking to me."

That one surprised Wil. "You've tried?"

"Of course." Dallin flicked Wil a quick glance, then pointed it back up to the ceiling. "They've reasons for everything They give us, even those things that look like gifts. I've been wondering what sort of price They were expecting of you for... for letting you choose."

When would Wil ever learn to stop underestimating this man's insight?

"So?" Dallin prodded tightly. "What will it be this time? More saving the world, or just being run over by it again? Surrender yourself to the Guild and let them lock you up for another few decades, maybe? Or no, better—let's go right to Penley and confess to Channing, throw ourselves on his 'mercy,' and take odds on how long before we're swinging in the gibbets. Really, the possibilities are endless."

He was *very* angry, and not just at Wil, it seemed.

"I can see to Channing." Wil waited for Dallin to say some-thing, or at least *look* at him, but Dallin would do neither. "I can see to the Guild too, if you choose. I can fix it all, make it so you can go back to being Constable Brayden, a hero in the One Day War of Lind. Your life would be yours, your choices your own, and you could bury the memories of everything that hurts you just as deeply as you buried your past."

Wil would never know how he managed to get the words out without tripping all over them, without slanting them either pleading or accusing, how he managed to keep his tone even, unaffected. How he managed to sit there, bare and exposed in every sense, and yet give nothing away.

"No more running." He kept his voice soft. "No more voices in your head you don't want to hear, no more dreams you don't want to remember, and no more—" This time, Wil did falter. "No more possession, no more soul-eater, no more gods who expect the impossible from you and then expect more. No faithful fold who look at you and expect you to know how to lead them, no blind faith, no Guardian, no Shaman of Lind. You can have your life back, Dallin."

Dallin was still staring at the ceiling, eyes slitted and mouth gone flat. "And how is this *your* price?"

Leave it to sharp, shrewd Constable Brayden to cut right to the heart of it all.

"Another Guardian would be Chosen." Wil opened his mouth to say more, but it dried in his throat, because he'd rather said it all, hadn't he? What more was there to say?

"Ah." Dallin smiled, though it was hard and rather cold. Finally he looked at Wil, though Wil wished he hadn't. Dallin's eyes were blazing rage at him like a physical blow. "And whose idea was this?"

It was strange how a tone so gentle could still be altogether lethal.

Wil was meant to back down and cower; he was sure that was the result that look usually got. Except he couldn't—not only couldn't but wouldn't.

"You were right before." Wil found himself sitting up

straighter. "I'm not Wil, I'm not Aisling, I'm not anything I was only days ago. I took him, and I—" Wil didn't flinch back, though he wanted to, because Dallin's whole body tensed as though he was ready to spring and pummel Wil into the mattress. "What was his is now mine. I *am* dearg-dur, I *am* daeva, and I *did* see your face when you realized what She was talking about when She told me to use all my gifts. I am everything you loathe, and you are no longer obligated to abet and protect what you loathe."

There. He'd said it. And had only got a pounding head, a racing heart, and a stomach that was trying to crawl out his throat for it. The walls hadn't caved in on him, and the earth hadn't opened to swallow him up. Whatever came of this, Wil would survive it. Because that seemed to be what he did best, one way or another, whether he wanted to or not, and to hell with whomever happened to be in his way.

Beyond all sense, Dallin was chuckling—low, rolling ripples that gathered in his chest and ground out his throat like a scree of gravel.

"Sorry." He snorted, darkly amused. "It's only...." He covered his face with his hands. "Show me enough rot and I'll eventually have to close my eyes, right? Wait long enough, trust too much, and in due course, the badger will almost certainly turn its teeth on me." The chuckles turned abruptly to a deep, grinding snarl. Dallin fisted his hands, then brought them down to the mattress so fast and hard it made Wil jump. "Fucking *hell!*"

Dallin snapped upright and leaned in, managing to somehow loom over Wil even while sitting.

"Soul-eater—a smaller, weaker copy of a creature who wanted to tear out your heart, gobble you up, and you've done so many horrible things anyway, you probably deserved it, right? And now you're just like him, of course, because obviously you're not strong enough and don't have enough decency to control it. I expect we'll need to start chaining you up at night to be sure you don't run about stealing babies and eating their hearts." Dallin clenched his teeth, an inarticulate growl seething out from between them, and his fists curled tight once more. "Mother's *tits*, Wil, grow the fuck up and stop being that little boy who begged for scraps from Síofra because he didn't know any better. You're *Drút Hyse*, for fuck's sake. Don't you know better than this yet?"

"I *saw* you—"

"You saw me grieve for what you were going to have to do. You saw me mourn that you were going to have to slog through more muck and darkness, and that I was going to have to watch you do it, and you saw me wish I could take it from you. I don't have to like it—in fact, it makes me want to puke—but you *will not* use some bloody 'choice' I never asked for and don't even want as an excuse to walk away from this because you're trying for some idiotic, twisted nobility and too scared to see what happens next."

"Walk away from—" Wil shook his head, sincerely bewildered. "What the hell are you talking about?"

That made Dallin stare, shock-silent, for so long it seemed he'd turned to stone again.

"You really don't know, do you?" He leaned back and away from Wil in mystified chagrin. "How could you not...?" He just kept *staring*, only he was more thoughtful than angry now, keen intent in his dark eyes. "I see." He nodded. "All right, then."

He stood slowly and just as slowly walked to the window to peer out, his face like granite. Wil could see Dallin's breath skirl from his mouth on a thin puff of vapor in the chill, the only thing that indicated right now that he was a living being at all, until—

"There was a young man, a corporal—one of Wheeler's men. Said he was on his way to earning his lieutenant's stripes. Wheeler had promised him a commission after this—" Dallin paused, thought about it for a moment. "—this mission. Only a little older

333

than Hunter. Said he had a wife and their first child on its way. He was hoping for a girl." A tight, bitter smile creased his mouth. "He didn't say all this easily, you understand. I got it out of him with... difficulty. I seem to have lost my aversion to pulling fingernails. Or refound my approval of it. I don't expect it matters which."

He huffed a soft chuckle that made a shiver walk up Wil's spine. Dallin caught the movement out the corner of his eye and turned to look at Wil, animation abruptly leaching back into his stony expression like a statue come to life. There was concern there, unnerving for its sincerity.

"Sorry." Dallin paced back over to the bed, retrieved the fur he'd swiped earlier, and wrapped it around Wil's shoulders.

And then he went back over to the window, resuming his tale and his strange remove as though he'd never stopped.

"You see, the problem is, we need everyone to tell the same story. A conspiracy of thousands. We need them all to state emphatically that they stopped an invasion of Lind by Ríocht, and that the Chosen was tragically killed in the melee. It would be helpful, of course, if Penley believed Constable Brayden died too, because anything less than a complete, final conclusion to this, without Lind actually having to secede from the Commonwealth, just won't do. We have to give them a firm statement of events and produce bodies. The Mother knows there are enough of those to choose from on both sides.

"So anyway, almost every one of them—Commonwealth soldiers, I mean—are willing to swear on their lives that what we want them to say happened really did happen. They believe, you see. Seems they all had a divine epiphany on the battlefields and could give the Linders a contest for faith. You should see it. It's bloody mind-blowing. Men who halfway believed all their lives, crossed the threshold of a Temple maybe twice, and now they're faithful servants to the Mother and the Father. They'll say anything I want them to say, and the funny thing is, most of them truly believe it.

"But this one young man, this corporal—Holden, his name is... *was*—he and Wheeler, I think there was something there between them. He was mourning 'the great general' like his world had ended, and he wouldn't—I mean *wouldn't*—say a word against him. He wasn't going to break, I could see it in him, and even if he had done, it wouldn't've stuck. He would've recanted the minute someone questioned him."

Dallin stopped, turned, and looked at Wil straight, dead calm.

"So I blew his head off."

His expression hadn't changed, his voice was still cool and matter-of-fact, so it took a moment for the sense of it to penetrate.

Wil blinked. Huh. Maybe that was what Marden had been talking about when he'd said there might be more deaths. Wil's eyes narrowed, and he tilted his head.

"Just like—?"

"Yes." Dallin's hand came up, thumb and forefinger extended, and rested against his own temple. "Bam. Quick and... well, not so clean." He shrugged. "Creighton held him for me, though by that time there wasn't much need. I don't know if Creighton'll ever get the blood and brains from off his coat. Though I suppose it's not so bad—it wasn't his surcoat."

Wil shook his head, quite unnerved—not by the story, but by the cold, emotionless recitation of it, the dull, flat look in Dallin's dark eyes. "I don't—"

"It wasn't the only time, just so you know. I've killed men before, and plenty of them in anger, rage... for vengeance. It's a fine line a man walks, the line between killer and murderer, and I'm not so sure it's a distinction that matters to many. In fact, I'm not so sure it's a distinction I've managed to maintain.

"See, the problem, as I saw it, was that Corporal Holden was holding a gun to your head, to my head, just as surely as I was holding one to his. I just beat him to the trigger. Just like you did. And I'll likely have to do it a couple more times before this is all through. And you know what? I'm not sorry. I won't *be* sorry."

Dallin paused to stare at Wil for a moment, gauging. When Wil didn't say anything, Dallin shrugged as if it didn't really matter.

"I may not like the way you did it. In fact, I could throttle you for having done it that way at all, and not because of what you think, but because it was bloody dangerous and almost killed you. But this misapprehension you have that I would somehow condemn you for having lived through it, survived, when it's the *one thing* I asked of you, it's—" Dallin shook his head, very obviously angry and frustrated, then turned back to the window. "It's incomprehensible to me. Insulting, really, though I haven't quite figured how yet." He thought about that for a moment, frowning. "See, I believe in you. Whoever or whatever you are, I believe in *you*, because I've touched your heart. I touch your soul every night when we sleep and you let me in. And so I keep thinking you believe in me, and when I have the fact that you don't, maybe *can't*, slam me in the face, it... well, it rather winds me, I think."

A long, shaky breath dragged into Wil's chest, and he held it for a moment, waiting until his heart slowed before he let it go. "I never meant—"

"Who chooses?" Dallin's tone was once again impassive, no trace of emotion. "By tradition, it's the Guardian who calls, but in this case...." His hand opened, waving vaguely. "Doesn't seem to fit, does it?"

"Dallin—"

"I've been thinking how odd it is that the Guardian has never been a woman, considering how devoted Lind is to the Mother, and She supposedly to it. None of the Old Ones, either."

"Please don't make this—"

"Strange, innit? Maybe you should consider Andette. You'd be able to push her around, at least, because she's still feeling like she cut out your heart just by being related to—"

"Damn it, Dallin, *listen* to me!"

Dallin finally stopped, eyes shut tight. He bowed his head and breathed in deep. "No." He lifted his head and shook it, looking right at Wil, his eyes no longer blank but on fire again. "I don't think so." It was flat, fury finally bleeding through the odd calm as Dallin turned and started for the door. "I've already heard more than I can stand."

"You've not heard a bloody word I've said!" Wil retorted sharply, and when it didn't stop Dallin's progress toward the door, Wil stood and aimed lower. "I'll come after you if I have to, and I still get dizzy, y'know. If I fall on my face, I'm going to tell Thorne and the rest of the Old Ones that it's entirely your fault. I'll tell them you pushed me!"

Aiming below the belt worked remarkably well.

Dallin spun, then stalked back over to Wil, hands fisted tight at his sides and teeth bared. "You can tell them I punched you in the mouth, because if I—"

"*I don't want a new Guardian!*"

Dallin was looming over Wil again, *this close* to actually following up on his threat, by all appearances. Momentary uncertainty made him pause before anger closed his face again.

"Well, it appears it isn't your choice, dunnit?"

Wil gritted his teeth, growling frustration. "It *isn't*, but—"

"I've fulfilled my calling, *She* told me that, and why I didn't guess—" Dallin snarled. "Fucking sentiment. Bloody hell, I've been a bleeding *fool*, haven't I?"

"*No*, it isn't what you keep—"

"And here I was, thinking—" Dallin's hand came up so fast

Wil almost flinched, but he only ran it through his hair. "Fucking *shit*! 'Choice' my arse, because I could hardly have made it any plainer, and if you *really* had to ask—" He leaned in until they were almost nose to nose. "What you're trying to do here, Wil, it's called letting a person down easily, and I have to tell you, you're really crap at it. At least have the stones to say what you bloody well mean."

It wasn't supposed to *be* like this, damn it.

"I *am* saying what I mean, but you won't bloody *listen!*"

"I've done nothing *but* listen—to Him when He told me She chose well, to Her when She told me to believe, and to you when you stood in front of me, lightning dancing in your hand, and told me—"

"I'm not done!" Wil shouted. "*That's* the price I have to pay. There's more to go, and I need you with me. I *want* you with me. Not just a Guardian, but *you*. And I know how unbelievably selfish it is to want it, but there it is, and I know if I loved you like people are supposed to love each other, I wouldn't want that, but I can only love how *I* love, and I had to give you the choice, I *had* to, and I *wanted* to give you a choice, but I *didn't* want to too, because why would you?—bloody dearg-dur, right?—and I desperately want you to choose to stay, but not out of... of *duty*, or any—"

Wil panted for breath and swiped at his cheeks. Damn it, he'd started blubbering back there somewhere.

"'Not meant,' everyone keeps saying that, and I used to think it was because they thought you were a danger to me—can't make good decisions with your cock thinking for you, can you?—but now I know it's because I risk whoever is standing next to me, likely for the rest of my bloody life, and someone like you, you're more important to the world than I am. All I am is the barrel of a gun, and I'm really fucking sorry, but selfish or no, I want the person standing next to me to be *you*."

Exhausted all over again, Wil sank back down to the bed, propped his elbows to his knees, and dropped his head into his hands.

"*Fuck!*"

He hadn't wanted to say it that way, not any of it, and he'd apparently shocked the shit out of Dallin, who stood like a rooted tree in front of him, staring at him with an expression Wil didn't quite have the courage to interpret.

Wil scrubbed at his eyes. "How you can even *think* I don't believe in you? I believe more of you than you do of yourself. You've no idea the things you can do, the things you are, and I wish I had the words to make you understand, but I can't do—"

"Shut up."

Wil snapped his glance up, blurry eyes narrowed. "I'm not going to—"

"I *said*—Shut. *Up.*" Slowly Dallin went down to one knee in front of Wil, jaw set tight, breath coming harsh and heavy. "You bloody *idiot.*" His teeth were clenched so hard it was surprising he could get a wheeze out, let alone the growl he'd just managed. "If you *ever* do this to me again, I swear I will pound you so hard you'll have to reach up to take a piss, and not even the Mother Herself will be able to hold me back. In fact I might just take a swing at Her as well. Of all the *stupid* bleeding ways to go about this, you had to pick the one that almost guaranteed I'd go off the deep end, and you don't even bloody know *why*, do you?"

Despite the fact that he should probably be pretty bloody pissed at all the slurs to his intelligence, Wil couldn't speak. He didn't trust his own voice or any words that might come out his mouth. He could only shake his head.

Dallin rattled out something between a growl and a sigh and a sharp, grim laugh, propped his elbow on the bed, and dropped his head into his hand. "Fucking *idiot.*" He shook his head. "Be*cause*,

Wil, you can be a cryptic little shit sometimes, and you have yet to learn that it's possible for someone to just want to be *with* you. Not for what you are, not for what you can do, but for *you*, and bollocks to whatever might come." Dallin looked up, calmer now. "I can't keep proving myself. I can't keep offering everything I am to you and have you blinking at me in bewilderment and disbelief. You either trust me or you don't. You either take my hand because I offer it, and you believe I'm doing it because I love you and I want to, or you—" His mouth tightened. "Or you don't. There *is* no choice for me. Haven't you twigged to that yet?"

We cannot teach you to accept an extended hand because you are worthy of it. Such a thing requires the patience and persistence of love.

Well... Dallin was the most patient man Wil knew. And damned bloody-mindedly persistent.

"I trust you," Wil said, small and cracked.

"Yeah?" Dallin flopped his face into the mattress, his shoulders sagging. "Good to know," he muttered, muffled by the furs. "Until the next time you don't, anyway. Bloody damn, you make my brain hurt. And you wear me to the bone. I feel like I've just run a dozen leagues. Underwater."

So did Wil. "There won't be a next time." Because he was sure now, and there really wouldn't. "I'm sorry."

"Don't be sorry. Just don't *do* that to me again. Say the 'I want you to stay' part *before* you say the other bit, yeah?"

Five minutes ago, Wil wasn't sure he'd ever have cause to smile again. Now he couldn't keep one from twitching at his mouth, and it only made his eyes blur more.

Not invisible. Not merely the sum of his sins.

"Yeah." He reached out tentatively and slipped his fingers into Dallin's hair. "I want you to stay."

"Good." Dallin sighed. "Because I don't think I can move just now." In direct negation, he turned and sat so his back was to the bed frame, flopped his head back this time, and peered up at Wil, upside down and with a frown. "I'm supposed to be feeding you and getting you ready for a trip down to the main common. There's a honking great festival for the Turning, y'know. They weren't going to have it, what with—" He waved his hand about. "—everything, but the Old Ones said it's more important now than ever, and I agreed. Our presence is... encouraged. Thirty minutes ago, I thought it was a brilliant idea."

Wil shook his head, trying to adjust his thoughts and emotions to this sudden relief, this new lack of tension. He'd been sure that, one way or another, there would be a good-bye back there somewhere. And then there just... hadn't been. Instead there was only... *this*—the same *this* that had been between them from the beginning—and there it was, still there, and it took Wil a moment to slide his brain from *Please don't go away* to *Let's go to a party*. It was, to put it very mildly, boggling.

The very thought of a festival made Wil tired all over again, but a honking great festival with a horde of Linders might help him pull his mind from the wad of cotton that had settled around it. And he always seemed to arrive at new places in Lind half-dead and unconscious. It would be a nice change to arrive somewhere awake and upright.

How had Dallin put it, back when they'd been trekking through the wilderness and undecided yet if they still hated each other? *Taking hold of life,* or something like that—*latching on and valuing it,* and if that wasn't *quite* right, it was at least close. Wil hadn't been doing much latching on lately. More like drifting beneath everyone else's surfaces and hoping they left him to it. Well, he'd got his wish, for the most part, and it didn't take much to show him he didn't really want it. He'd fought hard for life—had chosen *this* life, with *this* man—so he'd best start living it. Time, after all, had never been his friend, so making the time for a festival seemed one of the wisest things Wil had ever considered.

Later. Because there was time. For the first time in his life, there was *time*. And right at the moment, he was feeling a pleasant, slow-spiraling need to indulge himself—a need for something more immediate, something earthbound and close, just between them, just *for* them. A need for reclamation and affirmation. The feel of bare skin against his and hoarse whispers in his ear. Lind and the Turning could go hang, for the next... well, half hour, at least.

"Come to bed with me."

One corner of Dallin's mouth turned up, and his sandy eyebrows twitched. "Was that an order? Does the Aisling command his Guardian?"

And that was it—it really *was* over, and it really *was* going to be all right. Whatever came, Wil could stand anything, if only Dallin would always look at him like that.

Wil couldn't help the grin, soppy as it likely was. "I could make it one, if it'll help."

"Bossy." Dallin smirked, then sighed a bit dramatically. "Don't let this 'servant to the Aisling' thing go to your head. I'm not as easy as I look."

Wil's laugh came out a loud guffaw. "*Easy*. Yeah. Sure." As if that was a word that could *ever* be applied to Dallin Brayden.

Dallin gave him a wide return grin before he slid it wolfish. "I don't have to go about calling you Drút, now, do I?"

Wil's smirk crimped. "I wish you wouldn't."

"Good. Because that would be a little *too* twee, I think." Dallin started to lever up from the floor, but stopped. He frowned and sank back down. "*What's* more to go?"

Well, Wil had known that was coming. He was only surprised it had taken this long.

Wil's fingers were in Dallin's hair, stroking at whatever tension he'd put there.

"Ríocht." It was all Wil said, because just the one word more or less explained it, or at least it was good enough to be getting on with.

Dallin went a bit narrow-eyed. "Not marching on the Guild, I trust."

"No." Wil shrugged, tugging at Dallin, impatient, but Dallin still didn't join him on the bed. "I expect anonymously would be advised." Cautious, he peered at Dallin through the tangles falling over his brow. "Someone has to do *something*. It's gone on too long. The corruption's gone too deep."

Dallin rolled his eyes. "Too bloody right." He rubbed at his face. "Ríocht." His expression went predictably wry. "Bloody typical. Should prove interesting, at least. I hope you won't mind skittering about under rocks, because I'll be just a bit obvious over there."

"I know." Wil sank his fingers deeper into hair gone russet-gold in the weak strip of winter-thin sun threading in from the open window. He kneaded gently, satisfied when Dallin's eyes drifted shut. "It's why I shouldn't want you with me."

But I do. I'm sorry, Mother. I really did try.

Dallin quirked a weary grin. "Can't help yourself, I know. It's my carefully cultivated air of danger. A bloody magnet, me."

The grin was contagious. Wil clutched the fur around him and slithered down to the floor beside Dallin. He leaned in until his head was resting comfortably on Dallin's wide shoulder and slid his legs over Dallin's thighs.

"A lodestar." It was embarrassing how Wil very nearly purred it. "I followed your pull all down the whole of Cynewísan and didn't even know it."

Dallin was still for a moment before his arm came up and around Wil's back. "I don't think I know what that means."

Wil only closed his eyes. "'S all right. I do." He hesitated, cheeks heating the slightest bit. "I'm not starless anymore." It came out quiet, the rawness inside the truth of it discomfiting.

"Hm." Dallin pulled Wil closer. "If you say so." He dropped a kiss to the crown of Wil's head. "I thought we were going to bed?"

Wil grinned, lifted his head, leaned up, and kissed him. It was fairly well received—in fact, pretty enthusiastically received—so Wil kept kissing him until he turned himself dizzy, and it had nothing whatever to do with hurts and healings.

Eventually Wil found himself on his back, trying to curl around Dallin and at the same time stretch him out to get his clothes out of the way, because Wil wanted *skin* and *heat* and *touch me, please, don't stop.* It was easy to vanish, unafraid, inside kisses and hands and gently nipping teeth and words breathed with an urgency that set Wil's skin on fire. Their bodies rocked and melded together, arching one into the other, until all Wil could do was breathe Dallin's name over and over again like it was the only word he knew, and hear his own panted back, and *Please,* and *Yes,* as a sea of stars slowly unfurled behind Wil's eyes and melted his spine.

They never quite made it to the bed.

The festival was very different from Ríocht's. Turning Night, for Wil, had always been a strange mix of anticipation and dread. Once the shakes and spasms tapered off, and the cramps had died down to a dull, achy need, the call of seeing the stars again, and the hopeless but ever-present dream of escape—one way or another—would rise up and set his heart racing with life he'd forgotten was even in him. Faces staring up at him, an endless sea of faces, and he couldn't see a single one of them, not clearly, and he used to wonder if any of them might somehow see, might know. How many of them had he seen in dreams? And if he'd been in their dreams, how could they not understand, feel his pain, take pity, or even succumb to fear and hatred and send an arrow sailing up to the ramparts, strike him down as he mouthed blessings he didn't believe and didn't hear?

This—Linders and bonfires and music and beer and spiced cider and meat on a stick and joyous songs that bid temporary farewell to the Mother and welcomed the Father with praise and gladness—*this* was a festival.

Dallin hadn't trusted Wil on horseback yet—still too dizzy when he stood too fast—and though Wil didn't quite trust himself yet either, he put up enough of a fuss for show. Dallin drove them in a sled pulled by a furry gray stallion that looked like it had never seen a sled before and wasn't in the least pleased now that it had. Dallin only snorted and told Wil it was a bit of retaliation in Miri's honor.

They'd had a late start because Wil had insisted on a bath, and Thorne wouldn't let him leave the Temple until his hair was dry. He threatened to withhold clothes but relented when Wil promised. Eventually Thorne had handed over a fine white linen shirt that fit Wil surprisingly well, and deerskin trousers dyed black that were a bit long but would do. Sent especially for him by a man named Gecynd. Wil had remembered to ask this time, though he had no real expectation of tracking the man down and thanking him personally. Still, he'd try.

Dallin had stared, head atilt and eyes a bit intense, as Wil hiked up the trousers.

"What?"

Dallin merely shook his head, smiled, said, "Nothing," and handed Wil a thick pair of stockings.

The delay suited Wil, since it gave him a chance to meet some of the initiates and apprentices he hadn't seen while he'd been holed up in the room, and at least two dozen men and women who were a bit battered and torn and receiving care in one form or another. Those, Wil thanked with all the sincerity in him, and he returned their smiles and greetings with a warmth he didn't think he would've meant only days ago. Now he most definitely meant every word.

It took an hour before Thorne would hand over a thick, fur-lined suede coat from the same Gecynd. Wil's own boots—the ones from Locke—had luckily survived.

He didn't take the rifle when Dallin had Marden open the vestry for them to retrieve their weapons, but he did take the knife. He'd gotten used to its weight against his calf. Anyway, its significance had grown for him, and he wanted it with him. Dallin took all his weapons, because he was Dallin and he just would.

It was snowing again—great thick flakes that took no time at all to dust Wil's hair and shoulders in pristine white. The world was nearly silent with it, muffled somehow but sharpened too, every line of it fluffed and muted by drifts and mounds of the stuff but honed and stark, every sound heard as though filtered through cotton, yet clear and precise.

Wil made no apologies for scooping up a heap of it in his ungloved hands and giving it a healthy taste. Corliss chided him and told him it would give him a headache. It didn't, so he did it again.

Corliss and Woodrow had been waiting for them at the bottom of the Temple's steps along with Creighton, about whom Wil had heard but had never met. A wide, rough-looking man with big blocky hands and a thick, jagged scar that went right 'round his neck from ear to ear, as though he'd had his throat cut once or been garroted and lived to tell about it. Not that Wil would ask. Veteran, most likely. Wil could see the rust-brown stains on his deer-hide coat where Corporal Holden's head had splattered all over it, but he decided not to comment.

Creighton's smile was wide and full of square white teeth. His hair was an unremarkable brown going to an unremarkable gray that kept flopping down over a pair of *very* remarkable gray eyes that peered out at the world with a knowing depth and an easy acceptance of what he found there. He didn't seem like the sort of man who would hold another still so his executioner could get a clean shot. Then again, Dallin didn't seem like an executioner—*Diabhal Mháthair*—though Wil supposed it was all semantics, when you got right down to it, and depended on which side of Right you chose to stand. And really, who was Wil to judge? Creighton greeted Wil with an unembarrassed bow, then gripped his hand and arm both, but it was his eloquent gaze that held Wil.

"Wil," Creighton said, respectful, though it seemed his gentlest tone was an affable bellow. "A pleasure and an honor to finally meet you. A fitting companion for our Brayden, that I can see whenever one of these fine strapping folk speak of you, but it's Brayden's own eyes that convince me." Grinning, Creighton shot a look at Dallin, then back to Wil. He leaned in close. "You fought for your Guardian, Aisling—fought and won, and came out the other side. A good fight any soldier should respect. Just see to it you keep bringing him back, eh?"

That wasn't *quite* how it had gone, but Wil decided not to quibble. He merely nodded gravely and answered, "I'll surely do my best," and suffered a great booming laugh and a slap on the back that nearly sent him sailing into a snowbank. That was all right too, because it was Wil's sincere goal in life to do exactly as Creighton had said.

A guard contingent accompanied them down to Lind proper, because Dallin said they couldn't be sure all the Brethren had been captured or killed or converted, and he wasn't taking any chances. Wil was pleased to see Hunter and Andette among them, though the shorn hair made him wince.

"I had a talk with both of them." Dallin's mouth was set grim. "Even after I sent Hunter up to you, they both still had that... *look* to them. I don't know how much good it'll do, but I had to try. Anyway, if I hadn't made it clear they were favored, they might've been shunned." He shook his head. "P'raps it would've been better to let them—they both seem to think they deserve punishment, and I don't know that it's doing them any good not to give it."

"Shunned?" Wil turned to look at them both, then at those around them. They didn't *seem* to be acting any differently toward either Andette or Hunter. Then again, they were all concentrating on their surroundings and not on each other, so Wil doubted he'd be able to tell, anyway. "Seems very harsh for having merely been related to someone who did something wicked."

"There's a lot of work to be done here."

Wil slid closer, both offering support and trying to absorb some of Dallin's heat. "There'll be time."

"There's still Channing to see to." Dallin sounded all at once tired and unhappy. "Haven't figured what I want to do with that yet, but I expect there'll have to be a trip to Penley." He cut a sideways glance at Wil. "And likely Putnam first. I'll probably need Jagger for Penley. And I want to make sure he and Ramsford are all right."

Wil merely shrugged, unperturbed. "There'll be time."

"Mm."

Wil turned back again to eye Andette, her short hair flat beneath the weight of accumulating snow.

"I shouldn't've said I was sorry. I should've thanked her."

"Mm." Dallin squeezed Wil's knee beneath the furs. "P'raps you might make it a point to do that, yeah?"

Wil would've smiled, but it didn't seem appropriate. He merely shook his head and watched Dallin out the corner of his eye. How could Dallin even *think* Lind didn't need him as their Shaman? How could he think he wasn't exactly what Lind needed?

"Yeah" was all Wil said, and he leaned closer.

Their arrival to the common was, predictably, greeted with horns and cheers, and a song Wil didn't understand but that Dallin told him was meant as a lullaby to send the Mother to Her sleep in ease. They would sing the songs to welcome the Father after the Shaman lit the bonfire, which he would do when midnight arrived.

That had been more than an hour ago now, and Dallin had been pulled away immediately after to dance with the "Mother" and all Her maids. And a long line of young women who Wil suspected weren't Her maids at all. And a good smattering of young men who were most *definitely* not Her maids. They all waited with such delight and enthusiasm that Wil hoped Dallin wouldn't find the heart to refuse them.

Dallin didn't. He smiled like he meant it, sang the songs, and coiled through the steps with his partners as if he'd never done anything else in his life. Better at it all than Wil would've thought, though he didn't know why, really. He'd noticed Dallin's odd grace almost from the start. He'd just never before seen it applied to anything that didn't have to do with violence.

Woodrow was out there too. In fact he hadn't sat down once since the dancing started. And though he wasn't quite as graceful on his feet as Dallin, he had his own smaller line of both young men and young women waiting their turns. Not surprising. Woodrow was wonderfully friendly and perpetually cheerful, though Wil wouldn't be surprised if some of the Linders were hoping for stories of their Shaman along with their promised dance. And Woodrow would cheerfully comply, Wil had no doubt. Dallin might be annoyed, if it were brought to his attention, but Wil couldn't imagine it would be anything but a good thing. In fact, perhaps Wil would join the queue later himself. He wouldn't mind a few Constable Brayden stories to fill in some of the less important blanks.

Scattered in among the revelry were stone-faced men and women, weapons held at the ready and scanning continuously. More dark shapes stalked the perimeter. Wil absently wondered if their presence and obvious purpose were muting the festivities at all. Perhaps they were even more raucous and exultant when they weren't mourning and there hadn't just been a very brief war only days ago.

Wil peered about, marking the smiling faces, the hearty fervor with which the people threw themselves into the celebrations. He could hardly imagine.

"Are you cold?" Corliss asked, all motherly concern, which both warmed and embarrassed Wil.

"I'm not, really." He'd been freezing before, when they'd all stood around a great pile of wood and kindling annoyingly *not* on fire, their songs accompanied by the percussion of Wil's chattering teeth. Now he was quite warm, sitting at their own small fire on a pile of hide-covered pine boughs that weren't exactly comfortable but kept his arse off the ground, and as close to the fire as he could get without actually sitting in it. He supposed the beer and cider weren't hurting. And the mead too, now that he thought about it.

Creighton nudged Wil's arm with a flask. Wil took it, and swigged down a healthy swallow of... something really fucking *strong*. He blinked a few times, sucked a breath in through his teeth to hold back a cough, and handed the flask back. Well, if he hadn't been warm before, he was now. His gullet was downright *flaming*.

Creighton was grinning at him, like he'd been expecting Wil to hurl his guts into the snow and was heartily pleased that he hadn't. Wil only hoped he wasn't in for another back-pounding.

"Puts hair on your chest," Creighton told him with a wink.

"Or burns it off," Wil retorted, his voice more high-pitched than it had been a minute ago.

Creighton threw his head back and barked a deep, full laugh that came up from his belly, white teeth flashing gold in the fire-light, and—oh, fucking *hell*—gave Wil a swat between the shoulder blades that Wil thought might shove his spine out through his breastbone. Wil shot a glance to Corliss, but she merely shook her head at him and rolled her eyes in a way that Wil interpreted as *Serves you right*.

"So, Wil." Creighton was still smiling, but with a curious crease to his brow. "I've been wondering something, and I think you're the one to answer it." He set his elbows on his knees and leaned in, keen. "I know what happened, same as everyone else." He frowned, sharp gray eyes going a touch distant. "Like I was there, but I know I wasn't. It's all very strange." He paused for a moment, thoughtful, though he hadn't quite gotten to the question yet. He stared at his hand as Hunter had done.

"It was Dallin, you know," Wil put in. "Brayden, I mean." Perhaps Creighton was unnerved by it all and was trying to make sense of it. "He reached out to all of you, and he saved me. In a sense, you *were* all there, every one of you. He sort of... borrowed you."

And apparently everything that was in Dallin had somehow touched these people, shown them what he was about and what he had to do. Wil had once wished everyone in the world could somehow be touched by Dallin. This seemed a pretty good start.

"Mm." Creighton tilted his head. "But why did he have to?"

Wil frowned. Blame? Accusation? It didn't feel like either.

"Well... I wasn't quite strong enough to—"

"No, that isn't what I mean." Creighton shook his head. "I mean, why didn't the Mother just save the Father Herself? If you weren't quite strong enough, surely She was?" He waved his great hand around. "Here we sit, celebrating Them, promising our faith to Them because They love us and each other, trusting Them to watch over us, and yet." His eyes narrowed. "If my wife were dying—"

"Like anyone would marry *you*," Corliss put in.

Creighton snorted amiably, conceding the point with an easy nod and a small flourish of his hand. "If I *had* a wife and she were dying, and I had the power to save her, I'd do it m'-damn-self. And I sure as *shit* wouldn't send a—you'll pardon me—a boy to do a thing meant for gods, Constable Brayden at his back or no."

Ah. Interesting. Here was a difference between Lind and the rest of the world that Wil had known for some time now but hadn't really thought about in any specific way. Wil doubted any Linder had the same question. He was pretty sure they all knew the answer without even thinking about it, and even if they didn't, they'd hardly question it.

"In fact, I'm *not* the one to answer that." Wil nodded at Corliss. "You would've done better to ask Constable Stierne days ago. Likely would've saved yourself a lot of wondering."

Corliss blinked and lifted an eyebrow. "*Me?*"

"You're a mum." Wil held out his hand to Creighton for the flask. "Think about it."

Corliss did, frowning and staring into the fire.

Wil took another swig and passed the flask back to Creighton. It tasted horrid, but it did warm a person.

"She couldn't let him get Her too." Corliss finally looked up.

Wil merely gave her a small nod, and she went on, "She wasn't... expendable. Not with the Father so entangled. If She got caught in the enemy's spells too, we would've all been done for. And if it's a choice between your husband and your children—" Her eyes sharpened, honing in on Wil's, almost angry. "—or even one child, or all of them...." She pulled her gaze away and went back to staring at the fire for a moment, silent and thoughtful, then held out her hand. "Give me that flask, Creighton." Her voice was low and a bit rough.

Creighton wordlessly handed it over. Corliss likely hadn't realized the ability to make that decision was in her until just that moment. And by the looks of it, she wasn't sure how to feel about the fact that she now knew she *could* make it, even though she'd likely never have to. Not everyone wanted to know they had steel in their hearts somewhere, Wil supposed, even if they fancied those hearts were made of leather.

Well, they'd asked.

He was just getting over the pang at having silenced them both so thoroughly when he spied Andette walking slowly through the crowd on her watch. Wil sighed and opened his mouth to excuse himself—

"He's not coming back," Corliss said softly. "Is he?"

Wil followed her gaze to Dallin, his face flushed with exertion and spirits, that grin that made Wil's knees melt stretched across his face like it belonged there. Like *he* belonged.

Wil couldn't answer. What was he supposed to say?

No, he's not coming back; he's coming with me. He'll stay here for a while, get to know his people, teach them, and then he'll leave them again, because I'm not done and I need him. I know it's selfish, and I know it's unforgivable, but I love him, I need him, and it's poor consolation, but I'll spend my last breath to make sure he comes out the other side. Because he is not expendable.

I'm sorry for you, and I'm sorry for him, but I've got steel in my heart too, only I'm luckier than you, because he's got it in his hands, and there's no safer place for it. I'll try to hold his just as carefully.

"I think that's a question for him, don't you?" Wil gathered his legs beneath him. "If you'll both excuse me."

He rose slowly and carefully, because stumbling dizzily into the fire just wouldn't do. Woodrow, on his way to join his friends, greeted Wil enthusiastically as they passed each other, his open face bright red and sheened with clean, healthy sweat amidst the freckles.

"Now, *this* is a festival!" He grinned at Wil, echoing Wil's own thoughts of earlier.

Wil couldn't help grinning back.

Dallin caught him on his way over to intercept Andette, surprising Wil by wrapping his arms around him, lifting him off his feet, spinning him about, and planting a hard, sloppy kiss to Wil's mouth, to the delight of everyone around them. Wolf whistles and applause rippled into Wil's ears and rivaled the music.

Dizzy, oh yes, and not minding it one little bit. And not in the least bit cold.

"What was that for?" Wil asked when he could breathe again.

Dallin merely grinned and squeezed so tight Wil thought his head might pop off.

"For following the pull."

Dallin kissed him again, then finally put Wil down, but he didn't let go. He leaned in, took Wil's face between his big hands, and looked at Wil so hard it felt like he was looking right through to bone.

"For finding me."

There were spirits on Dallin's breath and a flush to his cheeks, gold fire sharding through his hair, and bright sparks of it burning in his deep-dark eyes.

Forest god, Wil thought, and he welcomed the dizziness that swept his head and heart.

"Just... for living," Dallin said, "for *surviving*, and for walking down the length of Cynewísan to find me."

Wil grinned, warmed right through and happier than he ever remembered being in his life.

"Well, it's only fair." Wil took hold of Dallin's shirt and dragged him down for one more kiss. "You helped me find myself."

He patted Dallin's cheek, shoved him away and back toward his admirers, swept a small bow to the still smattering applause, then went off to find Andette.

ABOUT THE AUTHOR

Carole lives with her husband and family in Pennsylvania, USA, where she spends her time trying to find time to write. The recipient of various amateur and professional writing awards, several of her short stories have been translated into Spanish, German, Chinese and Polish. Free shorts, sneak peeks at WIPs, and other miscellany can be found on her website.

Website: www.carolecummings.com

Join the Rocky Ridge Books newsletter to find out when the Aisling trilogy and more of Carole's work will be available.

ALSO BY CAROLE CUMMINGS

The Aisling Trilogy

Guardian

Dream

Beloved Son

The Wolf's Own Series

Ghost

Weregild

Koan

Incendiary

The Queen's Librarian

Blue and Black

Don't Fear the (Not Really) Grim Reaper

Wrestling with Love

Wrestling With Passion

Wrestling with Hope

www.ingramcontent.com/pod-product-compliance
Lightning Source LLC
Chambersburg PA
CBHW030916050726
47498CB00003BA/772